A . D .

Saab Lofton

III Publishing   Gualala, California

Cover and logo design: Saab Lofton
Cover art: Art Evans
Cover photo: David Hoffman
Made in the USA
First Printing—September, 1995

Library of Congress Catalog Card Number: 95-92155

ISBN 0-9622937-8-4

III Publishing
P.O. Box 1581
Gualala, CA 95445

This book is dedicated
to Tommygun,
the man who saved my life.

DISCLAIMER

This novel is set in an alternate future. Meaning that while the events throughout the story are in fact possible, they're also highly improbable. And though the persons mentioned by name are fully capable of the deeds performed within these pages, this book's intent is not necessarily to imply that said deeds are currently being planned or are about to occur. At least, not to quite the exaggerated extent that the author depicts.

INTRODUCTION

"Confessions of a Chomskyian Trekkie"

My earliest memories of *Star Trek* were circa 1974 or so. I remember distinctly watching an episode where a hairy, ape-like giant was pummeling a shuttle craft that was stranded on some moon ["the Galileo Seven"]. I also recall seeing an episode from the *Star Trek animated* series in which Captain Kirk and Mister Spock were floating in a water tank because they had been transformed into Atlantean water breathers ["the Ambergris Element"]. I had to have been around five years old and yet these images I watched on my TV at my house in Pasadena as a child are still with me to this day. Nevertheless, it took another 17 years for me to care about *Star Trek* again.

Not that I cared all that much as a child. As far back as I can remember I wanted to become a cartoonist (I got cured of that real quick; as soon as I saw how little they get paid, how little they get out of the house, and how little respect they garnered), so I'm pretty sure that the only initial attraction *Star Trek* had for me when I was that young was their bright colors, the fact that it was "fantasy," and that it had been a cartoon.

In the years to follow, however, my opinion of *Star Trek* lessened, and even sickened. Up until the very early '90s, I could not stand the "Trekkies" (as you'll see from reading my book, or anything else of mine for that matter, I am *not* politically correct nor have I ever been so you can forget about me saying "Trekker"). The geeks wearing the rubber, Vulcan ears, the amalgamation of "Trek" lingo into ordinary semantics ("Boy, we sure don't get weather like this on Romulus!" Corny shit like that.), and so forth. The worst without a doubt was an actual Trek wedding. I kid you not. On the front page of the Vacaville (California) Reporter's local section sometime during the late '80s I believe, they had a color photo of a couple dressed in *Star Trek* attire and I'm fairly certain the best man was done up like a Klingon. I think the main reason why I couldn't stand the Trekkies is because, at the time, I was knee deep in nerdom my damn self in trying to be a cartoonist and I didn't want to be reminded of how nerdy I still was. So while I did catch the first few episodes of *Star Trek: The Next Generation* in the fall of 1987, the fandom of Trek drove me away from watching many more than those first few.

And then 1991 hit. *Star Trek VI: The Undiscovered Country* was about to premiere and seeing as how Paramount was touting this as the last *Star Trek* movie, I was eager to see it. Outwardly, I was saying good riddance because I thought (as most everyone does) that the actors were way the hell too damn old to be going on as they had been. Inwardly—well, the idea of it being their very last one appealed to me because I have always loved a good ending, a good finale.

1

Saab Lofton

Everything from the tales of Ragnarrok from the Norse mythos to the conclusions of the *Star Wars* and *Back to the Future* trilogies to the last episodes of *Cheers* or *M.A.S.H.* I don't know what it is, but there's something about finales that just does it for me. Especially if they're done just right and the surrounding hype makes you feel as though missing that conclusion would be tantamount to missing Halley's Comet or the first Mars landing.

Actually, I do know what it was. From June 12th, 1991 to July 3rd, 1992, I was homeless. I was living on the streets and off the charity of others while going to Solano Community College full time (which meant I had no time for a job sufficient enough to pay for rent *and* food) taking on order of 20 units each semester during that period. The plan was to transfer (as I was *barely* able to) to San Francisco State University in time for the fall semester of 1992. The problem was during this period, known among my peers as "the Year of Hell," my uncle, the executor to my grandfather's will took his sweet time expediting my inheritance (which I had planned to live off of while going to college had it come when it was supposed to). Essentially figuring I should "pull myself up by my bootstraps" for the duration rather than count on him to do the job of executor that he volunteered to do. (If you ever wonder during the course of this novel, "why is he so radical?" Now you know.) Given all that was going on at the time, I would've died for such a happy, Ragnarrokian finale like the one in *Star Trek VI* to occur in my life which could've pulled me out of the hell my uncle (and his incompetent probate lawyer) had condemned me to.

When *The Undiscovered Country* came out on December 6th, 1991, I was in the very depths of the Year of Hell. Without access to regular transportation, or regular meals for that matter, I was in desperate need of some morale. I bummed the movie fare as I imagine people during the Depression did to catch the latest *Flash Gordon* serial, saw *Star Trek VI*, and came away very satisfied.

For you see, I was either too young or too alienated (no pun intended) by Trekkies to see what the *Star Trek* phenomenon was supposed to be all about: Addressing issues. This has been so as far back as the original series in the late '60s in which Frank Gorshin played an alien with two-toned skin, literally jet black on the left side of his face and chalk white on the right who died killing the last of his enemies; an alien who looked and dressed just like him except he was oppositely colored (white on the left side and black on the right). *Star Trek* has always been what William Shatner himself called, "a thinly veiled and substantive societal commentary" that speaks out to, "some fairly important, even controversial topics." In the case of the aforementioned episode, "Let That Be Your Last Battlefield," the writers were obviously addressing the idiocy of racism.

The Undiscovered Country was no exception. The press went on about how *Star Trek VI* was a parable of Glasnost and the end of the Cold War with Gorkon, the Klingon leader in the movie, being in the place of Gorbachev. There was little doubt, however, that the corporately-owned media in this country would've conveniently forgot to mention what the movie's story structure resembled more than anything else: The JFK assassination. *Star Trek VI* depicts a conspiracy orchestrated by all the highest echelons from the major powers of the galaxy (Humans, Romulans, Klingons, Vulcans) to kill off a leader (Gorkon the Klingon) who wanted to end the state of détente in the Milky Way. When they do so, the actual shooters of Gorkon are themselves killed off one by one and Captain Kirk is made the patsy (*Please* tell me this sounds familiar?). Besides all this being set in the year 2293 A.D., the only other deviations from real life the movie takes is that the good guys expose the conspirators for the world(s) to see and they live to tell the next generation about it.

One should know that such coup d' etats on the part of the humans of the *Star Trek* continuity is extremely rare (as opposed to our time when that sort of thing is the rule). *Star Trek's* creator Gene Roddenberry's utopian future in which Kirk and crew reside is one that even the most cynical anarchist would jump at the chance to defect to if they could. Starfleet, the folks in uniform whom you see in the stories defending the United Federation of Planets, must all adhere to a thing called the Prime Directive. Which states that you can never interfere in the natural, cultural, or technological evolution of a lesser developed planet in any way. I know what you're thinking, "what I wouldn't give to make the Prime Directive law in this country!"

After *Star Trek VI*, I started to watch the show whenever I could, so I guess one might say I became a Trekkie thanks to the movie. All that talk in the series about how they had eliminated poverty and hunger on Earth in the future gave my homeless self a source of inspiration to last until my inheritance finally did come. What made me a *die hard* Trekkie was the spin-off series, *Star Trek: Deep Space Nine*. As a proud and (relatively) militant Black man, I can't tell you how pleased I was to see Avery Brooks, a Black actor become Captain Kirk's heir apparent on the show. In the series, Brooks plays Commander Sisko, who takes charge of a space station near a wormhole that's basically a shortcut to the other side of the galaxy. He's also the single parent to his son, Jake Sisko, who is played by Cirroc *Lofton*.

There's no relation that I know of. However, if I wasn't an atheist (there's no hint of a God, "magic," or any other kind of mysticism in the Trek universe by the way), I would think it was an omen in that they just happened to cast Cirroc of all teens. Especially seeing as how one of the main reasons why I'm so much of an activist for the left is because I feel that I'm fighting in the here and now for a Roddenberryian future for my direct male descendants to come up in in peace. (I know that may *sound* sexist but I happen to be the last of my line and I did warn you before I am not PC.)

The problem with *Deep Space Nine*, however, has been—well, I'm not sure what the writers' problem is. Commander Sisko is, of course, the star of the show and yet only an infinitesimal amount of the episodes focus on him and as of this writing the show is going on its third season. Hell, sometimes you have episodes where Sisko isn't even seen or mentioned. It's scandalous! Now, is it racism? Possibly, but I'm certain it's something deeper than that.

Benjamin Svetkey of *Entertainment Weekly* wrote a piece on *Deep Space Nine* and reported on January 14th, 1994, "There were even charges in the press that the show's greedy Ferengi space merchants borne an uncomfortable resemblance to old anti-Semitic stereotypes."

As I've said before, *Star Trek* addresses issues. Issues like greed for instance. To demonstrate the ramifications of greed the writers came up with the Ferengi. But anyone with half a brain can tell from watching just one episode with an appearance by the Ferengi that they are clearly supposed to be satirizing White, corporate elitists. Republicans, nothing more. And certainly *not* the Jews.

The man who plays Quark, the lead Ferengi on *Deep Space Nine*, Armin Shimmerman, must surely know this as well as anyone. Unfortunately, all he had to say in response to these charges was that, "People are entitled to their opinions. Any time you're in the public eye, there's going to be gossip and stories. But that doesn't mean I have to take it seriously."

Why didn't Shimmerman just own up and tell the truth? That the Ferengi are blatant parodies of robber barons and captains of industry? Well, I imagine it's for the same reason why while the characters in *Deep Space Nine* will constantly elude to how there's no poverty or hunger in their time (circa 2370 A.D.), they'll hardly come out and say how they reached that state of fiscal nirvana. Each episode of *Star Trek* these days cost around $1.5 million to make, which includes the latest in FX and the salaries of top actors. So they must be too afraid of alienating corporate sponsors from the show whose dollars pay for all these things. Rather be vague about how is it Doctor "Bones" McCoy never charges you for a visit to sickbay or asks about your insurance and keep the advertisers coming back than explain in some episode how trips to see Bones are for free because at some point in their past (our future) the planet Earth has redistributed the wealth. Thereby pissing off some insurance company who wants to run their commercials within *Star Trek's* time slot.

When they announced that *Star Trek: The Next Generation* would cancel itself, I cheered. Now Paramount can quit dividing their attentions and devote all their time, money, resources, and best writers toward *Deep Space Nine*. Then they announced that yet another spin-off will take *The Next Generation's* place, *Star Trek: Voyager*. Will this *Voyager* business take away from the quality of *Deep Space Nine*? Since *Voyager's* premiere will be the spearhead for Paramount's new channel that will herald their entry into the super information highway in January of 1995, will this mean *Star Trek* will be less about addressing issues and more than ever before about capitalizing on what has been called the *Star Trek* "franchise?" I'm not sure, but I think it was when I started asking myself these questions that I decided to write the book you're holding in your hands right now. I figured if they won't write the stories of a Black Captain Kirk defending a utopian future my way, I would have to write them down my damn self.

* * *

I could end this introduction here (Lord knows my publisher probably thinks I've gone on long enough about *Star Trek* of all things) but I think it's important, for me personally anyway, to justify to you why I chose the venue of a science fiction novel as a form of dissenting protest instead of something more—*physical*. Like joining Greenpeace and riding shotgun in a motorboat alongside of a whaler or an oil tanker.

I feel the need to justify myself because this book is, in part, about my heroes, the Black Panthers. I feel the need because though I love the Panthers, were I alive and my current age during their peak, I probably would not have joined them for fear of imprisonment or being shot. And in turn, they probably would have dismissed me as an "armchair revolutionary" as the legendary Bunchy Carter, leader of the L.A. Panthers did Cal State University of Los Angeles sociology professor, Harry Truly.

According to Elaine Brown, who would later lead all of the Black Panthers in Huey Newton's place, Bunchy Carter once chastised Harry Truly saying, "weapons of words won't deal with 'the Man.' I think history has taught us that. The Man is a beast, and he's armed against us. The *only* [italics mine] thing that will deal with the Man is the gun, and men willing to use the gun."

I love Bunchy Carter. And I hate how that bastard Ron Karenga, with all his crap about Kwanzaa, had his US (which actually stood for United Slaves believe it or not) Organization murder Carter and fellow Panther John Huggins at UCLA's Campbell Hall on January 17th, 1969. But, but, *but* I do think the man was dead wrong stating that "weapons of words" are useless.

If words are useless, then why was the Fairness Doctrine struck down by Reagan in 1987? If the powers that be are so powerful that only bullets can take them out, surely they wouldn't mind giving somebody like Jim Hightower the same amount of air time that they give Rush Limbaugh?

If words are so useless, why is it that whoever's in charge of casting for CNN's *Crossfire* won't get someone like Ralph Nader or anybody with some balls to debate Pat Buchanan every night instead of that wimpy bastard Michael Kinsley? Even Kinsley himself confessed, "Buchanan is much further to the right than I am to the left." Howard Rosenberg put it best when he said, "*Crossfire* should at least get the labeling right: Pat Buchanan from the far right and Michael Kinsley from the slightly left-to-center."

If words are useless, why was it that during the Gulf War reporters only asked the man-on-the-street, "do you support the troops?" Instead of, "do you support our policy?" Why is it we still have parts of the country where novels on the banned books list are still at risk of being burnt? Why is it that Luther Campbell of Two Live Crew did jail time for rapping even as the Soviet Bloc was letting their poets out of the pokey? And can we say Salman Rushdie, boys and girls?

Hell, if science fiction, if *Star Trek* itself is so damn useless, then why was it that according to one William Galvin from the Republic of Ireland, an episode of *Star Trek: The Next Generation* was banned in the United Kingdom because the show's resident android, Data, made a single reference only a sentence long about how in the year 2025 A.D., Ireland is reunified ["the High Ground"]?

According to a piece Gail Collins did for *The Nation* on Edward Bellamy's science fiction/utopian novel *Looking Backward*, "By the early nineties [*eighteen* nineties], at least 165 Bellamy clubs had been formed around the United States to lobby for political changes that would transform the country into the sort of place *Looking Backward* describes." Could it be that "weapons of words," as Bunchy Carter put it, can work on "the Man" as well as guns and bullets?

Activist and MIT linguist, Noam Chomsky speaks of "the threat of a good example." He spoke of how a small country is found to be a threat to us (as in U.S.) if they either successfully repel efforts to turn them into a banana republic and/or if they provide social services for their people. If they do the latter and don't have nearly as many resources as we do, then people in our country (should they find out about this small country via *words*) will ask, "if they're dirt poor and can still provide certain services for their people, why can't the richest country in the world provide those same services for *its* people?" If that small country provides for its own, or if it protects itself from banana republicans, it constitutes a good example for others to follow, and therein lies the threat—to those in power usually.

But I think Chomsky should've went further with this and didn't. The threat of a good example can lie not just in some third world country socializing their economy, but in most anything. From truly leftist commentators on widely seen public affairs programs (which is why none are allowed), to our great leaders and speakers (which is why so many of them are assassinated), right down to our entertainment as well. Provided they all can offer a different, if not outright dissenting, alternative to the status quo of the time. This assumes that the status quo needs changing, of course.

If the characters of *Star Trek* would explain who controls production in their continuity and if it was also explained in detail exactly how was it the human race survived and thrived long enough to reach the stars as they have in the series, Trek would invariably become a threat of a good example. Because, like Edward Bellamy's *Looking Backward*, *Star Trek* would show that in order to avoid a dystopia and attain/maintain a utopia (or "Trektopia"), people must inevitably take the path on the left at the proverbial fork in the road and stay on it. Like the book, *Looking Backward*, Trek could truly become a soap box from which one can take a stand upon. It's just a shame that the Trekkies of today aren't as concerned with politics as those who made up the Bellamy clubs of the 1890s. Well, *this* Trekkie is. Which is why I consider this book a worthy contribution to the left and justifiable to those who call for (and might even succeed in) an armed revolution against this country, but would be doomed to live out the fate of Snowball from George Orwell's *Animal Farm* because they forgot to educate the masses *first*. And that education can begin with polemics like this. I see this novel as an arsenal of weapons of words amounting to a major threat of a good example. Because the utopia—and dystopia shown within these pages provides societal models as to how things ought (and ought *not*) to be like in our future. Noam Chomsky also said, "social action must be animated by a vision of a future society." If that's the case, then *A.D.* is my vision. I hope it inspires you all as much as Edward Bellamy did the people of a hundred years ago and as much as Gene Roddenberry inspired me.

The Mighty Saab Lofton,
King of the Impossible
San Francisco,
May 1994

8

What's past is
PROLOGUE

"What was the price of liberty again?"

When you forget history, it repeats itself.

They say unless the German people aren't constantly being made aware and reminded of the heinous crimes their forebearers made not that many generations ago, then history will repeat itself in Germany, most likely translating into a resurgence of Nazism that might match or surpass the scope of Hitler's Third Reich. Which is why there is currently a law on the books in Berlin stating that one cannot so much as preach Nazi ideals on a street corner.

Such laws are based on the erroneous presumption that it was nothing more than Adolph Hitler's charisma, his ability to turn a phrase, and his happening to be in the right place at the right time (a post-Versailles Treaty Germany) that elevated him to the status of would-be world conqueror. And while all these things were *minor* factors in what propelled Hitler's rise to power, to think that's all that it took *would be completely wrong.*

According to the works of Charles Higham, author of *Trading With the Enemy: An Expose of the Nazi-American Money Plot 1933-1944*, Anthony Sutton, author of *Wall Street and the Rise of Hitler*, and George Seldes, author of *Facts and Fascism* and *Even the Gods Can't Change History*, *American* industrialists funded and/or supported Adolph Hitler right out of obscurity. Without such sponsorship, the Nazi Party would have remained nothing more than a cult if not completely fading away over the course of time, just as so many other fascist groups did who were vying for attention in Germany back then.

Henry Ford, founder of the Ford Motor Company, funded Adolph Hitler in the early 1920s. Ford was a known anti-Semite and Hitler used passages from Henry Ford's book, *The International Jew*, (only one of many works by Ford Adolph Hitler had translated and collected in his antechamber—along with a huge portrait of Henry Ford himself circa 1922 according to *The New York Times*) in what has become known as the bible of Nazism, *Mein Kampf.*

The Berliner Tagesblatt, an anti-Nazi German newspaper demanded that the American ambassador at the time look into Ford's funding of the future fuhrer, but no action was ever taken. After all, you can't tell a rich man what to do with his own "hard earned" money, can you? To wit, Henry Ford never denied that he was a big donor to the Nazi Party. And in gratitude for seeing his party through its lean years, Hitler gave Ford in August of 1939 the highest honor any foreigner could officially receive from Nazi Germany: The Grand Cross of the German Eagle.

The du Pont family controlled General Motors during the 1930s. They owned 80% of the Opel AG—which made 30% of Nazi Germany's passenger vehicles. The Nazis rode in Opel trucks when Hitler's panzer divisions storm trooped across Eastern Europe. In the decade before World War II began, GM earned $36 million dollars through their dealings with Hitler alone. Capital flight was verboten in Nazi Germany, however (goes to show nobody's *all* bad), so $20 million of GM's profits were reinvested in Nazi controlled or owned businesses.

International Telephone and Telegraph was permitted to take the profits it made in Nazi Germany out of Germany, however, they chose not to. IT&T willingly reinvested their profits into German armament companies. IT&T had a 28% share in Focke-Wolf, a main builder of Nazi fighter planes, and also was the owner of factories that continued to sell products to the Axis from war-neutral countries such as Switzerland, Spain, and Portugal.

IT&T wasn't the only one helping Hitler even after the U.S. had entered World War II. Chase National (now Manhattan) Bank first arranged for other Nazi sympathizers in America to buy German marks with U.S. dollars at a discount only if:

1) Those doing so were willing to defect to Nazi Germany.

2) These Americans could prove to the Nazi embassy that they sincerely believed in Hitler's policies.

3) The marks would be used exclusively for Nazi interests.

Then Chase's Paris offices stayed open after all the other U.S. banks had long since closed. It was known by the Chase headquarters in Manhattan that the Chase bank in Paris was the nexus of major funding of the Nazi embassy during the entire Second World War.

Norman Solomon and Martin Lee in their book *Unreliable Sources: A Guide to Detecting Bias In News Media* pointed out that, "During World War II, General Electric was convicted of illegally collaborating with Germany's Krupp Company [which was built next to the concentration camp Auschwitz], a linchpin of the Nazi war machine." Solomon and Lee also state that there was, "a secret $400,000-a-year deal between Hitler and press baron William Randolph Hearst, which resulted in pro-Nazi articles in all Hearst papers. As late as December 1940, Hearst was ordering his editors not to include 'unnecessarily offensive' cartoons of Hitler and Mussolini in his papers."

The U.S. Navy prohibited aircraft industrialists from talking to foreign powers about dive-bombing techniques which our Navy had invented. To get around this rule in order to make a profit, the Curtiss-Wright Aviation Company coyly *demonstrated* the techniques in air shows to the Luftwaffe in 1934 rather than actually *saying* anything about them. The U.S. Senate investigated the matter and their finding was that, "It is apparent that American aviation companies did their part to assist Germany's air armament."

As late as that same year, 1934, Nazi Germany had no choice but to import some 85% of its fuel from elsewhere. A petrol embargo would have stopped the Nazis in their tracks, but to step around this potential obstacle, Germany started to convert coal into an artificial fuel using a process that the German chemical giant, I.G. Farben and *the* Standard Oil joined forces to create. Standard Oil taught the Germans how to make tetraethyl-lead, mix it with gas, and make leaded gasoline which was invaluable for mechanized warfare at the time.

Congress conducted an investigation after World War II and found that Standard Oil also helped I.G. Farben block synthetic rubber research in the U.S. so that Standard would have a monopoly in rubber-synthesizing in the Third Reich. The congressional finding? "Standard fully accomplished I.G.'s purpose of preventing the United States' production by dissuading American rubber companies from undertaking independent research in developing synthetic rubber processes."

To anyone willing to do the research and not wait for Dan Rather or Ted Koppel to interpret reality for them, none of this will sound that astonishing. We're talking about a time in which more than one third of the work force was unemployed and millions of people were ruined thanks to failed banks wiping out their life savings. It was a time when President Franklin Roosevelt responded to the grumblings of the people (and their stomachs) and nudged the country towards the left with such practices as taking the U.S. dollar off the gold standard, thus putting more dollars into circulation and allowing debtors to pay back bankers in "inflated" currency.

The business world called FDR "a traitor to his class," accused him of "fomenting class hatred" by supposedly attacking corporate America, and looked admiringly across the sea at the fascists in Europe. Industrialists *loved* how Hitler and Mussolini had outlawed strikes and unions and did their damnedest to emulate the Axis. Why not? They're all right-wing. Irenee du Pont had GM profits finance the Black Legion, urban terrorists who would firebomb union meeting halls and kill union members. In 1938, *Time* magazine declared Adolph Hitler its Man of the Year. And then there was the cryptic quote from the July 1934 edition of *Fortune* magazine . . .

> Fascism is achieving in a few years or decades such a conquest of the spirit of man as Christianity achieved in ten centuries . . . The good journalist must recognize in fascism certain ancient virtues of the race, whether or not they happen to be momentarily fashionable in his own country. Among these are discipline, duty, courage, glory, [and] sacrifice.

But the worst came in late 1933. Gerald C. MacGuire was a Wall Street bond salesman who, according to Curt Gentry's book, *J. Edgar Hoover: The Man and the Secrets*, had been traveling across Europe studying, "the role of veterans groups in the formation of the Nazi Party in Germany, the Fascisti in Italy, and the Croix de Feu movement in France." MacGuire and American Legion official

William Doyle had tried to seduce two-time Congressional Medal of Honor winner Major General Smedley Darlington Butler of the Marines into using his enormous popularity as a war hero to literally lead an army of 500,000 veterans funded by big businesses to overthrow the government. The veteran army was to act as a show of force in order to pressure President Roosevelt into creating a new position in his cabinet called the Secretary of General Affairs, who would in turn promote a Wall Street agenda by doing such things as returning the U.S. dollar to the gold standard. This secretary would really be the one dictating government policy whereas FDR would either have to stand back and become a figurehead or be removed, according to Jules Archer's book, *The Plot to Seize the White House*.

The du Pont family was ready to use its control over the Remington Arms Company to arm the planned coup. Heir of the Singer sewing machine fortune, Robert Sterling Clark, was a backer of the plan as was J.P. Morgan. General Butler said the Rockefellers and E.F. Hutton were also probably backers when he testified before the House Un-American Activities Committee on November 30th, 1934. The HUMAC's 1935 report on the matter found evidence "verifying completely the testimony of General Butler." And also said, "There is no question that these attempts were discussed, were planned, and might have been placed in execution when and if the financial backers deemed it expedient."

If all this *still* is too incredulous for a mind brought up on the Warren Commission and the Reagan Administration to conceive of, let alone believe happened, just remember that during the Gulf War the media called Saddam Hussein's army the fourth largest in the world. Remember how our government likened Hussein's invasion of Kuwait to Hitler's invasion of Poland. But most importantly, remember that for eight years we funded Iraq's war with Iran. Saddam Hussein didn't rise to power solely on his charisma or his being in the right place and so forth either. Therefore, having a law banning the preaching of Iraqi ideals on street corners probably would not have done too much to keep the Gulf War from ever happening. Words *are* important. But at some point, the acquiring of ducats is going to be necessary. Or as historian Howard Zinn put it so well in his book, *Failure to Quit:*

> What resources do you have to speak out? How many people can you reach? You can get up on a soapbox and no one arrests you, and you reach 200 people. Procter and Gamble, which made the soapbox, has the money to go on the air and reach five million people. Freedom of speech is not just a quality. It's a quantity. It's not a matter of do have free speech, like: in America we have free speech. Just like, in America we have money. How *much* do you have? How much freedom of speech do you have? Do you have as much freedom of speech as Exxon?

In other words, and this is going out to all the politically correct who thinks that censorship will stop a budding tyrant, allowing free speech for fascists was never the problem; *funding* them always has been.

It is entirely understandable for people not to grasp this most basic concept of poli sci. Mainly because it's not permitted to be taught in schools. Corporations own or control the publishing houses who print the history books that are to be read in junior high and high schools across the country and around the world. That being the case, no corporately-owned history book publisher is going to shoot themselves in the foot and allow millions of school children to be taught something as down right incriminating to the very concept of the corporation itself as what you've just read: That a wide variety of U.S. corporations (most of which are still in business today) were directly responsible for the rise of Adolph Hitler's Nazi Party and the loss of over 300,000 American and six million Jewish lives—even though it is a historical fact.

All too many political scientists are guilty of basically the same thing. They continue to this day to teach that somehow the mere existence of currency in a society and the ability to make money in and of itself is enough of a litmus test for democracy and puts one 180 degrees on the political/ideological spectrum away from a dictatorship. According to *The People's Almanac* by David Wallechinsky and Irving Wallace, "Adolph Hitler owned 8,960 acres of land in Colorado." He could not have afforded all that by fitting the stereotypical image of a currency-less dictator, that's for damn sure.

To be left-wing means to consistently support the best interests of the poor and/or oppressed whether you yourself are poor and/or oppressed or not. To be right-wing means to consistently support the best interests of the rich and/or the powerful whether you yourself are rich and/or powerful or not (the terms originated in a meeting of the National Assembly of Paris in 1789 in which those who spoke for the ignoble masses sat on the left of the speaker's rostrum and those who spoke for the noble elites sat on the right). Whether the existence of little green pieces of paper is allowed in a society or not has hardly, if any, relevance at all to one's ideology. If anything, it is how those green pieces of paper are earned and distributed that determines ideologies.

Unfortunately, these political scientists and the publishers of history books continue to tell the big lie, that somehow it was solely Hitler's great personality and winning smile that made for one of the biggest mass murderers of all time. Not only is this lie one that Josef Goebbels would've been proud as punch of, it wrongly turns people against the very idea of total free speech by letting folks believe either by omission or denial of all the aforementioned facts that words *alone* can cause some 25 million deaths worldwide. It also conveniently nips in the bud any possible call for more corporate responsibility. But worst of all, it also allows history—the one, true history, to be Orwellianly forgotten.

And when you forget history, it repeats itself. As we'll see . . .

* * *

In an alternate reality alongside of ours, barely a dimensional sliver away, there is a timeline in which their history is identical to ours, in every detail, in every conceivable way. In fact, it virtually *is* our timeline. For all intents and purposes, it is literally one with ours— up to a point. That focal point being an event, a single decision made by one man actually, that causes a hairline split from our history, which in turn causes the twin timeline that had always been a part of ours to branch off and diverge, heading in a parallel direction adjacent to our course in time from that divergent point on.

The point in question occurred sometime in the spring of 1996 when after having been begged by the Republican Party for the hundredth time to officially join their ranks and after having refused future offers similar in nature in our reality—

Ross Perot said yes in the other reality. Which is the reality our story is set.

In the mid 1990s, the American people were ridiculously petrified of political extremes. Despite the historical fact that it was political extremism that brought about the very things this same populace took for granted, like the eight-hour workday and an end to slavery, America had been bred to believe that the middle of the road is the best place to travel politically. This perverse desire to be a moderate was mainly the fault of the corporately-owned media in America who would just as soon not even let the populace know that the political spectrum extends to the left past the liberal zone. Seeing as how the risk of the populace's possible wide acceptance of the far left's policies was considered too great by those in power with the most to lose by said acceptance, any attempts to brand political extremists as "nuts" or "conspiracy theorists" were more than welcome in the corporately-owned marketplace of ideas, and such attempts were held up for all to see.

An example of this in the '90s was how the only choices in health care plans the media let the public know existed were the insurance companies' plan and then-President Clinton's plan, which was only slightly different than the former. The far left's plan for health care, a universally accessible nationalized fund, was hardly mentioned. By default, the American people assumed that the Clinton plan was the most leftward plan to choose from.

With this in mind, if anyone who already believed this lie had ever come across talk of that nationalized fund, they would have immediately reacted in kind, like Pavlov's Dog, "you must be some kind of extremist nut or something to want something radical like that!" And that kind of knee-jerk response suited the insurance companies just fine. So in a sickeningly impassioned effort to stick to the middle of the road, the American people figured, "let's have a health care plan that's *somewhere in-between* Clinton's and the insurance companies'!"

Since the far right is nothing less than a not-all-that-distant relative of the right-to-center, extremists on the right were also portrayed as "nuts" and so forth for much the same reason a crazy, drunk cousin is kept from sight during family reunions: To keep the greater whole from looking bad. In other words, extremists on the right might have turned the American people off and away from the far right. Not to mention the right in general and the right-to-center in particular (where the real movers and shakers of the country usually were), thereby possibly driving people to the left and even to the far left.

Which is why, for example, David Duke's 1992 candidacy for President only received as much media attention as, say, Duke's counterpart who was also running for the Presidency that year a 180 ideological degrees away, Lenora Fulani of the New Alliance Party. The reason why was that David Duke ran as a Republican. And that made *all* Republicans look bad, including the ones who weren't interested in cross-burnings, just "earning" obscene amounts of money.

In 1992, the Republican Party shifted further to the right and it cost them the White House because their very tactics of making Americans react badly to political extremes backfired when all their talk of "family values" scared the American people off. Whereas the Democratic Party shifted even further to the middle-of-the-road than usual and it won them the election. Learning from this mistake, the Republican Party decided that in 1996, they too would move to the middle in order to attract the voters. The Republicans no longer cared if, in the process, they would in turn alienate the likes of the Religious Right, who, for all their embarrassing idiosyncrasies, made up the very foundations of the Grand Old Party. The effect of this move would ripple across the future and change the world forever—but we'll touch upon that later . . .

As part of their campaign to let the American people know they were no longer extremists but moderates, the Republican Party succeeded in recruiting in the spring of 1996 the inexplicably popular H. Ross Perot, who had run an on-again-off-again Presidential campaign in 1992 as an Independent. Somehow that in itself was always, though not always accurately, perceived to be the sign of a true moderate in American politics. The GOP seduced Perot by offering him not only a disgustingly huge amount of money in a Swiss bank account that would be payable over the course of 20 years but also a secret guarantee, basically stating that he would automatically be the Vice Presidential choice of whoever would win the Republican Primary.

It was in fact Jack Kemp who won the primary that year and, as per the secret deal cut months before, it was a Kemp/Perot ticket that ran against President Clinton and Vice President Gore that November. The voters didn't know who to pick because they were both basically saying the same kinds of things. How one ticket was tougher on street criminals and immigrants and less likely to raise taxes than the other and so forth. To further accentuate this point, the election itself required a recount for the results were the most razor thin in American history. Even more so than the 1960 election between Kennedy and Nixon. Another reason for all this is because the left, for the most part, stayed at home on election day.

Clinton had spent most of his term promising the left that he was merely a proverbial Trojan Horse essentially chock full of liberalism. But unfortunately the Horse could not be opened until *his second term.* Clinton claimed that if he had went against the powers that be in his first term, he wouldn't have stood a chance at being re-elected, hence that Trojan Horse remaining closed shut. Only *after* the 1996 election would Clinton be able to enact all the liberal legislation he supposedly always really wanted to. This was the sort of thing that was told to various leaders of the left—in *private*, and away from the press, however, for the Democrats, too, feared the American people would believe them to be extremists.

The consensus from the left was that this was all too convenient of an excuse for Clinton to get his old job back and did not allow themselves to be blackmailed into voting for him just to keep Jack Kemp and Ross Perot out of office either. So they voted in protest for candidates from smaller parties the media purposely kept relatively unknown. But for the most part, all too many didn't bother to show up at the polls at all. The core of supporters Perot amassed in 1992 didn't bother to vote also, but only because they felt betrayed by his defection to the GOP. Ultimately, it was because of all these factors that the team of Jack Kemp and Ross Perot barely won the White House for the Republicans.

As if big businesses in America weren't given enough of a carte blanche, President Kemp alleviated more corporate responsibility to the world community and threw an even bigger party for the extremely rich in this country during his first term than Ronald Reagan did in his first and second terms put together. With a largely Republican congress, a conservative Supreme Court, and a fairly apathetic left as advantages, Jack Kemp had nothing to stand in his way.

Kemp employed much of the same, "don't dare look to the state for help" rhetoric that Reagan had used 17 years before to justify to an increasingly poverty-stricken public the gargantuan tax cuts and the many, new loopholes specifically manufactured for the very wealthy. Not to mention the infamous Kemp Act. Which essentially forgave all overdue tax debts owed to the United Sates or interests on said debts of any major corporation from either here or abroad.

Yet for all his talk as President of not wanting any "big government," Kemp definitely saw to it that government troops would protect various plants from unruly striking unions and laid-off workers who were protesting the loss of their jobs due to practices such as capital flight or "downsizing" caused by wanton mergers that were all rewarded by the government.

This sudden and unprecedented stepped-up blind support of corporate America on the part of the Kemp Administration, plus all the wild and barely regulated stock market and real estate speculation, plus the encouraging of businesses that came from Jack Kemp's bully pulpit to cut worker's compensation, pensions and other benefits, plus the strip-mining that increased tenfold of federal and state budgets allocated for Financial Aid for college students and General Assistance for welfare recipients, *plus* the *re*-deregulation of the Savings and Loans and other similar institutions all led to 1999 being known as "the Year of the Devil."

This was partly because of the Christian significance of what the 999 in the year looked like upside down, but mainly because it was in January of that year when the stock market fell further than it ever had in its history. This gave way to the Second Great Depression, which was, in every conceivable way, worst than the first with nearly half of the adult workforce in the U.S. unemployed and a little over a fifth of that same workforce homeless.

War hides poverty. This was something that all Presidents, including President Kemp knew well. Which was why to hide the obvious damage that his fiscal policies were doing, Kemp spent most of his first term drowning out the sounds of the American people's grumbling stomachs with the sound of gunfire. In the fall of 1997, when Great Britain wanted to extend their lease on Hong Kong till the year 2097 and the Chinese of course said no, President Kemp jumped at the opportunity to declare that it was America's job to offer a final solution to the problem. All in order for Kemp to keep from having to talk about the economy back home. The China War, as it would be known, cost some 18,000 American lives and 200,000 Chinese lives.

Alas, the China War only lasted a year, and the national consciousness had to be kept from thinking too long and hard about its collapsing infrastructure. The massive celebration of the extension of Britain's lease till 2097 was just enough cause for the media to give the numerous soldier parades across the country as much coverage as they had given Polly Klass, Tonya Harding, and O.J. Simpson, but it was still not enough of a distraction.

Which left for many of the Kemp Years the Drug War. One of the big problems with the Drug War was that too much of it was fought on the streets in the inner city. After a while too many started to notice, from all the televised images people were bombarded with of crack houses being raided, the blatant poverty neighboring all those crack houses and began to ask questions. So President Kemp came up with an insidiously brilliant idea: Invade the South American country most capable of growing cocaine (though not necessarily the one most responsible for processing or distributing it). Hence the Columbia War of 1998. Unfortunately, after costing the lives of approximately 12,000 American soldiers and 125,000 Colombians, the Columbia War lasted less than a year as well and, surprisingly enough, the drug trade itself stayed very much the same.

Then, after the stock market fell and the Year of the Devil began, Kemp came up with yet another wickedly great idea. During the Kemp Years, Castro's Cuba had undergone some radical, internal changes in the area of civil liberties and human rights. In addition to Cuba legalizing all drugs, free speech, freedom of religion, women's rights, gay rights, and the right to travel had all increased phenomenally while their socialistic economy remained unchanged. Seeing as how the Kemp Administration's social policies were as Reaganian as its fiscal ones, people across the country looked to Cuba as a good example of a societal model for the first time and a few even dared to ask, "why can't it happen here?"

Those few amounted to too many for Kemp's taste, and he also saw it was high time that new territory be pioneered for American industry anyway, so President Kemp decided to fuse NAFTA with the Monroe Doctrine and do what Presidents had been talking about doing for the past 40 years: Invade Castro's Cuba.

The justification was a masterstroke of evil genius. According to the Kemp Administration, the story had broke thanks to "reliable sources" who could not be revealed for reasons of "national security" that it was in fact the Cubans and the Cubans alone who orchestrated and provided the gunmen for the JFK assassination. The "proof" was doctored, of course, but it didn't matter. Most of the American people believed it enough to support going to war with Castro and any dissenters there may have been were simply not allowed onto the mass media's uneven playing field of debate or was branded a "conspiracy theorist" for correctly stating it was the CIA who killed JFK.

At some point during this period, a very proud Jack Kemp must have literally patted himself on the back—in private at least. He felt he had sedated any critics of the Warren Report once and for all with this excuse to go to war which, in fact, worked on both the people and their congressional representatives. And with Cuba turned back into the banana republic it once was, the tiny, island country would provide a fresh, new outlet for industry which, in turn, would keep Cuba from being a good societal example to be waved in Kemp's face ever again.

But President Kemp was one to learn from his mistakes. To keep the Cuba War from being as brief a distraction from poverty as the China War and the Columbia War, the Commander-In-Chief specifically instructed his troops to *tentatively* attack the tiny island as they did in Vietnam in order to supposedly give Castro a chance to surrender peaceably but in reality to prolong the distrac—war. This tentative approach prolonging the war would also mean all the more profits for the President's defense contractor friends at Lockheed and McDonnell/Douglas.

The one thing that no one counted on was how exactly the Cubans would respond to all this. Faced with an insurmountable enemy who intended on eventually conquering them and corrupting their way of life, the overwhelming consensus of the Cuban people was that death would be better than fiscal and social subjugation from their long-time nemesis, the U.S.—and fought accordingly, with little if any coaxing on the part of Fidel Castro himself or his hierarchy believe it or not.

History would remember Labor Day weekend, 1999 as "Castro's Last Stand." Since air strikes would have meant too swift of an end to the Cuba War, President Kemp sent in ground troops from Guantanamo Naval Base in Cuba to slowly take control of the areas surrounding Havana. What the troops did not expect was that literally nearly all the citizenry, both men and women as old as 60 or as young as 15, would be attacking them at every turn using all types of armament, mostly with very old or obsolete weaponry, while others had nothing more than machetes and aluminum baseball bats. What the ground troops found the strangest of all was that the Cubans who were the least armed were the very ones who fought the hardest and the most—feral.

Despite having been told to fight tentatively, the troops felt that they had no choice but to fire back out of self-preservation at those who were the least armed. The ground troops felt this way seeing as how they were not as suicidal as your average Cuban evidently was at that point. This less tentative approach on the part of the troops only fueled the tenacity of the people they were trying to subdue. And then, the Cubans tried to attack the Guantanamo base itself . . .

Two days later, Havana was (prematurely) taken and *one-third* of Cuba's population was dead, injured, or missing but almost none of the prisoners who were young and conscious surrendered willingly. Rather, they had to be dragged into the various makeshift jails kicking, clawing, and screaming since the idea of being at gun point seemingly no longer had the same psychological meaning it once had for them. The lives of over 25,000 American soldiers were lost in the Cuba War. President Kemp wanted the war to last at least until just past the upcoming election and instead it barely lasted a week.

The American people were outraged, even the ones in Florida. The Cuban people were now almost extinct and even the most rabid anti-Castro Cuban exile was incensed at this clear case of utter genocide. Between the Cuba War and the Second Great Depression, a growing consensus in America was that Jack Kemp had to hit the road. Over the course of the next few months, several failed John Hinkley-esque assassination attempts on both President Kemp's and Vice President Perot's lives by pro-Castro Cubans (in at least one case, an assassin was an anti-Castro Cuban who had shifted 180 degrees ideologically because of the Cuba War) took place until their public appearances were kept to an absolute minimum and security was beefed up. The team of Jack Kemp and Ross Perot's once certain chance at re-election was slowly but surely decreasing. The problem was that it looked as though the best the Democratic Party could offer against the Republicans were New Jersey senator Bill Bradley for President teaming up with Georgia senator and defense industry insider Sam Nunn as his Vice. Two more moderates to appeal to America's frightening fascination with the political middle ground. And then the delightfully unexpected happened. Sometime in the spring of the year 2000, the Reverend Jesse Jackson made a deal with former California governor Jerry Brown: Jesse Jackson would use his influence to call for as many people at the very left of the Democratic Party to defect, along with Jackson himself, to the Independent Party. Where the Reverend would become Brown's Vice Presidential running mate and make a run for the White House under an Independent ticket.

For the first time in the political history of the United States, the left-wing had a legitimate and reasonably well financed (yet entirely and phenomenally free of any major corporate interests) third party. Fairly decent candidates with name recognition, no scandals worth mentioning, and an iron clad platform that was both socially and fiscally liberal. The language had its intellectual appeal yet was still very clear to the barely literate and was not alienatingly politically correct in the slightest. But the amazing thing about this third party ticket was that it actually had a chance of winning.

It was as though all of America's entertainment industry had come out to back the team of Jerry Brown and Jesse Jackson both morally and financially. When the corporately-owned media predictably gave this Independent ticket the least amount of press coverage, numerous filmmakers of Steven Spielberg's and George Lucas' caliber filmed campaign commercials for free and saw to it that they aired before any theatrical release that they produced or directed. Madonna, Prince, and Michael Jackson joined forces to do a whole album dedicated to the ticket. Jerry Brown made a guest appearance playing himself on the last episode of *Murphy Brown*. And excerpts from Jesse Jackson's speeches were continually sampled and integrated into the lyrics of raps of all the top rappers of the time.

Yet Jackson himself had some unfinished business that had the potential of acting as a proverbial ball and chain on the Independent campaign. Namely, his past association with Louis Farrakhan, leader of the Nation of Islam. When the Independent Party's National Convention took place in San Francisco in August of 2000, not only were the NOI purposely not invited, but when Jesse Jackson's time to speak finally came on the convention's second-to-the-last night, he denounced Farrakhan as clearly and emphatically as anyone ever had. The results of Jackson doing so produced a rousing, standing ovation that even dwarfed the deafening one Noam Chomsky received after his keynote address during the convention's first night. The effect of this move would ripple across the future and change the world forever—but we'll touch upon that later . . .

The Independent Convention was an astonishing success considering how splintered the left had always been stereotyped to be over the years. Unions and environmentalists, disabled veterans and draft-dodging pacifists, Black radicals and Jewish liberals, the Green Party and the Peace and Freedom Party, anarchists and Marxist/Trotskyites, baby boomers and twenty-somethings, even the Hollywood left and the homeless all came together for just that once and collectively thought, "*we're* going to win *this* time!"

The campaign that fall was quite simply, without a doubt, the most seamless example of grassroots organization the country had ever known. It had to be. Because it had all of the Republican Party, the Democratic Party, and the corporately-owned media to contend with. The corporate elite of America and their soldiers of fortune, the CIA, however, decided not to pull out all the stops quite yet (assassination) for fear of appearing too blatant, for fear of appearing too desperate, and for fear of appearing in the national consciousness, period. It had been concluded that informing the public of the candidates' past discrepancies wasn't working that well (discreditation), so perhaps Brown and Jackson could be swayed to serve national interests should they actually win the election by some chance (bribery).

The powers that be didn't have to wait long to test those waters. Because on November 7th, 2000, history was made when the team of Jerry Brown and Jesse Jackson won a four year stay at 1600 Pennsylvania Avenue in Washington D.C. with even more of a razor thin margin than Jack Kemp and Ross Perot had slipped by with. There were no less than three recounts and on the final count the amount of those who voted for Kemp and Perot dropped by a digit— or two. Talk was even heard that still President Kemp would try to leave some kind of "political booby trap" set to go off the minute President-elect Brown took office. Since no one knew exactly what to look for, no one noticed anything that out of the ordinary during inauguration week besides that a man (who was truly) of the people was being sworn in for the first time in American history.

The most remarkable thing about the Brown Presidency was that since only a couple of the few Independents who ran for Congress off of the ticket's momentum actually won their seats, the Administration still had on its side a Congress that had become fairly split between Democrats and Republicans in the election. For the Administration was so immensely popular, all congressional attempts to block or dilute any of Jerry Brown's or Jesse Jackson's legislation would be thwarted by picketing droves of people informed of said attempts by Brown's televised "fireside chats" every Tuesday and Friday night, in addition to Jackson's own bully pulpit that he held every Sunday morning in various Black churches across the country. Any attempt made by some PAC, bloc, or lobby, however vague or veiled, to cut come kind of deal under the table in exchange for one of Brown's laws not passing the Hill was immediately made public— usually in a most humiliating way that more often than not borderlined on libel.

The Brown/Jackson supporters would then take over once any of this information was made known. Mass pressure that hasn't been seen in the United States since the 1960s was put on any congressmen or lobbies who stood in a given bill's way. And believe it or not, this usually worked. Essentially, the bloc of Independent voters was doing the job of the Congress.

The first thing Jerry Brown addressed was the simple, undeniable fact that the high echelons of the military might turn on him as they did Kennedy before Brown could do anything substantial. Which is why his first acts as President consisted mainly of efforts (made for the most part out of self-preservation) to siphon as much as he could from the budgets for defense in general and intelligence in particular. If Brown was ever asked to justify himself, he would point out that the Cold War had been over for 10 years.

The "peace dividend" was then parlayed towards various projects reminiscent of the New Deal to jump start the economy which, Brown hoped, lessened the chances by however much of an assassination attempt on the part of the military industrial complex. Taking this approach, President Brown miraculously managed a "nuclear freeze" and was somehow able to literally cut the CIA's and the National Security Council's budget in half. Brown freed up even more money for his different programs when he also legalized all drugs and dismantled the DEA. (This was the only issue during the Administration that had visibly split Jerry Brown and Jesse Jackson, since the latter had always been opposed to such a move. Fortunately, Brown won this particular argument.)

Unbelievable luck, backing long shots, and defying the odds seemed to be the most dominant trademarks of the Brown Presidency. The notorious Kemp Act which forgave all delinquent corporate tax debts was successfully repealed and augmented with raising taxes on the obscenely rich to their highest rates since the Johnson Administration. And in so far as the use of big government goes, President Brown did in fact send government troops to the offices of big businesses who owed back taxes and demanded that either a check be cut on the spot covering their debt or jail time would be served. This tactic, the few times it *was* tried, did not always work. But the fact that it ever did makes stating that the Brown Administration was charmed the ultimate in understatements.

Even Brown, and all his supporters constantly on the backs of congressmen, could not do everything, however. Finally putting an end to capital flight and breaking up corporate monopolies always seemed to be just beyond the Administration's grasp. Not because some deal had been cut in secret that granted concessions in certain areas but spared the aforementioned. It was simply because only so much could be accomplished in a President's first term considering all the forces Brown was up against.

While all the damage that President Kemp caused in the late '90s could not have been rectified in Jerry Brown's first four years, and though the Second Great Depression was still going strong, the American people felt that under Brown and Jackson the country was heading in the right direction. This national sentiment was never expressed more definitively than in the results for the 2004 general election that November.

For the first time in American history, the Democrats and the Republicans combined forces to form a single Presidential ticket in a joint attack against the Independents. This Democrat/Republican ticket consisted of Democratic senator Paul Tsongas of Massachusetts for President and Republican Warren Rudman as his Vice. In a landslide not seen in American electoral politics since Lyndon Johnson defeated Barry Goldwater, such an overwhelming victory was seen exactly forty years later when the team of Jerry Brown and Jesse Jackson left Tsongas and Rudman beaten, "like narcs at a biker rally" according to Independent senator Dick Gregory.

The painfully ironic epitaph to the 2004 race for the White House was that Paul Tsongas died of cancer on Inauguration Day, 2005. Jerry Brown's speech included a single sentence on the subject and then the re-elected President went on to promise that in his second term he would, "finish the job I started. And any unfinished business that *still* has to be done will be left for Jesse Jackson. Because in four years, *he'll* be standing up on this podium being sworn in as the first Black President of the United States!"

After the cheers from the crowd finally died down, President Brown went on to say how the Cuba War was agreed upon by the American people because of their ignorance or denial of history. The President's speech then took a more intense, impassioned tone and in a fevered pitch, Brown cried, "I refuse to be the leader of a nation where the truth is covered up. And *because* it was covered up, an entire people were wiped out. The Cuba War never would have happened if people were taught the truth in the first place! Castro couldn't have planned the Kennedy assassination by himself—let alone cover it up. He didn't have the means! *The CIA killed JFK*! I know it, you know it, we all know it! And as God as my witness, in my second term I'm going to open up all those CIA files, play all those damn Nixon tapes, and prove it once and for all! From this day forward, any history book saying that Oswald acted alone is to be treated just like a book that's claiming the Holocaust never happened!"

* * *

The idea of a future where capital flight and corporate monopoly would be illegal by 2008 was one thing, the notion that by such time, a former Black radical would be sworn into the highest office in the world was hard enough to take, but it was rumored that President Brown was going to start in his second term a National Education Standard. In which "history—not *his* story" as he euphemistically put it, would be required to be taught in every state funded public school and college. It would be required that children on the junior high school level would have to learn that Christopher Columbus wiped out the indigenous population when he sailed across the ocean blue in the name of greed. That President Kennedy was killed partly because greedy defense contractors wanted to prolong the Vietnam War longer than Kennedy himself did. That a wide variety of U.S. corporations were directly responsible for the rise of Adolph Hitler's Nazi Party and the loss of over 300,000 American and six million Jewish lives. Or that Wall Street tried to seduce a war hero into leading a coup against FDR.

At this rate, within a 100 years, the very idea of any profit-driven entity being in existence would appear so vulgar to a generation who would be the latest in a long line of those brought up with this National Education Standard in place, that such an entity could not possibly survive for long.

This was the consensus of the surviving Rockefellers, Morgans, du Ponts, Carnegies, Melons, Fords, and Hearsts, not to mention what little the Brown Administration had left of the military intelligence establishment. This current state of affairs could not be permitted to run its course, they all collectively thought. It was then just a matter of what exactly was going to be done about it.

So sometime in the spring of 2005 a plan was finalized with the following attitude behind it: If we can't have this country back the way it used to be, then no one would have it at all. At least, no one anyone would want to see have it. As usual, the backers of anything of this nature would remain in the background. Meaning there would have to be those who, at some point, would be in the public eye forcing things back to some semblance of how they used to be. And since the Independents were getting even more popular with each passing day, it was felt by all concerned that there was no longer anything left to lose by choosing the likes of Tom Metzger's White Aryan Resistance and various other White supremacist groups, the Religious Right the Republicans alienated in 1996 in their quest to be more moderate, and the Black Muslims of Louis Farrakhan's Nation of Islam.

The inclusion of the Black Muslims in this political rogues gallery may seem confusing at first to the layman but only because the mass media has purposely and inaccurately called Farrakhan a "radical" and tried to picture him as the sole voice of the Black community by not allowing any other extreme Black voices onto their uneven playing field of debate. The rationale? Any corporately-owned venue of the media would just as soon have Blacks adhere to the Nation of Islam's fundamentalist, reactionary platform consisting of, but definitely not limited to, bootstrap capitalism. Which would, in effect, alleviate corporate responsibility. As opposed to the Black community adhering to an extremely left-wing platform from an actual Black radical. This ideological bias was also why the newspaper of the Black Muslims had permission to circulate in the prison system of the sixties and seventies but the Black Panthers' newspaper didn't. And it's safe to say there was clearly an ideological bias behind why the FBI wiped out the Black Panthers as if they were buffaloes on the plains of the 1880s whereas their opposite number, the Nation of Islam faced no such extinction.

One might try to claim that the Black Panthers bearing arms in public is what ultimately caused their demise. Yet the Black Panthers armed themselves strictly for self-defense against cops guilty of Rodney King-esque beatings which took place on a daily basis during their era. The Panthers never arbitrarily killed anyone. However, if the FBI really wanted to shut down a clearly violent organization who had a long history of performing assassinations, they should have gone after the group who ordered the public execution of Malcolm X.

The Nation of Islam has since been implicated in the deaths of Malcolm X loyalists, whether they happened to be civilians or ministers of their own mosques. And if they decided not to kill a Malcolm X loyalist, or any other critic of theirs for that matter, the NOI would resort to harassment or terrorism. In 1970, Philadelphia's Uhuru Kitabu bookstore was firebombed because its employees would not take a Malcolm X poster from their store window after being threatened by local Black Muslims.

But if the following doesn't prove that the Nation of Islam is capable of being more of a threat to the community than the Black Panthers ever *dreamed* of being on their worst day, nothing will. This was taken from an article in *The Nation* magazine (1/21/91) written by Adolph Reed Jr., a professor of political science at Yale University:

> Most chilling, in January 1973 a simmering theological dispute with members of the Hanafi Islamic sect in Washington ignited into an attack of which only zealots or hardened killers are capable. Seven Hanafis were murdered in their 16th Street residence, owned by Kareem Abdul Jabbar; five of the victims were children, including babies who were drowned in the bathtub. (The Hanafis held the Nation [of Islam] responsible and four years later occupied a government building and B'nai B'rith center and took hostages to press their demands for retribution.)

So obviously, the FBI wasn't too concerned with an all-Black group causing mayhem. Else they would have assassinated Farrakhan as they did fellow Chicago native, Fred Hampton. Clearly the reasons why the Black Panthers were gunned down and the Black Muslims were left unscathed were primarily ideological. Or as Milton Kleg, professor of social science education at the University of Colorado in Denver put it, "unlike the Black Panthers, the Black Muslims are right-wing racists as opposed to the leftist, Marxist-Leninist Panthers."

The Nation of Islam has always shared the same, exact platform as their White supremacist counterparts. Stance by stance, right down to their opposition to Jewish life, socialism, and equal rights for women or gays. But the one position more than any other that has brought them together was their common belief that all the races should be segregated. And yes, they *have* come together—on more than one occasion . . .

In the fall of 1992, Tom Metzger was the sole guest on an episode of *The Whoopi Goldberg Show*, said that he had spoken with Farrakhan at length, and declared, as rapper Ice Cube had in the album *Death Certificate*, that the best thing for any young Black man in America to do was to join the Nation of Islam. Metzger also attended a rally in Los Angeles that Farrakhan gave in early October, 1985 and donated $100.00 according to both *Time* magazine and *The New York Times*.

Wayne King, who wrote that particular piece for the *Times* also said that, "cooperation between Black and White separatists is not without precedent." And he wasn't just whistling Dixie. On June 25th, 1961, George Lincoln Rockwell, "fuhrer" of the American Nazi Party appeared at the Nation of Islam's National Convention at the Uline Arena in Washington D.C. and contributed $20.00.

On February 25th, 1962, Rockwell was invited *again* to the NOI's annual convention. This time, the "fuhrer" was dressed in full Nazi regalia and was accompanied by 10 of his storm troopers *all of whom had front row seats*. Rockwell was one of the first speakers of the convention and said to hundreds of Black Muslims, "Elijah Muhammad [the leader of the NOI before Farrakhan] has done some wonderful things for the so-called Negro. Elijah Muhammad is to the so-called Negro what Adolph Hitler was to the German people. He is the most powerful Black man in the country. Heil Hitler!"

In a letter to his followers, George Lincoln Rockwell said the following:

> I have just had a meeting with the most extraordinary Black man in
> America: The Honorable Elijah Muhammad, leader of the Nation of
> Islam. I was amazed to learn how much they and I agree on things; they
> think that Blacks should get out of this country and go back to Africa
> or to some other place and so do we. They want to get Black men
> to leave White women alone, and White men to leave Black women
> alone, and so do we. The Honorable Elijah Muhammad and I have
> worked out an agreement of mutual assistance in which they will
> help us on some things and we will help them on others.

And then of course, there was the ever-popular Malcolm X, who while he had spent the last year of his political career (and his life) as a liberal, had also spent the previous 10 years of his public life as a minister and the national representative of the Nation of Islam. During this right-wing tenure, Malcolm himself was cutting a deal with the Ku Klux Klan according to a New York City FBI file dated 5/17/61, bureau file number; 100-399321. But Malcolm's own words, taken from a speech of his given on February 15th, 1965 in Harlem's Audubon Ballroom, would do the events more justice:

> The way they threw that bomb in there [referring to the NOI's
> firebombing of Malcolm X's home] they could have thrown it in a Ku

Klux Klan house. Why do they want to bomb my house? Why don't they bomb the Klan? I'm going to tell you why. In 1960, in December, in December of 1960, I was in the home of Jeremiah, the [Black Muslim] minister in Atlanta, Georgia. I'm ashamed to say it, but I'm going to tell you the truth. I sat at the table myself with the heads of the Ku Klux Klan. I sat there myself, with the heads of the Ku Klux Klan, who at that time were trying to negotiate with Elijah Muhammad so that they could make available to him a large area of land in Georgia or I think it was South Carolina. They had some very responsible persons in the government who were involved in it and who were willing to go along with it [Hence the FBI report?]. They wanted to make this land available to him so that his program of separation would sound feasible to Negroes and therefore lessen the pressure that the integrationists were putting upon the White man. I sat there. I negotiated it. I listened to their offer. And I was the one who went back to Chicago and told Elijah Muhammad what they had offered. Now, this was in December of 1960. The code name that Jeremiah gave the Klan leader was 666. Whenever they would refer to him they would refer to him as Old Six. What his name was right now escapes me. But they even sat there and told stories how—what they had done on different escapades that they had been involved in. Jeremiah was there and his wife was there and I was there and the Klan was there. From that day onward the Klan never interfered with the Black Muslim movement in the South. Jeremiah attended Klan rallies, as you read on the front page of *The New York Tribune*. They never bothered him, never touched him. He [presumably Old Six] never touched a Muslim, and a Muslim never touched him . . .
When the brothers in Monroe, Louisiana, were involved in trouble with the police, if you'll recall, Elijah Muhammad got old [James] Venable. Venable is a Ku Klux Klan lawyer. He's a Ku Klux Klan chieftain, according to *The Saturday Evening Post*, that was up on the witness stand. Go back and read the paper and you'll see that Venable was the one who represented the Black Muslim movement in Louisiana.

Yet another sacred cow of the Black community was guilty of very much the same thing. There is an actual photo, albeit rare, of none other than Marcus Garvey in an all-black, custom made Ku Klux Klan robe standing before a burning cross with half a dozen Klansmen around him. This move was similar to the one Martin Delany had made in the 1870s, according to Clayborne Carson, professor of history at Stanford University. Garvey's organization, the United Negro Improvement Association, shared the Klan's goal of the total deportation of Black Americans to Africa and even expelled members who married Whites.

Marcus Garvey met with the KKK's Acting Imperial Wizard Edward Young Clarke in Atlanta (where Malcolm X met Old Six) on June 25th (the date Rockwell went to the NOI's 1961 convention—strange . . .), 1922 according to E. David Cronon's, *Black Moses: The*

Story of Marcus Garvey and Robert A. Hill's, *Marcus Garvey: Life and Lessons.*

Garvey's second volume of his *Philosophy and Opinions* carried an advertisement for Major Earnest Sevier Cox's *White America*, a polemic calling for racial separation. Major Cox, in turn, wrote a pamphlet on maintaining racial purity dedicated to Garvey. Cox also spoke to UNIA audiences at New York's Liberty Hall during the mid-1920s as did John Powell, organizer of the Anglo-Saxon Clubs of America. Just as George Lincoln Rockwell would speak before the NOI 40 years later and as Tom Metzger would be teamed up with Louis Farrakhan some 40 years after that.

It *must* be remembered, however, that it was *not* the mere existence of extremism surrounding these figures which brought them together. The Black Panthers were extremists, but they were extreme *leftists*. Ergo they never would've had anything to do with these groups and never did. In the end, it was the fact that these Black and White reactionaries shared the same belief system, the same political platform, and the same world view, not much more. In the Nation of Islam's case at least, they had already joined forces with the CIA because they felt a shared need to kill Malcolm X. And what do they always say? "You never leave the agency, once CIA, always CIA . . ."

* * *

Since the general population was never taught in school or anywhere else what corporations were capable of, or even had the political will to fund fascists or overturn governments, no one thought it was unusual that by the summer of 2005, the Black Muslims no longer had to hawk their newspaper on street corners. Someone gave them the means to distribute it nationally via vending boxes that could be found right alongside the vending boxes which held copies of *The New York Times* or *USA Today.* The advertising in their paper, *The Final Call*, significantly changed as well. From advertisements for bean pie bakeries to full page car ads from GM and "plugs" for GE light bulbs.

No one noticed that the churches ran by the Religious Right were going as strong as they ever were at their peak during the mid-1980s even though President Brown began taxing them in 2002. And no one seemed to care that people were mysteriously going across the country bailing out of jail mercenaries, but mainly skinheads, by the hundreds, only to have them jump said bail.

Black gang activity suddenly dropped to unheard of levels as if the gang members had just disappeared off the face of the Earth and the rate of hate crimes likewise fell to almost nothing. Prison breaks were becoming more and more common in the fall of 2005. Except while the Latino and Asian prisoners were always caught right away, the Black and White prisoners were never captured. There were a few reporters who addressed these strange events but the stories hardly saw print outside of the alternative press. And even then, without ever having been taught the historical context into which to place these occurrences, reporting about them only confused the readers because their political imagination was too stunted by conventional wisdom to envision *why* these things might be taking place or what the ramifications could possibly be.

Which is why when Operation Domino *did* happen in the winter of 2005, everyone but the most canny of observers were caught completely by surprise.

Every exact, strategic detail of Operation Domino isn't needed in order to understand what basically happened. Which was that around three o'clock in the morning on December 18th, 2005, General Henry Fiorini and his immediate staff led dozens of members of the White Aryan Resistance, armed with Uzis, AK 47s, and 45 automatics past all the defenses of Lansdale Air Force Base in California's Orange County, and into the control room of an MX missile silo.

While the rest of the base was being evacuated as part of a scheduled bio hazard drill, Fiorini and the gunmen from WAR took the control room hostage. General Fiorini then began ordering the personnel on duty there to start arming the missiles' warheads and bringing their guidance systems on line. This was done only after a couple of defiant soldiers were shot dead as an example. And just as everything short of the two keys necessary to actually launch a missile was made available, several armed members of the Nation of Islam entered the control room ushering in the possessors of said keys, two generals still wearing pajamas, slippers, and robes. Both generals were forced at gun point to produce and insert each of their respective keys while they cursed Fiorini for being a traitor.

The single phone with an outgoing line in the missile control room rang and General Fiorini answered. Fiorini confirmed that the silo was very much under terrorist control and that they were entirely capable of firing all of Lansdale's twelve nuclear missiles towards multiple targets, at will, if their demands were not met. The general spent the remainder of the brief conversation assuring that what was going on wasn't a hoax of any kind and then hung up.

As it turned out, General Fiorini's discussion had been broadcast across the country and around the world alongside of the demands of Tom Metzger, whose men had commandeered a newsroom of the local NBC affiliate station in Los Angeles. Sitting behind a news desk in the anchorman's chair before a live camera, Metzger called for the immediate deportation of all non-Whites and non-Blacks from America's borders. He then went into great lengths describing what exactly was to be considered White and what was to be considered Black.

Tom Metzger also instructed all Black Americans to report to the following U.S. states: Illinois, Indiana, Iowa, Minnesota, Michigan, Missouri, and Wisconsin as they would embody a new, all-Black homeland called the Lost-Found Nation of Islam in North America. All of the other states in the Union would be collectively known as Aryan Amerikkka where only Whites could live.

In the name of maintaining the NOI's good PR in the Black community, the Orwellian lie was told by Metzger (and actually believed by an uncomfortably high amount of people) that originally all Black Americans were simply going to be put to death. But Louis Farrakhan supposedly somehow came through at the last minute and heroically bargained for the lives of all his people, as Oskar Schindler had done for the Jews during World War II, by negotiating for a homeland within Amerikkka where Blacks would be out of the Aryans' way.

Over the next couple of weeks the American people were obviously in a state of high anxiety and panic to say the least. Americans of all races were leaving the country in hordes, but only those who could afford to and then come back should the situation resolve itself. And as for those robber barons who funded the siege in the first place? Most of them flew away in private Lear jets to lounge in Switzerland and various resorts throughout the Mediterranean for an early retirement so they could still profit from afar off of whatever the aftermath of Operation Domino would be. The vast majority of people, however, financially had no choice but to wait for a military solution or for the terrorists to either be talked down and out of the silo.

President Brown contemplated all options presented to him while he made doubly sure that the commanders of all the other bases with nuclear missile silos in the U.S. were disconnecting their launching mechanisms as fast as they could. So that even if another base fell into the wrong hands, no other missiles would be able to leave its silos.

But the White and Black supremacists both decided that far too much time was being taken by the Brown Administration and the United Nations to officially relinquish power over the United States to the Nation of Islam and White Aryan Resistance or to expedite the mass national deportation they demanded. So one MX missile was launched from Lansdale on New Year's Day, 2006 at the first nuclear target they had mutually determined long in advance was the most fair place to be sacrificed. A country with both a White and Black population, one which they perceived to be far enough out of way ecologically to not cause any real, lasting damage to the rest of the Earth's atmosphere, but also someplace that would surely be missed by the world community.

The terrorists sent that single missile to Australia and it exploded over the exact center of the country before any anti-missile aircraft or weaponry could be deployed. The entire devastation to the area was indescribable but essentially every living thing on the continent of Oceania was dead. The Australian surface was literally wiped clean as though by the hand of God, leaving nothing but a simmering radioactive desert on the ground and, paradoxically, a nuclear winter overhead. Any people that were still alive in New Zealand and Tasmania were beyond help because the nuclear fallout was far too intense. And everyone within a two thousand mile radius of Australia's borders at the time of the blast suffered from either radiation sickness, deformed births, or sterility.

The United Nations and the government of the United States of America officially surrendered to White Aryan Resistance and the Nation of Islam on February the 21st, 2006. The racial populations that the NOI and WAR wanted to deport from America's borders were deported with all the haste the old government could muster. The Blacks that didn't escape the country or weren't killed for resisting the new order were reassigned to the states allocated to Farrakhan. Those Blacks who already lived in those states were told to stay there, of course.

Alaska, Hawaii, and other U.S. territories remained with the old order, however. Mainly because the new state of détente that would invariably exist between the rest of the world, the Lost-Found Nation of Islam in North America, and Aryan Amerikkka would make it too hard for the Black and White supremacists to hold onto these areas from a strategic point of view. Black Americans who had been living abroad were rarely let back into Amerikkka's borders in order to reach the Lost-Found Nation, even though Whites who wanted to defect from South Africa could do so with no problem.

And though Jews were assured that they would be able to leave either Aryan Amerikkka or the Lost-Found Nation of Islam in North America unharmed, all too many didn't make it out of what was once called the United States and were never heard from again by those waiting for them on the other side of the border.

When you forget history, it repeats itself. This is not America. Welcome to the future, albeit an alternate one. You may not like what you see.

Along with our insistence on self-defense, our attitude toward nationalism has made us notorious and unique. We're the only Black revolutionary group to build a coalition with Whites. We call our position "revolutionary nationalism," as opposed to "cultural nationalism," which limits the struggle for self-determination to appearances—dashikis, African names, talk about "new nationhood" and the Black nation. For us, such emphasis is real problematical. Dress and language are definitely *not* what Fanon has talked about in *The Wretched of the Earth*. Instead he insists that the only worthwhile culture is a *revolutionary* culture. We say we won't free ourselves through steeping ourselves in an African past and folklore but by aligning ourselves with other liberation fighters, movements that have won their freedom through political and armed struggle. We are about gaining economic and political freedom; after that, worry about what you call yourself.

David Hilliard,
Chief of Staff of the Black Panther Party

Therefore to be a revolutionary nationalist you would by necessity have to be a socialist. If you are a reactionary nationalist you are not a socialist and your end goal is the oppression of the people. Cultural nationalism, or pork chop nationalism, as I sometimes call it, is basically a problem of having the wrong political perspective. It seems to be a reaction instead of responding to political oppression. Many times cultural nationalists fall into line as reactionary nationalists. Papa Doc in Haiti is an excellent example of reactionary nationalism. He's against anything other than Black, which on the surface seems very good, but for him it is only to mislead the people. He merely kicked out the racists and replaced them with himself as the oppressor. Many of the nationalists in this country seem to desire the same ends.

Huey Newton,
Minister of Defense of the Black Panther Party

We don't fight racism with racism. We fight racism with solidarity. We don't fight exploitative capitalism with Black capitalism. We fight capitalism with revolutionary socialism . . . We don't care about changing what we wear; we want power—later for what we wear. Dashikis don't free nobody and pork chops don't oppress nobody.

Bobby Seale,
Chairman of the Black Panther Party

These quotes can be found in *This Side of Glory: The Autobiography of David Hilliard and The Story of the Black Panther Party*.

CHAPTER ONE

"A d a y i n t h e l i f e"

Even the best laid plans of mice and Klansmen don't always come together. As it turned out, it was unrealistic of Tom Metzger to demand that every other state (besides those that were collectively known as the Lost-Found Nation of Islam in North America) in the union be made his. After the majority of the mass deportations he called for were said and done, approximately 75 million Whites were left within the borders of what became Aryan Amerikkka. Out of that amount, only a quarter of a million included all of the actual members of White Aryan Resistance, the Ku Klux Klan, the Nazi Party, and the farthest of the Religious Right (the latter having been put in charge of regulating culture) who ruled Amerikkka with an iron hand.

This select few had to keep a policing eye on an area that stretched from Maine to Florida, from Los Angeles to Atlanta, and most points in-between. And the tighter their proverbial iron hand squeezed, the more rebellious Whites who didn't recognize Aryan authority slipped between its fingers. The maintaining of internal control over Aryan Amerikkka in the early part of the 21st century was a constant challenge. For Metzger and his ilk always wanted their vision of a White bred homeland to be fully populated with people who would be willing to fill up the scenery of said vision. Instead, Amerikkka's number one priority quickly became convincing the Whites who couldn't afford to leave the country to submit to the new order "by hook or by crook" as Tom Metzger's son and successor John had put it.

All of this was why right before the USA completely acquiesced to WAR in 2006, Metzger agreed at the very last minute to allow all of Northern California, Oregon, and the state of Washington to be left with the old order just like Alaska and Hawaii had been. Because just as the Aryans knew they wouldn't be able to maintain a real, strategic hold over them, they also correctly figured the less states within North America that had to be policed, the better. After all, nuclear blackmail was fine for repelling international invaders, but against one's own populace? In one's own backyard?

A Berlin Wall-esque wall was built all along the western borders of Nevada and Idaho. The wall also cut California in even halves and took the first decade of the new order's reign to complete. The fenced-in Pacific Northwest was euphemistically called by the Aryans the Divided States. Those within the wall in turn called Amerikkka, "the land where men are men and sheep are scared" and also called the Lost-Found Nation of Islam "New Africa" A label the Nation of Islam hated as much as they always hated the term "Black Muslims" because it kept them from feeling as though they shared the same legitimacy as orthodox Muslims. The use of New Africa didn't exactly sit well with those from the actual continent of Africa either.

Understandably, the patriotic residents of the Divided States tried their best to hold onto all that was the old order and every single vestige of what was Americana. Including the Constitution itself, with the actual hemp-woven piece of paper it was written on still perfectly preserved. Which was why when the Fourth of July rolled around, the general mood of the entire Pacific Northwest was uplifted to the 12th power. Spirits were higher during the days surrounding Independence Day than they were around Christmas time and certainly more so than New Year's Eve or Day which had become morbidly known as Nuke Year's Day because of the sorry fate that befell Australia.

But to one Elijah Isiah of the Lost-Found Nation of Islam in North America, July the 4th in the year 2030 A.D. was just another Monday morning in which he'd have to get up and go to work.

* * *

In English, the muezzin essentially meant "the one who calls Muslims to prayer." But to Sharrieff it might as well had been Arabic for "he who everyone in town wants to see left hanging from a tree." Though swear words had been nakon or forbidden for over twenty years, Sharrieff could still hear them in his mind's ear directed at him anytime he caught dirty stares from the brothers and sisters who happened to find out what poor Sharrieff did for a living. Which was to sound what once was known as an air raid siren every morning at sunrise (6 a.m. if the sky was overcast) in order to wake everyone within the reach of the cry of "Sharrieff's trumpet" as he called it. The siren was to let people know it was time to give praise to Allah in the form of the *Fajr*, the morning prayer, and get their day started.

There were seven of these sirens strategically placed across the city of Chicago but Sharrieff's trumpet in particular was heard all over Chicago's South Side and the sound wasn't welcome at all in the small three bedroom, two bath on the corner of Harlem and 125th Street. At the very least, it wasn't appreciated by Elijah Isiah. The previous day, Sunday, July the 3rd, was Elijah's 38th birthday and for a hot moment he thought that if it had fallen on a Monday instead, then that would be enough of an excuse to stay home from work. Wasn't there something in the Koran about a man not having to work on the day after his birthday? Especially if that workday fell on a Monday, Elijah jokingly thought to himself. Alas, the last thing Elijah wanted was to be reprimanded for befitting the stereotype of the lazy Negro, so even though he felt magnetized to his mattress, Elijah proceeded to crawl out of bed and stagger towards the bathroom.

Elijah wiped the snot out of the corners of his eyes before looking over at his wife Nayirah, who was already wide awake and impatiently waiting for him to finish using the bathroom. Since, as the man of the house, Elijah had to perform the morning ablutions before anyone else.

"In the name of Allah, I perform the ablution," Elijah said once he finally made it to the sink. He then scrubbed his hands as if preparing for surgery, brushed his teeth, and rinsed his mouth in an almost mechanical fashion that had evolved from years of routine. The only point in which this mechanized rhythm was broken was when Elijah hesitated with a barely detectable look of mild disgust on his face before rinsing his nostrils three times. A part of the morning routine that seemed to Elijah immune to the decades of repetition he had put into the process.

As Elijah was about to enter the shower, he stopped, went back to open the bathroom door that led to the master bedroom, and when the opened door gave him a clear view of the still scowling Nayirah lying on their bed, Elijah called out, "you know, Nay—you *could* be doing your ablutions while I'm in the shower."

Nayirah folded her arms at that. "As-Salaam-Alaikum, *dear heart*," she said with the last two words dripping with attitude.

Elijah's face fell as he sighed. The first thing that was to be said every morning was "peace be unto you," and knowing how adamant Nayirah can be, Elijah knew she wouldn't respond to anything else until he answered back "and unto you be peace," or—

"Wa-Alaikum-Salaam. Now, to save us some time, why don't you come do your ablutions while I'm showering?"

"You know that wouldn't be appropriate, dear heart," Nayirah responded. "And please don't call me 'Nay.'"

The reason why Elijah suggested what he did was because he wanted to spend slightly longer in the shower than usual that morning. Mainly to wash the proverbial cobwebs out of his head but also because of the especially hot, sweaty, and sticky lovemaking session Nayirah and he had had the night before. It was one of her birthday presents to him and Elijah had to put in more of an effort than usual because she had recently found out about an edict that stated a Muslim man is not permitted to leave his bed until his woman is—satisfied.

During said session, Nayirah wrapped her legs around Elijah's waist especially tight towards "the end" as if she was trying to entrap him. At the time, Elijah arrogantly thought this was merely the synapses of her thigh muscles clenching out of some sort of orgasmic reflex. While in the shower however, Elijah realized Nayirah had been trying to entrap him in a sense. All forms of artificial birth control were made nakon a few years ago (It would have been made illegal sooner except the amount of Blacks with AIDS within the Lost-Found Nation had to first be lowered to a small enough number to make discreet mass exile a possibility. Until that point, safe sex needed to be practiced.) and Nayirah was trying to get Elijah to secrete inside her in hopes of being impregnated.

Nayirah should have known by now how he felt about having another child, Elijah thought. Despite the call for the population to grow so the Lost-Found Nation of Islam in North America wouldn't look so barren in places, Elijah said to himself he couldn't care less if

35 million Blacks weren't enough to adequately fill up all of Illinois, Indiana, Iowa, and so forth. Little Elisha had just turned 10 on June the 23rd and it seemed as though the older he got, the more his high metabolism required that he eat. Though where all the food Elisha ate went was beyond Elijah since his only son was skinny as a post. In addition to not knowing if he could afford another mouth to feed, Elijah never was entirely confident of his parenting skills to begin with. He always feared those skills would be spread too thin if another child should enter the picture and Elijah had enough of a time protecting Elisha from the world around him as it was.

As Elijah stepped out of the shower, he decided to test his wife of 11 years. Without immediately reaching for his towel as he usually did, Elijah walked out of the shower stall in the altogether in plain view of Nayirah, who decided not to wait to begin her ablutions after all and was in the middle of rinsing her nostrils. Nayirah in turn predictably averted her eyes in silence, hurriedly stripped out of her pajamas, and ducked into the stall without looking back. Married over a decade and she still won't look at his naked body unless they were making love, Elijah thought. Doesn't she realize they haven't installed hidden cameras in everyone's homes (at least, not yet anyway) and you only have to follow the rules to the letter when in public? Or did Nayirah actually derive pleasure from not only following the rules but making up some rules of her own as she goes along?

* * *

In the living room Elisha Isiah had already emerged dried from his shower from the other bathroom in the house and in his prayer robes. The ceremonial rug was already spread underneath Elisha who was squatted on it in a position indicating to Elijah as he entered the room that his son was ready to pray. Except that unlike his mother, there wasn't any impatient scowl on Elisha's face. For like his father, Elisha knew what the world expected of him and only did just enough to get by without getting too anal-compulsive over whatever it was that had to be done. As Elijah knelt beside his son, he affectionately rubbed the boy's head, almost as if for good luck, as they did back in the days of old—before the Apocalypse a quarter of a century ago.

"Can't we just pray now and drink? I don't want to wait for mother to get out of the shower, I'm thirsty."

Elijah looked up out of reflex to see whether or not Nayirah could hear—as if she had the hearing of a female canine necessary to discern anything that was being said down the hall amidst running water. "Nay'll be done in a minute. And remember to say the greeting when she does comes out."

When a still damp Nayirah walked into the living room in her robes, Elisha did just that and called out, "As-Salaam-Alaikum, mother."

"Wa-Alaikum-Salaam," Nayirah answered in a soft but guarded tone as if to say "quieter next time." She parted the curtains of the living room window which had a view of the eastern skyline and the rising sun, then took her place on the rug and knelt next to her husband. The Isiahs all bowed their heads, raised their forearms slightly so their elbows were chest level, and cupped their hands as if catching rain.

"I perform the morning prayer to Allah, the most high. Allah is the greatest," Elijah began. "Glory to Thee, oh Allah, Thine is the praise. Blessed is Thy name and—and—*exalted*," Elijah said finally as if he had to recall the word first, "is Thy majesty. I bear witness that nothing deserves to be served or worshipped besides Thee." Elijah slowly glanced over at Nayirah, waiting for either her approval or a hard look. And sure enough, it was the latter.

"I really wish you would learn your Arabic, dear heart," she said softly. "Someday it will be our national language and you don't think the rest of our 750 million brothers and sisters in the Muslim world say the morning prayer in *English*, do you?"

* * *

Elijah drank his second cup of coffee, spied all the food he had in his kitchen cabinet, and already found himself wishing it was dinner—the one solid meal a day they all were allowed. Elijah then looked out the kitchen window and saw something he feared: He could tell even that early in the morning that there wasn't going to be so much as a wisp of a cloud in the sky to block at least some of that July/Chicago heat. Elijah stuck an index finger into his shirt collar and tugged on his bow tie as if a cartoonish plume of steam would vent itself into the air from between his neck and the inside of his shirt. Elisha mimicked his father in-between swallows of his orange juice and since the two were both drinking from cups while dressed identically because of the national dress code, the scene looked almost surreal. Certainly bewildering enough to Nayirah to keep her from making the usual "quit fidgeting" remarks.

Instead, she asked, "when are you going to fix that gas main, dear heart?"

Elijah looked up from mulling over whether or not a third cup of coffee would fill him up until 6 p.m. and then answered, "what do you mean *fix* it, Nayirah? You know I'm the least mechanically inclined man that was ever born. Besides, I don't hear that hissing you keep talking about anyway. Just call somebody that would know what to look for."

Nayirah was standing over the kitchen sink as if listening for something but when her husband said what he did, she put her hands on her hips in irritance. "That's your answer to everything, isn't it? *Call somebody*. As if the Nation didn't have more important things to do than to provide some special service to be at your beck and call for whenever you didn't feel like taking responsibility for what goes on in your own home."

"We pay our tithes, our tides, we pay our 'duty' at the temple don't we?" Elijah quietly commented without looking right at her, "we should get something back."

"When we had such *ser*vices—or just plain *vices* that we had to call the White man 'sir' to get, our people grew fat and lazy from their dependence on them, and that made us fall prey to the White man! Now that the Honorable Khallid Muhammad has completely privatized our economy, he has liberated us so that we can finally *do for self*. Mash Allah!"

Praise God for what, Elijah thought. That at some point he was going to have to find some technical manual, get under that damn sink, and tinker around where Elijah knew he had no business? Oh well, Elijah said to himself, at least finding a fix-it book would be easy, they didn't ban or burn those.

* * *

The Noble Drew Ali Elementary School (known before the Apocalypse as Trinity Christian College) was only around the corner from his house but Elijah still didn't like to see Elisha walk there all by himself. Mainly because it reminded Elijah that he wasn't getting any younger. But beyond that, Elijah missed all the walks and talks that he and his son once had on that short route to school—*alone*. For Elijah used the opportunity to inform any new teachers at the school that Elisha was not to be subject to the usual corporal punishments. And that if Elisha did do anything wrong, they were to merely inform his father, and his father only, because supposedly Elijah's "special brand of discipline" was far more severe than anything the school could conjure up.

There had been some close calls over the years and it didn't help that school was year-round, but so far Nayirah nor anyone else of any dangerous significance had found out about Elijah's one transgression against the will of the Nation. Elijah didn't protect Elisha from the world around him just because he loved his son so, which he did. It was fast becoming as of late Elijah's number one reason for living in that world at all.

On those days of schooling the school on turning Elisha over to only him in case of trouble or mischief, Elijah used to let Nayirah take the Isiahs' one car to her work while he would just take the bus to his job. But by the end of the last fiscal year, public transportation was viewed by all the ministers in all the temples across the Lost-Found Nation of Islam as interference with the Black man's independence and ability to pull himself up by his bootstraps. So since the last budget cuts, buses and commuter trains had been made nakon, leaving only taxi cabs, if one considered them public transportation. Elijah wondered to himself whether the elimination of public transportation was because the car manufacturers from neighboring Michigan wanted to make all the more money—because he didn't dare wonder any of this out loud. He was already taking more than enough chances at it was for covertly going against the school system's innate right to discipline Elisha.

Also, Nayirah read somewhere that it was common courtesy for the man to drive his woman around and drop her off at different places. So now Elijah had to watch his son walk off into the world and drop his wife off at her job. Which was teaching at the Muslim Girl's Training and General Civilization Class at a school that was once called Saint Xavier College. After the Apocalypse, it was renamed the Sarah X School for Girls after some martyr from the days when the slave names of Muslims were replaced with a "X" and before Black people were all assigned their true, Afro-Asiatic names by the ministers.

The ride to the all-girls school was relatively a quiet one. As was the case for the majority of Elijah's rides with Nayirah—unless of course they were arguing. To avoid an argument, Elijah tried to get to Sarah X as fast as the already heavy traffic would permit. When they finally did arrive at the school, Nayirah sardonically said, "you don't have to pick me up today. I have to get some things for dinner and I know how 'busy' you are, so I'll take a taxi to the market after school." Then she practically leapt out of Elijah's 2025 black four-door sedan, and flounced past the school's front gates with her white chador and roosarie flowing behind her in what little wind there was in the air on this balmy morning.

Though her robe and scarf were a solid white, Elijah's self-trained eye could still barely make out a silhouette of the hourglass shape of Nayirah's filled out body as she disappeared into a crowd of similarly dressed women and thought back for a moment to the day that they met.

Actually they never "met" in the traditional, eyes-met-across-a-crowded-room, romantic sense. They were "matched" by the Ministry of Love. Back in the 20th century, there was a time when light-skinned Blacks with keen facial features were treated by Whites better than dark-skinned Blacks with flat facial features. The lighter, keen-featured Blacks were considered better looking than their darker, flat-featured counterparts and whenever favors for Blacks *were* given by Whites, they would invariably go to any Black who appeared all the more White visually.

This dynamic had existed even within the Black community itself. The bias over nose bridges, lip sizes, and shades of skin color spilled over into the arena of interpersonal relationships between Blacks. According to all the ministers in the Lost-Found Nation, dark-skinned, flat-featured girls could never get suitors while their light-skinned, keen-featured rivals always could. To remedy this, the ministers decreed that in order to "even out the playing field," the Nation would take it upon itself to prearrange who would be allowed to date, let alone marry, whom. Light-skinned, keen-featured brothers would be paired by the state with dark-skinned, flat-featured sisters, and in the case of the Elijah and Nayirah it was the other way around.

Since Elijah was so dark and Nayirah was so very light, Elisha came out with an deep, even tan. Which was exactly the kind of result that was sought after by all concerned. For the consensus among the ministers was that within a few generations, everyone in the Lost-Found Nation would be a uniform shade of brown. It was both thought and taught that things were best this way because once everyone had the same skin tone no one would ever feel they were any better or worse than anyone else.

Elijah's eyes then fell on the front seat where his wife was just sitting, to see out of a perverse sort of curiosity, whether or not the extra couple of pounds Nayirah had put on lately had caused her to leave a still visible impression in the cushions. It was at this point when he noticed the book that she left behind. Nayirah's copy of *The Black Woman* by Dorothy Wedad was lying on the car floor on the passenger's side, and as Elijah snatched it up while hopping out of the car he thought for certain that this was an opportunity to coax a smile out of his demanding wife for returning her book before going to work himself.

Elijah didn't ask for permission to pass the school's front gate, he had forgotten he needed to. And because he had, Elijah found himself surrounded by women in white, flowing chadors that covered them from head to toe before he had gotten too far into the school's perimeter. It was almost like being accosted by a slew of ghosts in pale sheets from some 20th century Halloween, but Elijah remembered why he was suddenly being yelled at.

"You know the rules! Men are nakon!"

"No men are allowed here!"

"No men at all!"

"Alright, *fine!*" Elijah countered. He was slightly taller than the tallest woman there and felt like wading through the lot of them like Gulliver amongst the Lilliputians but he didn't want the Fruit of Islam called on him. Elijah didn't have a criminal record and he didn't want to start one over something this banal. "Will somebody just give this to Nayirah Isiah?" Elijah called out while holding up Nayirah's book for all to see.

"*I* will give the book to the sister," said the tallest woman there as she took it from Elijah. "As-Salaikum, my brother."

"Wa-Salaikum," muttered Elijah under his breath as he sulked back to his car.

* * *

Elijah thought he would never get on the expressway. Now that he was on it, Elijah was certain he'd never get off of it. Traffic was backed up for miles and he would be late for work for sure. As Elijah looked over at his fellow drivers nodding politely back at him whenever eye contact was made, Elijah noticed that most of them were driving Cadillacs, mini-vans, and sedans just like he was. It also occurred to Elijah that there was usually only one driver within each of the cars all around him and—if every four drivers or so would share a single car . . ? Alas, if people were to pool their resources like that, they might become too dependent on one another to get back and forth, and everyone in the Nation was supposed to be as self-reliant as possible. At least, so conventional wisdom would say, thought Elijah.

But he did wish that someone was responsible for fixing all of the pot holes that lay all along the highways and byways of Chicago. Elijah's drive to work every morning was akin to a soldier's trespass across a minefield and if it was expected of him to get to work on time so that he could be all the more productive, the Nation should step in with some kind of service to repair the roads.

While they were at it, Elijah pondered, it could also be looked into as to why it was one couldn't see the stars in the sky at night anymore. Or why temperatures continue to rise every year and why the summer of 2030 was the hottest on record? Or why the air tasted so stale and the horizon looked so hazy?

Could it simply be nothing more than all of the exhaust that was being put out by the extra cars on the road and all the smog one sees emanating from the city? There were a few who believed that, but they weren't heard nearly as much as the ministers who maintained either a silence concerning the issue or that everything was alright. People were told at their temples that complaining about one's eyes spontaneously watering at midday only made Blacks look bad. As though they were whining children who depended on some great power to take care of them. What would the Aryans from Amerikkka think of the Black man then?

As Elijah pulled into State Street he thought about how many times such concerns were fielded by those who claimed that no such services could be provided for the infrastructure or the environment because all of the Lost-Found Nation's resources were being diverted toward the protection of its borders from the White devils of Aryan Amerikkka.

It never made complete sense to Elijah why the ministers would be that worried about an invasion of the Nation. The peace has been kept for 25 years, so if Amerikkka were going to take over the states allocated to be the homeland, surely they would've done it by now, Elijah concluded.

When Elijah brought this up some months ago after a service at his temple, one of the ministers there explained:

> Sure our truce with the White man has kept the peace. But seeing as how they *always were* mortal enemies of the Black man, Metzger and his legions could decide at anytime to betray the agreement that was *grudgingly* hammered out *at the last minute* by Minister Farrakhan and the blue eyed devil during the Apocalypse. Luckily Minister Farrakhan and the Metzger were able to *temporarily* put aside their *many differences* so that our people could survive.

Nayirah believed the minister's explanation and accepted it as a rationale for why the Nation's attentions couldn't be focused on the welfare of its own people at home. But then, "Nay" would stand on her head if a minister asked her to, provided she could see to it that the ends of her chador were pinned to her socks so that her legs wouldn't be seen. Elijah wondered as he looked for a parking space if all the people he saw walking along State Street that morning were as accepting of everything that was told to them as Nayirah was. Or did some of them, *any* of them, ever question the authority of the Lost-Found Nation of Islam, the ministers in their temples, and the Honorable Khallid Muhammad—if nowhere but in the privacy of their own minds? Not disobey their edicts, just *question* them, and maybe dare ask if they're justifiable.

Elijah amazed himself with his ability to think such subversive thoughts when he looked the neighborhood surrounding the Old Water Tower on his long trek between his parking space and his job. The Tower was one of the few structures in the area to survive the Great Chicago Fire but just about everything else has changed in the past 25 years and it was hard not to feel overwhelmed by the Nation of Islam when you felt surrounded by every aspect of them anytime you came downtown.

The only form of art that the Nation saw fit to fund were the displays on the sides of nearly every other building for all to see depicting the likenesses of the Honorable Khallid Muhammad, leader of the Lost-Found Nation of Islam in North America; his retired predecessor, Minister Louis Farrakhan (though most of the pictures depicted him during his peak, circa 1984-2010, and rarely was he shown at his current age of 97); and the last Messenger of Allah himself, Elijah Muhammad.

Gigantic banners were also hung from lamp posts and flag poles with slogans like "Each One Teach One," "Unity," "Unity Nation," or "Unity in the Community," "Respect" or "Respect Your Elders," "Knowledge of Self," "Do For Self," "It's On You," "Wake Up, Black Man," "The Black Woman is the Queen of the Universe," and "Buy Black" which Elijah always found an incongruity because there weren't anyone but Black folks in the Lost-Found Nation.

And then there were the more religious slogans in both Arabic and English saying "There is No God but Allah," "God is Great," "Praise Allah," "God is a Black Man," "The Black Man is God," and "Allah Will Provide."

Elijah crossed over from State Street to the corner of Chicago Avenue and Rush Street towards his place of work, Mustafa Enterprises in the Akbar Office Building where for five days a week Elijah Isiah becomes a "dictator."

Elijah thought about how comically ironic the title of his position was to take his mind off of him having to walk up the 14 flights of stairs to his office because the building's elevators were broken yet again. Elijah mused over the fact that he was only a dictator in the sense that he took dictation from his editor, Mustafa Ali, and dictated what he said or wrote by typing it into a computer data base.

When Elijah finally reached the offices of Mustafa Enterprises on the 14th floor, he crept inside as to not draw attention to his tardiness. He was only 15 minutes late but it wasn't the first time and the last thing Elijah needed was to lose this job, which was probably one of the best Elijah ever had. As a dictator, he was part one of the Nation of Islam's first entries into the super information highway—an encyclopedic database that would contain the entire history of the world from the beginning of time to the modern era. Events, dates, famous battles, or even historical trivia could be available via internet and accessible through computer terminals that would be installed at every junior high and high school in the Lost-Found Nation within the next year.

It did bother Elijah that this move would mean schools would have all the less reliance on history books but Elijah still viewed his job as a venture that probably should have been made decades ago. And it would have too, except that the majority of the Nation's attentions went either towards defense of its borders or the strict enforcing of its Islamic fundamentalist edicts at home. Not to mention the 25 year old world wide embargo and sanctions put upon the Lost-Found Nation that were, according to the ministers, imposed out of spite because no one wanted to see an all-Black, independent nation succeed.

Elijah quietly slid behind his desk amidst the snide, whispered comments about him made by the four other dictators already behind their desks typing away. Dictating from hard copy was thought of as a form of secretarial work, which in turn was considered feminine, which was why the only other dictators in the office were all Muslimah. Each Muslim woman dressed as per the national dress code in her white chador looked up from what they were typing and gave Elijah a contemptuous stare but were all too submissive to alert their boss, Mustafa Ali in the next room that his only male employee was late again.

Elijah couldn't help but to grin. The fact was he had the fastest typing speed in the office and at 80 words per minute, Elijah's status as Mustafa Enterprise's most valuable employee was stiil unchallenged. He even had the one desk in the room closest to the window which made Elijah feel all the more important though he never liked the billboard that he was in plain view of. It was a cosmetic ad for Muslimah which showed nothing but a woman wrapped in a single-eye chador and her one, visible eye had on the eyeliner the ad was trying to sell. The caption to the side of the visuals read, "Power Products presents—Eye of Edwina, the only make-up you'll ever need . . !"

Nayirah never completely approved of Elijah being a dictator because as far as she was concerned it was not what she considered a very "manly job." "Nay" probably would've been happier if he was some burly member of the Fruit of Islam throwing transients in overcrowded jails all day to keep them from loitering and becoming eyesores for potential tourists. Then she could have something to brag to her girlfriends about. Elijah was certain that his co-workers, whom he hardly ever spoke to at all, felt the same way except they just wanted to be rid of him and didn't care if he was boasting material or not. The only woman who seemed to appreciate Elijah's presence at the office was Mustafa's personal secretary, a young girl with the most unusual African name Elijah had ever heard, Minitrue.

"Have you found anyone else with that unusual name of yours yet?" Elijah called out as he saw the 17 year old Minitrue in her white gown and headdress come his way with a stack of hard copy from Mustafa's office for him to dictate.

Minitrue giggled, "No, Mr. Isiah."

"Because you know sometimes Black folks make up African names as they go along," Elijah quipped. "I never did think anyone from the motherland was ever named "La-Ti-Quisha" or half of the names I've heard."

This caused all the other dictators to simultaneously stop what they were typing for a moment, look at one another for a moment or scowl at Elijah, and then resume typing. Minitrue seemed oblivious to all of this and laughed probably louder at Elijah's comment than conventional decorum would have had her.

"My name is going to continue to be the running joke in this office isn't it, Mr. Isiah?"

Elijah looked about at the four women typing around him, "Mini, it's probably the *only* joke in this office."

"Well, here you go," Minitrue leaned over to set the stack of papers Elijah was to type on his desk, then whispered, "I don't think Mr. Ali noticed you were late, Mr. Isiah," and walked back to Mustafa Ali's office.

Elijah glanced towards his boss's office. It had a tinted window with a view of the rest of the office but mercifully Mustafa Ali usually had his back to it. As far as bosses went, Ali was tolerable. Considering he used to be a speech writer for the Honorable Khallid Muhammad's most likely successor, Professor Griffith Muhammad, the former rapper who was kicked out of his rap group back in the 20th century for being uncompromising in his belief and support of Minister Farrakhan's teachings at the time.

When the technology finally became available to the Nation of Islam a year and a half ago to deposit an almanac of world history inside internet, the ever enterprising Mustafa Ali was able to use his connections to land an exclusive, private contract with the Nation for the producing of his computerized tomes of world history. But while a decent conveyor of ideas with an eye for managerial business, paradoxically, Mustafa Ali was never very computer literate. Hence his need for the dictators.

In a rush to get the historical data downloaded as quickly as possible, Mustafa would churn out as many pages as he could either by hand or on his electric typewriter, and leave correcting any syntax or grammatical errors for his dictators. Once the information was in the computer, it could be accessed by Mustafa to see if what had been imputed was to his liking and if it met with the final approval of the group of ministers who oversaw the bulk of his historical research. The accessing of the program, one which was intended for children anyway, didn't require that Mustafa Ali or the ministers possess any great amount of computer literacy so much as the ability to move a cursor and hit the return button.

These same ministers were also Mustafa's primary source of historical information seeing as how only ministers of temples had access to certain books from the past. Which made Elijah wonder every once in a long while about whether or not what he was typing into internet was the whole truth.

Elijah remembered when he first became a dictator one of the very first entries he had been told to input. It told of how Christopher Columbus had sailed across the Atlantic Ocean, landed in the Americas, and was wholeheartedly accepted by the indigenous population that he ran across once he arrived. Considering all that Elijah subsequently typed about the myriad struggles the same population had to face from others who came across the Atlantic in the centuries to come, something told Elijah that maybe Columbus had been just as bad as those who came after him. It didn't made much sense that Christopher Columbus was the *only* voyager who treated the indigenous people of the Americas well—especially if Columbus' mission was to bring gold back to his king by any means necessary.

Elijah brought his concerns to Mustafa Ali who in turn waved them off citing that the research that he and the ministers had done was thorough and that it wasn't Elijah's place to question their final judgment seeing as how, at the time, he had just started the job.

A little over a year later, Elijah had become the only dictator who ever asked questions about what he was dictating that were of a philosophical nature and not on strictly a grammatical one. It was only once in a long while when he would attempt this, but that was because Elijah only felt like pushing his luck in-between long whiles.

Elijah would've just as soon not had today be one of those days, but Elijah was the type of man whom life had to make sense to, otherwise it wasn't as easy to live through. And what he currently had to dictate struck him as a trifle senseless.

Elijah was plowing through the latest stack of hard copy about the post-World War II era that Minitrue had left for him and at 80 words per minute he was almost ready for another batch from her. And then he got to a point in the copy that spoke of the Jews and all that the Nazis had put them through.

He went ahead and typed the passages that had been given to him as they were, accounting for Mustafa Ali's occasional grammatical errors. But as soon as Elijah was finished entering what he had dictated into internet, he got up, knocked on his boss' door, and asked that he come to inspect what had just been written.

"I don't know if you noticed all of these books and papers in my office, Mr. Isiah, but they indicate that I'm a very busy man." Mustafa Ali fumed. Being in his early 50s with an afro that was balding ever so slightly, Mustafa was a diminutive sort of fellow who felt as though the presence of his charisma needed to over-compensate for his lack of size in order for him to be listened to. Elijah always joked to himself that this was why Mustafa always wrote speeches and never gave them. Because all the posturing in the world wouldn't have made him any more visible from behind a podium.

None of this meant Mustafa Ali couldn't fire Elijah at any time. Or worse, call the FOI on him for "interfering with the smooth running of a profitable business," so Elijah chose his language very carefully.

"Forgive me, Mr. Ali, I just thought that you might want to make sure that what I typed was worded exactly how you wanted it."

"Elijah, you know full well that the ministers and I will eventually go over all the entries in due time," Mustafa folded his arms and blew a frustrated breath out the side of his mouth. "But now that you've already bothered me, go ahead and show me what it is you're talking about."

Mustafa Ali then followed Elijah to his desk, where Elijah sat back behind his computer terminal and moved the cursor so that the last paragraph he had just typed would appear in the center of the screen so that it could be seen in its entirety all the clearer.

> It was believed for decades that an unimaginable six million Jews had died in the so-called "Holocaust" that the Jews claimed they went through during World War II. It has been found, however, that only a million Jews died during that time and not even by the means in which they claimed the deaths occurred. For instance, the infamous gas chambers the Jews described turned out to be a complete fabrication and no Jew ever died from being put into such a chamber.

"I don't see a problem with what you wrote," said Mustafa Ali. "That's exactly how I wanted it, minus the spelling errors, of course. Good job."

"The problem, sir, is that it doesn't make any sense," Elijah explained. "Who could make up such a thing? Why would anyone lie about something of that—magnitude? And where did you get this information?"

"To gain undue sympathy, of course," Mustafa stated simply. "They wanted people to believe that they had gone through more suffering than the Black race. But if you *must* know, Elijah, our main source for this material was from a 1976 book entitled, *The Hoax of the 20th Century* by Dr. Arthur R. Butz."

"Sir, it's just that—if only a million Jews died, then where did the other five million go? Were they in hiding?" Elijah's voice started to rise slightly. "And since the missing five million Jews must have surely had children—and *great grand*children by now, then are *they* all in hiding too?"

Mustafa Ali looked around to see if the women in his place of business appeared to be taken in by Elijah's defiance of him. The four other dictators continued to type and practically ignored the scene going on before them. Minitrue, however, had emerged from Mustafa's office and looked as though she felt sorry for Elijah. As a former speech writer, Mustafa Ali knew the importance of maintaining popular opinion or, at the very least, a consenting one. So an example would have to be made of Elijah in front of everybody.

"Mr. Isiah, I could have said something about you coming in late this morning. I could have said something about your lack of respect for your Black sisters as far as the comments you made earlier, and yes, I did hear you make them, but I didn't. Now you have interrupted the flow of this business day with your questioning of the historical facts that the ministers of the Nation of Islam themselves and I have painstakingly researched. Questioning that I see now I have tolerated too long.

"By all rights, I could call the Fruit of Islam on you and have you carted off for any of the offenses I just mentioned. Actually, I *should* fire you, but you know as well as I do how valuable you are. Therefore, I'm going to go out on a limb and do something as liberally communistic as to *give you one last chance.* I hope that you don't abuse the privilege. As for the rest of you, it's almost noon. Get ready for the *Zuhr* prayer." Mustafa Ali then spun on his heel, stormed back to his office, and slammed the door behind him.

* * *

"*The Black Woman* by Dorothy Wedad is one of the single most important books that any young lady in our great nation will ever read." Nayirah held up her copy of the book in question that she would've forgotten had it not been for Elijah. She waved it in front of her class at the Sarah X School for Girls as though it was a bible and she was an evangelical preacher from long ago. And if Nayirah's intent *was* to generate anything close to the kind of spirited reaction such preachers could stir up in their day, the effort would have been a complete waste. For the pre-teen girls who were in attendance knew all too well what could happen to them if they were to display too wildly emotional of a response in the middle of class.

"Soon this book will be required reading and you'll have to memorize it, cover to cover." Nayirah paced back and forth in front of the front row of desks while she tried to turn to a page she had intended to read from.

"Nineteen seventy three: The year when the old United States had just legalized the killing of Black babies and called it 'abortion' or 'birth control.' The beginning of an era when anyone who called for the extermination of the Black race was called 'pro-choice.' This was the era of Dorothy Wedad, a proud Black woman, a *strong* Black woman, who had the courage to face up to the so-called 'feminists' who claimed they were for 'women's liberation' but were actually as bad as Nazis and spoke the truth to the White devil woman's face." Nayirah stopped pacing in front of the class when she found the page she was looking for.

"For a time she wrote for *Muhammad Speaks* and this book reprints pieces from what was once our national newspaper. Here is something that she had written for Muhammad Speaks on March 2nd, 1973." And with that, Nayirah began to read.

> Prior to the coming of Almighty God, Allah Who came in the person of Master Fard Muhammad, and raised up the Honorable Elijah Muhammad, the Black woman in America was totally ignorant to herself and her role. The devil (White man) had done such a thorough job of destroying the Black family and forcing the woman into a more and more dominating role, until today she actually pictures herself as being equal to the man. In this so-called age of the "liberated woman," the Black woman following along behind the devil woman frowns on the idea of woman as homemaker, mother, and wife. She feels that [she] should have equal job opportunities in any field, the same as the man. The Honorable Elijah Muhammad, Messenger of Allah to all of our people, has been missioned to right the wrong that has been done to us by the White man. His teachings to the Black woman in America are designed to return her to her rightful role which is the "Mother of Civilization and the Queen of the Universe," a most beautiful role. But first he teaches her that the Black man is the first in the creation and she was next. And, that man being self-created, then made her for himself as a means of reproducing himself. Immediately she learns that she cannot be equal to man, when from the beginning they were created for different purposes. He further teaches her that she is the field in which man plants the seed, and another life is born. From this alone, she can see the magnificence of her role, to be the means by which human life is reproduced.

Nayirah closed the book, set it on her desk, and said, "On March the 23rd of that same year, sister Dorothy Wedad said, 'tell the White man we are not interested in women's liberation—another trick to steer our minds from motherhood.' It is because of proud, beautiful, Black sisters like Dorothy Wedad that we are able to live in the truly liberated Black nation as we all do today. Any questions, class?"

* * *

Without a doubt, the best thing about being a dictator to Elijah Isiah were the hours, 10 a.m. to 2 p.m. (Mustafa Ali despised keeping anyone on the clock when there wasn't much to do and dictating wasn't that demanding). This was not because he was as lazy as his wife Nayirah thought him to be, it was because those lax hours enabled him to be home at approximately the same time as Elisha and the both of them would be home at least an hour before he would usually pick Nayirah up from school. And Elijah didn't even have to today, because this morning Nayirah's general disgust for him made her decide at the last minute to take a taxi to the market. So now Elijah and Elisha had all the more time to *talk*.

Not that Elijah and Elisha were anything like the subversives that the Fruit of Islam were always scouring the city for and had something secret to say, they just wanted to be able to talk about father and son things without feeling as though the eyes and ears of the Nation were upon them.

Elijah also thought it was important that someone was in the house when Elisha came home from school rather than him being what they called in the 20th century a "latch-key kid." Nayirah would have been more than happy to fulfill that role as the ever-present homebody except that Elijah's penchant for cushy jobs forced her to pay the majority of the bills and he never wanted to exert his rank as husband to demand that she stay at home—as Nayirah would've wanted him to (Elijah only exerts that rank to keep Nayirah from ever beating Elisha).

Nayirah had occasionally threatened to call the FOI on Elijah throughout the years over her being made a breadwinner against her inclinations but after a while she began to like teaching school. Eventually Nayirah came to love it so much that not only did she not mind so much that at one point Elisha was a latch-key kid (she would have minded more if Elisha was a girl), but she settled into the habit of staying long after school to help clean up after the cooking classes. Which was why Nayirah was usually the last one home.

Elijah and Elisha were sitting at the kitchen table enjoying the buffer zone of quality time that they had alone together before Nayirah would have to enter the picture. Elijah told his son about how he was almost fired and then asked one the most cliched questions on record.

"So what did you learn in school today?" Elijah queried as he put his hand on Elisha's shoulder.

"Weird stuff, father." Elisha shook his head as he sighed, grimaced as though he was trying to recall something, and said, "Mr. Bogam said that Black folks were descen—*descended* from some folks called the Original Men. They could talk to giants from Mars and used to live on the moon *way*, long time ago back when the moon and the Earth were one, big planet. Then everything *blew up*," and with that, Elisha illustrated the explosion he was describing with his hands and a sound effect he made with his mouth. "And then the moon and the Earth split into two planets like now. Then the Original folks came down and built Mecca and they were all in the tribe of Shazam."

"You mean the tribe of Shabazz," Elijah frowned. This story was sounding all too familiar to him.

"That's right. Anyway, there was this evil scientist with a big, giant head named Yacub. He was real smart and the Original folks put him on punishment and then sent him to an island. Then Yacub got mad and made White people in his la—labor—*laboratory*. He made everybody, father! First he made brown folks, then he made red folks, then he made yellow folks, and *then* he made White folks. And you know what else, father?"

"What?" Elijah answered back unenthused.

"Mr. Bogan said the White folks were animals in caves and then Allah sent Moses to get them out of the caves and the White folks that Moses got out of the caves turned into Jews!"

When Elijah heard the door open just then, he found himself surprisingly relieved. Even though he knew it was Nayirah, at that moment he actually thought it might be easier to deal with her than the idea that they had gotten around to teaching his son Yacub's History. To Elijah, both events were things that he would just as soon avoid.

"What are you doing?" Nayirah demanded as she set two grocery bags on the kitchen table. Elijah and Elisha were sitting around. "Are you out of your minds? It's time for the *Asr* and you haven't gotten the rug rolled out or the curtains parted or anything!"

"We won't miss the late afternoon prayer, Nayirah. It's not even close to five o'clock yet," Elijah countered.

"I don't care!" Nayirah exclaimed, which was rare because of her usual parochial restraint. "We're permitted only one meal a day that I have yet to fix and I don't have all that much time *to* fix it because in case you've forgotten we still have service at the temple to go to tonight."

Nayirah then sent Elisha to roll out the family prayer rug and then muttered to Elijah under her breath, "Since you don't stay at work long enough to work up a man's sweat, the least you could do is see that everything is prepared for the end of the day. You can call the Fruit of Islam on me for disrespecting you if you want, for I would rather be fined or jailed for telling the truth than for sitting idly around with a child *like* a child."

* * *

As Elijah drove his family up Ridgeland Avenue to the neighborhood still known in Chicago as "Burbank" where the nearest temple to the Isiah home was, he wondered for a moment why would a Black nation such as the one in which he lived allow its streets to still be called something as Caucasian sounding as Burbank and then he remembered. All of the semantic remnants from the old order would simply be translated to Arabic once it became the national language in approximately a decade. With all of the Lost-Found Nation's other worries, linguistics simply hadn't been the priority that it once was in the days when the Nation was first founded. But making sure that everyone showed up to their Monday, Wednesday, and

Friday night temple meetings always was one of the Nation of Islam's top priorities.

After Elijah finally found a place to park, he, Nayirah, and Elisha all filed into Muhammad's Temple of Islam Number 42 (which used to be a movie theater until motion pictures were made nakon) behind the scores of other Muslims and Muslimah who were already in line heading for the front entrance. After a while, Elisha let go of Nayirah's hand and proceeded to hold Elijah's as the one line that they were all in became two, with the women parting to the left and the men to the right. Once everyone, male or female, made it to the front door, they were searched. Even the children were frisked from head to toe.

A man who stood in front of Elijah was told by the temple guard searching him to open his mouth so that the man's breath could be smelled. The man still refused to do any such thing after having been asked three times. In response to this, two temple guards who seemed to Elijah to appear from nowhere grabbed the man from behind and held him down as the guard who originally had a problem with the man pried open his mouth. The temple guard then smelled the man's breath as he originally wanted to and declared that he had to have been drinking. The man swore what the guard was smelling was the alcohol base of the medicine that he had been taking as of late. This story wasn't believed by any of the temple guards so the man was carted away and Elijah didn't see him for the rest of the night.

After uneventful searches of their own, the Isiahs entered the temple with Nayirah finding a seat on the left-hand side of the temple where the women sat, Elijah finding a seat of his own across the aisle from Nayirah on the temple's right-hand side where the men sat, and Elisha being escorted to a basement where all the other children were kept during services (Elijah had even schooled those in the temple at one point on not disciplining Elisha and to his astonishment it had worked so far). At the head of the temple was a simple, Spartan speaker's stand that seated six with a microphone and a podium in the center. Behind the stand hung the national flag of the Lost-Found Nation of Islam in North America, an all white field with a red star and crescent moon in its center. The temple guards and the ministers took their places on the speaker's stand as other guards posted themselves by the doorways.

When all of the seats in the temple were completely filled to capacity one of the elder guards took the mike and a roll call was taken. It took over an hour to go through the five hundred names on the list and to send guards out to see about calling the homes of the few people on the list who didn't answer "here" or "present," but once that was finished, the minister that was to speak for the night finally stepped up to the microphone and led everyone there in the Maghrib or evening prayer.

* * *

" . . . And we cannot even take our pilgrimages to Mecca, our Hajj because we are welcome nowhere in the world. We cannot leave this mighty Black nation that we worked and waited so long for so that we can make the journey to the Ka'ba like any other Muslim should be able to. Why? I'll tell you what *they* say, the Jewry, the camel jockeys, the faggots, the Euro-trash, and the Orientals, I'll tell you what they're talking about! So never let it be said that the Black man is any kind of a censor or whatever it is they call us. They restrict our travel abroad because they're all under the delusion that Minister Farrakhan somehow knew in advance that 'the Great White Demon' Metzger was going to bomb Australia. Can you believe it? What lies! There were Black people on Australia! We would never drop a bomb on *Black* people! In case they hadn't noticed, we *are* Black people!"

"Yes!" ,.. "*Teach*, minister!" . . . "Take your *time* up there, little Messenger!" . . . "You *right*!" . . . "Tell it—*tell it*!" All these and more were among the many cries from the temple's congregation. A couple of them even came from Elijah, but his shouts weren't Freudian slips so much as they were cried out out of reflex. Also, who knew what would happen if anyone noticed he wasn't shouting as loud as everyone else.

"*Then* they insult us and our intelligence by telling the lie that somehow, some kind of way, we *collaborated* with Metzger and his devils during the Apocalypse? And they say *we're* guilty of creating mythologies!" The last line garnered a great deal of laughter from the crowd in the temple. "All those conspiracy nuts need to quit smoking that marijuana and start living *right*! Maybe then they'll stop suffering from all these delusions!" Even more laughter than before rose from the crowd. "And what's with all these folks going around calling us 'right-wing' and 'rightists' . . . Just what does that Jewish psychobabble mean, anyway? 'Right-wing,' 'left-wing'—brothers and sisters, we are *Black-wing*! They need to know that their White-wing rules don't apply to *us*!"

At this point there was a standing ovation, at least from the men's side of the temple. Displays of this type were considered by the Nation of Islam throwbacks to the era of the Black Baptist and Christian churches and were actually supposed to be nakon but Elijah was at a more liberal temple. So every once in a while such emotionalism was permitted, but only among the men.

Elijah tried to looked over at Nayirah from across the aisle. He had deliberately picked a seat directly across from her so that she could always be within his sights. Yes, she could get on Allah's nerves, but sometimes Elijah just liked to gaze upon his wife and wonder what it would have been like if they had met completely at random because their eyes happened to meet across a crowded room. A crowded room like this temple, perhaps. What if they never knew each other and the look that Elijah was now throwing Nayirah's way marked the first time he ever laid eyes on her?

Just then, Nayirah returned Elijah's stare but no actual eye contact was ever made. Rather, she seemed to Elijah to be looking at something right behind him. And before Elijah could turn to see what it was, he felt two gloved hands twist his neck forward.

"Brother, there's a reason why we separate the brothers and sisters. To keep one another from being distracted. Now pay attention to the minister before we have to take you somewhere."

Before Elijah could give an obedient response, the temple guard had resumed his post by one of the fire escapes. Now that he was more than suitably shaken enough to not risk anything else for the rest of the evening, Elijah found himself clapping from a false state of euphoria as a couple of frightened and shameful tears started to involuntarily roll down his cheeks.

"If the rest of the world wants to try and ignore us, fine. If they want to continue this embargo of theirs, that's fine too. Because we'll know the *real* reason why, won't we brothers and sisters? It's because they're jealous of the Black man and what he's accomplished here—in the wilderness of North America! Jealous, I say! And *fearful* too—because they know that we provide the threat of a good example to all the many Black people in the world who would try and establish an all-Black republic just like ours. Because that's what we are, brothers and sisters—*Black republicans*, and the rest of the world can't stand it!"

* * *

Elijah couldn't understand it. He lived off of one meal a day and yet there was enough in his system to get him up at two-thirty in the morning to urinate. The trick now was to not wake Nayirah up in the process. Which meant pissing not in the center of the toilet water, which would obviously make a sound, but to hit the inside surface of the bowl itself and not flush the toilet. And all of this had to be done in the dark too.

But even the best laid plans of mice and Black Muslims don't always come together. For no sooner had Elijah stealthily wrested free from Nayirah's embrace, slipped out of bed as quietly as he could, and made it to the bathroom door did he hear his wife's voice sternly say out loud, "Isha."

The *late* evening prayer. The one every Muslim is bound to perform if he happens to get up in the middle of the night. Actually the rule stated *two* prayers, but "Nay" let Elijah slide—*this* time . . .

5 6

CHAPTER TWO

"The state of the alienation"

The only problem with praying outside was that the thin prayer rugs that were standard issue in the Lost-Found Nation of Islam didn't offer a lot in terms of cushioning one's knees. It would be one thing if there was some soft grass or a field nearby, but this was the infamous "Loop" in downtown Chicago. So Elijah Isiah decided to do his kneeling on the pavement inside the promenade of the Water Tower Place since it did have a relatively tranquil atmosphere and because it was permitted.

The Water Tower Place was an indoor/outdoor mall where people like Elijah whose jobs were in the Old Water Tower neighborhood could come during the Zuhr prayer at noon and also enjoy the gigantic fountain in the mall's promenade. It was a fairly popular fountain seeing as how it had been almost unbearably hot out and the sky was so arid that it was nearly enough to make one's eyes water. But excessive loitering around the artificial geyser or most anywhere else in the Nation was definitely nakon, however. So people usually only frequented the fountain when they were either on the way to or coming from work.

In essence, the Zuhr was the closest thing to a lunch break the Muslims and Muslimah had, seeing as how they were only allowed one meal a day. Since the citizens of the Nation couldn't actually eat anything, at least they could try to relax and bask in the ambiance the promenade had to offer.

As Elijah finished his prayer, however, he thought how even if the view inside the mall wasn't all that it was, he still would've had to pray outdoors anyway. Since as of a half an hour ago, Elijah no longer had a job to go back indoors to. About 20 feet away praying alongside a herd of white chador clad women was the lovely Minitrue, the personal secretary of the man who finally had enough of Elijah's "boat rocking" and let Mustafa Enterprise's fastest dictator go.

Everyone in the promenade started their prayers at approximately the same time and began to slowly rise from where they all had knelt like an opening scene from a musical. Those who had mobile, miniature prayer rugs rolled them up as they rose. As Elijah bundled up his rug, he looked over at Minitrue, and motioned for her to come his way. The elder women that the 17 year old secretary was with said nothing when she did so, but they did give both her and Elijah either puzzled or disdainful looks.

Minitrue sat some distance away from Elijah on the enormously circular bench that essentially made up the barrier between the pavement and the water leading up the mall's huge fountain. "You know if I have to shout over the sound of this rushing water so that you can hear me then everybody will know our business," Elijah called out. "Isn't there something in the rules against that?"

Minitrue grinned as if in understanding and slid closer to Elijah. "We're not alone, this is a public place, and Tuesday *is* Unity Day, so I guess it's alright," she said as she looked back at the elder women she had prayed next to. It could still be seen from afar that the Muslimah didn't approve but they left without saying anything. "I was running an errand and when I came back you weren't at your desk—and no one told me anything, of course. What happened?"

Elijah sighed. The next time he was going to have to tell this story to a woman would be late in the afternoon when it came time to pick Nayirah up from school. And the sad part was this young girl, who's last name Elijah still didn't know after working with her for nearly a year, would be more understanding (and merciful) than his wife would ever be.

"Well, I abused that last chance I was given yesterday and now I'm fired," Elijah said mournfully.

"But how," asked Minitrue. "What did Mr. Ali tell you?"

"It wasn't so much what he told me so much as what I asked." Elijah fidgeted where he sat.

Minitrue looked at Elijah. "Mr. Isiah, you asked him to justify some more of his hard copy didn't you?" She tried her best to sound scornful but had to fight to suppress a smile.

"But it didn't make any *damn* sense!" He looked around to see if anyone was listening and when Elijah saw no one was, he continued. "Sorry for swearing. Anyway, I was inputting an entry about of the assassination of one of the Presidents from the old United States. A 'President Kennedy,' I don't suppose you ever heard of him?"

"No," Minitrue shrugged.

"Well, he was shot while riding in the back seat of an open car. There was this other guy, a 'governor,' sitting right in front of Kennedy who suffered a few wounds himself when the shooting started. Now, according to Mustafa's manuscript, there was this one guy named 'Oswald' who did all the shooting. But what doesn't make any sense is how the three shots that this Oswald character pulled could've possibly caused the two wounds that killed Kennedy and the five or so this governor had. Mustafa says the first shot missed altogether, the second shot hit this Kennedy in the throat *I think*, I'm not sure, and then that last shot—this one other bullet hit Kennedy in the head, bounced back and forth in the car, hit the governor in the back, the arm, the wrist, and I forget where else.

"*But then* 'Mr. Ali' says that this bullet was found in *mint condition* on a stretcher in the hospital where they took Kennedy. Now, I thought this was a simple enough mistake, Mustafa must have just over-counted the amount of wounds or under-counted the amount of bullets there were. But instead of even considering that he might have made a mistake insofar as the number of bullets or wounds he went off on a tangent. The man was actually trying to explain to me how it was that this—*magic bullet* could have zig-zagged all these different places and then it showed up somewhere, *unscathed*—I thought he had lost his mind! And when I said so, he kicked me out."

"Oh, Mr. Isiah . . ." Minitrue wanted to put her hand on his hand to comfort him but knew how risky that would be. "Why didn't you just dictate what he wanted you to? It's only a historical encyclopedia. Just because it was going to be on internet doesn't mean it was that important."

"But don't you care that what's passing off as historical fact is sounding more and more . . . Fanciful? Especially since children will be reading what we're doing!"

Minitrue looked thoughtful for a moment and then spoke as if she was much older but not necessarily any more wise. "Mr. Isiah, I have been told all my life that a pig is a cross between a cat, a rat, and a dog. Now I don't believe, not for one minute, that a pig can be a three-way cross of three different animals. I know that only *two* animals, or two people for that matter, can mate and give birth to something new.

"The way I figure it, a pig is probably only a cross between a rat and a dog, but I don't expect the ministers to tell me everything because they don't *know* everything. Only merciful Allah has 360 degrees of knowledge. And since all the ministers already know that only Allah has the sum total of knowledge, there's no point in reminding them, is there?"

After a long moment of stunned silence, Elijah sensed that he wasn't being asked a rhetorical question and muttered, "I guess there isn't."

"It's not a question of anyone being correct or incorrect, it's just a matter of people not being perfect. Since only Allah is perfect and everybody else knows they're always going to be less than perfect anyway, why bother pointing it out? You see what I mean?"

Though this sudden outpouring of bizarre, twisted logic from the youthful Minitrue sent a chill down Elijah's spine, he would just as soon have this strange young girl as company rather than be left sitting all alone by the fountain in the mall. So he asked, "How much longer do you have till you get back?"

"Another 15 minutes, but I can't sit with you anymore if that's what you were going to ask."

Elijah looked genuinely hurt. "Why?"

"Because the FOI might have something to say about me spending so much time with someone I'm not matched with *and* who's already married." Minitrue motioned behind her and when Elijah looked for himself, he saw what she meant.

The Fruit of Islam. The ever-present security forces of the Nation of Islam who enforce its fundamentalist edicts to the letter. In the 20th century, they wore what all the Black men in the Nation were required to in the 21st; a two-piece suit and a bow tie. Since the founding of the Lost-Found Nation in 2006, they have all worn white uniforms, bow ties, and hats (that were reminiscent of the garb milkmen or ice cream soda jerks wore during the 1950s) with red stars and crescent moons on their collars and lapels. One of their members was at the far end of the promenade standing over a woman who was breast feeding her baby. Knowing the law as they did, Minitrue and Elijah correctly assumed that the woman was being told to move along and do her breast feeding in private or be fined. For no sooner did they notice the Fruit of Islam officer approach the woman did the woman herself get the message and begin to unsuckle her baby while straightening up her chador.

"Yeah, I guess we shouldn't attract any undue attention," Elijah lamented. He looked at his one friend from work who was less than half his age and said, "I guess this is goodbye."

"I may see you again, Mr. Isiah," Minitrue smiled.

"At any rate, the next time you do? Call me *Elijah*, alright? Damn the law."

Without saying another word, the young girl briskly walked away. Somehow Elijah knew he would never see Minitrue again and wondered what the future would hold for her. Would she continue to be a secretary even after she was matched at the Ministry of Love or would whomever they match her with insist that she stay at home? There wasn't much to wonder about because there weren't many possibilities for Muslimah. But after listening to Minitrue's warped rationale for not questioning authority, Elijah knew that somehow she would find a way to cope with whatever the world threw her way— however illogical that coping mechanism might be.

No sooner did Elijah finish imagining what Minitrue would be like in the future did he look up and see a woman who looked as though she could be a middle-aged version of his young girlfriend, albeit a shade lighter. If only Minitrue could have stayed a second longer to see this woman, thought Elijah, and then it occurred to him: He was staring at a woman he didn't know. And while that would not have meant anything ages ago, it could mean a fine or worse if the FOI caught him "disrespecting a Black queen by undressing her with his eyes" as Black men reportedly did often in the 20th century.

Though the Koran has always been the scripture of choice in the Lost-Found Nation, the Bible was cited and quoted a great deal as well. One of the Biblical concepts the Nation applied the most in its governing, essentially states that a sin conceived of in the mind is just as bad as one that was actually committed. That concept was one of the guiding principles behind the ministers teaching that the first step in an actual rape is to ogle at a woman from afar. In turn, those teachings are responsible for the Fruit of Islam's preemptive approach to policing: The practice of stopping a crime *before* it happens.

Elijah would not be able to explain to the FOI that the reason why this woman caught his married eye was because she looked like a future version of a 17 year old secretary he knew. He thought how it must have looked to this woman to see some man suddenly avert his gaze from her as if she could turn him to stone with a glance. But when Elijah opened his eyes again, he saw that the woman was about to have more to worry about.

The Pasdar, the female counterparts of the Fruit of Islam, had encircled this woman with a speed that befit the white, sheeted, Halloween ghosts that they resembled in their bleached gowns and headdresses. The chadors of the Pasdar differed from what every other Muslimah had to wear in that the Pasdar's headgear looked more like caps with draping scarves than simple habits or headties. Aiso, the Pasdar had both red stars and crescent moons on their uniforms, just as the Fruit of Islam did.

The surrounded woman sounded rather cagey when she asked, "Is there a problem, my beautiful Black sis—"

"Fix your *roosarie*," one of the women from the Pasdar barked.

"By all means," the woman said as she touched her scarf and felt a few hairs that were violating the national dress code by protruding from her headtie. Elijah marveled at how the Pasdar were able to see from only-Allah-knew-how-far-away a couple of strands of hair on a woman's head.

The woman smiled a painted smile and nervously told the Pasdar, "If that will be all, my sisters, I must be on my way."

"Just a moment," one of the elder Pasdar agents said as she reached for what looked like a spit curl on the woman's head before she could tuck all of the loose hairs back into her roosarie and fingered it. "This is awfully straight hair for a *sister* to have. And it has a reddish-brown tint to it too."

"I'm half White, I was born right before the Apocalypse," the woman responded.

The elder Pasdar frowned, "be that as it may, we'll still need to check and see whether or not you've been using any chemicals to straighten your hair because this looks too much like one of those 'jeri-curls' from the 20th century. We've been having a lot of cases of that lately. And—" The Pasdar agent then looked at the back of the woman's head and said, "I suppose those dark, wet spots on the back of your headtie came from you sweating because it's so hot, eh?"

"That's right," the woman stammered.

"I'm sorry, but you'll have to come with us."

Before any one of them could put a hand on the woman, she forcibly backed out of the circle the four Pasdar agents had made around her. The woman then kept backing away from the steadily advancing Pasdar yelling, "my hair is *naturally* like this! There's no grease in my hair and I'm not trying to look White either! I don't think I'm better than anyone else, I *swear*! I hate White people! I *hate* the White in me!" When the woman tried to make a run for it she tripped on her own chador. By the time the woman got back to her feet, the four agents each grabbed a limb of hers and carted her kicking and screaming outside of the mall.

When they were all out of view, Elijah found he was slightly short of breath and that his heart racing. He tried to calm himself down by reminding himself that he was a man and the dress code wouldn't ever be *that* strict on him. Just the same, Elijah thought that maybe he had sat by the fountain long enough—long enough to get something said to him by the FOI for loitering, but as Elijah stood up a hand dropped onto his shoulder and his whole body trembled.

"Excuse me, my brother, but your bow tie is crooked," a voice came from behind Elijah cryptically said. "You better straighten it before I have to write you up."

Wait a minute, Elijah thought, I know who that *is*. He turned around and couldn't believe his eyes. "*Ishmael*! Praise Allah, it's Ishmael Emmanuel!"

A tall, husky, light skinned Black man returned Elijah's joyous embrace with a big grin on his face. "Scared the White devil right out of you, didn't I, Eli?"

When Elijah finally let go of Ishmael's barrel chest, he stepped back and put his hands on his friend's broad shoulders. "Nobody has called me 'Eli' in—in over—"

"Fifteen years, at least. Look at you, Eli. You still look just like Wesley Snipes, even in your old age!" Ishmael laughed. "You remember him, that actor from when we were little kids?"

"Yeah! And you still look like that comedian, Sinbad! What did they always used to call us? The Celebrity Impersonators!"

"Actually we were so awkward in our youth, they used to call us the Hollywood Squares!"

Elijah laughed and then sighed as he looked his friend over. "You know, it's a crying shame so much is nakon these days. I really wish I could show Nayirah and Elisha some of those old moving pictures we used to watch—"

"'Nayirah?' 'Elisha?'" Ishmael interrupted, "This wouldn't be your family, would it? Eli's got a family?"

"I turned 38 this weekend, I don't think the Nation would've let me go this long without matching me up with somebody. Nayirah's my wife and Elisha's my 10 year old boy." Elijah beamed the proud smile of a father and then asked, "But what have you been doing all these years?"

Ishmael grimaced in chagrin as he sat where Elijah just had, by the waters of the enormous fountain. "You know, it's funny you mention the Nation matching somebody. 'Cause that's what I do for a living. I work in the Ministry of Love."

Elijah sat next to his friend stunned and with his mouth wide open. "You're kidding me!"

"I kid you not. I'm one of the folks who had to learn by heart, before it was put all on computer, that someone half Black and half White is a Mulatto, then someone half Mulatto and half White is a Quadroon, a Quadroon who's half White is a Sextaroon, a half White Sextaroon is a Septaroon and—"

"There's more?" Elijah asked incredulously.

"Oh yeah, a Septaroon who's half White is an Octoroon and *that's* it. But the main thing I do is I use all that knowledge to basically make sure folks like Octoroons or Septaroons mate with jet black Blacks so their kids will be darker."

"I still can't believe all of this is to see that someday everybody will be the same shade so there won't be any Black folks who'll feel inferior or superior like they did a long time ago," said Elijah as he shook his head.

"That's right, that's what I do for a living," Ishmael continued. "Match up dark folks with light folks and sharp-nosed folks with flat-nosed folks and light folks with flat noses with dark folks with sharp noses—"

"What do you do with the medium folks?" Elijah slyly grinned.

"Match them up with medium folks," Ishmael chuckled. "It's all very symmetrical!" Elijah leaned on his larger friend as they both laughed until tears came from their eyes.

"This summer air is so dry and hazy, isn't it?"

"Yeah it is, so you've been at the Ministry ever since—"

"Ever since I quit being a press boy at *The Final Call*, Eli. I just worked my way up the ladder and was so busy doing that I just— lost touch. I hate I did, though. I missed our days back when we were in the press room. Fooling around back when you could do that sort of thing, talking trash all the time, we did have fun, didn't we?"

"You just stopped coming by one day, Ishmael," Elijah sounded a little hurt. "How can folks just lose touch like that? We were pretty close!"

"It just happens sometimes," Ishmael said mournfully. "But hey, what happened to you after I took off? Are you still working for the Nation's only newspaper?"

"Well, right after you left, which was—when? 2017? I got kicked upstairs to the paste-up/layout department and I was there for about five years but I was only getting so much out of it. Then I lucked out and managed to get a job as an *assistant* assistant editor for *The Nation* magazine—"

"Eli! That's something else! That's really something!"

"The problem was I was only there for a year because *The Nation* merged with *The Final Call* and *The Nation* was phased out."

"I'm sorry," Ishmael apologized. "I remember hearing about that now. Go ahead."

"Then for about seven years I had to work for a copy shop called Kimbro's. I had a ladder of a kind myself to work my way up while I was there. Started out working the counter, then I was told to splice and layout designs for flyers, before too long I was typing people's resumes and business proposals for them and I just got good at it. And quick too. The next thing I knew I was being introduced to a guy named Mustafa Ali and for the past year or so I was working for him as a dictator but then I got fired today."

"Oh, Eli," Ishmael looked heartbroken. "What happened?"

"I don't want to get into it. But hey, what about you? You must be married by now, right?"

"Well, no kids as of yet. But yeah, I'm married, and I even got to pick my *own* wife too!"

"No . . ."

"One of the perks of the job. 'Course I still had to follow the guidelines and pick a girl who was as dark as I am light. Fatima and I look like salt and pepper together. Are you and Nayirah the same way?"

"She's half White . . ." Elijah became distant for a moment and then motioned in front of him. "Just like that one woman that the Pasdar picked up a minute ago."

"Uh huh, when my hair comes out it comes out kind of wavy because I'm mixed myself so I always have to keep my head shaven bald or else someone will think that I'm trying to 'conk' my hair or give myself a 'process.'"

"Yeah, Nayirah shaves her head too," Elijah said simply as a matter of fact but for some reason it came out funny to the both of them. So funny that the two friends began to laugh all over again only louder than ever before.

"Excuse me, my brothers," a voice said. "May I have a word with you?"

Elijah's and Ishmael's mouths were still hanging open and strains of laughter were still indiscriminately seeping from their lips as they both looked up to see a stern, stoic member of the Fruit of Islam standing over them. "What . . . What seems to be the . . . *Ahem*, what's the problem, officer . . ?" Elijah managed to get out in-between laughing.

"My brother, I'm afraid that you and your friend here are getting to be a little too gregarious."

"What . . . What's that supposed to mean?" Ishmael shook his head and smiled.

"It means that you're getting too loud and are disturbing some of the elder Black sisters, my brother," the FOI officer said as he motioned to the older women in question, all with scowls on their faces, sitting several feet away from the fountain. "I'm going to have to ask you to disperse."

Ordinarily a conversation of this sort would not have lasted so long between a member of the FOI and a citizen he was ordering but the facetious euphoria Elijah and Ishmael shared needed a moment to wear off. Once that happened, they saw the severity of the situation, cleared their throats, and both muttered, "yes sir, right away, sir."

When the officer from the FOI saw Elijah and Ishmael stand up from where they were sitting, he started to walk away as if sensing his job was done. The FOI member hesitated for a moment and started to turn his attentions back to them when he saw the two men hurriedly exchange addresses but then moved on after they hugged and finally went their separate ways.

"I can't believe you want to go to somebody's house after losing your job," Nayirah Isiah scolded. "I would be ashamed of myself to no end."

Elijah sat at the dinner table and sulked as he took his wife's abuse. Everyone in the Lost-Found Nation was supposed to try and befit the image of a hard working Black man at all times. Not necessarily to increase productivity so much as to continually dispel the 20th century stereotypes of Blacks being sluggish and dependent. Elijah felt lucky that the FOI didn't ask him if he had any work to do earlier. Ishmael had his job at the Ministry of Love to go back to but Elijah had to refrain from any more loitering or wanton wandering for the day for fear of reprisal.

Before the Apocalypse people were sometimes paid by the state while they were unemployed and even had a service to help them find other jobs but the Nation fined those who made the Black race look bad as a whole for not appearing industrious all the time while offering no such employment services.

"And I can't *believe* that you lost your job anyway! It wasn't even a real job so how hard could it have been?" Nayirah usually didn't raise her voice, especially at the dinner table or with Elisha also sitting there innocently for that matter, and this precedent increased the tension in the Isiah household ten-fold. "What are you going to do all day, dear heart? You know that idle hands are the White devil's handiwork and I *know* you're not going to fix that gas main so there's no point in me even asking again—"

"Nayirah," Elijah interrupted, "it's Unity Day, alright? Every Tuesday's supposed to be a time of fellowship and understanding, remember? Besides, Ishmael doesn't care that I'm unemployed, I told him already when I saw him today."

"I know, I know, and he felt *sorry* for you!" Nayirah put her hands to her face, "Allah, it's all so—*embarrassing* .. !"

"Fine, then it's embarrassing, but I'm still going to try and enjoy what's left of Unity Day anyway by going over to Ishmael's because I want to get out of the house for a while and enjoy some of that fellowship," Elijah put a hand on his son's shoulder from across the table and smiled, "plus, I want him to see Elisha too."

Ishmael and Fatima Emmanuel lived in an area of Chicago still known as Western Springs despite decades of (Nation of) Islamic rule. Their home was as suburban and visually unimpressive as the Isiahs' house, which led Elijah to believe that a minister of love such as Ishmael didn't make much more than a dictator or a teacher such as his wife did. Not that Elijah wished his friend any less but if Ishmael did in fact live in a bigger and better house, he would have never heard the end of it from Nayirah.

Ishmael stepped outside to meet Elijah as the latter pulled his sedan into the driveway. Elijah embraced Ishmael as Nayirah rolled her eyes at what she thought was an unmanly display and Elisha politely stood by his father's side waiting to be introduced while his stomach rumbled from having nothing but the one meal a day one was allowed to eat in the Nation.

" . . . And this is Elisha, Elisha this is Ishmael Emmanuel—"

"*Mister* Emmanuel," Nayirah suddenly, but predictably, added to what Elijah was saying.

"So, how are you doing, *mister* Elisha?" Ishmael jokingly asked.

Elisha looked up at the big man and said simply, "I'm still a little hungry, sir."

Nayirah's face went from its usual pale tan to beet red. "*Elisha*!" She would have snatched him from where he stood had Elijah not made eye contact with Nayirah in that instant and flashed her a hard look she knew very well which basically meant "don't strike my son." Despite Nayirah's firmly believing that the boy needed a swift lesson in discipline, those looks Elijah shot her in these instances always made her feel, however briefly, all the more feminine. Since such feelings were rare, she didn't ever want to discourage anything dominatingly masculine on Elijah's part, so Nayirah instead responded by only barking, "don't beg!"

"Oh, I don't think he was trying to beg," Ishmael diplomatically said. "Were you Elisha?"

"I was just answering your question honestly, sir," Elisha responded.

"There, you see?" Ishmael jovially pointed out. "And you don't have to keep calling me 'sir,' either. Now let's step inside before someone thinks something's the matter out here."

* * *

Elijah sat with his family on the Emmanuel's sofa. He looked over at the shy and demure Fatima Emmanuel standing over Ishmael's stereo switching one compact disc with innocuous Middle-Eastern instrumentals for another, and thought if his Nayirah was the picture of the maximum amount of aggressiveness allowed from a woman by the Lost-Found Nation of Islam then this Fatima was just the opposite. She may have nodded a couple of times while being introduced to everyone and murmured an "As-Salaam-Alaikum" or two but beyond that there was barely any other acknowledgment of the Isiah's presence.

What surprised Elijah so was the very idea that the happy-go-lucky Ishmael would pick and marry someone who was as quiet as he was congenial. Congenial to the point where Ishmael could even bring out what little of a pleasant side Nayirah had and coax her to talk about her day at school with a smile on her face. In spite of the very decorum Nayirah lived and died by which dictated that the women at a social gathering such as this one would have their own conversation going. But since Fatima wasn't much of a conversationalist, Nayirah had no choice but to break with convention just this once.

"Well, today was the first of our bi-monthly weight checks at Sarah X for everyone over 13, and as you know we charge a penny for every additional pound the girls are beyond each of their prescribed limits," said Nayirah.

"Is there some standard limit as to how fat you can be?" Ishmael asked. "'Cause they never had anything like that at any boys' school I ever went to," Ishmael then felt at his paunch. "Thank Allah," he said with a smile.

"Oh no, all the limits are decided on a case by case basis and are different from individual to individual," Nayirah continued, seemingly enthused that someone was interested in her work. "In fact, one of the extra duties I've taken on as of late in addition to helping clean after the cooking classes is helping decide what everyone's weight level is to be."

"Do you decide what your own weight level will be?" Ishmael queried with a straight face.

Nayirah blushed slightly. Since she knew she had put on a couple of extra pounds lately, Nayirah felt as though she had fallen into a verbal trap. It didn't help that she noticed that next to her Elijah was trying to repress a grin. Nayirah glanced over to make sure Elisha wasn't smiling but her son had only a blank expression on his face so she assumed that he didn't understand the significance of what had been said.

Elisha *might* have, since he was actually paying attention to the conversation. It was just that he was concentrating on a different aspect of it. How could it be that anyone could possibly be overweight with as little as people in the Nation were allowed to eat, Elisha thought. Elisha also remembered his father saying how his "high metabolism" was the reason he was thin and why he always wanted seconds and thirds at dinner. His mother on the other hand told him of how Elijah Muhammad himself said that all "Negroes were particularly susceptible to overeating" and that dinner was the only meal the Black man ever needed.

Elisha always kept from his mother how he felt otherwise, however, and was about to attempt a little trick of his that might actually be considered blasphemous. Something that would definitely mean being punished severely if he was ever caught.

"May I please go to the bathroom?" Elisha asked his family's host for the evening.

"Of course, Elisha," Ishmael boomed. "Down the hall and second door to your right."

* * *

The water from Ishmael's bathroom faucet was a lot colder than the tap water at home that Elisha was used to and for some reason it wasn't as filling. Since gorging himself on running water wasn't doing the trick it usually did, Elisha looked hungrily at the tube of toothpaste lying on the side of the sink. Elisha twisted off the tube's cap and squeezed as he held the tube over his mouth. The taste of fluoride proved too much for Elisha so he proceeded to fish around for mints or even some cough drops, hopefully fruit flavored.

As his eyes wandered across the bathroom, Elisha decided to look out the window to see what was out there since he had never been to this neighborhood before. The sun had still not gone down and because the sky hadn't darkened yet, Elisha had a clear view of an enormous apple tree even while it looked as though it was several blocks away. Elisha found himself salivating as his eyes fixated on the spots of bright red amidst the green foliage of the distant tree.

Elisha surprised himself as he found his fingers unhooking the latch on the bathroom window and then sliding the window open. The space was just big enough for a slim child to crawl through and before he could think of a reason not to, Elisha wormed his way out of the bathroom and hit the side lawn outside of Ishmael's house running. His hunger and certainty that he would make it back to the bathroom with a few apples in him before anyone knew he was missing counteracted the fear of punishment and the racing of his heart. Elisha stealthily sprinted block after block south on La Grange Road near the border of Chicago's Cook County towards the object of his desire, praying to Allah all the way there that no one would stop him or ask him anything. For not even his father would be able to protect him from what might happen if Elisha were to get caught trespassing onto someone else's property—let alone for the purpose of stealing something.

* * *

"So there I was, sitting in our temple, and I couldn't keep my head up to save my soul!" Ishmael laughed as he had Elijah in rapt attention. "First the guard came around and shook me awake saying, 'wake up, Black man, and pay attention.' That kept me up for a while, but pretty soon I went right back to sleep!"

Elijah was stunned at hearing such a thing as he recalled what happened to him just the night before at his neighborhood temple for doing nothing but looking at his own wife for too long. Who, Elijah noticed, was beginning to glare at Ishmael slightly as if his charming hospitality was wearing off. Most likely because Nayirah was starting to find Ishmael a potentially bad example on Elijah, whom she felt didn't take Islam seriously enough as it was. Hearing Ishmael's jocular take on temple life couldn't possibly help matters, Nayirah thought.

It was at this moment Elijah realized why Ishmael had picked someone as unassuming as Fatima to marry: So that he would never have to worry about her betraying him as Nayirah had occasionally threatened to call the FOI on Elijah throughout the years. Could this mean that when guests aren't over and only Fatima and he are around Ishmael talks of even more subversive things besides temple anecdotes that she's trusted to be privy to because of her quiet nature? Elijah would have to think about that but for right then he wanted to know, "what happened next?"

"Well, they woke me up again only this time they carted me off to the bathroom, bent me over against the sink, and splashed ice cold water all over my face and my bald head! It felt like I was being baptized!"

Instead of finding the punch line of the story funny the reference to the bathroom only reminded him of his son. "Where's Elisha?" Elijah said as he stood up from the sofa. "He's been in the bathroom for a long time." Everyone else's eyes in the room followed Elijah as he walked down Ishmael's hall, came to the second door on the right and knocked on it. "Elisha? Elisha, are you alright in there?" Elijah hated to do it but he turned the knob and opened the door anyway. Instead of invading his son's privacy Elijah found nothing but empty space and an opened tube of toothpaste. He stuck his head out of the bathroom window and called out for Elisha while trying to figure out which direction he could have possibly headed for the boy was nowhere in sight.

Ishmael, Nayirah, and even Fatima came down the hall when they heard Elisha's name being yelled by his father. "Where did he go?" Nayirah asked as she poked her head through the bathroom's doorway.

"I don't know, *I don't know* . . !" Elijah started to panic and then managed to force himself to calm down. "Alright, he couldn't have gotten far and I doubt anyone just *took* him so—" Elijah briskly worked his way through his wife and friends who were crowding the doorway and headed for the front door while saying, "Ishmael you look one way and I'll look another. Fatima, if you don't mind could you wait outside the house and watch for him?"

Fatima nodded in approval as Elijah and Ishmael stopped short of exiting the front door as Elijah turned and called back, "Nay, stay with Fatima and call the FOI."

Nayirah folded her arms, "he's only been gone for a few minutes. He needs to be missing for two days before we can bother the Fruit of Islam with this. And don't call me 'Nay.'"

Elijah stood in the front doorway staring at Nayirah in disbelief over how detached she had just sounded before finally following Ishmael outside and jogging off in a direction opposite of his. A direction that just happened to coincidentally lead Elijah towards the apple tree.

* * *

There was a sick moment when a cruel thought flashed across Elisha's mind. That somehow the red he saw in the tree would turn out to be some kind of decoration or even a kind of scarlet leaf he never saw before. But when he reached the white picket fence of the house whose front lawn the tree occupied, Elisha could see for sure his vision hadn't failed him. There were huge red apples at the end of nearly every branch and every one of them seemed to call out to Elisha because the mad dash there had made him all the more hungry.

Elisha quickly scanned the area to see if there were any people standing around in their yards who could become potential witnesses to the deed he was about to perpetrate or if the yard he was about to sneak into had a guard dog and found none of the above. Elisha had considered actually asking for one of the apples, or two, or three, but the risk of being told that he couldn't have any at all was too great in the face of the risk Elisha had taken in running away.

The picket fence was as tall as Elisha's five foot body so scaling it was a challenge but not much of one. He just had to make sure not to have one of the fence's sharp points end up in-between his legs while swinging his body over the top of it. Once he landed in the front lawn, Elisha stalked the circumference of the tree and tipped around the rotten apples all over the ground for a branch with an apple at its end that was low enough to the ground for him to be able to retrieve with a single leap since the trunk of the tree was too sheer of a surface for him to climb.

Elisha found such a branch low enough to the ground with an apple he could reach. The problem was it happened to be the one point that was closest to the front window of the house and Elisha's jumping up and down made just enough noise to be heard by the home's owner and sole resident, "Sister" Sweanea, who was walking past the window at that most inopportune moment.

Sister Sweanea couldn't eat apples since she was allergic to them and because of her abundant savings she never needed to sell them. Sister Sweanea didn't even have any relatives, children, or grandchildren to pass the apples on to and it wasn't as though she had been assigned a house with an apple tree in its front lawn against her will either. With all of her money, Sister Sweanea could have afforded any other house in the neighborhood she wanted. She purposely picked one with an apple tree merely to make her property all the more valuable and enviable.

She has grown obsessed with the sanctity of that property in her old age. Because of the relatively low crime rate due to the Fruit of Islam's preemptive approach to policing throughout the Nation, she never had to worry about investing in a security system, hidden cameras, or even a guard dog. Not having to deal with such things caused her to develop a taste for personally dealing with the few intruders she did receive herself. Since she only saw a little boy eating one of her prize apples and not a grown man, she thought the shotgun probably wasn't necessary, but as she reached for a four foot bamboo cane in the corner of her closet with a label on it which read "made in Singapore," Sister Sweanea did think of a discipline that would be appropriate.

* * *

What frustrated Elijah the further south he jogged on La Grange Road was the whole idea that while the Fruit of Islam and the Pasdar stood ever ready to enforce dress codes and rules of public (and sometimes private) behavior, they would wait two days before looking for a lost child. Elijah also thought how these same people would chastise him for not having a job and would never help him find one, at least not one he (or anybody else) would want. Were these backwards priorities on the part of the Lost-Found Nation? Was it even Elijah's place to ask if they were?

And Nayirah—without Elijah back at the house to restrain her nothing would be able to stop her from beating the life out of Elisha were the boy to show up at Ishmael's right then, especially given how embarrassed about the whole situation she must be by now. Fatima certainly hasn't demonstrated she would have the will to intervene and Ishmael himself might not have returned from his searching in time. Assuming he'd be so inclined to try and stop Nayirah to begin with. Since Elijah wasn't all that sure about his friend, who he hadn't seen in 15 years, he resolved he had to find Elisha before *anyone*.

When Elijah Isiah saw his son crying and running directly towards him, however, it was all too painfully clear someone had found Elisha first.

"Father . . !" Elisha shrieked as much in relief as in anguish when he ran into Elijah's arms with bits of apple still all over his mouth and his face caked with tears. "I'm sorry! All I wanted was an apple, I was starving! And she beat me with a *stick*—"

Elijah didn't need to hear anymore. Supposedly, one of the most afrocentric of family values that were lost during the enslavement of Blacks was if a child committed some crime and the parents weren't on the scene at the time but another adult was, the other adult somehow had every right to discipline the child however they saw fit. Whether the adult was of any genetic or personal relation to the parents and the child or not. This tradition had been revived by the Black community in the 20th century and made law in the 21st despite all the whippings Blacks endured during the 17th, 18th, and 19th centuries. It was the one law Elijah always feared someone who caught Elisha doing something would invoke and a law Elijah had absolutely no respect for.

This was why Elijah took all the criminally suspect measures he had over the years in order to keep his son from falling prey to this value. Always managing to keep Nayirah in check, interfering with the corporal punishment policies of Elisha's pre-school and elementary school on the sly, spending as much quality time with Elisha as he could rather than to let his son venture out into the world to play too far away from home and have the boy come back to him in tears and in pain.

Maybe the dry heat was getting to him. Elijah had been sprinting while still fully dressed in his nationally required suit and bow tie after all and never was what one would consider to be in good shape, but Elijah already felt as though he had been pushed beyond his usual limits as of late. And when he looked down at the boy still sobbing from that very first spanking in his arms, all of Elijah's pent-up frustrations began to boil over from deep within while forming a sensation which made him feel as if he was literally going to explode.

Elijah Isiah always tried to follow the Lost-Found Nation of Islam in North America's rules, even when they didn't make the least bit of sense to him. All he ever asked of Allah was that the world spare his son from any of its nonsense. But Allah failed him, and now Elijah suddenly found everything within his field of vision taking on a bright red hue, as though he had sunglasses on with crimson lenses. This would have appeared unusual to Elijah except in that instant he was in too much of a state of utter rage to pay the visual phenomenon much notice.

"Show-daddy-*where*," Elijah grumbled with an almost demonic tint to his voice. Elisha, noticing something different about his father, took a startled moment before trepidatiously taking his hand and leading him back to Sister Sweanea's home. Elijah stormed ahead of Elisha and let go of his hand once the house surrounded by the white picket fence and the apple tree behind it was in sight.

The wooden fence had been erected for its quaint look rather than for any actual security so it wasn't stable enough to withstand Elijah's foot when it sent a man-sized portion of the fence crashing down. Sister Sweanea was still standing in the front lawn with her bamboo cane in hand and instinctively swung it at Elijah. Who, in turn, caught the cane in one hand, snatched it out of her grasp, and shoved her down to the ground in the same motion.

Not quite sounding like himself, Elijah snarled in a feral tone, "So, you won't let a hungry little boy have an apple, huh? You greedy old *bitch!*" Elijah drew the bamboo cane back in a wide arch. "It's time you started sharing what you clearly have to spare!" And with that, Elijah struck the apple tree again and again and again, bringing upon him a deluge of apples with every violent swing.

Elijah couldn't believe how good this onslaught felt. It was as though he was ten, no, *twenty* years younger and all of the adrenaline that had been pumping through his veins was producing a euphoric high that deafened him to Sister Sweanea's screaming. It was only when enough of the apples rained on his head at one time that Elijah stopped what he was doing and advanced towards Sister Sweanea, backing her against the side of her house.

Holding the cane horizontally up to her face for inspection, Elijah's voice took on the rolling of thunder. "And another thing, I don't give a *damn* what they tell you, you do *not* have the right to touch my son! If you *ever* even *think* about beating another child again—" Elijah bent the bamboo cane into a bow until his adrenaline-powered arms caused it to snap in two with the labeled words "made in" on one half and "Singapore" on the other. "I swear to Allah I'll *break* your old ass just like I did this stick here!"

Elijah threw down the two halves of cane onto the ground and abruptly started to feel drained and nauseous. Elijah was beginning to come down from the rush he had been riding on which enabled him to do everything he did and granted him the fury that he did it with. What the hell was he doing, a very weak and fearful voice cried from inside Elijah. What was he *going* to do? Keep this woman outside her house and away from her phone forever? So that she could never call the Fruit of Islam as she must have obviously wanted to at that moment more than anything else in the world? And what of her neighbors? Would they be able to identify either of the Isiah men? Would word of what happened get back to Ishmael—or Nayirah? Elijah suddenly felt very deflated and craven. He started to become extremely conscious of everything around him, specifically the lights in the windows, the doorways, and even the carports of the surrounding houses. As far as Elijah could tell, no one had stepped outside to investigate the commotion. Possibly because it was Unity Day and people were out enjoying it, but that still didn't mean that he or his son were safe.

He had to get Elisha out of there, but they couldn't go back to Ishmael's, not just yet. Elijah was sure he would have to lose anyone who would try to follow him and Elisha first. Otherwise he might lead someone straight to his identifiable car in Ishmael's driveway and three people who could name the violent man and his mischievous son by their names. Elijah didn't know the neighborhood he was in well at all but he had to put as much distance between him and his son, Ishmael's, and the scene of the crime as he could just the same. At least until he thought things had cooled down and the coast was clear.

Elijah wasn't sure if this logic was sound but his head was swimming and the sound of his pounding chest was beating almost loud enough to keep him from hearing himself think so Elijah wouldn't have been able to be very logical at that moment anyway. As he scooped up Elisha and blindly ran even further south on La Grange Road while Sister Sweanea yelled threats from her front lawn behind them, all Elijah knew for sure was that he and his son could now very well be fugitives and had no idea what to do about it if in fact they were.

CHAPTER THREE

"H i s   e y e s   o p e n e d"

Not long after Elijah and Elisha got out of the eyeshot of Sister Sweanea did they run smack into a rather tall and thin imposing figure who seemed to step into the path from out of nowhere. He was a dark-skinned Black man, dressed in accordance with the national code just as they were, except that there was something different about him. He wasn't sweating from the heat for one thing and he also had an expression on his face that looked as though he had known the both of them for quite some time.

"As-Salaam-Alaikum, my brother," the man said as he extended his hand as if to shake Elijah's.

Elijah, sweating profusely with Elisha in tow muttered, "Wa-Salaikum," as he nervously tried to side step the tall man. The stranger's answer to this was to step back in front of Elijah and put his hand on Elijah's shoulder.

"Where's the fire, my brother?" The man asked as he eyed Elisha. "It looks as though your boy's been crying, do you need any—"

"We're fine and we're in a *rush!*" Elijah thought he'd meet the stranger's stare with an especially hard look in order to accentuate the point. However when he made eye contact, Elijah found that the thin man's gaze had fallen just to the rear of the Isiahs. As if someone was approaching right behind—

And then everything went black . . .

* * *

The first sensation Elijah felt when he regained consciousness was a sudden chill. As hot as it was that summer, this cold wind would have been welcome except that Elijah also felt a panic come over him because he was lying on his back in what looked like the mouth of a dark tunnel and no longer had any idea where he was.

Elijah sat up, wiped at his lip with his fingers and smelled a chemical he didn't recognize. He looked over and he saw the same tall stranger standing over Elisha cracking open some kind of capsule over the boy's nose. Elijah correctly assumed that the man was only trying to revive his son but didn't see the act as any great favor since this same man had just abducted them. Anger spilled over from within and Elijah growled out of impulse, "stay away from my son," as he tried to wave the stranger away from Elisha.

"He's *fine,*" the thin man assured. "He'll be awake in just a second." The assurance didn't seem to be enough for Elijah who then leapt up and took Elisha in his arms even as the stranger had finished administering the contents of the cracked open capsule.

Elijah cradled Elisha for a moment and when the boy finally started to cough his way to consciousness, Elijah asked, "Elisha, are you alright? How do you feel?"

"I'm OK, father," Elisha answered as he rubbed his eyes. "What happened?"

"Why *did* you grab us?" Elijah added as he shot his tall abductor a look. "And who are you anyway?"

"I'm Tom, and here comes my little brother Jerry." Tom motioned behind him to a second Black man heading towards them from around a blind corner in the tunnel—with a 45 automatic in his hand.

"She said they don't have to be blindfolded," Jerry called out as he put his gun in a vest holster. "She *claims* they won't decide to ID us later, but I'm keeping my shit on anyway."

"Well it ain't breezy enough down here for me to keep mine on and it's starting to itch," Tom replied and with that he literally peeled his mustache, goatee, and his short cut afro clean off of his bald head much to the shock of both Isiahs. "Welcome to the underground, fellas. Where the revolution *would* be televised if they hadn't made TV 'nakon' all those years ago."

* * *

The tunnel Elijah and Elisha had come to in was in fact part of what used to called a subway. As the Isiahs were led by Tom and Jerry around the blind corner, Elijah noticed the iron railways on the ground for the first time. When they all reached the mouth of the tunnel, Elijah felt as if he were on the site of a major archeological dig. Abandoned streetcars that looked like they could be as old as he was stared back at Elijah with broken headlights for eyes were stacked back-to-back on their metal tracks. Their interiors were covered with either broken glass or cobwebs. The four huge stairwell passages, two on each side of the huge subway valve, that might have led 20th century commuters to the turnstiles or the subway token machines on the surface were all blocked off by boulders and rubble. On the walls were gigantic cracks that seemed to have come from an earthquake, or a bomb blast, and along those same walls were advertisements of the time. Such as movie posters which read *Lethal Weapon Seven* and *Batman Retires* and there was another poster which read, "the best of both worlds—Paul Tsongas and Warren Rudman in 2004." Elijah had to fight back the reflex to cover Elisha's eyes from the sight of a lingerie ad from Calvin Klein on the side of one of the streetcars with a half naked White woman lounging on it. It had been so long since he had seen so many photos of Whites at one time that Elijah felt as if he had indeed stepped back in time somehow.

There were several people, some abiding by the national dress code but most were not, bustling about carrying open boxes to an end of the subway furthest from where Tom, Jerry and the Isiahs were. There was an enormous stack of these boxes and even more people were labeling or counting either the boxes or their contents, which

Elijah could tell even from where he stood were compact discs, video tapes, and books.

The last person Elijah expected to stop cataloging books and tapes in order to greet him was an old woman smoking a corn cob pipe. She was petite with very keen features but had the same, exact dark tint to her skin that Tom did. The woman also possessed a lion's mane of unkempt gray hair that frizzled down to her shoulders. The mane must have been too big to fit a headtie over so she went without one, something that would've been illegal for even a woman of her old age on the surface. Whenever one of the subway's drafty winds would pass through the tunnel, a few of her hairs would blow out of place and adding to her appearance of a wrinkled wild woman was her tattered, off-white dress and leather thongs that would certainly attract the unwanted attention of the Pasdar.

The same look of familiarity that Tom had given Elijah on the street seemed quadrupled by the old woman when her eyes fell on the Isiahs. Those same eyes almost started to tear, but as if she had to keep up appearances for anyone who may be watching, the woman only extended her hand to a still confused Elijah. Though when it was politely shaken by Elijah, the woman took the opportunity to warmly caress his hand and prolong the handshake as long as she could. "*Elijah Isiah*, is it? Lord have mercy, it's really you," the old woman said almost under her breath.

"Madam, do you know who could tell me why my son and I have been taken here against our will?" Elijah asked while he was pulling his hand away from the woman's embrace.

The old woman took a deep sigh then she looked down at Elisha and put her hand on his hand and affectionately rubbed it. Elisha didn't look as though he minded but looked to his father questioningly just the same. The woman looked about her as if she had forgotten herself and suddenly took on an authoritative yet cantankerous air. "*I* can tell you why you're here 'cause I'm in charge here. The name's Baines, do I look familiar to you?"

"No, ma'am," Elijah replied.

"First off, none of that 'Madam,' 'ma'am,' or 'misses' crap, alright? Next thing you know, you'll be calling me 'my Black queen' or some stupid-ass shit like that. *The African Queen* was a goddamn boat on a fucking Bogart movie! My ass is from *Dee*-troit." Baines stopped to note the shocked expression on Elijah's face and smiled. "You probably can't remember the last time you heard a woman talk like that, huh? We're revolutionaries. We don't live by the same bullshit rules you have to up there," she said as she pointed to the ceiling. "And we don't have the time nor the inclination to be politically correct."

While Elijah put a couple of fingers to his temple and rubbed it in wide-eyed disbelief, Baines motioned for Tom to step closer to her and out of the Isiahs' earshot. "Your brother said he went back to Sweanea's and told her that he saw the FOI pick up these two 'round the corner from her place," Baines quickly whispered. "The bitch is probably stupid enough to believe it, but I want you to go back above ground and stay up there for a while just to make sure. If everything's quiet and there ain't nothing going on, fine. But if her ass is in the front lawn gossiping to her neighbors about what happened or if she's called somebody after all, I want to know *immediately*, understood?"

Tom nodded and bolted back into the dark tunnel where Elijah had awakened. Noticing that Elijah no longer looked bewildered but suspicious because of the whispered conversation, Baines quickly turned her and his attention to, "*Elisha*, right? I bet you look just like your daddy did when he was your age. How would you like something to eat, huh?" Baines observed Elijah's apprehension and assured him, "the kid'll be alright."

Elisha again looked to his father but this time he was beaming over the prospect of being *given* something more to eat. Sensing how hungry his son must have been, Elijah found himself letting go of Elisha's hand while watching the young man known only as Jerry lead the boy off into the distance. "Bring him *right back!*" Elijah called out before they could get out of his range of vision.

When Elijah looked over at Baines again he found her grinning at him like a Cheshire Cat. After a moment she asked, "so, I hear you beat the crap out of an apple tree?"

"If you *are* in charge, will you please tell me why am I here?" Elijah demanded.

"Now *that's* a philosophical question," Baines smirked. "I didn't know old Khallid encouraged existentialism. Well, all I can tell you is you ain't come from no tribe from the moon or some such nonsense."

"That's not what I mean and you know it," an infuriated Elijah snapped. "Why did Tom and Jerry drag me and my son to this place?"

"Wait-a-minute—*Tom and Jerry*? Is that what they said their names were?" Baines abruptly went into hysterics much to Elijah's surprise. After she managed to calm herself down, Baines exclaimed, "Lord have mercy! Last week they were Heckle and Jeckle and the week before that they were Ren and Stimpy!" When Baines saw that Elijah was looking as though she was a madwoman, she explained, "they're cartoon characters, Jesus Christ! Animated drawings of cats and dogs and mice running around—aw, forget it. I imagine they were the first to go."

"Suffice to say those aren't their real names."

"No shit, Sherlock, they're *spies*. You must have seen 'Tom' pull his wig off. I sent them to watch over you—"

"You *what*?" Elijah roared. "Why? For what possible reason? What did I ever do to you?"

"Calm down, calm down, you didn't do anything," Baines replied as she took a drag off of her corn cob pipe. "They never went inside your house, which is more than I can say for the FOI, and they didn't follow Elisha to school or anything. "'Tom' and 'Jerry,'" Baines snickered and then cleared her throat, "only followed you from afar. They didn't interfere in any way with one iota of your life, they never opened your mail or went through your garbage or anything, and they've only been trailing you for the past couple of days.

"In fact, this was supposed to be the boys' last day of shadowing you. They were on their way back here for good until you decided to attack the apple tree. If they hadn't gotten you off the streets when they did, you'd have been picked up by the FOI for sure. Speaking of—" Baines reached over, grabbed Elijah by the arms, and walked him to an ancient looking, coin operated telephone installed on the side of a nearby wall. "You probably don't remember this either, but there was a time when these things didn't take dollar bills."

Baines slipped her gnarled right index finger into the "change return" slot, pulled out a quarter, inserted it into the coin slot of the phone as she picked up the receiver. She listened for a dial tone and the moment it could be heard the very same quarter could also be heard landing right back in the "change return" slot. Baines held up the quarter for Elijah's inspection and handed the receiver to him. "Amazing, isn't it? It still works, believe it or not. One of the main reasons we picked this place. Now, you need to call that big light-skinned fella's house the boys saw y'all go in tonight and tell him to quit looking around for Elisha before he starts attracting too much attention. Tell him that you already found Elisha and the reason why you're taking so long getting back is because you're giving him 'the whipping he so richly deserves' or some such damn thing."

Elijah simply glowered at Baines and huffed defiantly. "Why should I? You still haven't explained why you had two spies follow me around in the first place."

"Unless you want to hear that explanation right before one of the NOI's Kafka-esque, so-called 'trials,' I suggest you cooperate. I'll be glad to tell you everything you'll ever need to know but I won't be able to explain jack shit if—"

"If what? If you people were captured?" Elijah looked about him to see if the others in the abandoned subway were paying his outrage any heed. Some heads had turned but most of the people went about their business of taking inventory of the many boxes of books and cassettes. "Why should I care about a bunch of *criminals*?"

"In case you've forgotten, you're a 'criminal' too," Baines pointed out. "You're 'the Great Apple Tree Slayer,' Sister Sweanea's, not to mention Johnny Appleseed's, arch nemesis. But seriously, I guarantee you, you will not get out of here unless you make that call." Baines said as she fit the receiver into Elijah's hand. "Now reach out and touch someone."

* * *

"As-Salaam-Alaikum," a very anxious Nayirah said as she answered Ishmael's phone.

"Nayirah? This is Elijah."

"*Elijah*! Where in Allah have you been? Have you found that miserable little brat?"

Elijah frowned, "Nay, get off the phone and put Ishmael on if he's there."

Luckily, Ishmael had in fact returned from an obviously vain search for Elisha at just that moment and picked up the phone. "Did you find him, Eli?"

"Yeah, he's standing right here with me," Elijah lied while glaring at Baines.

"Hold on," Ishmael turned to Nayirah and Fatima. "He found him, alright!" Nayirah rolled her eyes, sighed, and plopped onto Ishmael's couch while Fatima quietly praised Allah to herself. Ishmael then turned his attentions back to Elijah. "Where you at, Eli? I'll swing on by and—"

"No, that's OK, we're taking the long way back on purpose. I've just—*disciplined* the boy and I may discipline him again for running away like he did. We're having a long, man-to-man talk, just the two of us, that might take a while, *but I will be back before too long*." Elijah looked Baines dead in the eye when he put the emphasis that he did on the last few words which were said but Baines only smiled.

"No problem, Eli, we'll be here. Just be careful, though. Word is the FOI found some guy in the area not too long ago who had a nervous breakdown in the middle of somebody's yard. As-Salaikum."

"Wa-Salaikum," Elijah replied before hanging up the ancient telephone. "We *will* be able to leave this place, right?"

"Oh yes, of course," Baines reassured as she sat on a bench that extended from the side of the wall. "Come, sit a spell." When Elijah simply stood over her with his arms folded, she stated, "look, the truth can't be summed up in 30 seconds or less so if you really want to know the whole truth and nothing but, I'd make myself comfortable if I were you and let an old woman ramble a bit."

Once Elijah sat next to her, Baines reached with her fingers into a pouch she took out of her pocket and pulled out what looked to Elijah like small, pale green twigs. She then gently stuffed them into her ever-present corn cob pipe and lit it with a match she had struck against the side of the wall. "What *is* that?" Elijah queried.

Baines waited until she had taken a couple of deep puffs before responding. "It's the stuff dreams are made of, kid. Chronic, hemp, weed, Mary Jane."

"You mean *marijuana*," Elijah condescendingly said as though he were addressing a child.

"That's right, it's for medicinal purposes," Baines retorted. "It deadens these pains that I have."

"I bet it does. I've heard that one before."

"I have cancer that's in remission," Baines observed that Elijah's face fell and waited for a moment of silence to pass before saying, "now that some of that Farra Shakka Khan self-righteousness of yours has fallen by the wayside and I've got your full attention, let's begin, shall we?"

* * *

"When I found out it was Sweanea's front lawn you went off in, it brought back a lot of old memories. On Easter weekend back in nineteen hundred and eighty eight A.D., I was, what, 28? Yeah, 28 years old and after the obligatory church services I went to Sizzler." Noting Elijah's perplexed expression, Baines added, "an all-you-can-eat restaurant?"

Elijah sounded incredulous when he repeated, "'all-you-can-eat?'"

"Just bear with me, alright? Anyway, I was in my Sunday dress sitting with some old spinster girlfriends of mine who hadn't found a man yet. I never had too much of a problem in that area, I was always slim and trim no matter how much I ate. High metabolism and all, though my mama chalked it up to hyperactivity. The reason why I hadn't gotten married yet was because all the men I ran into thought monogamy was a kind of wood."

"In the Lost-Found Nation infidelity is nakon," Elijah commented.

"I don't suppose you know Elijah Muhammad himself slept around, do you?" Baines correctly interpreted Elijah's shocked silence as a "no." "Birthed quite a few illegitimate kids? No, I didn't think so. I ain't surprised your Lost-Found Nation would keep that under wraps. I'll show you some proof of all that later. Until then, don't interrupt me no more.

"So there we were in Sizzler, eating some greasy *pork* chops—mmm *mm*! Just kidding, they never served the other white meat at Sizzler. And then this fine light-skinned brother walked into the place, but he walked in with this blond haired, blue eyed White girl on his elbow. Now I never cared about that sort of thing because . . . I had a life! I always had bigger and better things on my mind. What folks did with their own personal lives was their own business so long as they didn't keep me from living mine how I saw fit. But one of the gals I was sitting with I had just met that Easter Sunday. Her real name was Sarah—Sarah *something*. I can't remember, but she had just changed it to something African. Or something she *thought* was African, *Sweanea*. Which is supposed to be Kenyan for 'dark and lovely' or something. As if any of the slaves that made up the Black American population ever came from Kenya, in *eastern* Africa."

"This Sweanea, is the same woman . . ?"

"You damn skippy! Oh, she-was-ab-so-lute-ly-*infuriated* that this light-skinned brother had walked in with this White girl. Couldn't stop talking about it and couldn't keep her loud-ass voice down either. She was going on and on about how he was selling out the race by being with her. How he had no right and how there ought to be a law against that sort of thing. How because he was so light and she was blond *and* blue eyed, any kids they would have wouldn't be able to pass for Black, and, in effect, wouldn't know who or what race they were.

"It was at this point when I jumped into the conversation because as you can probably tell by now I can't keep my mouth shut. But also because a cousin of mine once took too long walking past a movie poster in Mississippi with Jane Russell on it. When this cop passing by discerned that my cousin was drooling over this picture of a White woman dressed like a hillbilly sprawled out on a haystack, that damn cop beat—well, old Jesse Lee never could walk straight after that.

"I told that story to Sweanea, reminding her that there *was* a time when a Black man didn't have the right to like who he wanted and there *was* a law stating who you could be with and who you couldn't. And all she had to say to that was how that light-skinned brother was supposedly disrespecting her by just being seen with the White girl. When I reminded Sweanea that this guy didn't even know her from Adam *or* Eve, she pointed out that everyone at our table was single at the moment and how if someone, and she named Farrakhan by name, would step in and take charge, we would all have men of our own. Because that someone would see to it that the brothers going with girls from other races would be taken away from said girls and turned over to us hapless old maids.

"And I remember—not being all that mad at Sweanea. I expected her to want to have a man handed to her by the church, as opposed to the state, seeing as how she always was an ugly motherfucker. No, I was more mad at the other girls at the table who just sat right there and said hardly anything at all as Sweanea and I went back and forth on this issue. That's all too often the case in life and the world we live in: You have yourself a good old ram, a bull who's full of shit, and a bunch of damn *sheep* just grazing by the *fence* in the *middle* of it all. Without any backup from my mousey 'friends' I was sitting with, Alicia, Shamica, and Ena, I decided to end my involvement in this little debate. My last words to Sweanea on the subject warned her that one should 'never sacrifice freedom in the name of security.'

"At the time, I was only referring to the security she sought insofar as being guaranteed a soul mate. But then I got to thinking, how many other instances in the Black community were our people sacrificing their freedoms in the name of security? There was once a form of singing called 'rap' and for the longest folks thought that it 'incited violence and promoted juvenile delinquency.' Every once in a blue moon, you would have two rival gang members go at it on the floor of a rap concert. Rivals who wound up at the same concert only because no one ever provided anything else for young Blacks to do at night, but that would never be looked at or addressed. So you had Black folks willing to eliminate rap altogether, and then you had Black folks who just said, 'keep rap, but let's have metal detectors at the doors and a dress code so no gang members can wear their colors.' This same line of thinking spilled over into just about every other aspect of Black life.

"When you had Black kids killing one another over these overly expensive tennis shoes that were so in back then, did anyone think to look at the poverty that these kids came from that would make them be that bad off? No, instead they told the kids not to wear Nikes to school any more. You couldn't even wear jogging suits because someone said, and enough sheep believed, that Black men in jogging suits might be mistaken for sweaty criminals on the run, especially if they were jogging past a rich neighborhood, so they were told to wear something more dignified in public.

"The premise was we wouldn't get as much respect from the Whites if we didn't stay dressed up all the time. That we ran the risk of getting fucked with by 'the Man' if we decided to let ourselves go or let our guards down. Well, I've always been a 'tom boy' and I never was the type to put on airs for *any*body, which is why I never stopped believing my civil liberties should not ever be hinged on whether I happened to look 'bummy' one day. I also never wanted those same freedoms dependent on the condition that I was descended from a royal family in some fantastic all-Black civilization way back yonder before the beginning of time. I don't care if all Black folks ever did in Africa was walk around with bones in their mouths, *any* human being deserves basic, human rights, and shouldn't have to impress somebody to get them. So it shouldn't matter how many cultural or technological achievements their Egyptian ancestors contributed to the world.

"As I recall, it did seem as though Black folks were going out of their way in trying to ape their conservative White counterparts in some over-consorted effort to prove to said Whites, 'we're not an inherently violent people. Our ancestral background is just as illustrious as yours, and we can be as respectable, as parochial, and as paranoid as you are.' What our people didn't realize was that that was the whole point. To convince Blacks, who had caused so much trouble for the establishment in the 1960s by being radical, to become reactionary instead. Someone out there was trying to shame Blacks into *proudly* giving up their right to receive welfare or any other financial aid because it supposedly would make them lazy. When in actuality, the greedy of the world would just as soon not give anyone who's needy *anything* no matter what the situation. Besides, the biggest welfare cheats in town always were the super rich with their tax breaks and all the other kinds of breaks the government gave them while Black folks were always made to feel like they had to bend over backwards to justify what little they did get. As if there weren't more poor Whites on welfare than Blacks anyway.

"Black folks *also* somehow got it in their heads that it didn't make a difference if they voted in elections if all there ever was to chose from were two or three White men. Even though Black voting blocs were notorious for usurping election results and changing the course of Presidential campaigns in the past. Somebody along the way had preyed on our feelings of alienation, sense of displacement, and powerlessness in order to turn us off of the decision making process altogether.

"This made all too many of our people believe that only a Black leader could ever help Black people. Hell, racists had been saying for the longest that we'd be better off in our own Black nation, but I'm certain all the powers that be really wanted was for us to be 'out of their hair,' especially when it came to fiscal issues. And that's why we have the mess we have now, all because too many Black folks were willing to sacrifice their freedoms for the security of having someone in charge who looks just like them. Whether that someone *thinks* or *feels* like them or not.

"Which was exactly why Farrakhan had as much light shined on him and as much free advertising in the Black community as he did. Oh, sure, most of what was said about him back in the 20th was negative, but negative attention is always better than no attention at all. Not to mention the fact that the negative attention was always centered on Farrakhan's racist social policies and never on his self-help fiscal policies—as if there's nothing negative about 'self-help.' And all that negative attention from Whites fooled Black folks into believing that they hated Farrakhan and, of course, anyone our people thinks Whites can't stand, we'll *flock* to him. But the hope actually was that the lure of the forbidden would kick in and it did. In reality, those who were rich and powerful enough to hype Farrakhan up as much as he had been *loved* that bootstrap message of his because it let the rich and powerful off the hook.

"In other words, 'the Wrath of Farrakhan' had all the coverage it did because he told those who were rich enough to own the major venues of the media what they wanted to hear. That those who own those venues need not worry about Blacks protesting the censorship or the monopoly of said media with the same fervor that went into protesting racism in the '60s. Or that those who were rich enough to afford to own those major venues wouldn't be demanded by Blacks to pay their fair share of taxes. Why? Because, like the Pied Piper of Harlem, Farrakhan would someday lead all those pesky Negroes to New Africa.

"Yes friends, *New Africa*! Where Black folks would live like the very so-called devils Fairy King claimed to have hated so much. New Africa! Where it's illegal for a man to be alone in a room with a woman who's not your wife! New Africa! Where women are put on a pedestal so high they can't be seen or even breathe! Or where a total stranger can beat the living shit out of your children! New Africa, ladies and gentlemen! Or should I say New *Afrikkka*, thank you very much! Brought to you in part by the CIA, the corporate imperial army and guarded by the Fruit*s*, *plural*, of Islam! With the Shiite social policy of 1984 Tehran, *Not Without My Daughter*, Iran, and Reaganomics, a fiscal policy from 1984 Amerikkka. Every year is 1984 in the Lost-Found Nation of Islam in Goddamned North

America, George Orwell would be pleased. Now that instead of Big Brother we have Big *Brother Man!*"

Elijah's head was spinning. Baines' Southern accented stream of consciousness, her juxtaposition of the slang and double negatives, of Black English and intelligentsia, plus her subversive tangents peppered with swear words were all spoken with a rapid-fire pace which was almost too much for him to keep up with. But Elijah did understand at least the gist of what she was saying, and could also appreciate what was said on some primal level, even if he didn't recognize some of the phraseology the cantankerous Baines used. "Those last few references you mentioned," he queried. "'Rea-ga-no-mics,' 'Orwell,' what does all that mean?"

"It's means you've been kept fucking stupid by this hollow world in a plastic bubble where everything is 'nakon this and nakon that!'" Baines took a couple of drags from her pipe as Elijah fumed. "Sorry, but while the truth will set you free, the first thing it'll do is piss you off," Baines said and then she asked, "they told me you work downtown, what do you do?"

"Well, I used to be a dictator—"

"No," Baines sounded genuinely disappointed. "Not one of folks who're working on that super information bullshit?"

"As a matter a fact, I was fired today."

Baines put her hand on her chest in relief, "Lord have mercy. You were a part of that new history whatchamacallit, weren't you? That thing where little kids can punch up historical events on computers at school? Elijah, honey, do you know what they had you doing? Let me guess, they had you say something like Nixon was actually a decent President or that there weren't any Jews who died at the Holocaust, didn't they?"

Elijah scratched his head. "Actually, they said only a million had died," he sounded almost apologetic. "But I told my boss it didn't make any sense to me."

"You damn skippy it didn't make any sense!" Baines calmed herself down a tad and then she added, "Elijah, they've had you telling lies, boy! Six million Jews died in the Holocaust, *six* million! Jesus H. Christ . . ."

"You're going to tell me they had me type 'one million' because Minister Farrakhan and the Honora—Khallid Muhammad are anti-Semitic, huh?"

"Oh, sugar, it's so much deeper than that. I remember the first time I heard Minister Farrah Fawcett Khan speak. He was basically saying how in order to build a strong, proud Black nation from scratch we'll need doctors, we'll need architects, we'll need engineers, we'll need accountants, but we won't need sociologists. He said we won't have time for philosophy or poli sci because there's nothing that an old Jew like Freud or Marx can teach a Black man living in this day and age.

"Now, at the time, everybody went off on how what he was saying was so anti-Semitic, which it was. But once again I got to thinking, I do that every now and again and it usually gets me in trouble," Baines smiled and then continued. "I could understand his call for more scientists. Hell, I figured if he *was* crazy enough to secede from the Union he'd need folks who knew how to build stuff. But no *political* scientists allowed? Why was that? Well, I'll tell you why it was. Even as politically uneducated as Black folks were in those days, most of them still wouldn't have fallen in with someone they perceived to be an outright fascist. Which was why Farrakhan, with the help of the media, kept everyone, and the Black community in particular, from perceiving that the Nation of Islam always were a bunch of fascists.

"It kind of reminded me of this science fiction thingamabob I saw *years* ago called *V*. *V* was about these aliens who were really lizard men and wanted to eat us, but they knew if they tried to invade they would lose the element of surprise. It also would've meant too much trouble keeping us in control and from fighting back. So they disguised themselves as humans. This worked for a while and everybody loved them but one by one the leading anthropologists of the world started to disappear. Do you know what an anthropologist is?"

"No," Elijah shrugged.

"Figures. An anthropologist would be able to prove Whites weren't eugenically created over six thousand years ago by some Ferengi/Dr. Sivanna-looking mad scientist. Anyway, an anthropologist is someone who studies the history of human evolution, and the aliens from *V* knew this. They knew the anthropologists would be able to tell that the aliens weren't humanoid but reptilian so the aliens started bumping them off. And that's what the Nation of Islam did, except they went after anyone who could prove that they believed in the same conservative things that the blue eyed 'devils' did so that the Black folks would still accept them.

"And our very acceptance of the NOI back in the day only goes to show that most of our people must not have been able to tell a liberal from a conservative. Therefore, the last thing Farrakhan wanted was someone in the Black community or 'some old Jew' who would've been able to teach Blacks the difference. Specifically some of the Jewish folks at the time who could've told us exactly what the Nation of Islam was really all about. Folks like Noam Chomsky, Howard Zinn, Jeff Cohen, Norman Solomon—"

"Who are *those* people?"

"My point exactly. Sure, he may not have liked Jews, but I believe a lot of that anti-Semitism back then was a big smoke screen. The *main* reason why Farrakhan tried to steer Black folks clear of any Jewish influence is because somebody like Chomsky might have been more popular in the Black community than the NOI ever was. More importantly, Blacks would have known that the kind of life and the kind of future Farrakhan wanted for them wasn't in their best interests. Now it's too late."

Baines hung her head down low, took a deep breath, and continued, "Elijah, what they had you doing was wrong. It was part of something that all conquerors do. The first thing any conqueror does when they invade is they get a hold of the means of communication and then they begin to control the ways folks get their information. That's what the aliens in *V* did, that's what the old United States did in Panama back in '89, and that's what you did as a dictator. You weren't typing history into that computerized whatever, you were typing *his* story, Farrakhan's, Khallid's, God knows what else they had you put in.

"Frederick the Great said, 'if my soldiers began to think, not one of them would remain in the ranks.' Which is exactly why the Nation'll be feeding the next generation stuff like that one-million-not-six-million garbage, so that they'll stay in line. Otherwise, if they were allowed to hear an opposing viewpoint—*like the fucking truth*—then they might start to think for themselves and may even want to leave the Nation, *in droves!* Hell, you don't know who George Orwell or Noam Chomsky is, you didn't even know what an anthropologist was, how the fuck can you be professing to type something about history for little kids? Goddamn, it's a classic case of the blind leading the blind!"

"Alright, fine," Elijah started to sound frustrated. "We're so blind, we're so stupid, and I'll even admit that the Nation is *far* from perfect. In fact sometimes it can be . . ." Elijah paused and Baines looked as if she was waiting for something. After a moment, he spoke again, though it was clear he wasn't going to finish his original thought. "Well, let's say we *aren't* that much better off than the Whites, what's the answer, hmm? What are we supposed to do?"

Again, Baines hung her head low. This time she also shook it in exhaustion. "I don't think there's anything you can do. The first thing to do would be to get Metzger's finger off the button and yes, Metzger and Farrakhan *did* in fact cut a deal back in two thousand and five, so get over it. But after that, I have no clue. As far as the Nation itself goes, killing Khallid or any one of the ministers won't help because you'll make them martyrs and then you'll have 10 thousand ignorant motherfuckers waiting to take their place. And why? Because they're all fucking stupid, just like you."

"Hey—"

"I really mean to say brainwashed. Y'all just don't know any better, that's all. Or that things can be better. The only thing I could think of would be is if there was some way to educate *every*body. Wake folks the fuck up and teach them—"

"What?" Elijah seemed intrigued. "What would you teach people?"

"Hell, I don't know. There's so much else that would need to be done too . . . I don't know, I've about given up on niggers myself."

"Alright, fine. If you were in charge, if you could do anything you wanted, what would you do?" Elijah insisted.

"What are you asking? If I could wave my magic wand and play Lenin for a while?" Baines sighed as she looked up at her semi-willing guest. "O.K., I'll indulge myself. Beyond the obvious? Beyond making the dress code and all those anal rules strictly optional, I would have it where you didn't have to pull yourself up by your bootstraps for every-single-solitary thing in your life. Where the most basic essentials of living were paid for and taken care of by the very folks who're *supposed* to be our chosen public servants, and not have those same public servants ask for anything Stalinisticly unreasonable in return."

"But that would be socialism," Elijah remarked. "And socialism is dead."

"You can't kill an 'ism,' boy! What's wrong with you?" Baines sounded indignant and then began again only calmer. "Look, anytime you have a bunch of folks like your boy Khallid, Kool Aid, whatever the fuck his name is, in power, they're naturally going to want to *stay* in power. Which means that pretty soon they'll get greedy, meaning when it comes time to distribute the resources the Nation has to offer, they'll throw up every excuse their ministers of information can think of as to why they have so damn much, and you ain't got jack shit.

"The problem is, the folks in the world who ain't got jack shit believes those laissez-fairy tales even more so than the folks telling them. Like that tired old line about 'socialism being dead' for instance? But it's like—" At this point, Baines started to chuckle knowingly and wagged a finger at Elijah. "It's like something a hero of mine once said, 'if you're afraid of socialism, you're afraid of yourself.'"

"Who said this?"

"A radical from around these parts, a little over 60 years ago. He was the leader of the Chicago Black Panthers in fact. I don't suppose they let you know about the Panthers up there on the surface, do they?"

"They do," Elijah beamed ever so slightly at the chance to sound knowledgeable in the face of Baines' wisdom. "They told us that the Black Panthers were just a common street gang who wanted to get into politics but were ruined when they decided to work with Whites."

Baines slapped her hand to her forehead in angst and let it slide down her face. "D-a-m-n . . ! No, goddamn it, they weren't a fucking gang! They were a radical, political group who worked *just fine* with other radical, political groups who happened to be White in order to make this country a slightly more tolerable place until the police and the government wiped them out. And the Panthers were *never* friends with the NOI either, in case they told you *that* lie too. *Anyway*, the leader of the Chicago Panthers? He used to tell the story of an old woman who, like you, was afraid of socialism. She was dirt poor, so she went to see the Panthers about some of the programs that they offered. Even as the woman was saying how she didn't trust socialists, she was gorging herself on the Black Panthers' Free Breakfast Program. When the old woman who claimed to hate socialism just as much as the next man wanted to check and see whether or not she had sickle cell, she went to one of the Panthers' free health clinics.

"Then the leader pointed out to her that everything that she had been bred to despise were the very things that were helping her out. How did he put it? 'This is what happens,' he says. 'First you have free breakfasts, then you have free medical care, then you have free bus rides, and soon you have—*freedom* . . !' Elijah, do you know who that leader was?"

"Should I?"

Baines put a hand on Elijah's shoulder and grasped it. "Yeah, you should. The leader of the Chicago Black Panthers was the man you were named after, Fred Hampton."

A shiver shot through Elijah's entire body and translated into him suddenly jarring. Almost as if he were riding in one of the derelict streetcars he saw before him and it had went over a speed bump. Baines drew herself closer to Elijah and began to sound less like her usual shrill self and more maternal.

"You don't even know who you are, do you? Lord have mercy, child . . . Well, I do, you are Fred Hampton Rush. Son of Bobby L. Rush, a bona fide congressman for these here United States and an ex-Black Panther. In fact he was the minister of defense of the Chicago Panthers, do you remember?"

"I—" Elijah looked shaken. As though something deep inside him, something unreconciled that he just as soon not have anyone else see, had just been exposed to the world. "I don't know what you're talking about," he managed to counter.

"Oh, yes you do. You may even remember me now. Amelia Baines, I was one of your father's biggest fans. I was one of the precinct leaders who helped him get elected to the House of Representatives in '92 and to the Senate in '98. I became a friend of the family before too long, though considering what happened later, I didn't turn out to be a very good one." Baines paused and then asked, "you remember what happened . . ?"

Elijah pursed his lips together tightly, shut his eyes, and shook his head.

"How you were *accidentally* left behi—"

"I don't want to hear it!" Elijah boomed and shot straight to his feet and stood over Baines. "Damn you! Is that how you know me? Is that why you had Tom and Jerry or whoever the hell they are follow me around?"

"You have to understand, your mama, Carolyn had six kids. Jesus, I lose track of my *three* sons sometimes."

"There's no excuse! There's no excusing the likes of *them*! The airport wasn't that crowded!"

"The hell it wasn't!" Baines stood up to meet Elijah's stare. "It was February of 2006, the country had just surrendered to these—

bastards! A 100 million people were being evacuated in a matter of months! *Months*! People were ripped from their homes, interracial families were being split apart, it was utter *chaos*, it was hell on Earth! And everybody who could afford to tried to get the fuck out of the city! O'Hare was a goddamn madhouse! Everybody who was working for the government, your pops included, had already been shipped out to either Europe or the Divided States as they call them. Bobby was waiting in San Francisco for Carolyn to fly the six of ya'll to meet him. And yes, it *was* that crowded! Crowded enough for—for you to be left behind . . ."

When Elijah sensed that his eyes were starting to well up, he put his hands to his face. Baines went on with her tale, however, as though what she was saying didn't effect the man who stood before her as it obviously did. "It was an accident. Carolyn probably didn't even realize what had happened until after the plane had took off because the planes themselves were butt-crowded too. You don't actually think she wanted to leave her 13 year old son behind, do you? You were her youngest child, her baby, of course she didn't! If you do still hate your folks after all these years, you shouldn't!

"I should have been there . . . I *would* have, but my idiot husband thought we could take a ferry to Canada and waited until the last minute to boot. God rest his soul, but the man could fuck up a free lunch. The minute the damn boat got out of the dock, they shut down the borders. Nobody else got in and nobody else got out. And for the most part that's the way it's been ever since.

"By the time I finally found out what had happened to you they had taken you to the Ostrowski Home for Boys. They wouldn't let me take you and they weren't about to go against their vision of an all-Black nation that early in the game by giving you back to your folks either. If they did it for you they would have had to do it for all the others with stories like yours. I tried to get you out of there, I really did. I . . . Heard all about how they used to beat kids until they renounced their birth names and accepted their new 'Afro-Asiatic' ones assigned by the Nation." At this point, Elijah's crying had become slightly more audible and Baines found herself having to talk over it if she was to be heard. "But as you could probably tell, the more Shiite or shitty things got for women around here, the harder it got for a loud mouthed bitch like myself to get around, so I had to go underground.

"I checked on you from afar from time to time, whenever I was in the area and when I could do it with the least risk of getting busted. I admit I hadn't done it in a while, not since Elisha was born, in fact. And I'm ashamed to say, that with everything else that's been going on in the past 10 years, I had almost forgotten about you. But this past weekend it hit me, July 3rd was your birthday. So I sent my boys to go check on you and see how you were doing."

Elijah wearily sat back down and by this point his face was drenched in tears. Baines put her arm around his shoulder and squeezed when she joined him on the bench. "Where's my parents? Where are they at?"

An apprehensive Baines turned away from Elijah in dread. "I was hoping you wouldn't ask that. I don't know about your five brothers and sisters but your mom and dad have . . . Passed on some years ago. I'm sorry." Baines then leaned her head on Elijah's shoulder. "I'm so sorry you had to find out like this," she whispered.

* * *

The tall man known only as Tom returned from the surface to find Baines and Elijah sharing the same bench against the wall wiping tears from their eyes. When Baines noticed Tom, she cleared her throat and authoritatively said. "Report."

"Well, as luck would have it, at the exact time Elijah here was in Sweanea's lawn, folks in the neighborhood were either having the eight o'clock Maghrib prayer or were just out of the house because it was Unity Day. You're a fortunate man, Mr. Isiah."

Elijah's eyes were red and cracked when he looked up at Tom. "I don't feel very fortunate, 'Tom.'"

"Actually, in a way, you should," Baines remarked, "you're now more knowledgeable about yourself and who you really are than anybody else in the entire Lost and Found Nation. Except us, of course."

Elijah looked about him at the different people who had been passing by Baines and him all along, moving those ever present cardboard boxes around or inspecting their contents and cocked his head to one side. "You never did say what is it you are doing here."

Tom gave Baines a look but she waved it aside with her hand. "I think we can trust Elijah. Besides, he's seen enough already to write a book—and have the book thrown at us." Baines stood and motioned Elijah to follow her to a nearby open box of paperback novels. "We're smugglers, nothing more. With all the stories I imagine they must tell about us on the surface, you must have thought we'd certainly have more guns and ammo than literature."

"You're going to tell me that knowledge is power and that it's more important to arm the mind than anything else." Elijah observed.

"Very good, Grasshopper," Baines didn't bother to explain yet another one of her archaic, pop cultural in-references to a slightly bemused Elijah, who raised one eyebrow above the other at being called an insect. "You see, the rest of the world knows that New Africa and Aryan Amerikkka burns books. And videos, *and* CDs, and anything else that teaches folks to think for themselves or even hints that one should question authority. Now the deal was that instead of burning all this stuff, and making the environment all the more polluted by doing so, the Muslims and the Nazis were supposed to simply turn any material that they would otherwise burn over to Europe or Canada or the Divided States. That way, everybody's happy—so to speak. The rest of the world can still benefit from the works of—no, I won't even bother 'cause you won't know who I'm talking about anyway. And the Metzger/Farrakhan alliance wouldn't have to worry about their people learning anything.

"But like true fascists, the NOI and WAR don't want anyone else to learn anything either. So whenever they think they can get away with it, and that's way the fuck too damn often, they'll burn the books anyway, just to spite! That's where we come in. We'll steal the books and videos and so forth that they're about to destroy before they're destroyed and smuggle them across the borders." A proud smile creased across Baines' wrinkled face as she glanced over at Tom. "We're kind of like *Hogan's Heroes* that way, ain't we?"

"Father!"

As if on cue, Elisha ran right up to Elijah and leapt into his father's open arms. "Father! I saw 'images,' 'visions' in a big brown and black box! People were moving in the box when Jerry put this black bar into a rectangular box on top of the big box. And we saw a play called *Sesame Street*. It had a little man with orange skin and a magic wand called 'Mumford the Magician,' and—"

"I see you had my son doing more than eating," Elijah interrupted Elisha's enthusiastic tangent.

The man known as Jerry shrugged. "What was he going to do? Go his entire life without ever having watched TV?" Jerry then turned to Baines. "What are we supposed to do with them now?"

Elijah still held Elisha in his arms when he asked, "you're going to let us go, just as you said."

Not able to understand why this issue could generate the tension it did, Elisha's added, "can we come back, father? I want to see some more *Sesame Street*."

"*Sure* you can come back," Baines reply left Tom and Jerry stunned and speechless as she approached Elisha and gently laid her hand on his shoulder. "So long as you promise *never* to tell *any*one about this place or anyone here. Not even your mom and you can't tell your friends at school about *Sesame Street* either. You have to keep everything about tonight a secret, do you understand?"

"That's OK, I don't have any friends at school," Elisha said mournfully. "And I never tell my mother any of the secrets father tells me."

"Now hold on!" Elijah bellowed. "You expect us to keep coming back here? I never said I was joining you people, I have enough trouble as it is. I mean, even though I . . . Alright, I'll say it, I don't like the Nation, but I'm still a Muslim. I actually *like* being a Muslim and no matter what else is wrong with the Nation I want to *stay* a Muslim. And judging by the way you—well, you people don't exactly seem all that, how you say, 'God fearing?'"

"We don't want you to join us. We won't be at this location much longer anyway 'cause we're mobile and I doubt you'd want to tag along with us," Baines stated. "Besides, Malcolm X defied Elijah Muhammad, wound up getting kicked out of the Niggers of Islam, and *he* stayed a Muslim."

Elijah scrunched his features together at Baines as though he was trying to discern something which perplexed him. "Malcolm who?"

Tom, Jerry, and Baines all looked at each other and while the two young men shook their heads slightly, Baines proceeded to rummage through the open box of paperback novels before her. "It ought to be in here," Baines mumbled. "This is—well, what do you know, it *is*!"

From her squatted position over the box, Baines handed Elijah a paperback with a Black man on the cover who was in a suit and tie and wearing glasses. It was entitled, "*The Autobiography of Malcolm X?* This is another one of those people I should know, isn't it."

"To say the least," Baines said as she stood back up. "Remember before I was telling you how I'd show you some proof of Elijah Muhammad's sleeping around? Well, here it is. I want you to take this home, *keep it to yourself*, and read it. You're unemployed so you'll have plenty of time to look it over."

"Wait just a goddamn minute!" Jerry blurted out. "Letting them go is one thing, but letting him walk out of here with one of our books that could be traced right back to us—"

"First of all, if we didn't let them go, they'd be missed and the search for them would lead back to us a lot quicker than some damn book." Baines scolded. "Second of all, I'm sure Elijah here is in no *rush* to let anyone know that he's secretly the Great Apple Tree Slayer. And finally," Baines caught Elijah's glance. "*I* trust him, because he comes from good stock, don't you, boy?"

Looking a bit shaken for barely a moment as if he was just reminded of something unseemly, Elijah only nodded.

"Tom, you and Jerry'll take them back up to the surface," Baines ordered. To wit, Jerry rolled his eyes and made a smacking noise with his mouth. When Baines shot him a look in response to this, Jerry stormed towards the tunnel.

"Anyway," Baines laid an affectionate hand on each of the Isiahs' shoulders. "I'm not trying to change you, I'm just trying to *add to you*. I just want you to know more than what you're already being told, that's all. Turning on us will only keep you from learning things that you wouldn't ever be able to find out about from anywhere else. You understand that, don't you?"

As Elijah held Elisha in his arms as though the boy were much younger, he looked all around him. At the broken down relics the streetcars had become over the course of time, at the cracked and cave-like subway, and at the casually dressed Black people categorizing the vast number of boxes of novels, cassettes, or discs. He then eyed Baines up and down and said, "it would be one thing if you were a bunch of violent terrorists about to run riot in Chicago, but the one man I've seen with a gun around here doesn't seem to have all that much say. As far as I can tell, all you people do is steal books from people who don't want them, which is just like digging in the trash, and that doesn't make you much of a criminal, *Amelia*."

"I hope that's not you just sounding diplomatic," Tom commented. "And telling us what we want to hear."

"No," Baines smiled. "Trust is a two-way street. He trusted Jerry, who was packing a 45, to feed his only son. And he trusted *me*, so the least we can do is trust him." She then took hold of Elisha's hand. "In a couple of days we'll let your father know when y'all can come back by and watch some more Mumford the Magician on *Sesame Street*! How does *that* sound?"

"Great!" Elisha exclaimed.

"Alright," Baines let go of the Isiahs and took a step back as Tom led Elijah and Elisha towards the tunnel from which they originally came. "Good bye, y'all."

"Good bye," Elijah repeated as he tried to think of the last time he used that particular farewell in a public setting instead of what was supposed to be said.

"As-Salaam-Alaikum," Elisha called back as he waved at the old, wizened woman.

"Allah-peanut-butter-sandwiches to you too," Baines replied.

CHAPTER FOUR

"S e d i t i o n !"

Elijah couldn't believe it had never occurred to him to blame the Nation of Islam for being forgotten in O'Hare Airport all those years ago and left in the hands of the old men at the Ostrowski Home for Boys. Old men who used to give beatings which would be nostalgically (and masochistically) bragged about as rites of passage by their recipients when they came of age, but only prompted one Elijah Isiah to secretly and silently swear to Allah never to see a son of his whipped for any reason.

If the old woman Baines was right, and if the ministers had been denying all along that Farrakhan *had* cut a deal with the Great White Demon Metzger, it would actually make perfect sense. In order for the ministers to be in any position of real power in the first place, let alone stay in power, it had to have been believed by as many as possible that any hardship that was suffered in the founding of the Black Republic, such as being abandoned by your parents, was the fault of someone else. *Anyone*'s, other than the fault of those in a position of power to actually effect events in one's life at the moment in question. In Elijah's case, it never made that much sense to completely blame the Jewry, or even the White devils themselves for all that ensued after the Apocalypse. So he had blamed his family, but he decided he wasn't going to do that anymore.

After the Isiahs were awakened with smelling salts above ground by the men known only as Tom and Jerry, Elijah looked about him to find they weren't on the same street where he had first ran into the tall, thin man now standing before him. The four of them all stood in a plot of grass in-between two houses, but then again, Elijah imagined that was the whole point. To keep him from pointing out to anyone the exact spot where he was originally drugged unconscious and taken underground. After he directed the Isiahs towards the quickest route to Ishmael Emmanuel's home from where they were, Tom sprinted like a gazelle with his long legs in the opposite direction whereas Jerry just stood and fumed until Elijah and Elisha headed on their way before taking off himself.

Nayirah was so furious she was about to risk Elijah's wrath and attempt to beat Elisha for embarrassing her so at Ishmael's house, but when she spied the welts that "Sister" Sweanea had inflicted upon her son, Nayirah remembered what Ishmael said Elijah had claimed over the phone—that they would be a while getting back because he was disciplining the boy. Never knowing what really happened, Nayirah was content that justice had been served in two ways. That her spoiled offspring finally received his first whipping and that it was, so she believed, administered by a husband she had almost written off as having no backbone whatsoever.

She still didn't like the fact that he was unemployed, however. But what would have doubtlessly given Nayirah a conniption was that Elijah neither looked for work or attempted to fix the occasionally hissing gas main near his kitchen sink in-between dropping her off and picking her up from the Sarah X School for Girls. While Nayirah was out of the house on Wednesday, Thursday, and Friday of that week, Elijah was at home reading *The Autobiography of Malcolm X*.

Though Elijah could tell the book was supposed to be a factual account, it certainly read as though it were an ancient saga. It was basically the story of a man in search of himself and how the three father figures in his life shaped that search. The first being his real father who was allegedly killed by the Klan. The second being a gangster called West Indian Archie who took in a young Malcolm as his apprentice in crime and helped school Malcolm in the ways of the streets. And his final surrogate father was Elijah Muhammad, who elevated Malcolm X to the status of no less than the national representative of the Nation of Islam until, just as Baines had said, it was discovered that Muhammad did in fact have several illegitimate children by cheating on his wife.

Elijah didn't know what was more shocking, finding out that *the* Elijah Muhammad was unfaithful or that the Lost-Found Nation of Islam had successfully wiped clean any record of this Malcolm X. The official history was that during that period Elijah Muhammad himself was the only nationally known representative of the Nation of Islam. But as Elijah read on, he found the Nation had long since been in the business of changing history to suit their liking.

It seems that the newspaper for the NOI at the time which proceeded *The Final Call* was called *Muhammad Speaks*, a paper that Malcolm X had founded. Initially, he would pick one day out of every month, lock himself in a room, and assemble photos and other materials for a printer that he found. Not unlike the projects Elijah used to work on at Kimbro's Copy Shop and the short-lived *Nation* magazine before his days as a dictator. But despite Malcolm single-handedly starting *Muhammad Speaks* from scratch, and even though he was their national representative, there came a point when the jealously within the Nation of Islam kept them from printing any of the many positive contributions Malcolm X made for the NOI. Any of them at all.

* * *

Wednesdays and Fridays were both nights the Isiahs had to show up at their temple or else. So Baines had her man Tom contact Elijah Thursday morning. Tom seemed to suddenly appear next to the driver's side of Elijah's black sedan in front of the Sarah X School for Girls just after Nayirah had cleared the school gates and Elijah was about to pull away from the curb. Tom told Elijah that he and Elisha could see Baines after Nayirah was picked up from school late that afternoon if they wanted. The thin man also told him where exactly in Ishmael's neighborhood the two of them and *only* the two of them were to be met.

Elisha was ecstatic at the prospect of returning to the underground and could barely restrain his enthusiasm enough to keep from drawing attention to themselves as the Isiahs stood that afternoon at the spot Tom designated for them to wait to be contacted. The man known as Jerry escorted them to a nearby alley way between two bombed out buildings where Tom was waiting for them as Elijah mentally braced himself for the smell of chloroform and the sensation of blacking out that he knew was to come.

Since all he did Wednesday and that Thursday was straighten up the house and read the autobiography, Elijah had gotten through a little over half of the book and had plenty of questions for Baines, mainly concerning all the different 20th century references that Malcolm X alluded to—such as Li'l Abner, the NAACP, and a place called Casablanca.

Baines interpreted all those terms and more. She also seemed to go out of her way to make doubly sure Elijah knew that not everything thing Malcolm X said was the gospel nor was the man a demigod. A preeminent example of this was when Baines went through the chapter of the book called Laura. The chapter begins with Malcolm describing how his "long-suppressed African instincts" to dance were loosened up at a party he went to and Baines was quick to point out Blacks never were a race of natural born dancers.

At the end of the chapter Malcolm X claims that the Black girl the chapter was named for "became a lesbian" because he had left her for a White woman. Baines corrected this too, stating that one is either born with a sufficient amount of either dormant or overt homosexual tendencies in order to be considered gay or not. She explained that one doesn't magically cease to become a heterosexual after having been straight all of one's life and certainly not after losing a boyfriend to someone from another race.

The afternoon of Saturday, July the 9th proved to be the third and very next time Elijah and Elisha would be taken to the underground. Elisha looked happier than he ever had in his young life. He was watching something on video cassette called *The Electric Company* with an unusual character known as Spiderman (or "Spidey" as his friends called him) who when he spoke somehow made whatever he was saying visibly legible in a opaque balloon that would appear over his head. As Elisha sat transfixed, his father, standing over the battery-powered television next to Baines, noted how surreal it all seemed to him and proceeded to walk alongside of the old woman who was lighting her familiar corn cob pipe.

"You didn't bring the book with you this time around?" Baines sounded a tad concerned. "Where is it?"

"I hid it inside this huge jar of pennies Elisha has," Elijah said assuredly. "Even Nayirah isn't low enough to go through a little boy's penny bank. I'm just about finished with it, and I would've given it back to you today except that I still want to read the epilogue but I haven't gotten to it yet. I hope you don't mind."

"Mind?" Baines snorted. "Are you kidding? Look at you, you're every teacher's dream. Somebody who's actually eager to finish a book assigned to him." She patted Elijah on the shoulder blade in a congratulatory manner and then asked, "speaking of teaching, do you remember the part in the chapter called 1965 about how Malcolm didn't vote for Barry Goldwater or Lyndon Johnson for President?"

Elijah thought for a moment and answered, "I think so, wasn't that when he called one a 'wolf' and another a 'fox?'"

"That's right, and Malcolm was talking about how neither of them could be trusted because the fox was only the lesser of the two evils. How the wolf was at least honest about his intentions and let you know where you stood but the fox would try and trick you?"

"What about it?"

"Well, it's a crock of shit." Once Baines saw the shock value of what she had just said register in Elijah face, she smiled and moved on. "Even though the autobiography came out after he quit the Nation, Malcolm still had some residual conservatism left over from being Elijah Muhammad's right-wing hand man for ten years. All the stuff he was saying about natural dancing instincts and folks 'turning' gay we went over the day before yesterday are examples of that. Not to mention Malcolm's distrust of us liberal foxes, so—"

Straining as though he was sorting out something in his head, Elijah blurted out, "wait, conservatives help people already in power, and liberals, liberals . . ."

"Liberals are supposed to help out folks who are being stepped on by people in power, like Black folks!" Baines impatiently huffed. "Reactionaries are conservatives with attitude and radicals are liberals who aren't watered down, got it? We've been through this! 'Every teacher's dream,' Jesus . . . Now, if you were White, rich, and *really* powerful, and you wanted to keep Black folks from teaming up with Whites who are liberal so your life won't be made more inconvenient, what would you do?"

All Elijah knew to say was, "I have no idea."

"You keep Black folks fucking stupid! You pump them up with a lot of shit about how you can somehow trust and respect a wolf like Goldwater because he says what's on his mind, no matter how detrimental to our people whatever he had in mind was. Like the policies he would implement the minute he got into office for instance, specifically the fiscal ones. Then you turn around and tell them, *or let a token tell them*, that they can't trust liberals because supposedly they're foxes that'll trick you into thinking they're your friends. Well, if you're wrong, if a liberal was sincerely an ally of yours, and you've just alienated them by saying they can't ever be trusted because they're some kind of damn fox, then your ranks are down one less ally for the struggle! And that's exactly what the rich and powerful want, for you to be alone and all the weaker from a lack of allies instead of acting collectively. But then, Earl Ofari Hutchinson did say in his book *Black and Reds*,'the Muslims demanded that Blacks reject any calls from the left to unite . . .'

"Malcolm then claimed that, 'Black people have advanced further when they have seen they had to rise up against a system they clearly saw was outright against them.' What a masochistic thing to say! In other words, since Black folks supposedly can't get ahead without someone constantly whipping our asses, we shouldn't have cared if a madman like Goldwater became the most powerful man in the free world at that time? I remember Farrakhan said the same thing about the Reagan Years and it made me wonder whether or not the boy always was some kind of plant. Talking about how the hellish economy back then supposedly lit a fire under Black folks to do more for themselves. Oh, it lit a fire, alright. And the fire burnt our asses up like we were crucified on a burning cross!

"In the days of the Black Panthers, in the days of your father, Bobby Rush, all too many Black folks like Stokley Carmichael—please, don't ask me who that is—said that the Panthers were crazy for teaming up with the Peace and Freedom Party and the Communist Party. 'They're White dominated,' they said. 'They ain't up to no good,' they said. Well, *that's* racist. Why? Because these people just assumed the Communists were bad just because they're White. 'It's too good to be true for them to like us, it doesn't matter what they believe in, they're White, so they'll eventually betray you.' *Wrong*, it *does* matter what someone believes in, and in the end, that's *all* that matters. The Black Panthers never had a problem with the White groups they allied themselves with but they *did* have a problem with the NOI, Ron Karenga and his US Organization, don't ask, and other Black reactionaries.

"We're in the trouble we're in because all too many Black folks believed that Blacks are so inherently good they'll never turn on anybody who's Black. 'The Black man is by nature divine?' Well, all that glitters is not gold and all that's Black is not 'down' as they used to say in the 20th century, and the Lost-Found, Lost Again, Found Again Nation of Islam in North America is stone cold proof of that. *Malcolm X* is proof of that because the people who shot him were Black Muslims. And Farrakhan himself, back then known as Louis X, was quoted in *Muhammad Speaks* calling for the death of this father of four daughters."

As if she was giving Elijah time to soak everything she had just said, Baines struck a match and used it to light her pipe. After a couple of drags, she mumbled something about wolves and foxes and then queried, "do you remember Minister James 3X, Elijah Muhammad's assistant? One of the original guard, old school, joined Muhammad back in 1940, was the one who said, 'the idea of private property gives the individual the incentive to work hard' because he didn't like communism—hell, what am I saying? Who in the NOI ever did?"

Elijah's head perked to one side in recognition. "Yeah, yeah I remember *him*."

"Damn . . !" Baines shook her head and her eyes widened as she raised one eyebrow above the other. "Didn't know about Malcolm before this week but knew about some obscure—well, I guess they only teach you about the ones who stayed in Elijah's favor. Anyway, this James 3X was the guy who said White folks' brains are only six ounces and Black folks' brains are seven and a half ounces?"

"He also said that, 'the White man's physical power is one-third less than that of the Black man.'"

Baines gave Elijah a look as she cocked an inquisitive head to one side. "You believe that, boy?"

"Well, I uh . . ." Elijah was clearly caught off guard. He didn't know what to say that would keep Baines from blowing up on him and going off on a tangent so he responded with a very neutral, "I don't know," and hoped in vain for the best.

"I *hates* a fence straddler, you ought to know *that* by now, don't you?" Baines snarled. "C'mon, it's time you met a buddy of mine."

* * *

Elijah followed Baines past an assortment of the same group of nameless faces busy categorizing boxes of books that had become somewhat familiar to him because of his previous two trips to the underground. Baines never bothered to introduce any of them to Elijah, but it now seemed as though that would change at least somewhat. He almost expected to be introduced to another one of her spies like Tom and Jerry, but whoever Elijah thought he was going to meet, he assumed that they would invariably be Black and assumed wrong.

Off in a corner with a small stack of paperback novels at each side of him was a blond haired, blue eyed White man of medium build, probably in his early twenties. He had a sparse, auburn beard, wore his slightly ragged dress shirt and slacks a size too large, and had a pensive look about him, as though he didn't like that someone he didn't recognize, namely Elijah, was coming in his direction. Whether that someone was being led to him by Baines or not.

Elijah felt his heart race just a bit. He could not remember the last time he saw someone who was White. The young man was seated "Indian style" on the cold ground of the abandoned subway station before him pouring through a copy that Elijah could see was entitled *America: What Went Wrong?* by two people named 'Barlett' and 'Steele' which may not, and shouldn't, seem as out of the ordinary as it did to Elijah, whose eyes widened in mild shock at the sight of the man.

Baines noticed this and briskly ran one of her hands in front of Elijah's face to get his attention. "Hello? Is there anyone out there? Just nod if you can hear me." An embarrassed Elijah shook his head and took his eyes off of the White man only long enough to give Baines a look of irritance. "He's an illegal alien, not an alien from another planet," Baines continued. "And guess what, he's got a *name* too! Eric Blair, this is a man who's got a long way to go, Fred Hampton Rush."

Elijah suddenly gave his full attention to Baines and looked at her with contempt, albeit mild. Up until this point, Baines had never tried to call him that for they both knew the connotations that came with the name. But at the same time, Elijah was hesitant about correcting her. In the end, as Elijah found himself shaking the young man's apprehensive hand and greeting the man under his breath, he didn't. But only because he figured it didn't make a difference what this man thought his name was since he probably wouldn't be seeing that much of this White person in the future anyway, or so he told himself.

"Eric here is a refugee from Aryan Amerikkka. Believe it or not, he didn't like it down there even though he's White and White folks run the show—into the ground that is. Now remember all that crap James triple X rated was saying about Whites being mentally inferior? Well, not that I've ever been one to feel the need to prove anything to anybody, but Eric can speed read and he has a photographic memory. Tell him why you're so invaluable to us, Eric. Besides the fact that you're a wonderful human being."

Eric sighed and put down the paperback in his lap. "I guess I'm like the old professors from the end of *Fahrenheit 451*, I commit to memory as many books as I can speed read in case some of them get lost." Eric then gave Elijah a nervous look and added, "I—haven't memorized the Bible, or the Koran yet, because I only have time for banned books."

"Oh, don't sweat my boy here," Baines reassured, "he doesn't care about all that, he's not like my ignorant-ass aunt. Who used to always get on my case talking about, '*child*, if you want to read about somebody with superpowers, why don't you read about *Jee-sus!*'"

Elijah blinked and wrinkled his brow for a moment as he tried to take all of this in. Then he sounded almost parental when he addressed Eric again and warned, "If they catch you here, they'll think you're an invader and kill you."

"Why do you want to scare the kid, huh?" Baines demanded. "They're not going to catch him and what the hell are you talking about an *invader*?"

Like a child who knew he was about to be corrected on some fine point in logic, Elijah held his head down. "Well, the *ministers* said that the reason why we don't have as many civil services as we used to is because all of our resources are going towards fortifying our borders against a White invasion."

"Man—goddamn it!" Baines felt at her side as if in pain and then lit her corn cob pipe again. Elijah lounged towards Baines as if to help her but she angrily waved at him to stand aside. After regaining her composure, Baines took a couple of drags from her pipe and exclaimed, "is that what they're telling you these days? Is that why you can't get the city to do something as simple as come to your house to take a look at a broken sidewalk or pick up a dead body before it starts to smell?" Baines waited until Elijah nodded and then she continued. "And I suppose they've been using the old bully pulpit to tell y'all that if you complained about it you'd be a bunch of whiners, huh?" Elijah nodded again. "As if the mere existence of basic public services will magically turn all y'all brainwashed motherfuckers into a bunch of sluggish minstrels lounging around on some porch down South somewhere. Goddamn it, how long will niggers continue to be conned into not demanding what's theirs by this same old, tired-ass shit about them being, 'too Black and proud to be dependent?' Let alone folks in general being conned by this boogeyman/scapegoat bullshit.

"I've *been* past the border, *many* times, and I can tell you, Metzger's got enough on his hands as it is without trying to invade somebody, which he ain't. Most of the White folks in Amerikkka don't like the way things are run. If Metzger's troops are doing anything, they're beating the crap out of their own people, trying to force them to fit into this wholesome, *Leave it to Beaver* vision they can't seem to get out of their heads. It's just like Farrakhan's vision only his is in 'blackface.' I'll *tell* you what's going on at the border, FOI and WAR border guards playing chess. *Chess*, saying corny-ass, one-up-man-ship shit to each other like, 'check, my iceman from the North,' and 'ah, checkmate, my warrior from the South' and so on. And of course, the Muslims always have the black pieces."

"But they won't even let us drive anywhere near the border," Elijah implored.

"Well, I imagine that's because they have a big lie to maintain, don't you think?" Baines snidely remarked. "Look, the reason why I introduced you to Eric here is because I wanted to drive home what Malcolm had said in the book about how when he went to Mecca he met Whites he could trust, who weren't devils—"

"Like any of us ever were," Eric commented.

"You know, with your photographic memory I'm surprised you don't remember that 'Ronald,' 'Wilson,' and 'Reagan' each had six letters in them. Triple six? If *any*body was ever the anti-Christ—" Baines turned her attention back to Elijah. "But anyway, the point I'm trying to make is that Whites are not *inherently* evil. Some of them, like Eric here, are invaluable."

"Thank you kindly, massa," Eric quipped sarcastically in a mock Southern accent. "I is so glad I could be useful around these parts."

"You know what I mean," Baines said apologetically. "Do you understand now that you've been told a bunch of lies all this time, 'Fred Hampton Rush?'"

Still not entirely sure how he felt about being called his birth name, Elijah changed the subject. "You were feeling at your side a minute ago. Are you alright?"

"It's nothing some more of this 'Indo' can't help." Baines lit her corn cob pipe after puffing on it a couple of times and added, "it's also nothing the Nation's lack of health insurance will help either, like I could be parading around above ground for very long anyway. But that's OK 'cause we'll be headed to Canada in a couple of days so I can get myself looked at up there."

"Canada?" Elijah sounded both worried and disappointed. "You're leaving?"

"I told you we're mobile. We've got to smuggle all these books and tapes and CDs and shit out of bonfire territory, ain't that right, Eric?"

"That's right," Eric said before returning his full attention to the paperback he was speed reading.

Baines looked Elijah up and down and smiled. "You're going to miss me, aren't you?" Before he had a chance to answer she walked back towards the niche in the subway where Elisha was watching *The Electric Company* to give Eric the privacy he needed to concentrate. As Elijah matched her steps, she talked with a sense of finality. "This will be the last time y'all can come down here, and it'll probably be the last time you'll ever see me again. You can go ahead and keep the book, just keep it out of sight."

"Are you sure?" Elijah asked.

"Oh yeah. We've got plenty of copies of Malcolm's book because of the big Malcolm X glut of '92." Baines' tone then became somewhat more serious. "If there's anything you always wanted to know about your father, now'll be the time—"

"Actually, Amelia, I think I know enough as it is," Elijah saw that she was about to scoldingly correct him so he quickly spoke again before Baines could say anything. "What I mean is, I'm probably going to have to spend the rest of my life in the Nation. That being the case, I'll spend the rest of my life knowing that everything around me is a farce. On the one hand I'll feel superior to everybody else still believing in Yacub's history and whatnot, but on the other hand, I won't be able to *do* anything superior . . . Like change anything about the Nation that I may not like. So it doesn't make any sense for me to learn that much more." Elijah took a breath and thought for a moment. "*If* things were to change, in a major and *violent* way—" Elijah looked for a revealing change of expression from Baines and when he found none, asked. "Will I be one of the first up against the wall?"

"Just open your mouth and say something intelligent that'll separate you from Yacub's sheep," Baines smiled. "With us revolutionary types it works just like playing dead in front of a bear. You'll be fine. Besides, revolutionaries don't arbitrarily kill people anyway. And then, of course, there's always that old cliché folks used to fall back on so."

"What's that?"

"That the revolution won't happen in any of our lifetimes."

* * *

As Elisha sat with Baines' agent Jerry and was transfixed by a White woman swinging on a vine and calling herself Jennifer of the Jungle, Baines motioned Elijah towards a small stack of video tapes on a bench that protruded from the wall.

"After Elisha gets done watching *The Electric Company*, I want you to watch this documentary on Malcolm called *Make it Plain*," Baines proposed as she held up the video in question for Elijah's inspection. "Seeing is believing, and even though Malcolm's face is on the cover of the book, it'd be good to actually see him preach and be interviewed and so on 'cause all the footage'll give you a fuller feel for the era, you know?"

"Actually, I was thinking as soon as Elisha gets done we'll head on home."

Both Elisha and Jerry did jarring double takes at Elijah from their television watching over his mention of leaving. Baines drew her head back as if to say something but Elijah cut her off. "Didn't I just finish saying it doesn't make any sense to learn anything else? Your point's been made, you stubborn old woman: The Nation is no utopia, 'least not for anyone who's not in power. Fine, you don't have to convince me anymore and you don't have to show me anything else that's going to make living here all the harder. You get to go off to Canada but we'll have to stay here. So you showing us how much better things could be is only going to make us feel worse because there's nothing we can do about it." Elijah then turned to his son and regretfully ordered, "Elisha, it's time to go, say goodbye to these nice people."

"But father," Elisha pleaded. "Everybody's going to eat in a half an hour. They're going to make something called a 'pizza' and some 'popcorn—'"

"And apples too," Jerry snidely interjected.

"We wouldn't give Elisha anything that would violate that string beans-not-lima beans, mustard greens-not-collard greens, lamb-not-pork, FOI-enforced food code y'all have up there." Baines assured.

"I'm not worried about that. How *could* I be after everything else about all this?" Elijah asked as he flayed his hands in the air all around him. "Besides you—*tantalizing* my boy with even more ideas he might never be able to see realized, I just as soon not have Nayirah sitting in the house for too long wondering why are we taking so suspiciously long coming back from 'a playground.'"

Baines put a hand on Elijah's shoulder before quietly saying, "if you remember, the reason why you wound up here in the first place was because Elisha was hungry. And seeing as how y'all ain't allowed but one damn meal a day, I don't think a little home made pizza is going to spoil his appetite. He'll still be plenty hungry by tonight."

"But Nay—"

"*You* go home and keep her from getting suspicious if you want to leave so bad, if you're that hell bent on not learning anything else," Baines raised her voice a notch. "You don't want us to put any more ideas in your head, fine. Let us at least put a little something your son's belly *one last time*." Reminded that this would be the last visit to the underground, Elijah's attention seemed to perk. Noticing this, Baines continued, "Tom'll take you back up to your car, when you get back home, just tell that old hatchet wife of yours you dropped Elisha off somewhere that's not that far from the house so he could play a little longer. Tell her he'll be walking home by himself and will be back in time for dinner or whatever the hell prayer it'll be time for."

"And what about Elisha?"

"In about an hour or so, Jerry'll take one of the cars that we have on stand by out to your place and drop him off just beyond y'all's view. Then he'll just walk in the door like he actually came from—*playing around*." Baines looked at Elijah and squinted her eyes slightly. "You do trust us, don't you?"

Elijah took a step back and rubbed at his temples in a circular motion with both of his index and middle fingers. He was lost in thought until he remembered that Elisha, Baines, and even Jerry were still waiting for him to answer. Elijah shook his head as though he were clearing mental cobwebs and said, "alright, fine. Elisha? If you want to and *only* if you want to, you can eat with Misses—"

"Ah, *ahh*," Baines interrupted. "What'd I tell you about that Miss, Ma'am, massa crap when you first got here?"

"—*Baines*. As soon as you're done she'll see to it that you're driven *straight* home and when you get there, you're to tell your mother that the reason why you didn't come home with me was because I let you play some more. Do you understand?"

"Hell yeah!" An ecstatic Elisha leapt to his feet from where he was sitting down next to Jerry and hugged his father.

As Elijah returned the hug, he glared at Baines. "*Hell* yeah?" He queried under his breath.

Baines in turn only smiled. "Lighten up, there's nothing wrong with saying the real name of the Lost-Found Nation. Funny, they always did say back in the 20th that things would have to get a hell of a lot worse before things got any better. Well, if this ain't 'a lot worse . . .'"

* * *

Elijah was never one for long goodbyes. He always thought they prolonged the inevitable, so when Tom led him and Baines to the mouth of the tunnel, Elijah briskly hugged Baines while sternly but softly saying for her to make sure that his son was to be returned soon and safely. As Tom was about to dab his chloroform onto the balled up hand cloth he had been placing over Elijah's face, Baines held up her hand and told Tom not to knock Elijah out. Her rationale was that since the move to Canada would leave this particular hideout vacant and obsolete within a couple of days, and Elijah was entrusting them with his only son, surely they didn't need to render him unconscious. Seeing as how he would be leaving the underground for the last time and never coming back.

Grudgingly, Tom agreed. After putting away his chloroform and the rag that smelled of it, he motioned for Elijah to follow him deeper into the tunnel. Elijah followed Tom for several steps before turning his head to see if Baines was still standing at the mouth of the tunnel watching them go only to find her nowhere in sight.

As it turned out, the damage that Elijah had seen done to the subway was not the doing of the Nation of Islam. The last time this particular subway saw regular operations was circa early 2005. Then-President Jerry Brown had just been re-elected and, in a destructive backlash that was almost a prelude to what would come in the following year, a little known terrorist arm of the Religious Right calling themselves the Sentinels of Life had stolen a small explosive device and detonated it near the subway right before their capture.

Tom explained to Elijah that the devastation to the area was so extensive, total excavation of the subway was never fully completed. By the time efforts were stepped up, the NOI had taken over the Great Lakes region, and between their privatized economics and backward priorities, the damage to the subway was simply left unattended. Especially since it was thought by the ministers from the beginning that public transportation would eventually be made nakon anyway. The few bodies left in the subway that hadn't decomposed had to be discretely buried or cleared out by the underground before they moved in.

Hearing Tom's account had brought back memories Elijah thought he had long since buried. He did remember being in school on the day of the explosion. When what sounded like a faint crack of thunder was followed by a low rumble had been heard in his classroom while the ground briefly tremored. Elijah mulled over the recollection while he climbed a long and winding rusted stairwell which was missing a couple of steps that led to the back of a cramped office of sorts which must have been where the subway's maintenance personnel used to gain access from the surface to the tunnels below in cases of repair. The maintenance office didn't have a door which led to the outside but a broken window instead. After Tom looked out of it to see if anyone was around, he motioned for Elijah to follow him through it. Once Elijah had, he grabbed Tom by the cuff of his shirt and demanded, "I know damn well you didn't drag me and my son's unconscious bodies through all *that* every time we came here!"

"Of course not," replied Tom. "And obviously we didn't fit all those books and videos through that window either. But we're obviously not going to show you all our little secrets, now are we. I may not be as much of a hard-ass as Jerry, but I'm not stupid either."

Nayirah felt like such a hypocrite. She preached in school how the White man used to "castrate" the Black man by paying his wife higher wages so that the man could no longer be the head of his family. And here she had been for ages it seemed supporting Elijah with the teaching position at the Sarah X School for Girls more so than he supported her. Nayirah really hated it when Elijah would remind her that the prophet Muhammad himself was what they used to call a "house husband." Imagine, the insolence it must take to use a book as holy as the Koran to excuse not doing something or doing something your way, she thought.

Nayirah found herself so flustered from thinking along those lines she began to pace across the living room of the Isiah home she had just cleaned from stem to stern out of boredom and take greater notice of the time. How long did that brat have to be out to play, Nayirah asked herself, since she recalled never having as much free time on her hands in her youth as Elisha did.

Nayirah also recalled that she never had an allowance like the one Elijah paid her son either. *Allowance*, Nayirah often huffed, when she was Elisha's age, she was *allowed* to go outside, by Allah. That lazy, *unemployed* man of hers still hadn't fixed that gas main, the occasional hissing and the peculiar smell that came with it was getting on her nerves, and Elijah was surely going to spoil Elisha into becoming just as inept as his father.

This is what was going through Nayirah's mind as she headed for her son's room, the one room in the house she wasn't supposed to clean up, the room Elijah said Elisha himself was supposed to keep clean. Nayirah correctly assumed that Elijah was more concerned with the boy's privacy than giving him the responsibility of the room's cleanliness and for once decided to defy one of the very few edicts her husband had laid down, such as not ever laying a hand on Elisha. After all, the boy ought to be grounded and his movements on restriction rather than being allowed to play only days after he ran away for reasons Nayirah still did not know, and humiliating her at Ishmael's. Therefore no one concerned should have anything to say about her walking into Elisha's room without him being there since the room was in a house that, thanks to his father's disdain for manual labor, she paid the rent for.

She wasn't too surprised to find Elisha's room nearly spotless after all. If there was one attribute the Isiah men had it was their neatness. And then there was that disgustingly huge mason jar that the boy kept his allowance in, all the free money his father liberally threw his way just squatting on the—closet shelf? As long as Nayirah could remember it was always on the floor because it *was* that big and at least half full of pennies and other coins, as it was now, making it possible to break any wooden shelf trying to support its great weight. Which is why when Nayirah went through Elisha's closet in order to find where the huge jar had been moved, she then hoisted it from the closet shelf and back onto its familiar spot on the floor. They ought to thank me, she thought, I just saved those two fools from having to buy a new shelf.

In jostling the heavy jar around, Nayirah could see through the jar's clear glass the coins flowing to and fro almost like water. Because of this jarring movement, she noticed something that looked like it could have been made of paper inside. Was it a dollar bill? If so, then Elijah had been paying that brat far too much money, she decided. The huge jar's tightly sealed top needed a nearby towel to be wrapped around it in order for Nayirah to have the traction necessary for her to twist it off.

But when Nayirah reached in to retrieve what she had thought was a dollar with Farrakhan's face on it, Nayirah only caught a hold of and drew forth the page of a book. The rest of the book surfaced from the sea of coins as she pulled further, of course, and once Nayirah could make out its title, she gasped in shock. Dropping the paperback novel to the floor as if it were poison before picking it up again after a cautious pause, Nayirah then sprung to her feet from where she had been kneeling by the mason jar trying to get it open and walked briskly toward the Isiah home's one phone in the kitchen. Holding *The Autobiography of Malcolm X* with her right hand's index and middle fingers as one would hold a dead rat by the tail.

* * *

"As-Salaam-Alaikum, this is the Fruit of Islam."

"Wa-Alaikum-Salaam," Nayirah answered back after having dialed 911 from her kitchen phone. "I want to report an act of—sedition."

"What is your name, my Black sister?" The FOI officer asked.

"Nayirah Isiah, I'm at 2247 Harlem Avenue on the corner of 125th Street in the South Side. I found a nakon book my husband Elijah had hidden in my son's penny bank."

"What's the title of the book, my sister?"

"*The Autobiography of Malcolm X. X*, was he one of the 20th century Muslims who never received his afrocentric name?"

There was a long, silent pause, and after an uncomfortable moment of her thinking that she might have done something wrong, Nayirah took it upon herself to be the first to speak again. "Hello? Is there some—"

"Do you have the book with you?" The officer quickly snapped.

"Why, yes, I—"

"You haven't read from it, have you?"

"No, I just—"

"Burn it! Burn it *right now*, right where you stand, I don't care who else is watching. We'll be right over."

"But there's no—"

"Don't argue, sister! And don't worry about proof either, we record just about all the calls we get and I happen to know for a fact this one *is* on tape. Get off the phone, burn that book this instant, and wait for us! As-Salaikum!" And with that, the officer from the Fruit of Islam slammed the phone receiver on his end down.

"Wa-Salaikum," a somewhat dazed Nayirah said to the dial tone after being abruptly hung up on. For a hot moment, as she held up the paperback novel for inspection, Nayirah tried to see if she could dare herself to crack open the book and peek at one of the pages, or maybe just a sentence, but it was for naught. Her devotion to the Nation was too strong, stronger than the devotion she had for her own family, or herself for that matter.

Since cigarettes were made nakon, cigarette lighters were nearly obsolete. So Nayirah looked through her kitchen cabinets until she found some common house matches. Once she had, Nayirah held the novel over the sink and lit one of the matches by striking it against the side of the oven, where she barely had time to notice that the sickeningly familiar odor and hissing of the gas main had gotten even stronger from it having been unserviced for as long as it had.

BA-BOHSSHH!!!

From the view of a neighbor across the street from what was the Isiah home who just happened to be looking out their front window at that particular moment, the fiery explosion resembled a miniature mushroom cloud. The neighbor was old enough to remember what exactly a mushroom cloud looked like since depictions of anything nuclear in nature were not necessarily nakon but rare and considered politically incorrect to dwell on because of what had happened to Australia on Nuke Year's Day in 2006.

The Fruit of Islam arrived on the scene some 15 minutes later. They appeared in two white minivans, each with a red crescent moon and a red star on its sides and the four officers who exited each van wore their usual all-white uniforms with the same crescent moon/star emblem on their shirt collars and caps. They, of course, found the residences 2245 and 2249 Harlem Avenue, but 2247 Harlem Ave, the house where they received the call about the forbidden text and were to report to was no more than a pile of ash and still smoldering cinders. Except for the assortment of various rusted pipes and plumbing fixtures coming from underneath, there was nothing to speak of that was left of the incinerated house.

When Elijah drove within view of the Fruit of Islam's minivans parked in front of the empty space where his house used to be a half an hour after the FOI showed, his heart was pounding as if it wanted to break free of his chest. He felt like hyperventilating and his head was swimming so with probable explanations for the Fruit of Islam standing around the charred ruins of what used to be his home he couldn't think straight. Elijah would've turned his sedan around and driven away except that an overwhelming demand to know what had happened to his house outweighed what fear he had of having committed some wrong in the Nation's eyes. Or some past wrong being found out.

Elijah brought his car to a dead stop in the middle of the street and staggered from being too drained by angst to run the rest of the way to where his home once was and the FOI now were. Dodging the few spectating neighbors that were standing around in the street and in his way, Elijah jogged out of breath right up to the nearest Fruit of Islam officer, a big, burly fellow holding a pen and clipboard, and panted, "what happened here?"

The burly FOI officer merely held the clipboard up to his face to read and asked, "are you *Elijah Isiah*?"

"Yes, yes," Elijah said impatiently. "Where's my wife, what happened to my house?"

"Your wife and son were killed when the house blew up because she tried to burn a nakon book that *you* illegally had in your possession," the officer motioned for two of his counterparts who were standing amidst the debris of Elijah's former home to come his way, "Elijah Isiah, you are under arrest for sedition, for the possession of that contraband book."

Those two officers the first burly one had signaled for grabbed a speechless Elijah by each of his arms and unceremoniously hauled him into the back of their nearest minivan. There was all so much to take in, Elijah thought that his brain would explode as he imagined his house must have from the sudden influx of bad news. When the two officers who threw him into the minivan piled in to join him, Elijah tried to grasp the idea that his wife was now dead. Dead. As the officers kicked at Elijah to sit only on the floor of the back of the van. He then remembered that in addition to the death of his wife he was being arrested for sedition.

Treason! They had found out about *The Autobiography of Malcolm X*—and Nayirah must have been the one who told them! Some sense could finally be extracted from the swirling chaos Elijah's life was fast becoming. The gas main that Nay complained about so must have filled the whole house with gas and when she lit a fire to burn the autobiography . . . Dear Allah, she died betraying me, Elijah thought, she called them up to turn me in. He didn't quite know how to take that yet, but one thing Elijah did not do was shed a single tear over her in particular.

Elijah's deepest worries were mainly centered around the fate of Elisha. The FOI officer had said his wife *and son* were killed when the house blew up, so however they came to assume that Elisha was at home at the time of the explosion, the Fruit of Islam would not think to try and pursue the boy. It then occurred to Elijah that one good thing would in fact come out of the Lost-Found Nation's privatized economy after all. In that the same Nation that wouldn't come out to the house to fix the gas main in the first place would be a nation too ill-equipped to accurately tell whether Elisha's remains were actually amidst the ruins of the house or not.

However if they were to ever find Elisha, he would definitely wind up in an orphanage. Like the Ostrowski Home for Boys which, as far as Elijah knew, was still in business to this day. And that, Elijah decided, must never happen. Elisha must never be made to live through the childhood that he had, Elijah resolved, no matter what.

With a new sense of purpose and self-sacrifice swelling inside him, Elijah began "psyching himself up" in order to steel himself against the beating and interrogation that was surely to come. The FOI would no doubt be demanding to know the exact location Elijah received a copy of the prohibited novel and for him to say where he did get it would also point them straight to Elisha since the boy was still with Baines and the others in the underground. And Elijah wasn't about to turn over his son as Nayirah had turned on him.

* * *

Forty-five minutes after Elijah had been driven away by the Fruit of Islam, Jerry had parked a car which belonged to the underground to the side of a curb along Harlem Avenue when his naturally paranoid instincts easily discerned that no small degree of carnage had recently taken place in the area. Then he noticed that the Isiah home could no longer be seen. In the car's back seat was little Elisha, wondering why Jerry was waving him silent and ordering him to crouch onto the floor of the back seat of the car. Once Elisha was curled in hiding in a fetal position on the car floor, Jerry threw a dark blanket over him, told the boy not to move, and stepped out of the car to stop an old man he saw nearby to ask what had happened.

"Well, it's like I told the FOI, I was looking out my front window when I saw the whole house go up like a mushroom cloud—you know what that is, boy?"

"Actually, I do," Jerry answered.

"Really? 'Cause you shouldn't. Anyway, the whole thing just went up in flames and singed the houses next door pretty bad. Then the guy who owned the place showed up and the FOI carted him off. I never really knew him all that well even though I've been living here for twenty years. Quiet brother, unassuming, got a wife and a kid I think. But he was probably a pork dealer, it's always the quiet ones, you know. Hope he gets what he deserves."

"Probably will," Jerry rolled his eyes and made a smacking sound within his mouth indicating disgust with the old man's ignorance. "As-Salaikum, my old and very wise sir."

"Wa-Salaikum," the old man answered as Jerry returned to his car, turned around, and drove back in the direction from whence he came.

* * *

What a week, Elijah thought. Seven days ago it was his birthday, he was carving a rather plain soy bean cake with white frosting, getting over turning 38 years old, and one week later, Sunday July the 10th, in the year 2030 A.D., he's sitting on the floor of a sweltering jail cell downtown, covered with swollen bruises from being beaten and saying nothing during his interrogation that lasted all of Saturday night. The smacks across his jaw, the cheap shots to the stomach, and the kicks to the groin were almost enough to make Elijah want to tell the Fruit of Islam that the sun was white with craters and the moon was red with fire if they had asked him to say so.

But anytime he sensed that he might give in, Elijah reminded himself how used they beat him at the Ostrowski Home for Boys until he said aloud that his name wasn't Fred Hampton Rush but Elijah Isiah. The Nation broke him into saying something he didn't want to once, but that was when Elijah was only a boy, and he decided they weren't about to break the man that beaten boy had become.

So Elijah tried his damnedest to pretend as though he had been a deaf mute all his life and remained absolutely silent throughout the entire ordeal, more for his son's sake than anything else. Self-preservation didn't really enter into Elijah's mind because since it was very likely he would never see Elisha again, Elijah felt that at least half of him was dead already, the other half would lay in the hope that wherever his son was, he would be alive and better off.

In addition to his other woes, Elijah was also to share the closet-like space his cell had to offer with at least a dozen other prisoners, whom Elijah didn't find quite as bad off as he imagined they would be or any harder to deal with than, say, their jailers. They were all in for various offenses as Elijah found out through the few conversations he dared to have with these people.

One stated an unwillingness to die for Allah in public, another wanted to become a Christian, a couple of the prisoners had violated several personal hygiene codes and never cleaned their houses, a few were in for disrespecting FOI officers and gossiping about the lives of their local ministers.

By late afternoon, Elijah had found that someone was actually in for adultery, which prompted him to laugh until he was forced by an indignant prisoner who grabbed Elijah by the front of his shirt and demanded he explain what he thought was so funny. When Elijah tried to tell them that Elijah Muhammad was also guilty of cheating on his wife, no one believed him. A fight nearly ensued over this fine point of historic truth when at that very tense moment, the guard outside opened the barred door allowing into the cell an elder officer from the Fruit of Islam who, after a pause, called for the indignant prisoner to let the scruff of Elijah's shirt go and ordered Elijah to come with him.

* * *

Elijah thought, rather he wished, he was being taken somewhere to be fed, but Elijah knew he wasn't that lucky. Instead Elijah had been led back to the very room where he had just spent the previous night having the living daylights beaten out of him. Elijah didn't know if it was possible for his heart to literally lose all cohesiveness and break up into crumbs, but that's exactly what he felt was happening when he had been pushed screaming for mercy into the room which had 101 marked on its door.

Elijah managed to calm himself a tad once he saw he was alone in room 101 until it occurred to him that their whole point might actually be to give him just enough hope to be snatched away by how many ever FOI interrogators would walk through that door in the next few moments. His shock was unparalleled, however, when after pacing back and forth in the room like a trapped animal for several all too suspenseful minutes none other that Ishmael Emmanuel walked into the room alone.

"Allah be praised! Ishmael!" Elijah hit the top of his head on Ishmael's chin when he leapt forward to hug the last person he expected to see. "You've come to get me out of here, right? We're leaving, right?"

Ishmael pulled himself away from his old friend and kept Elijah at an arm's distance from him. "I'm not here to let you go, Elijah."

"Oh, Allah," Elijah gasped as eyes grew wide. "They're locking you up too?"

"No, Elijah, I'm here to try and get what they couldn't beat out of you." Ishmael took a couple of steps back and leaned against the room's one, closed door. "Why don't you tell them where you got that book? You're in enough trouble already, and I may be able to use my influence as a minister of love to get you a lighter sentence if you would just tell me where you got it."

Elijah had been near tears for most of the past 24 hours. His wife's death, even being severely beaten all night long didn't cause him to shed one real tear. But the sensation of who he thought was his best friend stabbing him in the back was what finally made Elijah weep. "Please tell me," Elijah barely managed to get out as he slumped to the floor, "tell me that you didn't come here on your own and *volunteer* to, to—"

"To what? To do my job?" Ishmael retorted. "I may joke and clown a lot about things sometimes, but I never crossed the line. And in the end? I work for the Nation, I'm a *minister*! Yes, I work for the Ministry of Love, but that's still a legitimate ministry, it's still a state job, and I'm still a state employee. Which means that when I found out what happened *I* let *them* know I was a friend of yours—"

"'*Was*,'" Elijah snarled between tears.

"Damn it, Elijah, I *had* to. If I didn't step forward right away and they found out later on that I knew you . . . Look, we're not kids anymore. We're not the 'Hollywood Squares' anymore. We can't just go off half-cocked, pull some stunt and get away with it like we used to, which is what it sounds like you did. We're grown up now, we have to pay the rent, and this is how I for one do it."

"By selling folks out?" Elijah wiped away at the tears in the pits of his eyes.

Ishmael squatted down with his knees, lowering his massive frame so that he could be eye level with Elijah, who was still sprawled on the floor. "You're the one selling our people out."

"How the hell do you figure that?" Elijah snapped.

"Well, first of all, listen to you! 'Hell!' What kind of language is that? An occasional 'damn' is OK, but that's it. You can't just go around saying anything you want, you know."

"No, I *don't* know. So why don't you explain it to me?" Elijah began an attempt to be snide in the face of his situation. "Or aren't you allowed to tell me why even after a man is grown *and middle aged* he still has to watch his mouth like he was a smart child? Even in his own home?"

"Well, if you really don't remember then that *is* a shame," Ishmael finally sat on the floor "Indian style" next to Elijah, who angrily slid a few inches away from the attempt to sit by him. Ishmael looked disappointed for a moment and didn't try to get any closer to Elijah. "I know you must think you were beat up last night over a book, but that's not the whole story. They came down on you because no one in the Nation wants all the chaos that Black folks had to go through back in the 20th century to come back."

"What the hell are you talking about Ishmael?" Elijah's facial features scrunched together in frustration. "People could read and say just about anything they wanted to back then!"

"Exactly! And do you want to go back to that anarchy?" Ishmael saw from Elijah's confused expression he would have to explain himself. "There was a time when words like—oh, I see I'm going to have to say them." Ishmael's voice lowered a tad, "'Nigger,' 'coon,' 'jungle bunny,' 'porch monkey,' 'roach stomper'—'*hell*,' all these words were actually legal if you could believe it. Now, back in the day, the White man claimed if you illegalized those words then you would take away their 'basic rights.' Well what about Black folks' right to feel good about themselves? What about that? Black people were made to feel subhuman for so many decades, *centuries* even, and why? Because those White devils were allowed to call us whatever bad names they wanted to because of their precious 'First Amendment.'

"Things got so bad, you actually had young Blacks taking advantage of this 'amendment' that some blue-eyed devil wrote hundreds of years ago. Oh yes, our young men were going around disrespecting their Black sisters, their Black *queens*, by calling them 'bitches' and 'hos,' which was short for 'whore' in case you don't remember, and actually addressing *themselves* as niggers! As if was 'nigger' was some kind of term of endearment or something! Can you imagine?

"Well, I shouldn't have to tell you the damage that all this caused. The lack of morality, or common decency and self-respect for that matter, within our own community just kept building and building because we allowed that sort of language to flourish. Then, thank merciful Allah, Minister Farrakhan and the Honorable Khallid

Muhammad led our people down the straight and narrow path towards *true* freedom, not the White man's 20th century freedoms, and made certain books nakon knowing just how bad some of them could make our people feel.

"Elijah, don't you see? White folks read all the nasty books and say all the nasty things they want because they're immoral. That's why they're called *devils*, and you don't want to be like them. When they call for more of their 'civil liberties' none of that stuff applies to you. What they really mean to say is they want the permission to call you names and make you feel bad. But it doesn't have to be like that. Right here, in the Lost-Found Nation of Islam in this Wilderness of North America, for the first time in history, Black folks can feel good about being Black. Really good, Elijah."

Elijah shook his head, put his fingers to rub the bridge of his nose, and sighed. "I never thought I'd hear a sermon out of the likes of you of all people. You used to draw caricatures of the different ministers back at the Ostrowski Home for Boys, where I now wish I had never met you. But about what you were saying, 'friend,' what about Black folks feeling good about being *themselves*—instead of feeling good only because they just happened to be born Black? What about *that*?"

Elijah waited for an answer and received only silence from Ishmael before continuing. "The way I figure it, in order for Black folks to feel good about themselves, they have to *know* themselves. In order to know themselves, they have to *think* for themselves. And Black folks can't think without first exposing themselves to something other than the Koran or what the ministers have to say. Which is why folks ought to be able to read something different once in a while that'll make folks want to think for themselves."

"Books make you think, alright, but they also make you think of different ways to make Black folks feel bad." Ishmael interjected.

"Well you know what, 'Ish?' I for one would rather risk feeling bad about myself for however long from hearing a different point of view than to go my whole life never knowing other views existed."

"Speaking of risking feeling bad, would you risk getting executed at your trial for not telling these people where you got that damn book?"

"*What* trial?" Elijah barked. "A trial is when you get a chance to defend yourself before your peers and hear other arguments besides the Nation's. No, what we have here is somebody being placed into custody in some temple where nobody else is allowed in except for a minister, a FOI captain, and an entire section of the FOI. The charges are read, you can't say anything in your defense, and when the verdict comes down, there's no appeal. What's the point in even having a trial? Trials in the Nation are just formalities, but then, that's what we Black folks love to do: Stand on formality, right?

"But you know what 'kills' me more than any execution? Is that you've been in here all this time, defending the interests of the Nation with your two-faced self, and you haven't even offered your condolences yet. You would have walked right out of here without asking me how I felt about the destruction of my home or *the death of my family*, wouldn't you?" Elijah now hoped that Ishmael too thought Elisha was dead.

"Elijah, I'm sorry, I—"

"Get out," Elijah stated succinctly. "Get the *hell* out, and don't ever let me see you again, traitor."

"Like I said, *you're* the traitor," Ishmael said as he rose to his feet, went to the door of room 101, and knocked on it to let the guard outside know he was ready to leave. "Just like brother Malcolm was."

"Wait a minute," Elijah stammered. "How do you know who Malcolm was?"

"I'm a minister, Eli," Ishmael said just before slipping out of the room once the guard had cracked open the door. "And membership has its privileges."

* * *

Elijah's trial was held the next day, the morning of July the 11th at a downtown temple in Chicago's Loop which was almost walking distance from the Akbar Office Building where he used to work for Mustafa Enterprises, a bit of trivia Elijah found most ironic. Elijah wondered if Mustafa Ali knew, through his connections as an ex-speechwriter for the Nation, that his most argumentative and rebellious dictator was about to face charges for sedition. Knowing Mustafa, he would probably be pleased and not the least bit surprised.

All the temples in the Lost-Found Nation were built for jam-packed capacity crowds, so it seemed strange for Elijah to walk into one with only a dozen or so people occupying it. For the most part, this dozen consisted mainly of Fruit of Islam officers, a couple of whom Elijah recognized right away as the officers who arrested and later interrogated him. He also remembered the elder FOI officer who came to his cell to take him to see Ishmael. The elder officer was standing next to and going over notes with the only other person in the temple besides Elijah who wasn't in a Fruit of Islam white and red trimmed uniform. Elijah correctly assumed that this middle aged man dressed as per the national code (except that his suit looked as though it was brand new and custom made) was the minister the Nation had appointed to judge the trial.

The FOI captain and the minister sat next to each other at a long table at the head of the temple. They adjusted and tested the microphones installed before them for sound as Elijah was escorted by a particularly burly Fruit of Islam officer to a seat at a front row pew on the left-hand side of the temple, the side where women would otherwise be seated during ordinary services. The burly FOI officer didn't bother to remove Elijah's handcuffs, nor was he ever ordered to, and stood over him while the rest of the officers sat in pews on the all-male side of the temple and glared in his direction with contempt from across the temple's aisle.

After the minister led everyone into a brief opening prayer, the recording of the phone call Nayirah made to 911 was played over a stereo system for all to hear. For his part, Elijah only shook his head and rolled his eyes upon hearing his traitorous wife's voice for what would most likely be the last time. He was then startled but not shocked to hear that the charges against him that were read by the Fruit of Islam captain had gone from just sedition to sedition, murder (of both Nayirah and Elisha), wanton property damage (the destruction of the Isiah home), withholding valuable information (not breaking during the interrogation), and the chronic use of obscene language.

Part of Elijah wanted to actually laugh, the whole exercise suddenly looked utterly ridiculous to him, and witnessing what was looking more and more like a sorry attempt at a judicial system seemingly making up their rules as they went along only made it harder for Elijah to hold back his laughter. But he pursed each lip together tightly knowing full well his lips could get even more swollen than they already were from a quick rap across the mouth by the burly officer still standing over him if any laughing were heard during the trial. Or any other sound emanating from Elijah for that matter, since neither he nor anyone else was allowed to speak on the defendant's behalf.

Once the many charges against Elijah were read by the captain, the minister said a few words about how Elijah ought to be ashamed of himself and something about how they would eventually find out where he had gotten the nakon book without his help so any last minute pleas to exchange information for mercy would be in vain, and then the minister declared the final verdict: Permanent exile. Presumably to Aryan Amerikkka, though the minister curiously never actually said exactly where Elijah would be exiled to, which brought out a reaction of disappointment from most of the officers across the aisle that was barely registerable because their strict decorum kept them from reacting any more visibly and strongly than they did.

Since there was never an appeal in a trial held within the Nation, the hearing was over and the officer who had been standing over Elijah hoisted him to his feet. Seeing this as the one opportunity for an audience, and also not seeing anything else to lose, Elijah made direct eye contact with one of the FOI who had beaten him Saturday night and called out across the aisle, "you couldn't break me, and you never will! You people did break me once, I'll admit, when I was a kid and you made me change my name to something Afro-Asiatic, something that didn't even make any sense, because *Elijah* and *Isiah* are two *first* names, you *idiots!*"

"Shut that brother up!" Cried the minister.

"No! *You* shut the hell up! My name isn't Elijah Isiah, it never was! My real name is *Fred Hampton Rush!* And from now on that's the only name I'll answer to, damn it!"

"I said *shut him up*!" The minister angrily reiterated.

"I am Fred Hampton Rush! I am Fred Hampton Rush! I am Fred Hampton Rush! I am—" Fred managed to get out before his burly escort from the Fruit of Islam was finally able to restrain Fred's squirming form enough to secure a hand over his mouth in order to cover it while dragging him outside of the temple.

* * *

"Report."

Tom stripped out of a FOI uniform and then proceeded to slip into a more casual shirt and slacks as he answered Amelia Baines who sat before him on a bench in the subway that was "the underground" while everyone around them seemed to be in the process of hastily moving crates, belongings and themselves out of it. "The good news is that, as far as I could tell, he didn't betray us. The bad news is we couldn't get to him."

Tom then motioned to Jerry who was also dressed like a member of the Fruit of Islam. "Tom's right, there was no way in hell we could have gotten alone with him long enough to do anything."

Baines shook her head as she hung it low, "those bastards didn't beat him too bad, did they?"

"He looked pretty fucked up at the trial," Jerry remarked.

"And how was 'the trial,'" Baines mournfully quipped.

"Speedy," Tom replied. "They sentenced him to exile, but the thing is they didn't say where. They carried him out back and took off like they were in a hurry which is why we couldn't tail them without being made."

"*Carried* him?" Baines repeated inquisitively.

"'Cause he was going off," Jerry explained with half a sly grin on his face. "At the end he starting hooping and hollering about how they couldn't break him and yelling, 'I'm Fred Hampton!' 'I'm Fred Hampton!' Over and over again."

"Yeah," Tom added, "could he have remembered that from seeing Spike Lee's *Malcolm X* back in the 20th? You know that bit at the end when he had all those little kids yelling, 'I'm Malcolm X!' 'I'm Malcolm X!'"

"I doubt it," Baines stated simply. "Besides, Spike swiped that whole spiel from something that happened right after Fred Hampton got shot. All these little kids here in town were asked by some preacher, can't remember who, what Fred Hampton meant to them and the kids started yelling how each of them was Fred Hampton. I doubt Eli—Fred could've have known about that either."

"Speaking of little kids," Tom looked about him, "where's Elisha?"

Baines felt at her trademark corn cob pipe anxiously. "Laying in front of the TV. It seemed to take his mind off of things for a while at least, but the last time I checked on him it looked like he went and cried himself to sleep again."

Jerry took note of all his fellow smugglers bustling about in a hurried effort to evacuate the subway and transport all their cargo, be it the many boxes of books and tapes or the few personal belongings they allowed themselves. He then eyed Baines and asked, "well, junior ain't coming with us, is he?"

"We can't just leave him on somebody's doorstep in a big old basket with a note safely pinned to his bib," Baines admonished. "someone accidentally left his father behind in this Lost-Found Nation of ours when he was around the same age and look at what happened to him. I'll be damned if I see the same mistake repeated *on purpose*. And you can take that scowl off your face, Jerry, nobody's going to ask your ass to chaperon him on his first date or anything. *I'll* take care of the boy. Now, let's get a move on, fellas, the land of the Single Payer awaits"

* * *

Fred's ride in the back of the Fruit of Islam's minivan was already uncomfortable enough. Still handcuffed, the FOI also had a thick strip of duct tape over his mouth because of the outburst he made in the temple. In addition, Fred was made to sit on the floor of the van by the occasional kick to his side from either of the two Fruit of Islam officers in the back with him whenever he tried to look out the window. He kept risking those kicks because the terrain the minivan was traveling across began to look frighteningly familiar from all those peeks through the minivan's windows. They were heading west on the Stevenson Expressway when they had got off of it and onto 47th Street—and Fred knew this was the surest way to get from downtown to Ishmael's neighborhood.

Once Fred managed to discern that the FOI van had made a left turn on La Grange Road and was heading south, he became very *very* nervous. The underground was near Ishmael's neighborhood, could the Fruit of Islam have somehow found out where Baines and her crew were hiding? And if Elisha was still with them . . .

The further and faster the minivan sailed south on La Grange, the more Fred calmed down. If they had found the underground surely they would have at least slowed down by now, Fred thought, but where *were* they going? The route being taken was far from the quickest to the Aryan Amerikkkan border, Fred pondered, were the FOI going to pick up more prisoners since Fred himself was the only convict aboard the minivan?

The van finally slowed down as a building Fred did not recognize loomed ahead. Before Fred could tell (from the view he had from being made to sit on the floor of the minivan) if the building looked more like a hospital than it did a university, a place to park was found, the back doors of the van flung wide open, Fred was unceremoniously ushered out onto the pavement, and hauled over to the front entrance of the huge complex that stood before them all.

A transparency that looked to be as thick as bullet proof glass separated a visibly bored and unconcerned young man thumbing through a huge appointment book from anyone entering the lobby of the complex via its automatic sliding doors out front. With Fred in tow, too confused to put up much of a struggle to resist walking with them, the officers from the FOI strode up to the glass. "As-Salaam-Alaikum," the oldest and seemingly highest ranked among the officers addressed.

"Wa-Alaikum-Salaam," the young man dully responded. "Is this the permanent exile from this morning?"

"It is," the elder officer answered.

"Take him to the showers, all the way down this hall and to the right. The doctor should already be there. As-Salaikum."

"Wa-Salaikum, my young brother."

Someone was already waiting for Fred and the trio of Fruit of Islam officers. He had a blue-green surgical cap, mask, and gown on with rubber lined transparent plastic bags over his shoes. His arms were bent at the elbows from holding his sterile, rubber gloved hands up to around eye level, which for him was pretty high. Fred dared say the man was around 6'2" and easily 200 pounds though his weight appeared evenly distributed throughout the man's large frame. The man had broad shoulders and a barrel chest just as Ishmael Emmanuel but wasn't quite as rotund. He seemed older to Fred, possibly in his early fifties, yet his eyes had the gleam of a wicked little boy who was about to burn an insect with sunlight directed from a magnifying glass.

"Strip him," the man in surgical wear ordered, "but go ahead and leave the handcuffs on. They might come in handy and I'm certain you can spare them."

The man stood nearly motionless as the three agents of the FOI passed around a switch blade one of them had produced from their pockets and used it to first make strategically placed nicks in Fred's coat, shirt, and slacks before using said nicks as starting points for literally ripping his clothes off of him. Fred's shoes, socks, and bowtie were all violently snatched off as was his boxer shorts and the strip of duct tape that had kept him silent up to this point.

"I thought I was supposed to be exiled!" Fred exclaimed after letting out a cry of pain from having the tape ripped off his lips. "Where the hell am I?"

"You're in the Argonne National Laboratory of course, I'm Dr. Batala, at your service, and just look upon all this as your sentence being commuted," Batala grinned from under his surgical mask, "after a fashion." Once Fred was completely nude save his handcuffs, Dr. Batala added, "so unless you want to risk being gunned down the minute you cross the Amerikkkan border, I suggest that you always remember to fully cooperate with us here whenever you're asked to from this moment on, do you understand, Mr. Isiah?"

"The name's Fred Hampton Rush."

The bemused look Dr. Batala had when he turned to the FOI officers for an explanation for Fred's comment was only met with shrugged shoulders and shaken heads. Batala then sighed and laid a sterile hand on Fred's shoulder blade gently pushing him past the double doors besides them while following him inside leaving the officers in the hall.

* * *

Fred had heard once about how if one was joining the military in the 20th century someone with rubber gloves would hold a testicle while asking for a cough. When it was happening to him while standing next to a metal tray on wheels with various medical instruments in the frigid, pale pastel tiled shower room, Fred thought that was what Batala was doing: Preparing him for some kind of secret mission, most likely the kind Fred wouldn't be returning from. After coughing, Fred asked, "am I being recruited for—"

"You're not going to be sent behind enemy lines as it were," Batala cut in, "however you are every bit as expendable as someone who would be sent on such an excursion."

"Then what am I doing here?" Fred waved his handcuffed arms around in frustration.

Batala's tall form rose from his one bent knee from feeling between Fred's legs, reached over at his metal tray, and readied a hypodermic needle.

"What's *that* for?" Fred demanded.

Dr. Batala's only response was to grab Fred's right forearm, draw it forward, and jab the needle inside.

"Allah," Fred muttered in pain as he watched the doctor draw some of his blood. "Just what are you doing?"

"I'll need to see if you have the dreaded HIV virus," Batala answered as he labeled a small vial of Fred's blood he had removed from inside the tube of the hypodermic needle and laid it on his tray. "Fortunately in this day and age that sort of thing won't take but a couple of hours to be found out." Dr. Batala then looked about him, "especially with all the resources I have at my disposal."

"What's that supposed to mean?"

"Well if you must know, I was made the minister of science and technology not too long ago for my years of service to the Nation but I'd like to think it was mainly because of my extremely prodigious intellect." Batala's eyes gleamed proudly behind his surgical mask and one could tell he was smiling as well. "Since I'm the very first to ever hold such a post, I've been given an incredible amount of leeway. In addition to my usual state subsidized endeavors to turn homosexuals back into heterosexuals and deprogramming atheists and other heretics, I've recently been allocated an extraordinary amount of funding for my own personal projects so long as they remain classified. Luckily for the Nation's hierarchy, I never really needed to work with too many assistants because of my supra-genius and all. So only a select few ever have any knowledge, or any clue for that matter, of what I am up to."

The doctor's megalomaniacal ego didn't phase Fred so much as the sudden realization of his place in the current scheme of things did. "I'm to be a guinea pig . . . Aren't I?"

"Oh, 'guinea pig' is such a *harsh* term," Batala remarked. "I prefer to use the word, 'volunteer.'" He then handed Fred an orange bar of medicated soap. "Now, I hate to sound like your parents but I want you to scrub yourself quite thoroughly with this. Especially inside your buttocks."

"What about my handcuffs, doc?" Fred held up his still bound together wrists.

"Deal with it," Dr. Batala snorted. "And don't call me 'doc,' Mr. Isiah."

* * *

The sterile padded cell Batala led Fred to after he had somehow managed to bathe and dry himself off while still handcuffed didn't have a clock or a window from which the time of day could be told by looking outside, but Fred could still tell that it had to have been past nightfall. When he had awakened on the floor of a jail cell that Monday morning, Fred was being dragged off to stand trial. Now he was in the nude, but very clean, in yet another kind of cell. What a day, he thought. No one had even bothered to come by and uncuff or feed him either, so Fred decided to resign himself for the night by trying to lie on the empty cell's white padded floor, and then the door suddenly swung open.

"You can't sleep here I'm afraid," Dr. Batala called out from the doorway. "Come with me if you're tired, I'll take you somewhere you can retire." Batala's medical gown was still on but his gloves were off as were his surgical cap and mask. Fred could see that Dr. Batala was in his late forties to early fifties. He had a robust, graying mustache, a short cut afro, and somewhat gruff facial features that resembled a dark brown bear.

Fred trepidatiously stepped towards the doorway, Batala and someone else, presumably one of the doctor's assistant, who held out a pair of sandals for the still naked Fred to wear. "Where we're going it'll get a bit rocky and I don't want you cutting your feet."

As Fred put the sandals on he quipped, "Allah forbid I bleed on your precious rocks."

"Ah, speaking of your blood you'll be pleased to know that you are HIV negative. I told you the results wouldn't take any time at all."

"Terrific," Fred sardonically said as he walked with Batala and his assistant down a nearby flight of stairs cupping his genitals with his handcuffed hands for some degree of privacy. "I don't suppose you're ever going to give me anything else to wear, are you."

"Well, there's really no point, is there? You're going to sleep, remember? Who'll see you? Besides we're all men here at Argonne, even the dictators and the nurses. There's no need to be embarrassed." Batala assured.

Fred saw what Dr. Batala meant when they reached the bottom of the winding flight of stairs they had been descending. There was an enormous cave that stretched almost all around them and the stalagmites of the cave floor might very well have cut Fred's feet were they still bare. Laid diagonally against the side of the nearest cave wall was a huge and foreboding mechanical apparatus that resembled a cross section of a man-sized capsule with a slightly cushioned interior leaning alongside a metallic tank with a battery of gears, consoles, wiring, and tubes which were occasionally hissing or belching out blasts of cold air stemming from it. Fred had never seen anything as technologically advanced as this before, and all he could think to ask from being so bewildered was, "what is it?"

"It's a bed," Batala lied, "note the matted lining? Step in, lie down, and relax. But take your sandals off first, we can't have any unnecessary foreign objects or organisms in there."

"Do you actually think I'm *that* stupid? The padded cell upstairs has a damn matted lining," Fred reminded the doctor. "So why couldn't I sleep up there? Unless of course this is the part where I'm supposed to *volunteer* to get into this thing."

"You know, I'd really hate to have my assistant here run and call the FOI on you as if you were a child for not cooperating with us." The doctor chimed in a very sing-song, condescending tone of voice. "And *look*, I even have a key to your handcuffs. Now if you'll trust me, I'll trust you and set your hands free, so shall we trust each other, 'Frederick?'"

Fred saw there was no point in either asking Batala a second time what the apparatus was or arguing over whether climbing into the coffin-sized capsule might be fatal. Apparently the doctor didn't like his guinea pigs suffering from too much anxiety right before an experiment, or didn't see the point in explaining to someone he considered to be a lab rat the purpose of a maze that was to be run, so a straight answer would have been out of the question.

It also went without saying that if he tried to run away while buck naked and handcuffed he wouldn't get far, even in sandals. So whatever this device that Dr. Batala was so anxious to see him climb into, Fred knew his only choices at that moment were to either eventually be shot or capitulate. The only real reason why Fred accepted the key from Batala, uncuffed himself, slipped out of his sandals, and opted for the latter was that *anyone* could be gunned down. And after everything that he had already been through; the destruction of his home, the death of his wife, the beatings from the Fruit of Islam, and the prospect of never seeing his son again, Fred figured he was no longer like anyone else. So he might as well leave this world in a manner unlike anyone he knew ever has: Via an experiment which would no doubt go awry at some point, and that looked to Fred like something straight out of what used to be known as "science fiction."

The moment Fred laid back in the slanted capsule, a transparent plexi-glass cover slid over its top half, sealing Fred inside. Freezing cold fog emanating from barely visible vents inside the capsule immediately flooded the compartment and out of reflex Fred screamed. But the cover was sound proof and neither Dr. Batala or his attendant would have paid the scream any mind anyway. In a matter of seconds, Fred found he could no longer bang against the capsule's glass cover because his once shivering limbs were frozen immobile. He could no longer see through the glass from it being too fogged over, and as everything within his field of vision took on an icy white hue, Fred Hampton Rush tried to recall if the current state of affairs he was in could be traced back to one, seminal event. One past deed that, if it had been done differently, would have made it possible for him to still be with his son today.

And suddenly he wasn't conscious of anything at all.

CHAPTER FIVE

"B l a c k   t o   t h e   f u t u r e"

It had been as if Fred was asleep. He might as well have been, he had no sensation of the passage of time between the last thing he remembered—suddenly being frozen solid without warning—and him batting his eyelids until they stayed open. Since Fred wasn't aware of how much time had passed, he assumed the reason he was strapped down onto a hospital bed still naked and under white sheets in a very dimly lit beige colored room was because he had somehow miraculously survived Dr. Batala's experiment, and was now being observed for his response to the treatment by the middle-aged woman who stood over him. Fred quickly surmised however that he was no longer at the Argonne National Laboratory and that this woman could not be one of Batala's attendants. Not just because the doctor himself had said Argonne was a male-only facility but mainly because this woman, whoever she was, wasn't covered from head to toe by a chador and was White.

"Am I in—" Fred stopped when he heard how raspy his voice sounded, as if he hadn't spoken in ages. "Are we in Aryan Amerikkka?"

The woman leaned towards Fred's face, smiled pleasantly, and shook her head in the negative. "We're in Chicago. Chicago, Illinois."

"I know what state Chicago's in," Fred grumbled. "Are you with," his voice then sank to a cautious whisper, "the underground?"

"'The underground?'" The woman reared her body back at Fred's remark, which let him see that she was wearing what could be taken for a doctor's smock. "Which underground would *this* be?"

"Allah," Fred muttered to himself in angst. Could this have been some sick, elaborate trick on the part of the Fruit of Islam? Baines said they and the Aryans were in fact ideological soul mates, could they have gotten this strangely dressed White woman from Amerikkka to lull him into divulging the whereabouts of the underground? The thought of his interrogation not yet being over caused Fred's breathing to get heavy as he began to strain at his restraints. "I don't know of any 'underground,'" Fred nervously lied, "I just wanted to know if that's where I had been taken to now. I—"

"Calm down, calm down," the woman soothed. "I'm not here to judge you and I'm not going to punish you. I just found what you said curious, that's all. No one's going to hurt you."

"Who are you anyway?"

"I'm Dr. Cohen, but you can call me Joanna if you want. I'm a friend."

"Then why am I tied down to this bed, 'friend?'"

"I don't want you getting too excited and hurting yourself when you hear what I have to tell you," Dr. Cohen explained. "I had the lights dimmed so you wouldn't be startled by a lot of bright lights when you came to and later on I'll bring them up gradually so that your eyes can adjust. I didn't want to cause any kind of a shock to your system at all because what I have to tell you is already going to be more than shocking enough as it is."

"Fine, now, what the hell is it you have to tell me?"

"Easy," Dr. Cohen motioned gently with her hands for Fred to calm down. "First, I'd like to know the last thing that you remember before waking up here."

Fred looked away from Dr. Cohen and up at the ceiling. After a lapse of silence he sighed and answered, "I don't suppose you know who a Dr. Batala is?"

"I do, and you don't have to worry about him anymore."

"Why? What's that supposed to mean?" Fred demanded.

"I'll get into that later. Now, you were put into one of his devices. A tube or a capsule of some kind, right?"

"Right."

"And once inside of it you were—"

"Blasted with freezing cold air," Fred interrupted.

"Now, what was the date when all of this happened?"

One of Fred's eyebrows rose above the other as he shot Dr. Cohen a cockeyed look before asking, "are you serious?" When he took her silence as an affirmative, Fred answered, "just now. Well, yesterday maybe. I don't know what time it is now, but as best as I can figure it, it had to be around night time when he came to get me out of that padded cell and take me down to that 'ice capsule' or whatever it was."

"Then I want you to tell me exactly what you think today's date is," Dr. Cohen grimly stated.

"Fred frowned in frustration and said slowly, "July 11th, or 12th, one of the two."

"What year?"

"The year two thousand and thirty A.D., damn it!"

Dr. Cohen took a breath and inquired, "Do you know what cryogenics are? Or what it means to be put into a state of suspended animation?"

"No," Fred remarked. "What the hell was that bastard trying to do to me? Find out how much cold the human body could take?"

Dr. Cohen took an even bigger breath before sighing, "evidently it can take a great deal." Clearing her throat, she then spoke to Fred in a more scholarly tone. "If one is in suspended animation it means that all of one's bodily functions are slowed down to such a degree that they are put in a kind of stasis. And as long as someone is preserved in that kind of stasis, their body does not age in the slightest." Dr. Cohen laid her right hand on Fred's shoulder, "I want you to brace yourself because what you are about to hear may very well take you the rest of your life to truly comprehend and adequately cope with. Are you ready?"

"What-*is*-it-already?"

"Fred Hampton Rush," Dr. Cohen paused before continuing to note Fred's visibly surprised reaction upon hearing his full real name from this woman he barely knew. "Dr. Batala was somehow able to put *you* in a state of suspended animation by freezing you in that capsule at Argonne National Laboratory and left you perfectly preserved in stasis where you have not aged a single day—in three hundred and eighty years." Dr. Cohen's hand slightly tightened its grip on Fred's shoulder. "I want you to believe me when I tell you, Mr. Rush, that you are now alive and well in the year 2410 and it is now the 25th century. Do you understand everything that I'm saying to you?"

If anything, Fred initially thought he had absolutely no reason to believe anything this woman was saying. Besides not having in his life the amount of experience dealing with Whites needed in order to trust them as someone like Baines had, both his wife and his best friend had turned on him within the span of a weekend. So as of late his ability to trust was severely crippled to say the least. And yet, there was something about her that he couldn't quite put his finger on, something that said to him this "Joanna Cohen" person stood nothing to gain by deceiving him.

It then occurred to Fred that this couldn't possibly be a ruse on the part of the FOI because if they weren't imaginative enough to think to hypnotize the knowledge of where he had gotten *The Autobiography of Malcolm X* out of him, they definitely would not have been able to concoct a story such as the utterly incredulous one he had just been told. So if this wasn't some kind of a joke and if what Dr. Cohen was saying *was* in fact true . . . "Are you trying to say that I am now—" Fred took a moment to do the arithmetic in his head, "four hundred and eighteen years old? And this is the *future*?"

"The future from your point of view, the present for the rest of us," Dr. Cohen said simply. "But yes, that's correct. The exact date is Wednesday, March the 4th."

"But that's *insane*!" Fred cried out. "I don't remember any time passing between now and last ni—between now and then!"

"But that's just it, your bodily functions were slowed down to a near-death state. Which meant all your sensory outputs, including the mental faculties responsible for discerning and being conscious of time, were slowed to a halt too. So you couldn't have been aware of anything. You were preserved—"

"Like meat in a locker," Fred quipped. "I know, I heard you before. You're still going to have to prove all this, though."

"That you're now in 'the future' as it were?" Dr. Cohen put her hands in the pockets of her smock and looked about her. "I think for starters this will be benign enough to try without coming across as too much of a shock for you: Computer, gradually bring up the lighting by 25 percent."

When the room slowly illuminated by exactly that much, Fred's eyes widened and his lips bowed to form a tiny circle. With the lighting that much better, Fred could see how Dr. Cohen's clothes were more—*futuristic* than anything he had ever seen. Her doctor's smock was a very pale blue and underneath she had on a spandex body stocking with a blue and white pattern he couldn't make out without her removing the smock. Dr. Cohen also wore what looked like matching socks except somehow Fred had the feeling that the soles for these socks were a lot thicker than the kind he was used to.

"Computer, raise the lights by another—*seven point five* percent." When they were raised that much more, Dr. Cohen turned her attention back towards Fred. "Have you ever seen technology like that before?"

Fred regained the composure he momentarily lost to being astonished by the increased lighting and took on the scowl of a Doubting Thomas. "As a matter a fact, I have. In Dr. Batala's lab."

"Well, Batala has been dead almost as long as you've been frozen. And his lab, Argonne, is now being turned into a park. Which is actually how we found you. For hundreds of years, Argonne had been left completely untouched so it could be an everlasting monument and a constant reminder of Dr. Batala's cruelty. But the Agrarian Party has gained a lot of strength in the area in recent times and demanded that even more trees be planted in our cities—forgive me, I'm getting ahead myself and *far* ahead of you. Suffice to say when the building was being cleared away around a month ago for planting, we accidentally found your capsule, and so far we haven't found any others. You've been asleep and—*thawing out* for a couple of weeks now. The bottom line is, if you happen to be thinking all of this is part of one of his 'experiments,' I can assure that it's not."

"But—how did Batala die? And why—"

"Mr. Rush, you have to realize I can't explain one thing that happened while you were frozen without having to explain ten other things which lead up to it in order for what I'm explaining in the first place to make complete sense. You're going to have to be patient and I want you to come to grips with the idea that it may take a very long time for you to be completely caught up with everything that's happened in the past 380 years.

"You also have to understand that for all the advances we have made in all that time, we have never come across a case like yours. We don't really work with cryogenics in this day and age and we definitely did not think anyone had the technology to do so in your era. What I'm trying to say is we'll try our best to bring you up to speed but if we seem like we're not doing all that we could, it's because we're new at this. No one outside of the realm of science fiction has ever had to help someone who hasn't aged or seen the light of day in almost 400 years.

"The only reason *I* was picked and not an actual psychiatrist, and in your case a historian, is because my area of expertise lies in coma patients and helping them adjust to life after they awaken, I only wish I had more years in my field is all. We also decided that it was best for you to only have to deal with one person at first instead of you feeling surrounded by a bunch of doctors."

"I'm not going to be a guinea pig?" Fred wearily asked.

"Not unless you want to be," Dr. Cohen smiled. "I don't think you're going to be a danger to yourself either so I'm going to take off your restraints—as soon as I get back with some chicken soup. It's going to be a while before you can handle a lot of solids, and besides, it's the best thing for a cold."

"That's not funny," Fred snorted.

"A little sense of humor will go a long way in helping you cope with everything that has happened to you. But most importantly it will keep you from getting too depressed. I'll be back in a second and then we can talk some more."

* * *

Dr. Cohen had brought the lights all the way up when she returned with a bowl of chicken noodle soup for Fred to eat. When she had also released him from his bonds, Fred was able to look over to find that the bed he had been lying on was literally floating some four feet in the air. "I'll have to tell you more about anti-gravity some other time," was Dr. Cohen's only response to his surprise.

The bed could also recline and with the touch of a touch-a-matic button on its side, the doctor had the bed rear vertically from Fred's torso up so that he could sit up and have the bowl of soup rest on his lap. After being told not to try to eat too much too fast, Fred sipped at his soup and actually found it quite good.

"First, let me say that we do know who you are—and who you were. Let me assure you, however, with all certainty that you will not be made to pay for anything you did in your era. What I mean by that is, well, we do consider Farrakhan's reign to have been a bad thing—to say the least. If you were a member of, say, the Fruit of Islam, or one of the ministers we might have had to look at the possibility of pressing charges against you for being a war criminal.

"But like I said you haven't anything to worry about. From what we can tell, the worse you ever were was a 'dictator.' And while that's nothing to completely dismiss, since you weren't actually in charge of putting that 'historical' encyclopedia together, it's been decided that you are to be allowed all the rights that any of our citizens have."

"I guess it's safe to assume that the Nation of Islam has been overthrown," Fred looked up from his chicken noodle soup, "and if you think I'll miss them let me assure *you* that these bruises," Fred felt along his jaw and forehead and found them smooth, not swollen, "well, the bruises I imagine you people must have healed that *were* on my face were *not* self-inflicted. But who are the 'they' and 'we' you keep talking about? Who is in charge now?"

"From what we know about your experiences with Amelia Baines—" Dr. Cohen stopped when Fred did a double take upon hearing that all too familiar name. "I think you may already have an idea of the kinds of people who run and make up our society today. Our system of government is euphemistically called L.S.D., after the drug? But in this case it stands for libertarian socialist democracy—"

"Wait-a-minute, just hold on," Fred held a hand up to interrupt the doctor. "Before you tell me what all *that* means, if you do know about the underground—"

"'The underground,'" Dr. Cohen cut in. "*That's* what you meant before, Baines' book smugglers!"

"If you know about Baines, then you must know what happened to my son, Elisha Isiah? He was 10 years old and we were separated—"

"I'm sorry, I was going to save this for later, but I guess that the first thing on your mind would obviously be the fate of your son. And since he was so intricate in how things have changed, I figure we could talk about both because, in a way, they're interlinked. After your 'trial,' your son changed his name from 'Elisha Isiah' to Fred Hampton Rush *Junior* to honor you and to spite the Nation."

Fred leaned back on his bed and sighed in awed disbelief, "Allah—"

"In our time, we're taught not to attribute the triumphs or tragedies of history to one individual or a select group of individuals, rather we're told to look at what was the general mood of the time or the consensus of the masses to find out what were the causes of change in history. It's a sound enough philosophy, it reminds us to give historical credit where credit is due and it teaches us not to guru worship but to each be our own guru. But most importantly, it keeps us from throwing all of our faith into a chosen few, or the one, to solve all our problems and from allowing too much power to become concentrated in the hands of those few. But if there was ever any figure in our history that could make you throw that philosophy out the window it was your son, Fred Rush Jr.

"Despite what we're taught, we still love a good legend, and Fred Jr., or Junior as he's affectionately known, certainly fits the bill. Amelia Baines and her ragged band of smugglers went on to raise Junior like one of their own. After Baines died of cancer in 2035 a man by the name of Eric Blair took her place in Junior's life as his 'primary source of parental guidance' as Junior himself put it."

"I remember him!" Fred shot out. "I *met* him! He was the White boy who could remember everything he sped read!"

"'The Living Library,' 'The man with the photographic mind,' they called him. Eric Blair became the Merlin to Junior's King Arthur. The Doc Brown to his Marty McFly—"

"Doc who?"

"Never mind, the point is your son was never alone. He always had someone to take care of him, though life with the book smugglers was far from easy. But eventually after countless successful border runs Junior finally moved to London, England to go to school at Sussex where he joined the World Socialist Party. By 2040, this prodigy of yours rose to the rank of minister of information, the youngest in their history to hold that position.

"Now at the time things in the rest of the world had gotten all the better because of the threat of a *bad* example Aryan Amerikkka and the Lost-Found Nation had provided. I mean, who in the world had the heart to burn a book or ban a film when Junior and the other smugglers were risking their lives to sneak them across the border? Not many. Who in the world would continue to be anti-Semitic when one heard the stories of those in Amerikkka who were discovered to be Jewish and were also lucky enough to make it out? Not too many. And who in the world could ever think of making another nuclear missile after what happened to Australia? Not that many at all.

"Then, of course, once Oliver Stone's movie *Domino* came out in Europe and the Divided States in 2010 everyone had no choice but to at least acknowledge that US corporations had funded WAR and the NOI in 2005, so there wasn't too much corporations could get away with any more in the light of day after that point. And they certainly couldn't get away with propping up death squad-running thugs to head puppet governments in the third world anymore. Which meant that without the covert support from the *old* United States to back them up, all the banana republics that once littered Latin America began to fall one by one, and *that* finally gave the folks down there the freedom to socialize their economies without any fear of retribution.

"Things were better in the 21st than they were in the 20th century, but it was the World Socialist Party that had formed during the Brown Administration to keep him from selling out that went around reminding everyone that things could always be better. It was Junior who led the charge which pointed out that as good as a liberalized economy was, a socialized economy would be even better.

"Always demanding more, Junior, the WSP, and a multitude of others would try to back administrators and management further and further into the corner of obsolescence by having them acquiesce more and more with each passing year while calling for businesses to be worker owned or controlled. Junior's first hand testimonies of life with you in the Nation and of his smuggling across Amerikkka taught people of the dangers of privatizing economies and made people think twice before making the same mistakes over again. His charisma and speaking skills were on par with Martin Luther King and today some say Junior's fame and popularity has surpassed King's as well.

"When the time came in 2045 for a covert strike to be made against the one missile base Metzger had blackmailed the world with for forty years, it was Junior who was asked along as an 'advisor' to keep the undercover operation from becoming too Machiavelian. As things would turn out, Junior actually wound up getting physically involved in the operation code named Justified Cause at the ripe old age of 25 and called upon all of his experiences as a smuggler in order to sneak his way into Lansdale, disable the launching system, and fight his way out. This left both Aryan Amerikkka and the Lost-

Found Nation of Islam wide open for an invasion by the European Hegemony, a relatively liberal bloc of nations comprising nearly all of Europe who had replaced the old United States as *the* world power.

"The funny thing was, more resistance was faced by the European troops in the Nation than in Amerikkka. Since the vast majority of Blacks still couldn't tell the difference between ignorance and knowledge, between freedom and slavery, between being left-wing and being right-wing, the man on the street tried to fight back the invasion force as if they actually had a stake in the Lost-Found Nation, as if Khallid Muhammad, his successor—some ex-rapper, I forget his name, and all the other ministers hadn't *immediately* escaped to Libya at the first sign of trouble. The Libyans eventually handed them all back over for trial. After they lost that trial, they all died of extreme old age spending life terms in one of their own prisons.

"The only exception was the minister of science and technology, Dr. Batala, who for some reason decided to stay with the sinking ship as it were. When the bombing started, he was in his lab and a shell landed close enough to Argonne for some debris to have fallen on him. They later found his body and I think he's actually buried somewhere here in town. The last thing the NOI had him working on was some kind of gene splicing 'experiment' where they were trying to prove that this Yacub of theirs *had* eugenically created all the other races besides Blacks. They had kidnapped a Latino, an Indian, an Asian, a Jew, and Aryan Amerikkka had even handed over one of their White prisoners for this 'experiment.' That prisoner was unfortunately none other than Eric Blair. He stayed behind and continued to smuggle long after Junior had left for London and they caught him in the middle of a border run. None of the 'experiment's' participants survived.

"Once Junior found out about Blair he came to Chicago with the invading troops from the European Hegemony to see the mutilated body for himself and it was at this point the World Socialist Party split into two factions, a split that exists to this day. It also marked the formation of the principles that are the backbone of our society. The first faction, the party's vanguard, had claimed that since the Nation of Islam was allowed to speak freely, their message of hate was able to spread throughout to the Black community, and *that's* how they rose to power. The vanguard's final solution was to prohibit any speech or any press which put Farrakhan or the NOI in a favorable light and they also said the same should apply to any material concerning Metzger or WAR.

"That's what the party's hierarchy thought was best for the reconstruction of North America, whereas the followers of your son knew better. 'The Junior Woodchucks,' as they were insultingly called by the old guard knew their history. They knew that Farrakhan had been a *relatively* harmless staple in the Black community for 40 years, and for those 40 years he had been calling for the same thing he always called for, a separate state. But he couldn't *get* that separate state until after he had the funding of the du Ponts and the Rockefellers and so forth. So your son pointed out that all that was needed was a rule saying you couldn't excessively fund a fascist. Junior then pointed out that a rule barring free speech for fascists was not only unnecessary but would be fascist in and of itself.

"The Junior Woodchucks said that the reason why the Black community was so susceptible to Farrakhan's wiles was because there wasn't anything countering the deluge of coverage the NOI was getting from the corporately-owned mass media of the time. Having to constantly hear that one voice left Blacks with no choice but to think that what the man was saying was gospel and it also left Blacks with no choice of leaders either.

"Junior's solution to that was to make sure everyone knew better. His goal was to make sure that everyone was intellectual enough to see Farrakhan for what he really was, ideologically speaking, and if Blacks still wanted to join the Nation of Islam it would be because they themselves were right-wing to begin with and not because Blacks mistakenly thought they would be joining a radical organization. He believed that given the choice, given an *unscathed* choice, people would willingly pick a group like the World Socialist Party over the Nation of Islam at least eight times out of ten. Despite everything that Junior had lived through, he still felt that the human race was essentially a moral one, and those morals would automatically kick into gear if people were given a clear choice between a democracy and a theocracy/oligarchy or a theoligarchy.

"The hierarchy of the WSP on the other hand were far too cynical to believe that people were basically moral at heart, let alone trust that those morals would cause people to choose them over the fascists 'eight out of ten times.' They were absolutely convinced that a *counter* counter revolution would be inevitable if any propaganda from the other side was ever allowed to be disseminated by the public again. Junior used to try and explain to the vanguard all the time, 'just because you let the darkside have their *say* doesn't necessarily mean you'll let them get their *way*,' but the WSP would never listen.

"The old guard also began to make the issue personal for Junior, citing Eric Blair's death in particular as an example of how you can't be 'soft on fascism.' When your son called for Argonne to not be torn down so it would remind people of what the NOI did, members of the party who never even met Eric Blair were saying that Junior was being politically incorrect and insensitive to his own comrade's death for wanting Argonne to be left standing.

"Once the mudslinging started, the division bell rang, and the split between Junior's Woodchucks and the vanguard became official. Luckily, Junior's forces within the World Socialist Party not only outnumbered but outpowered that of the old guard, and it was the Woodchucks who 'dictated' policy in the Reunited States of America. Junior stayed in Chicago, married a White woman named Jill Holland who was part of the European invasion force," Dr. Cohen looked almost apologetically for an adverse response from Fred and continued when she found one that was only barely registerable, "and oversaw the reconstruction of what was the Lost-Found Nation.

"Instead of harassing, censoring, or even brainwashing the Muslims loyal to the Nation of Islam, Junior always made sure that the occupying forces allowed the Muslims' voices to be heard in the political arena during that reconstruction period. Your son gambled that if the people in what was the Nation were given a better alternative rather than European troops, or the vanguard for that matter, shoving it down their throats, they would choose it, and for the most part the people did, much to the NOI's dismay."

Fred looked both surprised and dismayed. "You're telling me that you people let the Nation of Islam still exist even after you took the Nation over? What kept history from repeating itself in all this time and them taking things over again?"

"I'm trying to tell you that given the choice in the form of debate after public debate during the reconstruction, people, *Black* people, chose what Junior and the European occupational forces were offering over what they were used to, so none of the strongarm tactics that the vanguard wanted to try were really necessary. Knowing history *kept* history from repeating itself."

Fred sounded worried and maybe a bit paranoid when he asked, "there aren't still NOI temples in this day and age, are there?" Fred knew that the idea of someone from the Nation of Islam wanting to exact retribution upon him after some 400 years wouldn't be unimaginable in the least.

"I think there is one in Detroit," Dr. Cohen thought for a moment, "maybe there's still that one here in town, I don't know. You don't hear from them much because they're such a paper tiger, their membership is a shell of what it used to be because people know better.

"Know better *how*?"

"*All* religions are taught and studied with neutral respect in our schools. And in the face of all the other theologies and mythologies throughout the history of the world, Yacub's History looked kind of puny. Therefore, all the fewer people today see any point in joining the NOI."

"Or being Islamic in general, right?" Fred scowled slightly at this prospect. "Tell me the truth, because of everything that the NOI has done, cutting a deal with Metzger, having folks 'experimented' on, and so forth, I can't see anyone in a post-Farrakhan future being too kind to someone like me, who fully intends on practicing *orthodox* Islam as Malcolm X did."

"Mr. Rush, I can assure you that we have the utmost respect for everyone's freedom of religion. You will not have anything to worry about insofar as anyone coming along and persecuting you. You have to understand, Junior knew he wasn't going to be around to teach people about the tolerance of different beliefs forever, and if after he died only one voice or one set of voices began to dominate the means of communication, then all he ever worked for would have been for nothing.

"So Junior picked up where President Jerry Brown had left off and revived the concept of a National Educational Standard. In which all sides of an issue and all worldviews of history—that of the far left, the left, the middle of the road, the right, and yes, even the far right—would be required to be fairly given an equal amount of time to be heard and disseminated by the public. That standard still exists today and it, more than anything else, has kept the Reunited States of America together during the reconstruction and has kept our whole civilization together for all these centuries.

"The premise is that once the choice is put to them, the majority of every succeeding generation will continually be moral enough to pick the leftwards path at the political fork in the road time and time and time again. However that choice really couldn't be made in your era because of the lack of a Fairness Doctrine or an equal time rule. Without such a rule, there was no stopping the left, particularly the far left, from being marginalized or kept from the public eye by the corporately-owned media. And since folks can't very well choose what they don't know exists, those of the late 20th and early 21st centuries had no choice but to continue to pick between the only political options ever presented to them: Outright fascism or diluted fascism with a friendly face painted on it pretending to be *democratic*.

"But we've changed all that, and have seen to it that every child on the face of the planet and on all our colonies and space stations—" Dr. Cohen saw the bewildered look on Fred's face and decided to bring her conversation back down to Earth, "anyway, we make sure that every child knows everything there is to know about history, political and social science, civics, philosophy, ideology, propaganda, hierarchies, atrocities, ethics in journalism, issues in free speech, and even legal precedents, so that literally everyone would be the intellectual that your son wanted them to be and what he helped forge during the reconstruction would always be maintained."

Fred folded his arms and smirked. "If everyone is some kind of super smart intellectual, who gets their hands dirty and does the *hard* work around here?"

"Believe it or not, we the *intellectuals*," the doctor shrugged, "the only difference between your time and ours as far as that goes is that because they *are* intellectuals no boss—'boss,' as if almost everything today wasn't worker-owned anyway—would ever be able to con them into being paid a microbe less than what they're worth. We still have custodians but they are compensated and benefited very, *very* well. We wouldn't have it any other way."

"You're still saying 'we' a lot. Is 'we' the state, the government? That LDS you were talking about before?"

"You mean *LSD*, and what a libertarian socialist democracy means is that we have the social policies of a libertarian, the fiscal policies of a socialist, and everything is decided via direct democracy. It was your son who initially coined the acronym/phrase. Junior wrote in his autobiography, *Tales of the Reconstruction*, 'in order for a democracy to be a democracy, everyone must participate, everyone must be well informed on every viewpoint in order to participate, and everyone must have equal access to every viewpoint and the actual democratic process itself in order to participate.'"

Fred felt at his temple as he took all of this in. "That's quite a mouthful. *My* son said all that?"

"Like everyone else, I had to learn all this by heart by the time I got out of junior high. In our society, politics isn't the big business it was in the 20th and it's definitely not anything that one has to first be 'into' in order to know something about or be interested in. Being politically active or at the very least politically knowledgeable isn't a hobby anymore, it's practically required. But I want to stress however it is *not* required for one to be left-wing, and the reason why that's not required—as the old vanguard of the WSP would've wanted—is because history has proved your son's gamble right time after time. All we ever ask is that every citizen becomes an intellectual, what you do with that intellect is your business. You can either be a Noam Chomsky kind of intellectual or a William F. Buckley kind of intellectual, just be *an* intellectual. Where we've been lucky over the centuries is that there has always been more Chomskyian intellectuals than there were Buckleyian intellectuals. And since the bulk of every past generation has chosen the Chomskyian over the Buckleyian over and over again, we're confident that *most* intellectuals will choose to stay on the leftwards course we've been on for the past 400 years or so."

"'Eight out of ten,' right?" Fred quipped.

"Yes, so there's no real fear that the right-wing will ever regain the power it had in your era—people are just too damn smart for that. Or as Junior always used to say, 'an uneducated populace votes one way, an educated populace votes another.' If the price of liberty is eternal vigilance, and if all the billions upon billions of people on the planet are eternally vigilant, how can you go wrong? Governments can only get away with what their people *let* them get away with, and if *everyone* is politically savvy, then governments can never pull the wool over their people's eyes. That's right, Mr. Rush, when I say everyone in school is required to memorize, say, both the platforms of the Black Panthers *and* the Ku Klux Klan for instance, I mean *every single person you will ever see*. Unless, of course, you run into someone who hasn't graduated from high school.

"Now considering that our system will not let anyone starve or go homeless, food and shelter would be all we would allow that high school dropout to have. In a LSD, everything is divided into two camps: Rights and privileges. You'll never need a job in your life in order to get the equivalent of a studio apartment and three all-you-can-eat meals a day because we decided a long time ago those were rights. Health care, day care, public transportation and higher education, all of these things are now guaranteed rights that every citizen on Earth, and beyond, has access to. But without a high school diploma, that dropout can't get accepted into one of our free colleges, or even get themselves a decent job, and without some kind of a job, there's no way they'd be able to afford the privileges in our society. Such as a house of their own as opposed to a cramped apartment, good furniture, fine cuisine, the latest in fashion, shows, concerts, sporting events, trips to outer—trips *abroad*, etc. We do permit free enterprise, but there are so many rules one has to follow with every business venture that people usually don't bother, so it's pretty much been regulated to the status of a hobby over the years.

"We have only one form of currency world wide, a World Currency." Dr. Cohen reached into a slit in the side of her spandex body stocking and pulled out a pale green, small rectangular piece of paper that looked as if its fibers were woven from some kind of hemp. "This is a ducat. They come in ones, twos, fives, tens, twenty fives, fifties, on up to hundreds and thousands. There's never any interest on them, and they're not backed by any gold. Just trust and honor, however naive that may sound.

"And we have a World Government, complete with a constitution covering everything from one's right to bear certain small firearms to one's right to partake of most any intoxicating or hallucinogenic substance."

Fred cocked his head to one side. "Don't tell me drugs are legal here?"

Dr. Cohen, sensing this might be sensitive ground for a Black Muslim and not wanting to enter into a heated debate, chose to ignore the question and move on. "There aren't any more 'states' as you remember them. We'll say the name of a given state for geographic reference in order to give directions and all, but there aren't any more state governments and a state's borders no longer have any legal meaning as far as jurisdiction goes. Each city, town, or collective has its own elected leader and legislature and while they're in charge of their own particular spot, the World Court, the World Council, and the World Committee all supersede them.

"The World Court is made up of 24 judges all democratically picked by the people and they help interpret the World Constitution I just told you about. One representative is picked from every recognized populated area in the world and all those representatives make up the World Council. The same goes for the World Committee except that a representative is picked from every *country*.

"The indescribably high amount of checks and balances we have in place to keep those representatives in line only goes to show how paranoid we are of any kind of concentrated power. The low pay our politicians get and the perk-free, minimalist lives they lead, like monks almost. The fact that they can't accept any campaign contributions over a set-in-stone amount. How every official political hearing or meeting is open to the public and never held in private. How 'the state'—for want of a better phrase seeing as how we *are* the state—makes sure that *all* the parties have the same, exact amount of equal time as one another on the air and in the press. How we only go by the popular vote and have eliminated the electoral college ages ago. How our primaries and election seasons are only allowed to last a couple of months at a time at the most. How one can only stay in any office a maximum of two years, and how even *then* they're all subject to instant and total recall should they ever start to mess up."

When Dr. Cohen stopped to catch her breath, Fred rubbed each of his temples with his index fingers from having to absorb and understand concepts of such enormity. His chicken soup long since finished, Fred handed the spoon and empty bowl to the doctor and sounded exasperated when he said, "I can't believe that all this came about because of my little 10 year old boy, my little Eli—Junior."

"Maybe I shouldn't have painted him out to be such a George Washington/Alexander the Great type," Dr. Cohen frowned, "it wasn't as if Junior was like Atlas and held up the sky. Don't get me wrong, you have everything to be proud of, you gave the world a fine son, but he *did* have plenty of help. And nothing he ever dreamed of would have been possible if it wasn't for the infinite amount of sacrifices that were made along the way by the countless individuals we'll never know the names of who took to the streets en masse. All of whom calling for fairness in the media and fiscal change in the world with the same amount of fervor, if not more, that people had when they marched for *social* change in the sixties.

"I also hope I didn't leave the impression that there haven't been any stumbling blocks between his time and now either. Things haven't been easy, trying to convince the more reactionary cultures in the world we weren't trying to assimilate them, that we were just trying to give their people a choice. Like for instance, around the 22nd century the world's population hit something like 15 billion—"

"And you weren't able to build any spaceships yet to get to any of those colonies or space stations in outer space you accidentally mentioned before?" Dr. Cohen frowned even more as Fred managed a slight grin. "I might find a lot of things shocking at first, but I'm not made of glass and I won't melt, doctor. I kind of figured we'd have all those things by the 25th century."

"*Anyway*—" Dr. Cohen was actually as flustered as she looked. After nervously scratching the back of her auburn-haired head she finished her last train of thought. "We had to take serious steps to control our population. So we went to the Pacific kim and the Middle East to try and explain to them that their women could no longer dwell behind the veil of ignorance—no pun intended, and had to have some knowledge of birth control. Well, the men who led these countries reacted predictably and said not just no but *hell* no.

"All we ever wanted to do was to give these countries the choice they never really had before, nothing more, but the principles of fairness and the equal time rule escaped these people. They fought us every step of the way until the succeeding generations in these countries finally decided on their own to be a little bit more receptive in allowing regular, unscathed public debates on birth control. These days learning about B.C. as we call it, is required world wide, and at last count I think our population, both here and—*beyond*, is somewhere around 12 billion. But there was a time where we were dancing on the brink of World War III—over condoms and diaphragms of all things. So, like I said, we weren't always on a bed of roses.

"And about you being able to handle culture shocks, Mr. Rush? Just as today we talked about some of the sociological advances that have been made in the past 400 years, tomorrow we'll talk about some of the technological advances. I think I've actually rambled on far too long about far too much for you to be able to take in. Why don't you give what I have told you so far a chance to sink in and go to sleep?"

Fred wasn't listening to how much of a child he sounded like to the doctor while arguing with her. "Sleep till tomorrow? I've been asleep for four hundred years! I want to see *something*, this room is bare empty! My eyes aren't going to burn out of their sockets if I see some more of this future! Why can't I—"

"Mr. Rush, we haven't even seen whether your legs are too weak from inactivity to stand on yet."

"Well let's find that out right now," Fred went to slide off of his floating bed and Dr. Cohen immediately met him halfway, grasping his bare legs and drawing the bed sheets back over them.

"Not-right-now, *tomorrow*," she said sternly, "and don't make me put these restraints back on."

"*Nayirah*," Fred mumbled under his breath.

"I didn't catch that," Dr. Cohen glared. "Was that some kind of Islamic curse? Are you swearing at me, Mr. Rush?"

"Nothing, forget it."

Dr. Cohen took a calming breath before explaining, "listen, I know you're anxious, but we have got to take this slow. Culture shock could cause permanent psychological damage. Even though you seem more enlightened and better at critical thinking than most of the Black Muslims of your era, we still have to proceed carefully. I promise, first thing tomorrow morning I'll bring a couple of things to give some color to this Spartan room and will show you what lies in store for you. We'll see about getting you on your feet, but don't you try anything before I come back, I mean it. You could step wrong, twist your ankle, or even break your leg so just lie still, please?"

Fred's only answer was him folding his arms and sulking.

"That's better," Dr. Cohen said, "now if by any chance you *really* need someone, touch this stud on the side of your bed, but only if it's an emergency. If you need to go to the bathroom, turn yourself over on your stomach, pull back that flap on the bed you feel at the small of your back, and use the hole underneath. There's a built-in bed pan within the bed itself. Beyond that, I want you to rest, alright?"

"Fine," Fred shut his eyes as if to showing how willing he was.

"Good night—*Fred*." Dr. Cohen smiled, and before quietly slipping through the room's door with the spoon and empty bowl in hand, she called out to seemingly no one in particular, "computer, dim lights by 45 percent."

Fred knew he shouldn't have been so harsh with this woman towards the end of their talk since the doctor was only trying to help him and had his best interests at heart. Upon reflection, he saw her point insofar as getting some rest, recalling that he wasn't being bored by the doctor explaining the differences between the World Court, Council, and Committee, but was in fact becoming tired. Perhaps one couldn't spring forth fully awake from having been in suspended animation for 380 years after all, and maybe sleeping one more night before taking his first steps into this brave new world wasn't such a bad idea.

Still, he didn't like the feeling that he was being handled with kid gloves. Fred wanted to feel as though he had *something* under his control and then he remembered something the doctor had said. Fred's eyes darted about him before mouthing the words reminiscent to those he had just heard a few moments before. "Computer, increase lighting."

For whatever reason the computer didn't respond to his voice, and when the room didn't illuminate in the slightest, Fred really felt like a kept child. But then he remembered his age, a ripe 418, and tried to do as the doctor ordered, to relax and think about all that was said today.

The doctor described a world where everyone had a keen mind, where no one was a dullard. This sounded ambitious but would it mean that Fred would be a Lilliputian among a world of Gullivers? Evidently, Fred only had a grasp of the most basic fundamentals of poli sci despite the 'education' he received from the Lost-Found Nation, did this mean he would have to go back to school? And if he refused, what would become of him?

According to Dr. Cohen, Fred would never be totally without because he was now in a time when housing and food were free world wide. A concept that would have been considered blasphemously inconceivable by those who ruled the era Fred knew best, in which if you didn't work you didn't live for too long.

For all her talk about everyone's rights being respected and the people themselves keeping their leaders in check, Fred still wondered if there really wasn't a class of—*overseers* out there in this 25th century who were a cut above all the rest and policed this liberal society democrat or whatever it was called. Dr. Cohen sounded as though a utopian paradise was right outside this hospital room. But surely there had to be at least a couple of malcontents out there, and if so, who, if anybody, kept the peace on Earth now?

Man exploring the stars . . . Sure, Fred acted as though the prospect didn't faze him, but nevertheless, he pondered which worlds were conquered? Mars? The moon? Jupiter? Saturn? Did all of this space travel mean that aliens had been encountered by intrepid explorers?

And then there was Elisha, little Elisha, who spent all the formative years that should have been spent with his father with that seditious, cantankerous, sacrilegious old woman Baines and went on to be these people's savior. As much as he hated having been separated from his only son, it occurred to Fred just the same that one could look upon the separation as a comforting and almost philosophical pun. In his most imaginative moment to date, Fred tried to compare leaving his son behind to having left a seed *underground* which sprouted into a tree, branched out as it grew, and shot up to the stars taking the rest of mankind with it. Every father wishes their sons will find and fulfill a grand destiny, but how many fathers get to see how those destinies turn out. And how many of those destinies involve the sons becoming legends? Not enough to keep a wave of patriarchal pride from completely drenching Fred and leaving tingly goosepimples behind as he laid back on his floating hospital bed/bed pan with his fingers interlaced behind his now "swelled" head.

Oh, the people of 2410 would deny that any one man had more of an effect on the course of history than the masses who rallied behind him, but from what Dr. Cohen had described, those masses followed Elisha's vision and not necessarily Elisha himself. Meaning while one probably shouldn't put too much stock in one man, it should be alright to put everything behind a vision, because unlike a man there's no danger of a vision ever corrupting or dying.

Dying. Dear Allah, Fred couldn't believe he had just now realized the obvious: That unless he was a man in his hundreds just like his father, there's no way Fred Hampton Rush Junior would be alive today! Elisha has been dead for centuries no doubt, and Fred wasn't sure if he should blame Dr. Cohen for not bringing the death up during the conversation or himself since it should have occurred to him right away without her pointing the obvious out. The pride only a father could feel fell away from Fred leaving a man who was trembling and shedding tears in mourning. It didn't matter if his son had died some three hundred years ago, it still meant Fred would never see Elisha ever again, and the thought of this kept him crying for most of the night.

After he cried himself to sleep, Fred awoke in what he could only imagine was the middle of the night, since Dr. Cohen probably saw to it that his room didn't have a window which could give him some clue as to what time it was for fear that something outside that window might give him culture shock. The reason why he woke up in the first place was because he needed to urinate, and while Fred turned himself over as he pulled back the flap at the base of the bed revealing the hole he was to excrete in, something came to him.

If Elisha or Fred Rush Junior did marry a—*White* woman (Fred shook his head as he took a moment to imagine how Nayirah would've reacted to that) after defeating Farrakhan, and if they had kids, and if their *kids* had kids, then maybe, just maybe, somewhere out there a descendant of Fred's was still alive and well in 2410 A.D. Logically, after all these centuries, the direct lineage should have long since been bred out, and the family name of Rush was probably lost in marriage generations ago. But Fred still thought "what if" despite the odds as he tried to go back to sleep.

* * *

It wasn't the middle of the night as Fred had miscalculated from not having a room with a view, it was still Wednesday, March the 4th but only late in the afternoon, around dusk. It had been a beautiful spring day that now had an even more beautiful sunset to look forward to.

Flying in the direction of the setting sun from downtown Chicago towards the Cicero district in his red Saturn four wheel drive decorated with the very sorts of decals indicative of a law enforcement vehicle was Captain Huey P. Rush. The sirens built onto the Saturn's roof were wailing like banshees as he sliced through the aerial traffic soaring over Douglas Park and Ogden Avenue consisting of cars, buses, trucks, and shuttles along the elevated paths and intersections upon which one "drove." The sky lanes as they were called were lined horizontally in grid-like patterns with brightly glowing bulbs floating via anti-gravity which shinned either green for "go," yellow for "slow," or red for "stop." These bright buoys that linearly marked these highways were ignored by Huey Rush however who, when on the kind of mission that he was currently on, could disregard the color of the lights.

Just below the stream of automobiles whizzing back and forth along the sky lanes lied a sprawling metropolis who's architectural layout would have made perfectly accurate clairvoyants out of the futurists of the World Fairs of the mid 20th century were it not for an obsession with the ecology that was before their time but all too present in the 25th century that insisted on the presence of a park or at least an arboretum every few blocks or so. Huey looked down at the city he had sworn to protect searching for the turn-off he was to take in order to land his car on Cermak Road and drive the rest of the way to his latest assignment: A hostage situation involving someone who "can't handle his high" according to one of his lieutenants already at the scene, Cheshta Castelblanch.

This was a rare thing on Huey's beat, or the beat of any "peace officer" for that matter. Not someone being incapable of coping with their inebriation, but a conceivably murderous incident. Because scarcity has almost become a thing of the past—and since every human being in 2410 was either lower middle class, middle class, or upper middle class—white collar, capital crimes and poverty induced crimes had become nearly extinct.

Which was why the jobs of the peace officers are akin to that of a small town sheriff despite the sizes of the cities or colonies they police. The lack of strife across the country, around the world, and beyond the stars made the common soldier or sailor, the National

Guardsman, the policeman, the security guard, even the bodyguard and the bouncer practically obsolete. Leaving the peace officers to pick up the slack and having to have the training necessary in order to be a Jack, or Jane, of all the trades of the aforementioned—everything from giving mouth-to-mouth resuscitation to getting a cat down from a tree.

In his youth, there was a certain rush that Huey felt whenever he was generous or helped someone. It was a feeling he quickly became addicted to and juxtaposed with his affinity for the golden aged heroes of the past. Robin Hood, the Scarlet Pimpernel, Zorro, the Lone Ranger, Popeye, Dick Tracy, Buck Rogers, Flash Gordon, Superman, and the like. He was always a well built lad who seemed born to lead and resembled an actor from the 20th century who played the very kinds of men of action Huey longed to be, Mario Van Peebles.

With such a blatant personality makeup, it seemed that Huey's original goals, charting the stars or terraforming planets for colonization, would be no trouble at all for him to attain. Except that Huey found out early on in school the hard way that he was probably the least mathematically and mechanically inclined person alive, something one couldn't afford to be in outer space. This left the only other career option the 25th century had to offer the adventurous likes of a Huey P. Rush—that of a peace officer.

Huey never came to regret his decision to become one, despite the contempt some in 2410 felt for *any* form of hierarchy with authority over people, despite there not being much to do (once he was actually called in to help an old woman across the street), and despite the prospect that someday even the peace officers would be made obsolete. Being as politically and philosophically intellectual as everyone else in the human race, Huey knew better than to wish for something bad to happen just to sedate his boredom and to justify his place in the world. All he really wanted to do was leave his mark as his ancestor did all those centuries ago, Fred Hampton Rush Junior.

Between his world famous lineage and his position as a public servant, Huey Rush was something of a celebrity. And though the anarchist nature of 25th century society usually shied away from exalting people in power, Huey could never resist wallowing in what little attention he got now and again. Which is why the citizenry regard Huey as something of an egotistical eccentric. What makes him even more of an oddity to the casual observer is the fact that he had turned down promotion after promotion for the past seven years so that he could remain a captain, and the reason why, were it widely known, would only feed into Huey's reputation as a pop cultural dinosaur.

The fault lied in the kinship he still felt at 45 years old with the superheroes of his youth in that regardless of how many times they've saved the world, the likes of Captain Marvel, Captain America, Captain Midnight, and Captain Freedom were never been "promoted" either. Huey simply thinks the title of captain has a certain ring to it and likes the sound of it so much that he's willing to pass up an extra thousand ducats a month to maintain it.

Huey was hearing that title called out over and over again as his red Saturn pulled into the crime scene, a modest, two story home near Naragansett Avenue, because as he stepped out of his car after parking it across the street from the house, the media immediately recognized him and began a deluge of questions.

"Captain Rush, can you tell us anything more about the situation?"

"Captain Rush, have you been in communication with the suspect?"

"Captain Rush, are you here to negotiate for the hostages?"

"Captain, what are his demands?"

It was during times like this when Huey could truly empathize with someone who was on a diet passing by the window of a deli. As much as he'd like to stay and be filmed by the reporters' camera helmets, with goggle-like lenses and antennae which transmitted any voices and images they picked up back to their studios, Huey had a job to do.

"Sorry boys, you know how much I'd love to oblige, but I know about as much as you do, honestly." Huey shrugged and excused himself from the crowd of reporters. "I got to go get briefed my damn self."

Huey had to remind himself that he was married everytime he laid eyes on his tawny skinned subordinate, Lieutenant Cheshta Castelblanch. For the past 150 years or so, people's everyday wear had consisted of either rubbery, cotton/spandex bodystockings or more baggy, East Indian influenced wardrobe to go over said bodystockings in colder weather. In this particular instance, it was near the end of a balmy spring day so the standard uniform for a peace officer consisted of a form-fitting bodystocking, and the buxom San Salvadorian Lieutenant Castelblanch always wore hers well.

Standing just inside the force field the other peace officers had in place to surround the house, Lieutenant Castelblanch let her captain step through the seven foot high fence of transparent static energy by switching off a button on one of the black and gray metal poles installed into the ground which kept the field energized. Huey strode through before any of the reporters could, watched the lieutenant switch the field on again, and ordered, "Tell me what I want to hear, Castelblanch."

"As best as I can figure, here's what happened," Lieutenant Castelblanch began in that Spanish accent of hers Huey found so familiar. "This guy, David Kornblatt, broke up with his girlfriend this morning—some girl named Sandra Lursah, and no, we haven't been able to get a hold of her. Anyway, David got a bunch of his friends to come over to comfort him and do some peyote shrooms with him so he could take his mind off of Sandra. Well, like I said when I called you, this guy can't handle his high. Everybody else was having fairly mellow visions, seeing dead ancestors, cartoon characters, the usual, except that our boy David starts really tripping out.

"According to the one hostage that managed to escape on her own, Heather Baytorn—who's now at the Medical Center District for a laser wound she took in the shoulder—David started going off about how life, the universe, and everything is all fictional, and was written by an angel just to entertain God."

Huey genuinely looked taken aback. "That's pretty deep."

"He says he's tired of God wanting to see people go through suffering—and heartache—in the name of life having more conflict and thus being more of an exciting story for His amusement."

"And of course, he's pissed off because the angel wrote in 'the script of life' or whatever that his girlfriend was to dump him this morning, right?"

"Right, he's says he's 'onto God's scheme now' and got a high powered laser rifle aimed at all five of his friends in the upstairs master bedroom. He's threatening to shoot them if God or this angel doesn't show up by sundown today and relieve him of having to jump through any more literary hoops for His entertainment. Heather Baytorn managed to sneak out through the bathroom window, got shot for her troubles, and that's when anyone knew to call us."

Huey looked up that the setting sun and saw that the deadline for the divine to make an appearance was fast approaching. "Then I guess I'm just going to have to play God. And I don't mean tinkering with eugenics."

"Sir?"

"Take my paratranquilizer gun, lieutenant," Huey handed Castelblanch a small firearm that had been attached to a patch of Velcro on his spandex uniform. "I'm going in."

Once she realized her superior officer was serious, Castelblanch stammered, "Captain, you can't—"

"Lieutenant, I know a little something of the fictional, you've been to my house, you've seen my collection, believe me, I can relate to this guy. Hell, *I've* sometimes wondered whether all of this," Huey waved his arms about, "is just some entry from the diary of a madman." He then leaned closer to Lieutenant Castelblanch and smiled. "Trust me, I'll be back in a minute."

As Huey slowly headed for the front door of the house, Castelblanch stayed at her post at the force field and swore a couple of oaths under her breath in Spanish before muttering, "coming on like some damn buckaroo with this 'cowboy diplomacy' of his is going to get him killed someday."

* * *

Whoever this David Kornblatt character was, he had squeaky steps on his side that let him know if someone was heading upstairs, which was strange for a house with union/collective-built quality. A quality the house no doubt had since it couldn't possibly have been constructed more than two hundred years ago. No sooner than Huey reached the middle of the one flight of stairs leading to the house's only other floor did Kornblatt suddenly appear in the doorway of his bedroom which directly faced the mouth of the stairwell with the laser rifle in one hand and the hair one of the hostages, a blond girl around 19, balled up in the other.

"Get the fuck out of my house you fucking pig!" Kornblatt raged. "Before I blow your fucking head off!"

"Take it easy," Huey soothed as he dared to take another step forward, "I just want to talk. As you can see, I'm unarmed."

"Yeah? Well what the fuck do you want to talk *about*?" Kornblatt blared with glazed eyes. "Do you want to ne-go-ti-ate, huh, pal? Do you want me to let these asshole friends of mine go? Well fuck *no*, it ain't going to happen! Not unless God or that dumb-ass angel writer of His shows up before the sun goes down in," he glanced back for an instant to look out his bedroom window behind him and quickly turned his attention back to Huey, "the next couple of minutes!"

Huey took a single step closer. "Well I'm here to tell you . . . *Two* reasons why God's not going to show up." To anyone else who was sober, Huey would've clearly sounded as though he were "reaching"—which in fact he was. "Reason number one? Reason number one is . . . Because God is like the Greatest American Hero."

"What?" Kornblatt was beginning to feel patronized and his finger felt for the trigger of his rifle. "What the *fuck* are you talking about?"

"*The Greatest American Hero* was a 20th century TV show about a guy who was given a bodystocking with a cape by aliens. When he wore the bodystocking it gave him superpowers, flight, superstrength, superspeed, invulnerability, the basics. *But*—" Huey's index finger shot upwards as if to accentuate a point, "but this outfit the aliens gave him didn't have a mask. So the Greatest American Hero had to always act *covertly*. He would capture the bad guys and then take off before the police or any press would show up and if the bad guys tried to describe how some guy in a red suit came out of the sky and captured them, they'd get sent to the nut house.

"Now God works the same way. He hasn't left any proof of His existence since Biblical times because if He did, He'd make liars out of the few religious leaders still around in this nondenominational/agnostic world of ours because the world's different religions' descriptions of Him can't have possibly all been right, *right*?"

Whether it was the peyote shrooms he took which were partly to blame for his current warpath or the inherent logic behind what Huey was relating, Kornblatt actually calmed down and responded, "right . . . Right . . ."

"God has to keep acting covertly so that he won't make all the religions of the world—besides the *one*, if there ever *was* one who accurately guessed what He looked like—obsolete. Even more so than our historians, who can prove that Jesus was just an ordinary man and that we did evolve from ape-men. If He were to show up right now, He'd blow His cover, and He's not about to prove you right after countless philosophers have been trying to find Him for a millennium. Not with all those reporters outside, that's for damn sure. But the bottom line is this: If He, or even that angel were to show up right now, He'd take away mankind's free will to chose not to believe in Him, and even He wouldn't do that. Do you understand?"

"What's reason number two, man? What's reason number *two*?" Kornblatt demanded, obviously engrossed by what he was being told.

"Yeah," one of the inebriated hostages called out from Kornblatt's bedroom, "what's reason number two?"

"Reason number two is going to cost you," Huey took two more steps towards Kornblatt, bringing him a couple of meters closer to Kornblatt's position. "You want to hear it? Let everybody go and take me as a hostage instead. God doesn't want to see me dead any more than He does your friends."

Huey was certain this ploy would never work, which was why he had to fight to keep the expression of shock off of his face when Kornblatt ordered everyone out of his bedroom.

As one of the last of the hostages filed down the stairs past Huey and Kornblatt, one sounded genuinely disappointed when he commented, "damn, I wanted to hear reason number two."

After he watched all of the captives make their way outside, Huey gritted his teeth underneath an uneasy frown when he turned to see the laser rifle aimed directly at his head. "There ain't no 'reason number two,' is there, pig?" Kornblatt cynically sneered.

"There is too," Huey took a calming breath before speaking again and taking yet another step towards Kornblatt. "Reason number two is—God's not showing up because He doesn't see any point since He has no intention of ever making your life any easier. Don't you see? The lives of ordinary people are boring as hell, and that's probably exactly where they'll wind up after they die, for boring God to tears. But you—look at you, you're going to be on the news tonight! That's drama, that's pathos! You're going to Heaven, son! Valhalla! To ask God not to want to see you suffer just so he can be amused would be like asking one of us not to want to see Indiana Jones go through the motions he goes through. Just as Steven Spielberg put Indy through hell so we could be entertained, that angel who writes for God is doing the same to you!"

"I know, man! I know!"

"Well, even if Spielberg knew Indiana Jones actually lived on another plane of existence he would still probably say, 'tough break, Indy. I'm entertaining too many people to make your life any easier.' I bet he wouldn't even have the heart to say that to Indiana's face and that angel's not going to come down here and say anything to you for the same reason."

Kornblatt lowered his laser rifle slightly, his facial expression was calmer, and even his body language seemed more sedate. "I never thought a piece-of-shit officer would understand, but you do, don't you?"

"Yeah I do," Huey tried to smile as he held out his hand. "Now why don't you let me have the gun, huh? What do you say?"

"You *don't* understand!" With new resolve, Kornblatt reaimed his laser rifle at Huey. "Goddamned *pig* trying to get in good with me!" In the millisecond that Kornblatt managed to squeeze off a shot, Huey's left arm swatted the rifle's nozzle sending the single fiery red beam that emanated from the nozzle's tip through the roof. In the same motion Huey's right fist came crashing onto Kornblatt's jaw in the form of an uppercut and sent him to the floor unconscious.

"Calling me, a direct descendant of Black Panther Bobby Rush, a 'pig,'" Huey said to himself as he picked up the rifle. "he *must* have been high to have *that* much gall."

* * *

Huey didn't bother suppressing the feeling that he was some kind of a big game hunter of old stepping out of the house with Kornblatt's laser rifle in one hand and Kornblatt's unconscious body slung over his broad shoulder. After Lieutenant Castelblanch switched off the force field and let the press through, she darted ahead of them to take Kornblatt from Huey and cart the assailant off to her car, similarly labeled with decals indicating it was a peace officer's vehicle just as Huey's was.

" . . . And I want to stress that it wasn't entirely the fault of the peyote shrooms he took. Why, I've been known to take some myself once in a blue moon and I've never decided to up and make a bunch of folks my hostages, but then, I've never had a girlfriend break up with me like Kornblatt did either. *No*, we can't ever allow ourselves to slip back to the days of yesteryear, when everyone blamed everything on the very existence of drugs and demonized anyone who experimented with them. Well, David Kornblatt may have had inner demons to excise, but-he-himself-was-no-demon! Folks know better than that and we need to make sure that they continue to, thank you."

As Huey proudly strode away from the crowd of camera helmeted reporters and headed for his red Saturn across the street, one reporter waited until after Huey was out of earshot before asking another reporter who stood the closest to her, "I'm new in town so maybe you can explain something to me because I'm confused: Did we just interview Captain Rush or Captain Kirk?"

"It does sound like William Shatner was his speech teacher back in high school, doesn't it?" The reporter who was asked the question snickered as he removed his camera helmet. "Huey Rush's infamous around these parts for his Wagnerian soliloquies. One of the oldest jokes in town is that the real reason the few Black Muslims in town can't stand to listen to Rush speak is that all the ham in his dialogue violates their no-pork diet. Welcome to Chicago—*miss . . ?*"

While the male reporter was trying to ingratiate and find out more about the female reporter back on the ground, Huey was airborne once again and flying along the sky lanes in his Saturn. As he was flying over Garfield Park, Huey spoke into thin air, "computer, get me the office of Dr. Joanna Cohen at the Loyola University Medical Center."

A moment later, Dr. Cohen's face appeared on a small screen embedded inside of Huey's Saturn above his stick shift and below his car stereo. "Good afternoon, Mr. Rush. Or should I say good evening?"

"Doc, has . . . Has he waken up yet?"

"As a matter a fact he did wake up a few hours ago—" Dr. Cohen saw she only had a second to finish her thought before the enthusiasm she could see building within Huey Rush from her table top screen would drown her out, "but he is by no means ready to be taken anywhere."

"Well, hell, I want to see him!" Huey protested. "This is my ancestor for God's sake!"

"I'm afraid not, I've *just* told him about his son, Junior, and I'm ashamed to say that the fact that he's obviously been dead for hundreds of years never came up in the conversation. So I have no idea how he's going to react if he sees that the son he only remembers as a 10 year old boy is now completely decomposed and has a living descendant in the 25th century."

"He's a Rush," Huey beamed. "He can handle it."

"I'm sorry, but I can't afford to be that cavalier," Dr. Cohen insisted. "As his doctor, I have to be concerned with the possibility of him suffering from culture shock—"

"Culture shock, culture shock, that's all we've been hearing for two goddamned weeks," Huey was beginning to get incensed. "He needs to be with his family, not being poked and prodded at while cooped up in some damn cell and spoon fed bits and pieces about what's happened over the past 400 years! He'll adjust, he'll adapt, that's what human beings have been doing for a million years!"

"So what do you want, Mr. Rush, hmm? Take him home with you as if he was some puppy that caught your eye in a pet store window and have him have a heart attack the first time he sees a Melkotsurakian? My God, he hasn't used his leg muscles for 380 years!"

"So ya'll got my boy laid up like some kind of invalid, is that it?" Huey glared. "Get him walking already, Jesus! Did it occur to you, *doctor* that the longer he ain't walking the worse his legs'll get?"

"Yes, and we were actually going to try and stand him up tomorrow—"

"Good, I'll be there!" Huey snapped.

"Mr. Rush, this is, by all rights, a member of your family." Dr. Cohen blankly stated. "And technically, I can't stop you from coming here."

"'Technically,' you can't stop me from taking him home to meet the rest of his family either." Huey pointed out.

"But I implore you to at least wait a couple of more days before picking him up."

"I will come by this time tomorrow, no ifs, ands, or buts about it," Huey fumed. "He's probably dying of loneliness right now wondering why the hell won't anyone come and get him."

"Mr. Rush, I have to wonder do you care more about your ancestor's mental state or your own curiosity?" Dr. Cohen commented bitterly. "I can understand the media, the scientists, and the historians who can't wait to paw all over him, but you're his flesh and blood. Don't you care enough about him to keep your impatience in check?"

Huey took a deep breath before finally saying, "If you were able to be with your great, great, great, great, great, great, great, great, *great* grandfather, how much patience would *you* have, doctor? I'll see you, and Fred, by this time tomorrow. Computer, end transmission."

CHAPTER SIX

"Looking blackward"

Fred was already awake when Dr. Cohen entered his hospital room, extending his naked legs and then bending them at the knees while lying on his bed. They felt perfectly fine to him, and that point of fact would have been the first thing Fred mentioned to the doctor after she wished him a good morning while commanding the room's computer to turn on its lights were it not for something else that weighed heavier on his mind.

"When did my son die?" Fred glared directly into Dr. Cohen's eyes. "When and how?"

Dr. Cohen set a large tray onto the ground next to Fred's bed that she balanced with one hand while the other had opened the room's door. Its contents protruding from under a small tarp which draped the whole tray, the doctor had to remember not to step on it when she stepped up to Fred and said, "on December 8th, 2080, he was 60 years old. During the late 2070s, when it was found out that HIV was a form of biological warfare, this corporation, G.M.E., General Medical Engineering, or 'Gimme' as they were sometimes called, claimed that AIDS could never truly be cured. GME came up with an inoculation which would immunize people who never had AIDS and kept those same people from *ever* getting it. All the while they would swear that that was the best that anyone could do.

"Well the gay community didn't believe GME and a few even had proof that GME was holding out, so the gay community asked your son to lend his fame towards seeing whether or not there was still a way for those already with AIDS to be cured. And sure enough, between Junior's presence and all the pressure from the gay community, GME was forced to release their previously top secret data to other doctors who were more willing to keep searching for a final cure and not settle for just immunizing people who never caught HIV.

"When the cure was found shortly afterwards, GME became plenty embarrassed to say the least. Which was the last thing they needed because at the time, GME was also pioneering the field of cloning and they needed all the public support they could get—uh, do you know what cloning is, Fred?"

"I do," Fred sighed, "I remember being told about it in school at some point . . . Before the big evacuation in 2006."

"I'm sorry if I brought up any bad memories," Dr. Cohen apologized before continuing, "GME wanted permission to clone *people*, hence their need for the public to be on their side. Their argument was that people wouldn't ever have to work anymore because you could clone all the workers you needed to work a field or mine a cave. Junior on the other hand thought that while cloning a single piece of tissue, an in vitro culture cell for instance, to test different things on would be an acceptable alternative to testing on animals, cloning human beings to be beasts of burden would never be acceptable.

"In debate after debate after debate, Junior led the charge calling for very strict codes of ethics and regulations. Laws were then passed regulating what could and couldn't be done with eugenics that we still adhere to today. Between their AIDS inoculation fiasco and their refusal to develop any other technology that might have been more humane, GME lost billions and went bankrupt, marking the collapse of the last of the big corporations of the 20th century.

"Finally, in the most bizarre drive-by shooting in history, the CEO of GME, Chris Miller, had a nervous breakdown, literally drove by your son in the back of a white stretch limousine, rolled down his electric window, and—shot Junior in broad daylight as he was coming out of a building on La Salle street. If it's—any consolation, I can tell you that Junior didn't suffer, the bullet hit his head so death was immediate. Also, Chris Miller, obviously not being able to get too far in a limo, was caught immediately afterwards and spent the rest of his life in jail."

A long moment of silence passed between Dr. Cohen and Fred Rush. Fred, for his part, had shed all the tears he had in him the night before, so he only hung his head low and drew his knees to his chest. "Please tell me he managed to have children before he—"

"And you wouldn't mind hearing that your son had them by his White wife?" Dr. Cohen brought up. "Because he stayed with Jill Holland until he—until death did them part."

"I don't care," Fred looked up at the doctor, "I just can't stand the idea that—hell, I don't know, I can't explain it."

"I think I understand," Dr. Cohen nodded. "You'd like to feel that a part of him, and even an indirect part of you, survived everything you both went through. If that's the case, I can tell you that Junior did have three sons."

"It's just that I was thinking last night about how maybe there's a Rush that's related to me out there somewhere." Fred, not knowing any better, mistook the look of dismay on Dr. Cohen's face for the doubt she may have had that what he was proposing could be possible. "Now I know that the chances of my last name *not* being bred out by 400 years worth of marriages are slim, but is there anyway that we could see if there was a descendant of mine still around?"

"Let's talk about the possibility of that later," the doctor stammered, "for right now, I want to show you a little something." She then reached for the tray covered with a small tarp she had set on the ground beside the bed. "Remember yesterday when I said I'd bring a couple of things to brighten up this room?"

"A window would do the trick," Fred quipped. "I'd also be able to at least guess what time it is."

"It's a little before noon and it's Thursday, March the 5th, 2410 A.D.," Dr. Cohen laid the tray on Fred's initially unwilling lap. Though confused, Fred proceeded to go along and sit "Indian style" so that the tray wouldn't fall off. Dr. Cohen pulled the small tarp off of the tray revealing a model of a city, except it was unlike any city Fred had ever seen. The architecture was stereotypically futuristic, consisting of sprawling white, pointed towers and amphitheatrical domes, monorails, art deco bridges between the top floors of skyscrapers, and then it occurred to Fred where he had seen a cosmopolis like this before: During the one trip he took to Disneyland in his life when he went to their Tomorrowland exhibit, only this model city boasted far more park land.

"This is what Chicago looks like now, Fred. And this," Dr. Cohen picked up something small and red from the tray the model city rested on that looked at first like a scarab, "this is what our cars looks like, except," she then held the miniature car with her thumb and index finger while moving it in a figure eight pattern over the model city, "now they can be flown as well as be driven. Do you understand?"

"Once again, a window would have told me all of this," Fred fumed, "and if I had a room with a view, I would have something to look at other than a bunch of toys."

"This, *Mr. Rush*," the formality that was in the doctor's voice when Fred first awakened and had since left now returned with a vengeance, "this is to keep you from going into culture shock, to keep you from feeling overwhelmed beyond belief. But if you think that you're ready for all the future has to offer, for all the future has in store for you," Dr. Cohen reached deep into the model city as she spoke, "then take a look at this one last 'toy.'"

Dr. Cohen held up for Fred's inspection a figurine around an inch high of a bipedal creature that looked to be half man, half dolphin. It was naked and the tone of its smooth skin was the strangest mix of blue, silver, gray, and turquoise. "What is it?" Fred asked.

"That, Mr. Rush, is a Melkotsurakian," Dr. Cohen answered very slowly and deliberately. "They come from another planet, one that is completely made up of water, except for its core, of course, and the Melkotsurakians are one of the alien races who are part of the Interstellar Community." She handed the figurine to Fred for him to hold as she said, "they're a lot bigger than that figure. Usually the Melkotsurakians are around six feet tall and 200 pounds and quite a few live right here in Chicago. So you see, Mr. Rush, the future is going to be a lot more complex than you realized."

"This 'Interstellar Community,'" Fred murmured, "are they all *friendly*?"

"They are," Dr. Cohen stated. "Their ancestors have been monitoring our broadcasts off and on ever since they first could tell whether we had the technology *to* broadcast, which would've had to have been around the 1920s. Needless to say, they didn't begin to even *contemplate* making contact with us during the 20th century or during your era. It wasn't until the year 2350, a mere 60 years ago, before they finally decided to make first official contact with us, and even *then* it was on a very trepidatious basis."

"Why would they wait so long for us to get so technologically advanced?" Fred queried. "Why didn't they just move on to some other planet and forget about us?"

"First of all, they weren't waiting for us to get more technologically advanced, they were waiting for us to get *sociologically* advanced," the doctor pointed out, "second of all, there aren't that many planets that can sustain intelligent life. Least, not many in this part of the galaxy, anyway. So since the Interstellar Community already made contact with the few inhabited planets in this corner of the galaxy—most of which make up the Interstellar Community—and not having the capability to go any further than this corner of the galaxy, they must have figured, 'we don't have anything else better to do but wait until these humans get their act together,' and that's what they did."

"What are the rest of them like?" Fred inquired. "Are they ugly, are they—"

"*Scary*, Mr. Rush?" Dr. Cohen anticipated. "Well, who's to say *what* you'll find scary about the future. This is why I'm trying to take things as slow as I have, so you *won't* get scared. That's why I have these 'toys' for you to look at." She dipped her hands into her pockets, pulled out more weird figurines, and set them on the tray that held the model city. One by one, the doctor held up figure after figure for Fred's inspection before handing them to him. "This is a Quidoc, and as you can see, they evolved from octopuses just as the Melkotsurakians evolved from dolphins. In fact they're both from the same planet. This one here is a Jorcon, they're from an all-Arctic world and evolved from polar bears, which is why it looks like a cross between a polar bear and a Viking. And this is a Bastian—"

"He looks like he could be Black . . !" Fred blurted out incredulously.

"The Bastians literally evolved from black panthers into the bipedal form you see here. They're also one of the few members of the Interstellar Community who wear as much clothing as we do." Dr. Cohen sighed and began again, "but they do take them off on occasion, coming from an all-tropical, steamy jungle planet as they do. They are in the habit of stripping on compulsion—as are we in this day and age."

"What do you mean?" Fred looked astonished. "Are you talking about taking off your clothes?"

"Mr. Rush . . . Fred, the main reason why I'm so worried about the potential for culture shock is that you come from an era when random public nudity was—simply inconceivable. I'm not saying that you're some kind of closet Farrakhan loyalist or anything, you couldn't be after all they put you through, but you can't deny that you were under his puritanical, parochial influence for decades. And seeing as how that's the case, there's no telling how you'll react the first time you see someone on Polk Street or in Humboldt Park decide to—strip out of their spandex. It *is* the spring, the Ides of March as they say, and the weather has been perfect for it."

"Doctor, I don't know how I'd react to it, but I'll never know how I would if I'm going to be stuck in this room without a view and not allowed to walk around," Fred handed all the figures of the aliens back to Dr. Cohen. "But I don't think I'll have too hard of a time."

"You say that now, but when you're actually out there—"

"Doc—Joanna, is it? I want you to see something." Fred then lifted the tray with the model city on top off of his lap and handed that back to Dr. Cohen as well. Before the doctor could open her mouth to protest, Fred had whipped off the one white sheet he had been under to one side, planted his two bare feet onto the floor while supporting himself by holding onto the edge of the bed floating thanks to anti-gravity, and let go of the bed altogether. Dr. Cohen repressed a gasp as she saw Fred stand up, albeit a bit wobbly, and walk several steps by himself for the first time in 380 years.

"And look, I'm *naked* too," Fred quipped, "but you're my doctor, so I don't mind. Just the same though, could I borrow some clothes if it's at all possible?"

* * *

The bodystocking that Dr. Cohen gave to Fred was olive green and rustic brown. It also seemed thicker than the bodystockings that she, and everyone else Fred saw while escorted by the doctor down the hall had on. Almost as if the ever-protective Dr. Cohen consciously gave Fred a suit of spandex that would be warmer than everyone else's. The motherly doctor also held Fred's hand the entire way from his room to the exercise room, which was two doors away.

Inside were devices and apparatuses Fred didn't even try to understand but the one thing he did recognize was a tread mill. But when he let go of Dr. Cohen's hand to stagger towards it, she caught up with him and steered him towards a different contraption. "I thought we might start off with this first."

It was a flat bed that protruded from the wall with two blocks which emanated from the wall and were a couple of feet above the bed. Dr. Cohen laid Fred onto the bed and planted the soles of his feet onto the flat of each of the blocks. The doctor tapped a touch-a-matic button on the side of the wall and Fred suddenly found the blocks pushing against his feet, causing his legs to bend slightly at the knee. "Try to push as hard as you can—but not too hard, I don't want to wear you out."

Fred did as he was told and quickly found himself alternating between having one block pushed into the wall and the other block push his foot, hence bending his leg at the knee right back at him, as Dr. Cohen nodded with approval at this alternating pattern.

Fred on the other hand grew weary of this within a couple of minutes and stopped to ask the doctor, "I just thought of something. I only saw a couple of folks in the hall just now, and you said yesterday that health care was free, so how come this place isn't jam packed? You told me that there were 15 billion people now, well, where is everybody?"

"What I said was there was 15 billion in the early 22nd century, it's only 12 billion now. Rather, 12 billion on *Earth*, and another six billion live on space stations, lunar colonies, and Martian colonies. The main reason for that big boom in the 22nd century was because, like I told you this morning, the cure for AIDS was found by the late 21st. And as you can probably imagine, the population went through the roof from people not needing to use a condom during casual sex for the first time since the 1970s.

"Remember I also told you how we went to the Mid East and the Pacific Rim to try and get them to teach birth control? Well, while we were waiting for them to come around, we also took it upon ourselves to build climate controlled cities in the Sahara, the Mojave desert, Antarctica, the Arctic Circle, and by the late 23rd century we even had underwater cities in the Atlantic built.

"Originally, these cities were only going to be political extensions of whichever country had the most to do with its construction. But as time went on, we found that not all of these Island Cities could be built within a specific nationalistic border for geographic, seismic, and other scientific reasons. This was when the concept of a world government was taken seriously for the first time so that the concerns of these nearly autonomous Island Cities could be fairly addressed. Which is why each of these cities are recognized as a country onto itself, so that it can have equal representation in both the World Council, which has a representative from each town/city/etc. *and* the World Committee, which has a representative from each country. This notion of airspace, nebulous borders, and national jurisdiction really came into play when the subject of space stations and colonies came up in the 23rd, but today they're treated the same as the Island Cities insofar as representation goes in that each station and each colony is considered a city and a country onto itself just as the Island Cities are.

"The thing is, no matter how far out they are or how autonomous they think they are, they all have to adhere to our Universal Code of Justice. Which says what can be justified by a country's cultural idiosyncrasies and what can't. Faith healing, ceremonial mutilation, and suicide can be so long as there's mutual, prior consent, whereas caning, torture, and marital rape can't."

"But . . . How is it that you can provide all of these billions of people with *free* health care?" Fred asked, sounding very incredulous. "Let alone free housing, free *food*—"

"We're not allowed to clone or eugenically alter people but we *are* allowed to clone food," Dr. Cohen said as if it was the simplest thing in the world. "Livestock, fruits, vegetables, seeds, plants . . . By end of the 23rd century, in fact, we had completely reforested all of the rain forests that had been cut down. That's how we're able to feed everybody. And as far as health care goes, believe it or not, there's not all that much for us to do these days. Without the brush wars or the drive-by shootings of your time we have less gunshot wounds to patch up. With most of our plants being worker-owned there are less accidents on the job. With more education and understanding between the sexes there are all the less instances of rape and injuries from domestic violence to deal with. So you see, there's more than enough for everybody and everybody has a place in the world. Be it on land, under the sea, or in the heavens."

"That's very poetic," Fred snorted, "and I'll believe it when I can see it for myself."

* * *

Over the next couple of hours Fred had graduated from pushing the blocks into the wall with his feet while lying on a flat embedded in the same wall to the tread mill he originally wanted to try and finally wound up riding on a bicycle immobile from being installed into the ground. By this point his legs were as well circulated as they ever were in the 21st century and he was thoroughly exhausted.

It was at this point when Dr. Cohen brought Fred a meal on a tray like the one she had the model city balanced on, a meal which consisted of clam chowder, a green "Granny Smith" apple, and a tall, cool glass of cranberry juice. Sweating as he was, Fred removed the top of his bodystocking to give his torso some air before eating. As he fanned himself and took a drink, Dr. Cohen sat down on the matted floor next to him while handling one of the miniatures, the red car that resembled a scarab.

"Remember when you were asking about whether or not you had any living descendants? Whether there was someone with the last name of Rush that was directly related to you and your son?" The doctor waited until she saw Fred nod before continuing. "Well, you're in luck. Not only are there still Rushes but there's one family, and one person in particular, who is right here in town and wants to meet you."

Fred's eyes bulged as he gasped, "who? Who is it?"

"Boy, I couldn't make my timing any more cinematic even if I tried!"

The door of the exercise room was only cracked ajar when Huey Rush poked his head inside but when Dr. Cohen's and Fred's widened eyes fell upon him, the peace officer swung the door wide open and strode in.

"You said 'this time tomorrow,' captain," Dr. Cohen leapt to her feet. "Which is to say that you wouldn't be here until around sundown since that's when we talked yesterday."

"I actually said '*by* this time tomorrow,' doctor. Which meant I would be here *before* the time we talked," Huey rationalized.

"You peace officers really do have a lot of time on your hands, don't you?" Dr. Cohen spat back.

Huey ignored the insult the doctor levied his way as his full attention fell upon Fred, who in turn gazed back at him. Fred slowly rose to his feet, never taking his eyes off of Huey as he stepped towards the peace officer. Huey met Fred half way, extended his muscular arms to grasp Fred's shoulders, and squeezed them fondly. Fred tried to take in as much as he could with a single, awed sweep of his eyes until they finally fell on the embroidered name badge on the left breast of Huey's bodystocking which read: Rush.

"I'm Captain Huey P. Rush," Huey said solemnly. "And I'm your direct male descendant. I'm your great, great, great, great, great, great, great, great, great grandson. Or great-times-nine-grandson, for short."

He knew by now that none of what he'd seen or been told was a dream and yet Fred still couldn't quite believe this was one of Elisha's, *little* Elisha's distant descendants. Butterflies the size of pterodactyls were beating their wings in Fred's stomach as he ran a full gamut of emotions ranging from pride to surprise to child-like wonder. Finally, when he managed to calm himself down, Fred looked up at his far flung progeny and said, "this is amazing . . . Absolutely amazing."

"You want 'amazing?'" Huey enthused, "come with me, I'll *show* you amazing! Everybody back at the house is just dying to see you—"

"Hold on, captain," Dr. Cohen stepped between the two Rushes and glared at Huey. "Before you drag him off without letting him know he has a choice in the matter," the doctor then turned to Fred, "Captain Rush here wants desperately to take you home with him, and *technically*," she eyed Huey once more before turning back to Fred, "you can go with him only if you want to, but I would strongly suggest that you stay here with me maybe two more days so that I can tell you more about the future so that you won't be so shocked by it once you see it. I know you're curious, I know that you're a little excited, but Chicago, Captain Rush, and his—your family will still be around in two days time."

In his best sarcastic tone of voice, Huey mocked, "she's right. I'm certain you won't miss a single thing."

Fred didn't notice the dirty stares Huey and Dr. Cohen were momentarily exchanging from being too lost in thought. If he did stay in the hospital, he would be better prepared for all that lay in store for him. Fred looked around at the exercise room and noted that he could only recognize the tread mill, what if he went to this Huey person's house and didn't know enough about 25th century technology to use the bathroom? Unless Huey had a hospital bed/bed pan, something he already had some experience with, Fred would be a 418 year old who had to be shown how to use the toilet.

And yet—it was boring at the hospital, hearing Dr. Cohen go on like some propagandistic tour guide through time about things that went on while he was asleep for 380 years. But there was something about this Captain Huey Rush that titillated Fred, maybe it was the idea of a scion of his being of some great importance just as Elisha was, and there was a whole other family waiting to see him. Waiting— unlike the last family of Rushes he knew who couldn't wait for a young Fred and left him behind in the Lost-Found Nation of Islam. Left him to get beaten in an orphanage, marry an utter bitch, work a job where he had to tell lies for a living, be beaten some more over a novel, and become frozen alive by a madman. No, these Rushes had to be different, these Rushes just had to be better off than the last ones, and whatever the future held couldn't be any worse than what he's already lived through.

"I want to go with Huey, doctor," Fred found himself saying, "I want to see what's out there."

"Alright!" Huey grabbed Fred and hugged him tightly. After letting him go, Huey faced Dr. Cohen and said, "unless there was some luggage he was frozen with, we'll be on our way."

"You might want to put this back on," Dr. Cohen sorrowfully picked up the top to Fred's bodystocking that he had taken off from being sweaty earlier and handed it to him. "It may be the Ides of March but it could still get chilly at night."

"Joanna," One of Huey's deviled eyebrows rose above the other upon hearing Fred call Dr. Cohen by her first name. "I should be alright, and I want to thank you for all your help. I'll try to remember all those facts and figures you threw my way."

"If you start to feel overwhelmed—by *anything*, I want you to go up to any screen and ask the computer to call me just like I ordered the computer in your room to cut on the lights. Or take a bus back here, public transportation's free, remember?" Dr. Cohen hugged Fred herself, marking the first time he was ever embraced by a White woman and his bemused facial expression showed it. "Damn, I haven't even shown you one of our screens, or a hologram, or—"

"I assume you mean a television screen of some kind," Fred tried to sound confident, "I still remember what those look like even though they eventually became nakon in the Nation. I'll muddle my way through."

* * *

One thing that Dr. Cohen did fail to discuss with Fred was the fact that he had been kept on a private, guarded ward of the Loyola University Medical Center from the people in the media and the historians who had been waiting around the hospital off and on for weeks to talk to the 418 year old man. Fred should have anticipated this, the doctor did say when he first woke up that there had never been a man kept in stasis for as long as he had. What he couldn't have expected was for the reporters to look so strange. The dozen or so who ran towards Huey and Fred when they came out of the elevator and walked onto the first floor were all dressed in bodystockings like his or baggier, almost East Indian-looking garb, except that two thirds of the people who made up this deluge had on helmets with goggles and antennae which made them look to Fred as though these people were part insect.

Huey did see this coming, mainly because he saw the reporters in the waiting room when he first walked in, but saw no alternative but to simply ask them when he was recognized as he first entered the hospital not to harangue Fred too much. There were backways that could have been taken by the Rushes to avoid the reporters and historians, but Huey didn't want to have to tell his distant ancestor that they had to sneak out of the hospital that Dr. Cohen didn't want Fred leaving prematurely anyway.

The reporters were civil enough and didn't actually block the Rushes' path, but they did fire dozens of questions at Fred about a variety of things, all of which Fred ignored primarily because he was stunned silent from being so confused despite Huey's vague warnings of such a scene during the brief ride in the elevator. He merely followed Huey's lead out into the parking lot where once the helmet wearing crowd saw neither Rush would say anything for the record after all, they thinned out and dispersed in a manner Fred found surprisingly polite.

There was one individual, however, who knew which car belonged to Huey and was leaning on the side of it with his one of those goggled helmets cradled in one arm waiting for the Rushes to show. "Fred Rush Senior, father to *the* Fred Rush Junior? I'm Adam Hecht, I go to Chicago State, and I'd *love* to do a documentary about you. I would need to follow you around wherever you went, and—"

"Sorry kid, we're going to hold off on talking to anybody until after Fred here gets settled in," Huey tried to sound sympathetic but firm to the college student. Turning down all of this attention wasn't easy for the peace officer who usually was anything except press shy. But besides thinking about Fred's best interests Huey simply didn't want to share his ancestor with anybody else right then.

"But this is the biggest news since Jesse Helms came out of the closet in 2003—"

"Sorry, I wish we could talk, but . . ." Huey shooed the young man away from leaning against the passenger's side so that he could let Fred inside the red Saturn. A moment after Huey had gotten in himself, the car began to hum and let out a mechanical whine as it lifted off. Fred's heart was trying to beat its way out of his rib cage the higher the Saturn rose. Between breathing hard he regularly checked how secure his seat belt was fastened. He dared to look out the window and saw the hospital get smaller and smaller. Soon Huey had the car driving within the sky lanes lit with their floating buoys and flew south high over a point where Salt Creek meets the Des Plaines River.

"Computer, play 'Can You Feel it' by Michael Jackson," Huey beamed as he looked over at Fred with a big grin on his face. As the song in question piped in seemingly from nowhere, Fred's features strained until what he was hearing sounded familiar to him.

"I remember this!" Fred blurted out. "From when I was a *little* kid!"

"Before the Apocalypse, or whatever Farrakhan called it, huh?" Huey asked. "Back when you were still living with your pops, with Senator Bobby Rush. What was he like, you know, as a father?"

To Fred, Bobby Rush was only a man who wasn't there the day his 13 year old son was lost and drowning in a crowd of tall strangers in O'Hare Airport. Bobby Rush was someone Fred's mother, sisters, and brothers were presumably able to rendezvous with and Fred never saw again. "I don't want to talk about my family right now." Fred's eyes fell upon his sock-like shoes resting on the car floor.

"Well, let me tell you about mine," Huey seemed almost oblivious to the frowned expression on Fred's face. "I've been married to a beautiful Hindu gal named Marta for almost 20 years now, I've got a short haired tabby cat named Mr. Whiskers, and we've got one son who's 15 years old named Bobby, after your father."

"Why are you a 'captain?'" Fred asked in an attempt to change the subject. "Are you in the army or something?"

"There hasn't been an 'army' for ages," Huey smiled. "I'm a peace officer."

Fred thought back to the beating the Fruit of Islam inflicted upon him the weekend before his trial for sedition and winced. "You're a policeman?"

"There hasn't been a policeman for ages either," Huey explained. "Or a fireman, or a Marine, or even a bouncer. The peace officers are a combined service. Since there's not as much trouble as there used to be in, say, back in your day, there's no need to keep all those different occupations up and running. But the few times trouble *does* come up, 'who ya gonna call?'"

"The peace officers?" Fred thought he'd respond.

"That's right, we have to know everything that a paramedic knows, everything that a bodyguard knows, and everything that a National Guardsman knows in case something does go down."

"You mean to tell me," Fred began with disbelief in his voice, "that the world is so much at peace that there's only *one* form of law enforcement left in the world—"

"And they're trying to say even *we're* obsolete, yeah," Huey lamented. "Or the anarchists say there's too much of a temptation for the peace officers to abuse our authority. Either way, most folks ain't all that fond of us. Mainly because everyone is taught from kindergarten to automatically distrust authority."

"Have you ever—*beat* people?"

"No!" Huey cried, "*hell* no! Not even the damn ACLU is more schooled in civil liberties than the peace officers! Shit, you can't even get your badge until you get at least a C on a test on the history of police brutality in America!"

Fred saw that he had hit a sore spot of Huey's, even if Huey didn't sense he had when he asked about Fred's father, so Fred decided to bend the direction of the conversation slightly, "so there's not many cases for you peace officers to solve, is there?"

"For the most part, we operate on an on-call, auxiliary basis," Huey answered, "but we still have to be at our headquarters at least 15 hours a week." Huey looked over at Fred from his driving/flying, "what did Dr. Cohen say? That society doesn't need the POs anymore?"

"We talked about how the government runs on LSD," Fred paused a moment to wonder why Huey was repressing a giggle before continuing, "but when I asked her today why wasn't the hospital crowded with people since health care is free she said it was because things are so peaceful there's not much for doctors to do either."

"Ha!" Huey let out a guffaw. "What did she say? 'You peace officers really have a lot of time on you hands, don't you?' Well, you doctors must have a lot of time on y'all's hands too!" Huey squinted at Fred and grinned slyly. "Actually, I shouldn't talk shit about 'Joanna' like that, judging by the way you two hugged back there, y'all might want to get together later."

When Fred saw the Freudian gist of what Huey was implying, he blushed and fumed, "I would never . . . I mean—"

"It's alright, great-X-9-granddad," Huey nodded knowingly. "Seriously, no one cares if you're friends with a White woman or not. This is the 25th century, you can do just about anything you want."

"You must be able to *say* anything you want too," Fred commented. "I haven't heard the word sh—I haven't heard it spoken out loud in I don't know how long."

"Well, don't get too uptight about that sort of thing," Huey cautioned. "In the 25th century we have to let other people do just about anything they want to too."

* * *

It was around three in the afternoon when Huey picked Fred up from the hospital but by the time he had driven/flown Fred on a tour all around 25th century Chicago it was long after dark, pointing out which buildings were the old fusion plants and which were the newer solar power conductors. Fred didn't believe Huey's testimony that nearly everything was recycled in 2410, even half-eaten food is ground up with other wastes into a kind of manure for farming until Huey pointed out that the entire Burbank district, where Fred's temple used to be, was now a string of recycling centers.

As long as light permitted, Fred was able to clearly see the many minute changes Chicago underwent in 380 years. Besides the sky being so much cleaner than Fred remembered, there wasn't a bombed out building in sight. The only incomplete buildings were those in the process of being constructed or renovated. Also, the structures weren't all the stark white or the glassy steel silver that Dr. Cohen's model city suggested, a few of the buildings had commissioned murals and elaborate graffiti painted on the sides of them. One mural in particular made proud tears well up in Fred's eyes when Huey pointed out that the stately portrait along the side of a high school wall of a painfully familiar looking Black man in his early 30s with a mustache and goatee who wore a black beret over his long dreadlocks was in fact supposed to be little Elisha Isiah, Fred Rush Junior.

Cars weren't the only things capable of flight. Fred could see several people with packs strapped onto their backs with fiery exhaust strewn behind them. Huey said they were called rocket jockeys and those who were especially proficient flew in races with obstacle courses for sport. One of the rocket jockeys Fred observed had on one of those camera helmets that Huey had described and edged closer and closer to the red Saturn until he could be recognized as Adam Hecht, the student who wanted to do a documentary on Fred. After Huey angrily fanned him away and cut on his Saturn's sirens as an intimidation tactic, Adam finally veered off and flew into another sky lane.

Huey lived at 666 East 79th Street, which Fred almost found comical: The idea of a cop from the future living in the South Side of Chicago, a neighborhood that was always rough, even under the rule of Farrakhan. But this was the future, after all, and Fred noticed right away how much more clean and suburban the South Side was as opposed to what he recalled it being. Huey's house also looked rather quaint and reminded Fred of the way his looked in 2030 before it exploded. There was a blue Geo Metro already in the driveway, presumably Huey's wife's car, and also something that looked like it could be a bicycle, presumably Huey's son's.

Before Huey could land his car, a filled-out woman of medium height with long, raven hair buttoned up the East Indian Salwar-Kameez she wore as she stepped out of the house and briskly walked the length between the front door and the driveway. When Fred found he didn't know how to open the passenger side's door of the Saturn she opened it for him, reached in, and hugged him tightly. She introduced herself as Marta before Huey had a chance to and led Fred into the house with Huey walking proudly behind them noticing all his neighbors who poked their heads out of their houses to see what was going on.

"You were on the news! I taped it and I've got it playing on continuous loop so you can see," Marta said as she slipped her arm around Fred's so that the pits of their elbows were touching and their arms were linked like two rings in a chain. "How are you feeling? Should Huey have gotten you out of the hospital so soon?"

"Hey, now!" Huey called out in mock offense as he followed behind them.

"Are you hungry?" Marta rhetorically asked. "Dinner's just about ready, I just wish Bobby was back." As she and Fred were about to enter the house, Marta saw her guest motion for his shoes when she said, "you don't have to take them off if you don't want to."

Fred didn't know what he expected the inside of a house from the future to look like but he was ever so slightly disappointed to find out not all that much has changed as far as interior design went in 380 years. There were still chairs, tables, curtains, desks, and a sofa (with Huey's orange cat, Mr. Whiskers sleeping on it), all of which looked different but not quite what Fred would call futuristic. The only exceptions Fred could see were the wide movie screen which was draped across the main wall of the living room and repeatedly displaying—*him,* and Huey, from the shaky point of view of one the reporters from the hospital on a newscast, and something very unusual.

In the corner was a flat, black cylinder that looked like a hockey puck the size of a manhole cover, and standing on top of it was a silent, transparent White man with dark blue hair and a spit curl dangling from his widow's peak in a red and blue bodystocking except, unlike any of the other residents of the 25th century Fred had seen up until this point, this figure had a cape. Then that man simply faded away and was replaced by a smaller, translucent figure with a mask who was making the white stallion he was mounted on rear up and kick its front legs about in slow motion.

"Don't you recognize a holograph of Superman or the Lone Ranger when you see one?" Huey sounded a tad despondent at noticing that Fred was looking dumbfounded at the images being projected by the large black disk on the floor. "I know they were both White, but my God, did Farrakhan *completely* deprive you of any superheroes? Jesus, I see now my work's cut out for me."

"Well it's time for dinner," Marta called from the kitchen, "so don't show him your comic book collection until after we eat."

"You ought to feel privileged, Fred," Huey motioned for his ancestor to sit down at the long banquet table he was pulling up a chair to. "Marta usually doesn't cook, but she figured since you came from a time when all women did was stay in the kitchen—" A balled up pot holder suddenly flew from the kitchen and hit Huey upside the head. Marta gave a wiry smirk after having thrown it and Huey chortled, "actually, she just wanted to whip up something special since I told her you would be coming here tonight and to celebrate your arrival in the 25th century. Now if only that boy of mine was here. . ."

"Bobby just said he'd be out," Marta answered, guessing what Huey would ask next, "he said he'd be back in time for dinner."

Fred leaned over the table and asked Huey who was sitting across from him, "I don't want you to take this the wrong way, I appreciate you taking me into your home and I thank you, Marta, for cooking dinner—in my honor of all things—but . . . Am I to *stay* here? We never talked about, well, where I was going to *live.*"

"Oh, yeah well," Huey's voice suddenly sounded more gruff and more authoritative but jokingly so, "see that mantle up there? Well, we're going to have you stuffed and put you up there, that's what we're going to do." Huey savored the slightly alarmed look on Fred's face before speaking again in a less exaggerated voice. "I'm kidding, Jesus. Fred, you can stay here as long as you want. We got plenty of room, and no, you won't be putting us out. I'm your direct male descendant, you're my 400 year old ancestor, we-are-fam-i-ly."

"He could get a place of his own for free, though," a voice from the front doorway said. When all eyes turned to face it, everyone saw the 15 year old Black youth wearing an East Indian Kurta-Pyjama close the door behind him as he came into the house. Bobby Rush stripped out of the Kurta-Pyjama and hung it on a post by the door revealing a skin-tight, red and silver bodystocking with black trim underneath.

Fred thought he was going to fall over in his chair. Huey's complexion was a light tan and Marta seemed to be a dark, rustic brown and between the two have produced a young man who looked astonishingly like Elisha. Or at least how Fred imagined Elisha looked like at 15 since when Elisha was 15 he was with the underground and his father was lying in Dr. Batala's cryogenic capsule.

Huey eagerly leapt out of his chair to sprint around the dinner table and put his arm around his son's shoulder, "Fred, this is my boy, Bobby Hutton Rush—*the first!*" Huey chuckled a bit before turning to his son. "Or Li'l Bobby as we call him. Bobby, here he is, *the* Fred Rush Senior, in the 400 year old flesh, in person! Can you believe it, boy? This is your great, great, great, great—"

"I know," Bobby cut his father short, "he's my great-X-*10*-grandfather." Bobby then looked Fred up and down, "so you're the Grand X, huh?"

"That's what he's been calling you ever since they told us they found you under Argonne," Huey thought he'd explain, "X is the Roman numeral for 10 and you know they used to give Black Muslims Xs for their last names and you're his distant *grand*father so—"

"I think Fred understands, Huey," Marta stated.

"You never can tell," Bobby amended his mother as he picked a seat at the table which was furthest away from Fred. "The Romans weren't Black so they probably weren't allowed to even talk about them in the Lost-Found Nation. Isn't that right, Grand X?"

Fred was too enthralled by Bobby's resemblance to Elisha to answer, his only response to the question put to him was, "you look just like my son . . . But you're 15, and the last time I saw Elisha he was 10 years old."

"Really?" Huey sat back down in his chair across from Fred. "You think so? I always thought Li'l Bobby here looked just like Cirroc Lofton from *Deep Space Nine*."

"Who's that?" Fred looked utterly bewildered.

"Hold on," Huey turned his attention to the wide screen on his living room and Fred turned around in his chair to look where Huey was facing, "computer, take the newscast you taped off of continuous loop and play any scene from *Star Trek: Deep Space Nine* with a frontal facial view of Cirroc Lofton—and play it in slow motion!"

The image on the screen immediately went from Fred and Huey bustling by helmeted reporters in the lobby of the Loyola University Medical Center to a Black teen amidst a field of stars in an outfit similar to the bodystockings of the 25th century who looked a lot like Bobby, and Elisha. "There, you see?" Huey beamed as Marta passed out plates under everyone's noses. "People say Marta here looks like that actress Salli Elise Richardson, except darker, older, and maybe a little chunkier—oops!" Once again, Huey found himself playfully hit in the head with some soft object by Marta.

"This is the most amazing technology I've ever seen," Fred marveled, "is there nothing we can't see?"

"Actually, yeah, there are limits to what we can do on TV or holographs," Huey proceeded to explain. "In theory, we have the means to take the Rodney King video—you do remember the Rodney King vid—"

"Yes, I do," Fred felt Bobby's stare as he was starting to get just a little tired of everyone assuming he didn't know *any* of the finer points of pre-Apocalyptic history.

"Well, anyway, conceivably we have the special effects technology to completely re-edit the video and make it look as though there were five Black cops beating up on a White guy. Now, if one was doing that for artistic purposes, like it was the plot of a movie or something, that's one thing. But one of the biggest sins you can commit in the 25th century is do something like change the King video like I just described and actually go around passing it off as a legitimate historical account, as if that was what *really* happened, and Rodney King somehow had us all fooled for over 400 years.

"Or warping the Zapruder film to make it look as though Kennedy's head went forward instead of backwards when that last, fatal shot hit him in the head." Huey proudly tugged at the waist of his bodystocking, "'cause if anybody *was* going around doing that, that's where I'd come in, and *I'd* have to take you downtown. Ain't that right, honey?"

Before a smiling Marta could answer, Bobby interjected, "you're not hoping that anyone Orwellianly changes history just so you peace officers can have somebody to lock up, are you, Huey?"

"No, son," Huey shook his head, "Li'l Bobby here is one of those bomb-throwing anarchists I told you about," Huey squinted at his son and grinned somewhat, "who seems to think that we don't need any leaders or hierarchies of any kind. How two liberals like Marta and myself ever came up with someone with as big an authority complex as my boy here, I'll never know."

"I just think that even a benevolent dictator is still a dictator," Bobby picked at his food while he spoke, "and we all know what the first syllable of the word 'dictator' is." The boy then looked up and into Fred's eyes as he said, "I don't see why we need *any* kind of an authority figure to keep folks in line. People these days are intellectual enough and moral enough to keep *themselves* in line."

It was so strange for Fred to see someone that looked so much like the mild mannered 10 year old he once knew have the kind of flippancy Bobby showed towards his parents, while a guest was over, and at the dinner table of all places. The Ostrowski Home for Boys would have tried to break his spirit for such a display while Nayirah would have found the nearest gun and shot the boy on sight. But this wasn't Fred's house, and it certainly wasn't his time, so he thought the best thing to do for now was to try and find out more about this new family of his.

"I noticed Bobby called you by your first name, is that the way it was when you were his age?" Fred asked of Huey.

Bobby fumed silently as if he were seeing something he'd been dreading unfold while Huey answered, "oh, hell yeah. My pappy, John Huggins Rush used to tell us about how when that crooked preacher from the 20th, Jimmy Swaggart was a little kid he had to call his parents 'sir' and 'ma'am' and told us how there wasn't any point to being all that formal because all that formality didn't make Swaggart any less crooked. Swaggart also had to dress in a three piece suit to dinner every night, he wasn't allowed to sing, he wasn't allowed to *dance*, he couldn't even play simple board games like checkers, *or read comic books*, not even the newspaper funnies! Can you imagine? No *This Modern World*?"

"God forbid," Marta quipped, her sarcasm aimed specifically at her husband's pop cultural tastes.

"Fred, the point is Swaggart's folks had him so uptight you could stick a lump of coal up his ass and in two weeks come up with a diamond. And look at what he grew up to be: An adulterer, like Elijah Muhammad, and one of the major contributing factors to the fall of organized, born-again Christianity, mainly because of that repressed childhood of his."

"Imagine a whole society of Black folks being forced to live just like Jimmy Swaggart did, everyday, for the rest of their lives?" Bobby snidely put to Fred, "wouldn't that be horrible?"

Fred tried to ignore Bobby's remark and asked Huey to, "tell me about *your* father, Huey, John Higgins . . ?"

"Huggins, John Huggins," Huey corrected, "he was named after the Black Panther. Just like all of the Rushes after you, in fact." Huey laid a hand on his son's shoulder and squeezed fondly. "Li'l Bobby's middle name is the last name of the first Black Panther to ever get assassinated. Bobby *Hutton* had surrendered after having lost a shoot out with the cops and as he came out of this house unarmed with his hands up they opened fire and gunned him down anyway."

"What did you mean, 'all of the Rushes after me?'" Fred looked puzzled.

"Junior, your son, was raised by Amelia Baines—after they handed you over to Batala, you remember her, of course?" After Fred nodded Huey continued, "well, you were named after a Black Panther who got assassinated and when Baines told that to Junior he changed his name from Eli . . . Shai . . . Isiah Thomas, or whatever it was, to Fred Hampton Rush Junior. Not just to honor you but to honor the Black Panthers, because people in the 20th and 21st centuries had either forgotten about the Panthers or thought they were just some gang due to a lot of bad press and disinformation." Huey didn't notice Fred's eyes fall to the floor at this point ashamed of having been taught the latter while living in the Lost-Found Nation. "So your son made his son, Fred Hampton Rush the Third promise to name at least one of any of the kids he had when he got older after a Black Panther, any Panther, and that's just what he did. Fred Rush the Third named one of his sons David Hilliard Rush, David named one of his sons George Jackson Rush, George named one of his sons Charles Garry Rush; who wasn't one of the Panthers but was a White lawyer who saved their asses more than a few times and Bobby Seale once called him, 'the Lenin of the courtroom.'

"Charles named one of his sons Geromino Pratt Rush, Geromino named one of his sons Mark Clark Rush, Mark named one of his sons Franco Thompson Rush, crazy old Franco named one of his sons Bunchy Carter Rush, Bunchy, my grandfather, named my father John Huggins Rush, and here I am!"

Fred looked exhausted. "I am *not* going to be able to remember all of those people."

"They're *all your children*, Fred," Huey teased, "you ought to remember them!" He then wiped the corners of his mouth with a napkin, reached into a slit in his red, white, and blue skin-tight uniform, and pulled out a thin, green stem almost the size of one's little finger. "Thank you, Marta for the best, damned home cooked Hindu cuisine I've ever tasted. Who's for an after dinner joint?"

Fred wasn't sure what the small green object that Huey had produced was until Bobby took a burning candle from the center of the table and lit the end of the object for his father while the other end was between Huey's lips. After Huey took a couple of puffs off of the smoking green stem, he handed it to Bobby, much to Fred's dismay. "You let your son do *drugs*?"

Huey shrugged, "well, we know Bobby's not *16* yet, but—oh, wait! No, Fred, listen, it's legal now. You don't have to worry about the Fruit of Islam busting down your door anymore, everything's alright."

"If you don't want any, no one's going to force you," Marta reassured Fred as the burning stem was passed to her, "but Huey's right, you never have to be paranoid or feel trapped ever again."

Fred found reminding himself that Baines used to smoke marijuana slightly comforting until it occurred to him that she might have turned Elisha onto it while the boy was under her care. Fred looked at the stem being passed back to 'Li'l Bobby' and thought was that how a 15 year old Elisha would've looked, taking drugs with the rest of the underground while his father was frozen in Batala's cave? Actually, Fred didn't know what to think and turned away from the Rushes to look at the image of Cirroc Lofton still moving in slow motion across Huey's screen.

* * *

Fred didn't know why, but somehow he found himself flung back in time to the Biblical city of Gomorra. Everywhere he looked scenes of wanton debauchery whirled about him until the Earth began to quake beneath his feet and a fissure split opened right between his legs. The entire city, every building and every person, Fred included, fell into the gaping chasm that quickly grew from the crack in the ground and, after a long fall surrounded in darkness, landed one by one into a great river made up of fire. The flames were so caustically searing that all of the buildings immediately disintegrated into ash upon contact but the people of Gomorra weren't treated so mercifully. They all remained intact, despite the "river" burning as it was with a white-hot intensity. And because they couldn't simply vaporize as the buildings had, Fred and the others continued to feel the searing heat on their flesh—for all eternity . . .

Then Fred awoke in a cold sweat in the guest room of his direct male descendant's house back in the 25th century. A guilt-ridden nightmare as blatant as the one he had just escaped from needed no interpretation: Fred had been in the year 2410 A.D. for two whole days and he hadn't prayed once or thought to watch what he was eating for any "impurities." Fred guestimated by looking out of the guest room's window that it was around three in the morning so he staggered into the living room where the black disk on the floor was still projecting holographic images of golden age icons; this time a deformed White man in an early 20th century sailor uniform holding a can with something green and leafy inside in one hand and a corn cob pipe in the other.

Fred tried as disoriented as he was to discern which direction was east while he instinctively grabbed a nearby throw rug to rest his knees on. Fred wound up kneeling near Huey's large, silver screen and, unbeknownst to him, facing the north instead. With his arms bent at the elbows and his hands cupped, Fred began to chant quietly, "I perform the late evening prayer to Allah, the most high. Allah is the greatest . . ."

"I thought *Muhammad Ali* was the greatest," Bobby whispered to Huey while Fred had his back bent to them as they both spied upon their distant ancestor from around the corner of the hall connecting the bedrooms and the living room.

"Hush," Huey admonished.

"Is he going to be doing this every night?" Bobby asked, barely above a whisper. "If so, what if I want to get something to drink in the middle of the night, *like now*?"

"Then we'll just have to wait until he's finished," Huey said so softly Bobby had to strain to hear his father. "And since it'd be disturbing for us to be walking all around him while he's doing this, we probably shouldn't be spying on him either. So let's go back to bed before he notices us." When Bobby proved slow to acknowledge what had been said and continued to stare at Fred, Huey put his hand on the boy's shoulder and quietly reiterated, "come on, let's leave him alone."

CHAPTER SEVEN

"H i s t o r y—n o t *h i s* s t o r y . . !"

Fred didn't have any more nightmares after he fell back to sleep and when he did awake the next morning Fred remembered the computer in the hospital and decided to try something the Rushes had yet to instruct him was possible. "Computer, is there any way you can you tell me what's today's date—and what time is it too?"

Scarcely a moment later a mature, feminine voice articulated, "It is March the sixth, 2410. It is now 6:56 a.m."

Almost seven o'clock, Nayirah would've lynched him for getting up so late, Fred thought. Then again, he couldn't be blamed, since there weren't any air raid sirens acting as "trumpets" blaring the people of Chicago awake every morning as was the case in 2030. Fred wasn't quite sure yet what exactly it meant to be an orthodox Muslim, the only impressions he could discern from having read *The Autobiography of Malcolm X* was that the orthodox views Yacub's History as a myth at best, Muhammad, not Elijah Muhammad was the last prophet of Allah, there are Muslims of all races, and worshipping Allah wasn't an exact science nor was it to be done on compulsion as Farrakhan dictated. And seeing as how Nayirah was no longer around to say otherwise, Fred decided to skip the ablutions, at least until he felt more comfortable with the fixtures of his descendant's futuristic bathroom, and go straight to the morning prayer.

Feeling pretty liberal about himself, Fred also thought as he headed from his room for the living room that he'd partake of two meals instead of just the one-a-day he was used to. And then he saw what he saw as he rounded the corner when he came out of the hall all the bedrooms were along and walked into the main of the house.

Huey, Marta, and even Li'l Bobby were already eating breakfast at the dining table and they were all completely naked. There were smiles on Huey and Marta's faces until Fred let out a yelp out of reflex and quickly averted his eyes. The married couple stood up from where they were sitting and stepped towards Fred while Bobby remained seated and continued to eat.

"I am so sorry," Marta apologized, "we should have realized that even though you're not a NOI loyalist or anything you'd still—"

"It's just that we've been eating breakfast naked whenever it's warm for—hell, I done forgot how long it's been," Huey explained.

Marta turned to Bobby who was still sitting at the table and said, "'C'mon, Bobby, let's go put some bodystockings on."

After a pause in which Bobby tried in vain to see if his parents would leave him be as they went to change, the teen protested, "damn it, what's the point? We'd be putting on *skin-tight* outfits anyway!"

"Bobby . . ." Huey let the stern tone of his voice trail off for effect.

"Goddamn it," Bobby shot up from his seat, stormed towards, and then down the hall, all the while grumbling under his breath, "here we have a tradition we've had for ages and now we have to give that tradition up because of *his* traditions. Where's the tolerance? Where's the diversity . . ?"

"We'll be right back," Huey informed as he followed his wife and son's lead.

Fred tugged self-consciously at his own bodystocking, the same green and brown ensemble Dr. Cohen had loaned him and wondered for a moment if everyone in the 25th century ate breakfast in the nude and if he had just committed some taboo. Did he have a right to upset these people's normal routine because of how unnerved he felt when his eyes immediately fell upon Marta's breasts and nipples? The only reason he came out to the main living/dining room area in the first place was out of reflex since that was the area in his old house where he, Nayirah, and Elisha always prayed. As Fred kneeled on the same throw rug that he knelt onto last night, he resolved that if he was to live in Huey's house he would pray in the privacy of his room from now on. Whether he would actually confine himself to the room every morning until he thought the others were dressed would have to be decided when the time came, Fred thought.

* * *

After Fred had finished praying, he sat at the table alone and sat on his hands nervously, without touching neither the juice in the pitcher nor the bagels on the platter before him, waiting for at least one of the Rushes to return. Huey was the first to, in his red, white, and blue peace officer bodystocking with Marta and Bobby emerging from the hall soon afterwards.

"Fred, we don't want you to ever feel uncomfortable," Marta sat back at the same place she had at the table when Fred first entered the living/dining room. "If you ever do, I want you to let us know right away, alright?"

Fred only nodded and looked up hoping someone would offer him something to eat or drink without him having to ask.

"How come you ain't got something to eat yet, Grand X?" Huey boisterously asked as he slid a glass towards Fred and filled it with cranberry juice. "Help yourself, make yourself at home now."

Bobby rolled his eyes at the idea of his house now being Fred's home also and suddenly announced, "I'm going to school early. I haven't ridden my bike in a while and I want to take the long way there." Bobby then leapt out of his seat and bolted out the door snatching up a satchel that appeared to have books inside as he went.

"See you later, son," Huey called out after the boy and then looked over at his ancestor with a grin. "So, what you want to do today, you old, 418 year old man, you?"

Fred suddenly felt defensive, he shouldn't have expected to be able to stay in this man's house for long without paying some kind of compensation. This had to be the part when Fred would be asked what kind of contribution he planned on making to the household and he already started to brace himself for the possibility of having to find a job in a time he still knew only so much about. "I don't know," Fred tried to sound diplomatic, "I'm not sure what there would be for me do to earn my keep."

"'Earn your keep?'" Huey sounded as though Fred's choice of words both startled and amused him. "What are you talking about? All I wanted to know was did you want to go check out Marta's work, roll with me on patrol, just kick back at home." Huey then shook his head in mock disgust, "Jesus, you've been hanging around them damn bootstrapists too long, 'earn your keep . . .'"

"I think he should come with one of us, at least for today. He'd get lonely if we left him in the house all by himself," Marta offered, "Fred, you don't have to worry about paying any rent, like Huey said last night, you can stay here as long as you want."

"Yeah, Marta's the breadwinner in this house," Huey leaned over to lay his hand on hers for a moment. "Remember I was telling you yesterday how there ain't too much for a PO to do? Well, we used to live in Detroit until crime there got so low that PO HQ relocated me here, and if we had to live off of what little I make being on-call and all, we wouldn't be able to afford a second car."

"These days cars are purposely taxed so they'd be more expensive in order to keep traffic down and to encourage people to take public transportation," Marta thought she'd elaborate.

"So being the gold digging, house husband that I am I married one of the best Interstellar Consulate Counselors there ever was. Now *they* make bank!" Huey laughed.

After blushing, Marta explained, "I work at the Interstellar Community Consulate here in town. Basically I help the Melkotsurakians, the Jorcons, the Quidocs, and the Bastians learn more about the idiosyncrasies of human culture and sometimes I teach people what I know about their cultures."

Fred's mouth gaped, "you get to see these aliens every day?"

"I talk to them with this," Marta produced from a satchel similar to Bobby's she had near her chair on the floor beside her a thin, black wire headset with a single antenna that looked to Fred like something telephone operators of old would have worn around their heads. "Most of them can't speak English, and a couple of them don't even have the vocal cords for it, so I use this universal translator. It translates anything they say to English, but sometimes the words come a lot slower than how they're speaking, and what you hear—sounds—drawn—out—like—this—" Marta smiled as she verbally illustrated.

"So do you want to hear dolphin men and octopus men speak in slow motion or do you want to come fly with me on patrol?" Huey invited. "Today is your day."

"Actually I think I will go with Huey," Fred looked to see the big smile on his descendant's face. "I don't think I'm ready to see two-legged dolphins in person yet."

"Yeah, you damn near had a heart attack when you saw us naked," Huey observed. "Ain't no telling how you'd react to some naked aliens, huh, old man?"

* * *

The one peace officer headquarters in the city of Chicago was located at Hilliard Center on the corner of State Street and Cermak Road. Fred couldn't get a complete view of the building because Huey had landed his scarab-looking red Saturn on the roof. Following Huey down a roof top entrance, Fred began to see other men and women of varying races wearing the same, exact design of bodystocking Huey had on. Except that while Huey's skin-tight uniform was red, white, and blue, the others Fred saw either had yellow-orange-brown, lime-green-olive, or pink-burgundy-violet outfits.

"'Case you were wondering," Huey noticed Fred's bemusement, "rank is color coordinated. The yellow and browns are corporals, the lowest rung on the peace officer ladder; raw recruits. The greens are lieutenants; the next step up. And the pinks are majors; they're higher than me. There's only one other rank, higher than a major, and those are the commanders who wear silver and black."

Fred watched a corporal pass right by Huey as if he wasn't there and nearly bump into him as she did so before asking, "you people don't salute?"

"Why should we?" Huey shrugged. "We just say the rank, the rank then the last name of whoever, or 'sir' when addressing our superiors. If you ain't got nothing to say you don't say anything. If you're talking to someone the same rank as you or below you you can say just their last name, the only thing is you can't say first names while you're on duty."

"And this is the last vestige of military protocol, huh?" Huey wrinkled his brow as he raised both eyebrows and thinned his eyes in observation. "So what should I call you, captain? Captain Rush?"

"The last messenger of Allah will suffice—no, Fred, I'm playing. I'm playing."

Huey and Fred reached the bottom of a stairwell that led all the way to the first floor where a few people sat behind a series of desks with computers atop them. A couple of those people rose from their chairs upon seeing Huey emerge from the stairwell's entrance.

"Captain, Major Byrne wants to see you about Wednesday," Lieutenant Cheshta Castelblanch regretfully informed.

"What does that asshole want . . ?" Huey muttered to himself before turning to his subordinates. "Everybody, this is *him*. This is Fred Rush Senior. Take care of my ancestor while I go see what this damn bastard wants with me, alright?"

As Huey walked off to an office at the end of a long hall on the first floor, Fred found himself surrounded by Huey's junior officers. Lieutenant Castelblanch acquainted herself with Fred right away, a trim, lean, well built man with light brown hair introduced himself as Lieutenant Harlan Kendle, another White man, wild eyed with long hair and a graying beard introduced himself as Lieutenant Bill Breeden, then a young, Black corporal said his name was Tercel Jackson and immediately let Fred know that he did in fact realize he was named after a car.

Everyone was friendly enough but they soon started to barrage Fred with a number of questions and made him feel as though he were back with the reporters in the hospital lobby again. Before Fred could answer any of them he saw something out of the large, clear glass windows and doors which made up the front entrance of peace officer headquarters and led outside to a huge park. Strolling in the distance along a grassy knoll was . . . A Melkotsurakian. It had to be, unless Dr. Cohen's model of one was wrong. Fred found himself slowly drifting from the crowd of peace officers, who for their part were wondering why was he suddenly walking in a trance for their front door.

Fred saw that the creature was moving fast and knew he had to move faster than he was if he were going to ever catch up with it. But the closer Fred got to the Melkotsurakian the more nervous he became and the more he felt as if he were moving in slow motion, like running from something in a nightmare. He wanted to call out to the creature and ask it to stop but even if Fred knew what the polite way to address someone whose half man/half dolphin, his throat had turned hoarse from fear and he couldn't form a sound.

Luckily for Fred, the Melkotsurakian noticed him trying to flag it down and stopped for his benefit. It was an upright dolphin, with arms and legs where fins would otherwise be but had mitten-like hands and feet with no fingers or toes. It was naked and its skin seemed to change color depending on where the light struck its body from a silvery steel blue in the highlights and a grayer blue-green where there was shadow.

Fred inwardly prayed it wouldn't mind him putting his hands on it, to both see what it felt like and if it was in fact real. His hand slowly reached out and made contact with its chest. It felt like a wet, smooth rubber ball, and when it finally registered that this creature from another planet was actually standing before him, Fred thought his brain was going to scream, blow a fuse, and shut down. He only thought this for a moment, and after Fred saw it was still there and hadn't gone away, he began to get over the initial shock of its physical presence.

* * *

"What the hell did you think you were doing, Rush? Clocking that poor boy across the jaw Wednesday night, almost breaking it, and walking out of his house with him slung over your damn shoulder like some great White hunter for all the press to see? Have you finally gone insane?"

Huey could only stand there and take the abuse from his superior, Major Byrne, a pale, balding man Huey always thought resembled a ferret or a weasel because of his long nose, sloped forehead, and lack of chin. "Major, I had no choice but to knock the suspect unconscious. He had a 12 gauge laser rifle aimed directly at my head—"

"You already got the hostages out, *through negotiation*, all you had to do was be just a *little* patient and talk the gun out of his hand. But *no* . . ! You just had to be a big shot! A showboat! A regular Demolished Man!"

"*Demolition Man*, sir," Huey corrected, "the movie you're thinking of is *Demolition Man*."

"Whatever! Don't think I don't know why you've turned down all those promotions, *Captain* Rush! Captain Chaos, Captain Thunder, Captain Whiz Bang, you just *love* being called a *captain*, don't you? Not to mention the *red, white, and blue* uniform that coincidentally comes with the rank of captain, which *must* make you think you're one of those patriotic, star spangled, all American super guys from those halcyon days of the 20th century, isn't that right, Rush?

"I decline to answer that question, sir."

"You can 'decline to answer' all you want, because I already know it's true. Which is why from now on you're going to be known as *Lieutenant* Rush." Major Byrne would've been even more pleased than he already was if he only knew how shaken to the core he had made Huey, who for his part stood perfectly at attention and showed no indication the major affected him so. "How heroic does 'Lieutenant Rush' sound, huh? Will that lime and olive uniform you'll be wearing be awe inspiring enough for you? Oh, come now, *lieutenant*, you've been passing up promotions for the longest, obviously you don't need the money, so surely you won't mind a demolition—I'm sorry, demotion."

"Major Byrne, I know that there's not much for us peace officers to do, but I know you can find something else to do other than persecute one of our best officers."

A tall, stately man with a thick mop of white hair and full beard addressed Major Byrne with a thick, regal Scottish accent as he strode into the major's office with a silver, gray, and black peace officer bodystocking.

"Commander Shelby, I—"

"Save it, major. I don't know why you're threatening this man with a demotion knowing full well I never would've approved such a thing." Commander Shelby then looked down at Huey, who was a full head shorter than he was. "I want you to disregard everything Major Byrne's been saying, son. I read your report and Castelblanch's, I even caught you on the news, and I have to say that under the circumstances there was nothing else you could have done. Nor did you act improperly, good job."

"Thank you, sir," Huey beamed.

"But sir, he's so—theatrical!" Major Byrne pleaded.

"Major, in an age when young men can walk right up to a peace officer, give them the finger, and say, 'get down on those knees of yours that are already dusty from all that hero worship and suck a bloody fart out of my ass you fucking bastard' with total impunity, don't you think it's a good thing that Huey loves being a PO as much as he does? That kind of dedication to public service is rare and should be encouraged. Don't you think, major?"

"Yes sir," Major Byrne answered.

"Now, captain," Huey's eyes sparkled at hearing himself addressed as such by Commander Shelby, "if Major Byrne is finished with you, and it's a pretty safe bet he is, we just got a call from Craig Hulet Junior High—"

"My *son's* school, commander?" A note of concern could be heard in Huey's voice.

"Don't worry, it's not about Bobby, it's that reactionary friend of yours James Finley. He's refusing to send his son Daniel to school again."

"That fool's no friend of mine," Huey explained as he walked the commander out of the office of a fuming Major Byrne and back down the hall to the series of desks where he left Fred with his lieutenants. "I knew *of* him back when I was in college, is all."

"Well, you still know him better than any of us, so we want you to handle it," Commander Shelby smiled. "Just as the peace officers have to act as police officers and military officers we have to act as truant officers as well, huh?"

"Sir, has anyone ever told you you look like Donald Sutherland but you *sound* like Sean Connery?" Huey observed.

"All the time, son, all the time," Shelby patted Huey's back and then pointed out something up ahead. "It seems that there's something going on in front of headquarters."

Commander Shelby didn't recognize Fred standing next to the Melkotsurakian in the middle of a crowd of lieutenants but Huey did, and he didn't know what to think of the spectacle. "I still remember Finley's address, I'll get right on it, commander," Huey assured as he lightly sprinted ahead of Shelby, went through the double glass doors that were the headquarters' front entrance, and when he stopped at the grassy knoll, Huey rhetorically asked Lieutenant Kendle, "what's going on?"

Huey could see for himself that Fred seemed oblivious to all else and was immersed in the process of running his hand along just about every part of the Melkotsurakian's smooth naked body, who for its part didn't seem to mind, so the captain was actually surprised when Kendle responded, "it seems that this 21st century man of yours has met his first alien, sir. I think he's looking for a point of entry."

Whether it was Lieutenant Kendle's Freudian remark or the presence of Huey, Fred snapped out of his stupor and took his hand away from the Melkotsurakian. "Huey! This is an alien! He's from another planet!"

"I know all this, Fred," Huey smiled and sighed. "I've known about Melkotsurakians all my life." Huey then looked about him at his lieutenants, "y'all just been watching this the whole time, watching my poor great-X-9-grandfather make a fool out of himself, and none of y'all bothered to go get a universal translator from inside, huh?"

"I'm sure the Melkotsurak doesn't mind, captain," Lieutenant Breeden said as he stroked his beard. "Everything's copacetic."

"Yeah," Corporal Jackson agreed. "It would've cast a force field and flew off if it did mind, sir."

"It can fly?" Fred asked incredulously before turning back to the Melkotsurakian. "Can you really fly?" Fred tried to illustrate by having its pinball-looking eyes follow as he reared his hand upwards as though he were making one of Dr. Cohen's toy cars "fly."

Amazingly, as if both in understanding and on cue, the Melkotsurakian took two steps back, closed its eyes in concentration, and a transparent, phosphor blue bubble simply appeared around its whole body. The bubble, with it inside, began to bob in the air, hovering three feet of the ground, before finally lifting off and telekinetically flying away.

Fred was completely stupefied, his eyes widened, and his mouth agape when a nearly unimpressed and perhaps even jealous Huey laid a hand on his shoulder, "'c'mon, old man, let's go. I got a call to go on so now you can see what I do on the job."

"How can watching you bust somebody possibly compare to this?" Fred muttered, still looking skyward.

"I can see now you're going to want to go visit *Marta's* work come Monday morning," Huey grinned, "but in the meantime we got to head out."

* * *

En route to the residence of James Finley, Fred was told a little something of the man by Huey. Finley and Huey both went to Chicago State and vaguely knew of each other only in passing with Finley being an upper classman and much older than Huey. Finley wanted to become a lawyer but became extremely disgruntled when lawyers were officially made obsolete and could not receive a degree in his major. Disbarred before having even practiced, Finley proceeded to act as counsel in different trials on an unofficial, freelance basis anyway. He specialized specifically in defending known right-wingers and was willing to travel anywhere an ultra-conservative was being accused of anything. Over the years, Finley went from being considered a moderate to becoming an outright fascist himself, and Huey warned Fred to be prepared for anything that might be seen or heard at Finley's abode on Columbus Avenue and 76th Street.

Finley was semi-retired and spent most of his time working out of his home raising his only son Daniel alone. No one knew what had become of Daniel's mother and there were those who suspected foul play, though these suspicions were hardly ever brought up because no one wanted to be accused of picking on one of the few reactionaries left in Chicago. Huey also told Fred that Finley's somewhat reclusive lifestyle prompted many rumors to be circulated about him from both ends of the horizontal political ideological spectrum: The right believes Finley to be a plant from the left who's in place to make the right look like clowns because he's so overtly right-wing, whereas the left views Finley as a plant from the right whose purpose is to push the envelope by seeing just how much overt fascist behavior one can still get away with in a libertarian socialist democracy where free speech is guaranteed to be unlimited.

Fred was about to ask what exactly did Huey mean by overt when Huey's red Saturn began to land across the street from Finley's house. The first thing Fred could notice, even while the car was still airborne, was the enormous red flag with the white circle and the black Nazi swastika in it waving from a huge flag pole on one side of his front lawn. On the other side of the lawn was a nine foot by five foot cross with a small computer terminal on a podium a few feet away from it. When Huey thought Fred saw the cross, he said, "one time I had to serve this asshole a warrant after dark, he was standing behind that computer panel you see off to the side there, pushing some buttons, right? And viola! The cross set itself on fire! Can you beat that? I hear he cuts it on every night."

Guarding the force field fenced-in front lawn was both a German Shepherd and a Doberman Pinscher, neither of which looked as though they'd been fed recently. The two dogs were barking at the Rushes from inside the force field's perimeter until James Finley himself stepped out of the front door and waved the both of them away with his walking cane.

"Better than a doorbell," Finley chortled as he strolled up to one of the black and gray metal poles lining his walkway and switched the energy off of the transparent force field surrounding his house. "I kind of figured they'd send you, Huey. They must figure I'd be all the more cooperative if I had to deal with a vaguely familiar face."

"You don't know me that damn well, 'James,'" Huey scowled, "address me as Captain Rush."

"Whatever you say, officer, sir," Finley then spied Fred standing behind his descendant. "Is this a trainee?"

"That's *Mister* Fred Rush Senior," Huey answered for Fred.

A gleam of recognition could be seen in Finley's eyes upon hearing Fred's name. "This . . . Is the Nigra Dr. Batala froze! From Farrakhan's time!"

"Watch who you're calling 'Nigra,' Finley!" Huey glowered.

"You're forgetting I know the law, captain," Finley admonished, "which means I don't have to be PC, or polite and courteous as I call it, none of us ever does. And certainly not on my own property."

"Well, we'll be *getting* off your property just as soon as you get little Daniel out here so I can escort him back to school." Huey said through gritted teeth.

"But I didn't know you were going to bring Elijah Isiah himself!" Finley gushed. "I just *have* to show him the things in my collection from the Lost-Found Nation."

"The name's Fred Hampton Rush," Fred corrected.

"Really? That's a shame," Finley shook his head. "'Elijah Isiah' is a nice African name, and since Africa's where you people should all be anyway, you should still go by that."

"Now look," Huey cut in, "just send Daniel out here so I can take him to school."

"But I have to show Eli—Fred the pieces I have from the Nation."

"We ain't got time to go in your house," Huey blared, "nobody wants to hang out with your ass!"

"Actually, Huey," Fred tapped Huey's shoulder, "I would like to see what he has from the Nation."

"Why? Anything he's got we can see in a museum," Huey pointed out, "and besides, you would think you had enough of the NOI after all the motions they put you and Junior through."

"I'm just curious, that's all," Fred looked at Huey and spoke quietly, "most of my adult life I've been told to beware of Klansmen, beware of the White devil. Well, here's a chance to see one's house without worrying about getting killed. Because if you go in with me I know he won't try anything."

"Oh, great," Huey rolled his eyes, "now I'm getting sucked into this too." After fuming a bit, Huey finally resolved, "alright, fine, but only for a minute. And if you do try anything, Finley, you'll wish you could go back in time and keep your parents from meeting. Understood?"

Finley only scowled and nodded as he re-energized the force field surrounding his house, shooed his two dogs away a second time, and led the Rushes through the front door of his domicile. The interior design looked very Nordic and Bavarian with swastikas, crosses and crucifixes, brass busts of wolves and eagles, and portraits of George Lincoln Rockwell, Tom Metzger, and Henry Ford on the wall with a giant portrait of Adolph Hitler in the center of the living room's main wall. In what must have been the den, were photos of Klan rallies and cross burnings next to a library of books including *Mein Kampf, The International Jew, This Time the World*, and *The Hoax of the 20th Century* by Dr. Arthur R. Butz—a title Huey immediately picked up on.

"So what was the big hoax of the 20th?" Huey slyly grinned. "That Farrakhan was some kind of radical?"

"Crack your jokes, captain," Finley sneered then turned to Huey's ancestor, "Fred and I know how great of a man Farrakhan was, don't we, boy?"

"I think I'd know what kind of man he was a little better than you would," Fred responded, "and don't call me 'boy' or 'Elijah' again or I won't answer."

"And then we'll *leave!*" Huey added. "Now hurry up and show all that NOI stuff you were talking about so we *can* leave—with your *son!*"

"It's right here," Finley reached with both hands for the edge of the huge bookshelf and pulled. Huey was immediately reminded of the entrance to the Batcave that Bruce Wayne had used in his manor as the bookshelf spun on a central axis 180 degrees to reveal—what could only be called a shrine. In the center was a portrait of Elijah Muhammad, to the right of it was a photo of Farrakhan and to the left was a photo of a Malcolm X minus his goatee. "Here's a shot of Malcolm before he sold us out," Finley said to Fred.

A copy of *The Final Call* newspaper laid diagonally on a shelf in a tall, airtight, glass box with the headline reading, "Free at last, free at last, thank Allah the greatest, we're free at last!" The photo showed Khallid Muhammad on the steps of the United Nations building holding several official looking documents while flanked by a dozen of his men and date on the paper was February the 21st, 2006.

There was also a beat up copy of the Koran in another airtight glass box opened to the first page which was autographed by Elijah Muhammad himself along with various other knick knacks including a sweat stained bow tie with a placard next to it which read a claim that the tie in question actually belonged to Farrakhan himself. Fred looked on with some degree of curiosity whereas Huey looked about as though he found everything around him suspect. "If you love Farrakhan so much, why is it you got all this stuff hidden away in back of some bookshelf/trap door?"

"He was a Nigra after all," Finley explained, "I mean, I have a great deal of respect for the man, but come on . . ! You can't expect me to parade pictures of a Nigra around for all to see, do you?"

"Why not?" Huey demanded. "'Birds of an ideological feather flock together,' your ilk *did* cut a deal with him way back when. Nuke an entire country, you know, the usual."

"Well somebody had to do something!" Finley began to sound incensed. "That pinko commie Brown was about to start up that National Education Standard bullcrap, requiring sex education and teaching folks that they can't trust the government! God only knows what would have happened if that Nigra Jesse Jackson made it to the White House."

Huey bore teeth in his first genuine smile since he entered Finley's home. "And you know, it's funny, because even after all you fascists tried to do, we still wound up having an education standard after all."

"Ah, yes," Finley exclaimed with overly dramatic sarcasm, "the Compulsory Curriculum!"

"That's right, and speaking of school, where's Daniel?" Huey folded his arms.

"How do I know these liberally biased schools of ours ain't brainwashing my son to be some kind of pinko?"

"First of all, if you know the law as you claim you do, you know that *any* form of brainwashing, deprogramming, subliminal advertising, even hypnosis are all big time felonies. Any one of which'll get you at least ten, uninterrupted years in the pokey," Huey ranted. "Second of all, our school system is *not*, nor has it ever been 'liberally biased.' You know damn well by now that everybody's taught *everything* there is to know about the Klan, the Nazis, the NOI, the Illuminati, you name it! Don't act like you didn't go to school right here in Chicago along with the rest of us, Jesus H. Christ . . !

"You know better, but you're just like the Religious Right, all y'all just plain greedy. They cried, 'we want Christianity taught in schools,' so to make it fair and keep from violating the separation of church and state, folks said, 'fine, we'll teach all religions and all the mythologies too.' And the Christians were the first ones to say, 'no! No!' At first folks thought the Christians were afraid that the teaching of Christianity would be slanted, so folks made doubly, hell, *triply* sure Christianity was taught with a straight face. But that wasn't it at all! And then folks finally realized what it was: The Christians wanted their religion to be the *only* religion taught in the religious classes! They didn't want to share the stage with all the other religions, let alone be taught alongside of mythologies! Like any right-winger, they wanted a goddamned monopoly!"

"Why shouldn't we?" Finley retorted. "It's the best damn religion there ever was!"

At this point Fred looked up from perusing Finley's shrine to the Nation and squinted his eyes at the ex-lawyer. "And what about Islam?"

"Well, I uh," Finely stammered, "you know what I mean! Fred, you know I have nothing but the utmost respect for—look, no one wants things put back the way they were back in your day more than I do!"

"What makes you assume that *I* want things the way they were too?" Fred asked.

"Yeah, Finley!" Huey jumped in. "Don't you realize if the Reunited States of America was still Amerikkka and the Lost-Found Nation was still around you wouldn't be allowed to live in this house! This is Chicago—*Illinois*? Remember how the geography worked back then? If they caught you here who knows what they'd do to your ass!"

"They would only deport me," Finley proudly stuck out his chest and jutted his chin forward as if he had pointed out some great flaw in Huey's argument. "Then I'd be in Aryan Amerikkka, the land that my ancestors fought the heathens and savages off of for me to have, and don't try to claim the Indians knew what to do with all that land! They didn't need *or deserve* all the space they squandered because they were ignorant! They were nowhere nearly as civilized as—"

"They knew the habits, markings, breeding grounds, and seasonal fluctuations of all the edible animals, fish, and birds of their hunting grounds," Huey interrupted. "They knew the external—and some of the less obvious properties of rocks, stones, waxes, gums, plants, fibers, and barks. They knew how to use fire to harden some woods and soften others. They knew how to apply heat to relieve pain, stop bleeding, and delay the putrefaction of fresh food.

"They knew the phases of the moon, the movement of the tides, the planetary cycles, and the sequence and duration of the seasons. They knew wind systems, annual patterns of humidity and temperature. They made intelligent and economical use of the by-products of the animals they killed food. They used leg-bones as—what's the word? *Fabricators*, for stone tools and as pins, the sinews were used for speak bindings, the claws were made into necklaces with wax and fiber that are now sought after by archaeologists the world over and are more priceless than any of that shit you got behind your bookshelf. So tell me, Finley, can you, a proud Aryan warrior, do *any* of the things I just said these 'savages' could do? Can you name *one fucking thing* I mentioned that you can do too, huh, pal?" After a long, silent pause, Huey took a breath for his sermon exhausted him and said, "I didn't think so. And another thing: Even if the Indians didn't know all that they did, it was still *their* land to 'squander' to begin with! Capice?"

Finley's cheeks and neck became red as a beet from frustration over having been clearly bested and searched inwardly for something he could say that would at least allow him to save face in his own house. "Back then, a man could be proud to be White. Now-a-days you're not even allowed to celebrate any White heroes or have a White history month."

"Finley, you know damn well we hold White Power Day every year when Columbus Day used to be where we celebrate people like Upton Sinlcair, Eugene Debs, Mary Mother Jones, General Butler, Jim Garrison, Karen Silkwood, Harvey Milk, Ben Bagdikian, Jello Biafra, Barbara Trent, Matt Groening, Eric Blair—"

"Those folks don't count!" Finley protested. "Those are all leftists!"

"You don't actually expect a state sanctioned holiday to celebrate bastards like Nixon, Hoover, Reagan and Thatcher do you?" Huey remarked. "Now where's Daniel? We ain't got all day."

"They *would* celebrate Reagan on White Power Day if 'the state' wasn't so liberally biased," Finley countered.

"Yeah, yeah, et cetera, et cetera. Now, for the last time, *where's-your-son*?"

"He's not home," Finely stated. "He's at my brother's ranch—*in Texas*."

"Great, just great," Huey paused as he took his thumb and index finger and rubbed the bridge of his nose with them in angst. "Alright, here's what going to happen: I'm going to the principal right now and I'm telling her that Daniel will be back from Texas by the weekend and in class *on time* come first thing Monday morning. If he is *not*, I'm going to personally file charges and I will get my ass a court order to get him out of his uncle's ranch or wherever the hell else you got the boy holed up in. Knowing the law as I know you do, you know you can fool around and lose custody of Daniel if you keep on. This is the billionth time you've pulled this, Finley, you better get your shit together and quit fucking around."

"This is nothing less than the indoctrination of our children," Finley declared. "In 1950, an Illinois congressman named Harold Velde said, 'the basis of communism and socialistic influence is education of the people.'"

"Harold Velde, huh? Funny, that sounds like something Fred Rush *Junior* would say," Huey glared right into Finley's eyes before finally turning to his ancestor. "C'mon, old man, let's get the fuck out of here."

As Huey and Fred both left Finley where he stood to walk back the way they were led in, Finley followed a few steps behind them and called out as he did, "well, I forgive *you* for coming up with a subversive son like Fred Rush Junior, Fred! As you can see, descendants ain't all they're cracked up to be! You come on back by here whenever you get tired of all that political correctness out there! C'mon back and we'll talk about the good old days, you hear?"

* * *

"I cannot *believe* that I spent as long as I did holding a conversation with that sick fuck bastard son-of-a-bitch!" Huey raged as his scarab-looking red Saturn shot along the sky lanes towards Craig Hulet Junior High. "'Political correctness!' Jesus H. Christ—the gall that motherfucker's got trying to imply political correctness is somehow inherently a left-wing thing! He knows *damn* well anybody from the left *or* the right can be PC! Hell, David Duke was being PC anytime he didn't say 'nigger' in public even though you know he wanted to and said 'African American' instead! Semantics, that's all being PC ever was! But the thing that kills me the most is that he had *Wagner* playing in the background! I *love* Wagner! Why did that fuck have to spoil it for me?"

"I'm sorry I asked to see his collection," Fred apologized. "It wasn't even much of one, really."

"Aww, well," Huey waved Fred off with a free hand, "at least you didn't want to go in there because you had some latent urge to be with your old brethren or some such thing. I know you're not that masochistic—*right* . . ?"

Seeing that was a question to be answered, Fred finally responded after an unintentional pause, "oh, yes, of course. I'm an *orthodox* Muslim now. So—what's next for today?"

"Next we go down to Li'l Bobby's school. I'm going in for just a minute so I can let the principal know what happened with Finley and I'm going to drop you off," Huey noted the doubletake Fred made before adding, "I want you to walk home with Bobby today so y'all can get to know each other."

"Huey, I hate to say it, but . . . I don't think 'Li'l Bobby' likes me—that much."

"'Course he does, you're his Grand X," Huey smiled with certainty, "it's just that Bobby's used to being the only child, the only center of attention in the house. When I got my holographic disk he got the same way, thought I was spending more time programming the holograms of the different superheroes and pro-wrestlers it projects than with him, but eventually he started to like the disk. Same thing with you, once he gets used to you being around, y'all will be just like apple butter on grits."

"If you say so," Fred said, sounding unconvinced.

* * *

Even though it was only one o'clock in the afternoon, Huey informed Fred that because of the amount of material one had to study, school was "year round" but it is only four to five hours a day. Huey also explained that from five years old to 10 years old one is in elementary school, from 10 to 15 years old, as Bobby was, one is in junior high, from 15 to 20 years old one is in high school, and after that one has the option to attend college for an additional five years. After which, one may spend how many ever years necessary in some kind of post graduate study to achieve a particular career goal, as Huey had to in order to become a peace officer.

The Compulsory Curriculum wasn't just a moniker James Finley had insultingly labeled the school system of 2410, it was in fact the official title of a program which has been taught to every human being that was born within the past 300 years. Just as Dr. Cohen had described, Fred could see just from Huey leading him down the halls of Craig Hulet Junior High to the room where the last class Bobby had for the day was held that the people of the 25th century took their education very seriously. Unlike the times that Fred could remember when Farrakhan would stripmine the budgets of public schools to parlay all the more money towards the imaginary border skirmishes with the forces from WAR in Amerikkka, Fred saw that out of all the buildings in this futuristic Chicago that his eyes had yet to fall upon, this—*junior high school* was by far the cleanest, most spacious, the best lit, and most acoustic of them all. It even smelled of potpourri.

"I can't even begin to describe how—*lovely* this place is!" Fred was spellbound as he spun around to take in as much of the atmosphere of the school as he could.

"Hurumph," Huey snorted, "I couldn't wait to get out of here when I was a kid." Huey saw in the expression on Fred's face that he needed to explain what he meant. "I was Bobby's age when I went here, which meant in another year I'd be 16 and in high school— which *meant* that I'd be old enough to vote and to drink and I'd be old enough to smoke what I want and sleep with whoever I wanted, no matter how old they were."

Fred's head began to swim, every one of his Muslim sensibilities were struggling to stay afloat because of the thought of 16 year olds being allowed things that were nakon to even grown men in his time. Huey didn't seem to notice how disoriented his ancestor was as he called Fred's attention to a classroom labeled, "Differing Views on Classic Black Icons." "Well, here we are," Huey said quietly, "looks like they've got another 10 minutes or so so just wait for Bobby here. I've got to go talk to the principal, see you when I get home, Grand X."

Before Fred could say anything Huey had briskly darted further down the hall and rounded a corner, removing him from Fred's eyeshot. It would've been unseemly for him to run after Huey, Fred thought, so he might as well try to slip into this Classic Black Icons class without interrupting the lecture so there wouldn't be any chance of missing Bobby, who was now his only way of getting back to the house.

A White woman of around 40 stood in front of the class amidst holographically projected, three-dimensional portraits of various Black leaders and statesmen, most of which Fred was ashamed to admit he could not recognize. She didn't seem to notice or mind that a stranger had just slid into her classroom and continued with her lesson without missing a beat.

" . . . So many in the Black community had disregarded Martin Luther King and had written him off as something of a milquetoast, as a wimp whose dreams and visions didn't substantively speak to the concerns of Black people, particularly the Blacks from the inner city. And we all talked about both the pre-Mecca Malcolm's view and 20th century conventional wisdom's view of MLK Jr. yesterday and the day before. But the facts suggest that MLK Jr. was much more. In a *Playboy* interview with Alex Haley in January of 1965, MLK Jr. didn't only speak of, 'peace on Earth and good will towards men,' as the likes of Elijah Muhammad would have one believe. In the interview, MLK Jr. described an outright socialistic program for both Blacks and poor Whites."

At this point a few in the class oohed and ahhed as if hearing some great revelation for the first time. "I say again, MLK Jr. laid out in some detail to Alex Haley a very precise plan to better distribute the wealth for all people, the interview essentially implied that Affirmative Action would eventually be rendered obsolete if America's wealth had been redistributed."

"So not only was he a preacher but he was a prophet," a teenage girl commented, "'cause it sounds like he predicted how things would be today. The sharing of the wealth, Affirmative Action being as obsolete as lawyers . . ."

"You could say that Susanne," the teacher encouraged as Fred stood fairly unnoticed in the back of the class wincing at the

(Nation of) Islamic ramifications of Martin Luther King Junior, a man who he was taught by The Lost-Found Nation to despise as an Uncle Tom, being called a "prophet," even though it was said without regard by a teenage girl he didn't know.

"As I'm passing copies of the Playboy interview for you to take home to study, let me read you a little of what MLK Jr. said to Alex Haley, 'We must develop a Federal program of public works, retraining and jobs for all—so that none, White or Black, will have cause to feel threatened . . . The unemployed, poverty-stricken White man must be made to realize that he is in the very same boat with the Negro. Together, they could exert massive pressure on the government to get jobs for all. Together, they could form a grand alliance.'

"Now it sounded before as though a couple of you were shocked at the idea of Martin Luther King of all people being called a socialist, but if you look at the way MLK Jr. was covered by the corporately-owned media of his time, you'd quickly find that your cause for shock is not all that surprising. In the 20th century and even in the 21st, most people never knew that he was anything but some country preacher. According to *the* Norman Solomon, whenever MLK Jr.'s birthday rolled around back then, the corporately-owned media always presented a very sanitized King with only one thing on his mind: Bringing down Jim Crow. They always used to repeatedly play the same old footage of him giving the famous 'I have a dream' speech, leaving one with the overwhelming impression that desegregation was all King had ever wanted.

"But they would never emphasize the leftwards slant that the majority of his speeches took which lambasted us as in US for spending more on the War on Vietnam than we did on the War on Poverty. Which just goes to show that King wasn't the moderate conventional history usually depicted him as. In fact, I have a quote right here from 1963 where he had this to say about the once much vaunted middle of the road:

> I must confess that over the last few years I have been gravely disappointed by the White moderate. I have almost reached the regrettable conclusion that the Negro's great stumbling block is not the White Citizen's Councilor or the Ku Klux Klaner, but the White moderate who is more devoted to "order" than to justice, who prefers a negative peace which is the absence of tension to a positive peace which is the presence of justice, who constantly says, "I agree with you in the goal you seek, but I can't agree with your methods of direct action," who paternalistically believes that he can set the timetable for another man's freedom.

"No wonder he got his head blown off," gawked a rather unkempt and awkward looking Black teen who sat next to Bobby, "niggers couldn't say no shit like in the 20th century."

Just then a steady chime signaling an end of not just the end of the school day but the beginning of the weekend sounded from out of nowhere, and the teacher saw she could only hold her students full attention for another few seconds. So what she had left to say she said rather quickly. "Remember, have the interview read for Monday, we'll talk more about how the far left views King, your mid-term papers on the Roaring '20s Black icon of your choice are also due Monday, and for the rest of next week we'll talk about how Hugh Pearson, Elaine Brown, and David Hilliard all viewed Huey P. Newton. Have a nice weekend!"

Bobby turned his head to see his great-X-10 grandfather still standing in the back of the classroom, turned his head back to the front of the class, and silently groaned. Since he was sitting in the front row there was no chance that Bobby could blend with the exodus of kids who were filing out the only door out of the room and slip by Fred. Bobby also knew if he did he'd never hear the end of it because he correctly assumed Fred was dropped off for the express purpose of being walked home. Bobby would have to remember to thank whichever of his parents were responsible for not letting him know Fred would be lain in his lap in advance.

The teacher seemed far more glad to see Fred and acted as though she knew him as well as Bobby did, rushing right up to the 418 year old man and pumping his surprised hand vigorously as she did. "Mister Fred Rush Senior, I presume? This is an honor, a historian's dream! I'm Lori Elizabeth, Bobby's teacher! Oh, this is such a thrill!"

"Why, thank you," was all Fred could think to say.

"I recognized you the minute I saw you come in and I wanted to run right up to you and introduce you to the class, but I didn't want to embarrass you or Bobby in front of everybody!"

"Good call," called out Bobby, still seated at his desk now the only child left in the classroom.

"I have so many questions to ask you . . . Is there any way I could persuade you to come and guest speak in front of the class when it comes time to cover your son?"

"Oh, I don't know," Fred blushed, "I never did like speaking in front of an audience. I mean, I've *done* it, but I've always gotten nervous, and—well, I just wouldn't know what to say."

"Just talk about what it was like living in the Lost-Found Nation. 'Course, you're probably booked till the year 3000, being the world's oldest man and all!" Elizabeth clasped her hands together and chuckled softly.

"Actually, I haven't—"

"Got the time," Bobby cut in as he leapt from his desk and sprinted to the back of the class, "that's right, he *is* busy as hell! Speeches, appearances, tours, oh, he's going to be tied up for a long, long time." Bobby took Fred's arm and proceeded to usher him out of the classroom. "And we're running late, too! Got to be back at the house before moms gets home. Bye, Lori, see you Monday."

Elizabeth was soon left standing in the doorway of her classroom and found herself waving farewell to Fred being whisked down the hall by his distant descendant.

After they were outside the building, Fred followed Bobby to a row of unchained and unlocked bicycles and asked, "you call your teachers by their first names too?" Bobby simply turned his head and shot a look at Fred whom he had his back to while kneeling before his bike to remove what looked like a kind of kickstand. Fred saw this question wasn't going to get an answer so he changed the subject. "Thank you for getting me out of having to speak, I never was very good standing in front of a big crowd. Even if it would be a bunch of children."

"The dumbest of those 'children' knows more about history in general and your own time period in particular than Farrakhan ever allowed you to know," Bobby scowled, "which is exactly why I didn't want you embarrassing me by speaking in front of them. If you got up there and started talking about how a pig is one-third cat, one-third rat, and one-third dog, I would have been a laughing stock."

One thing this Li'l Bobby knew well was how to skate the border between insulting someone and pointing out a matter of undeniable fact, Fred thought. Fred wasn't sure how he should take the boy's comment, mainly because he had made it a life-long point not to be as anal about having children "respect" him as someone like Nayirah always had been. Maybe all the boy needed was a little clarification on where Fred stood on the matter at hand. "I'm an *orthodox* Muslim, like Malcolm X," Fred offered, "I don't believe that a pig is one-third anything."

"Orthodox, NOI, what's the difference," Bobby looked even more frustrated at having to hover his bicycle, which could only levitate a couple of feet off the ground, in an occasional circle to keep from leaving Fred behind who was on foot. "Orthodox is just the lesser of two evils. Both of them are still opiates for the masses."

Fred gasped, and sounded genuinely shaken when he stammered a response to his distant scion's blasphemy. "I—I can't believe you just called Islam *evil* . . !"

"Look, old man, you have the right to believe in that shi— Shiite Muslim stuff and I have every right not to."

"I can't believe that you," Fred was at a loss for words and then finally blurted out, "young man, for all you know Allah just might exist. And if He *does* exist, what are you going to say if He asks why you called Islam 'evil?'"

"Old man, you know all those superheroes my pops is so into? Well, cartoonists back in the 20th century wrote extremely detailed continuities around most of those characters. Entire self-contained universes where the superheroes and all their supporting characters lived in. Including aliens, mad scientists, mutants, etc. Sounds way out there? *No more so than giants from Mars, big headed Dr. Yacub, or Whites being eugenically engineered 7000 years ago*!

"The Bible and the Koran were two *books* written by *men*, just like *comic* books were. Just because a comic book writer can imagine, envision, and conceive of superheroes living on some other plane of existence alongside of ours doesn't mean that they actually *exist* on some other plane of existence. And seeing as how that's the case, it's just as ridiculous to expect Allah to live in another dimension as it is to expect to see Superman when I die."

Fred frowned as he shook his head in disbelief of what he'd just been barraged with while glowering, "and who taught you all this, *Li'l Bobby*?"

"My father," Bobby stated simply, "who else would be so into superheroes as to come up with a Nietzscheian philosophy around them? There's the house up ahead, the door's never locked because, unlike your time, folks don't need to steal now-a-days. Anybody asks, I'm out riding." With that, Bobby hovered away on his bicycle and left Fred standing by himself down the street from the Rushes' South Side residence barely able to recognize the house from it being so far in the distance.

* * *

Because of the shorter work weeks unions in the past fought so hard for, Fred wasn't alone in the house for much longer before Marta finally came home. Fred thought he should mention something about the tone Bobby took with him earlier but Huey had called Marta while they were both driving/flying and had told her about how he had met a Melkotsurakian. She wanted to hear all about that so that's where the conversation was steered until Huey came home and Bobby walked in soon afterwards. When Fred tried to tell him that Bobby had called Islam evil, the vain complaint fell on deaf ears because of the big news Huey had to announce.

"I just got a call in the car from the Alexandrian Time Travel Consortium and they said they had a bunch of folks cancel their reservations this week, and since we've been at the top of the waiting list, we get to go tomorrow, *yeah*! I hope ain't nobody got nothing planned Saturday . . !"

"Are you kidding?" Bobby exclaimed upon hearing the news after having walked in the door right after his father did. "*Hell*, no! I'm fucking *there*, man! Way to go, Hu-*ey*! Hu-*ey*! Hu-*ey*!"

Fred saw that there wasn't any point in pursuing this any further. It wasn't as if Bobby had committed any grave insult, he just let Fred know what his opinion was concerning Islam, is all. And everyone was far too excited over the prospect of actually going time traveling to really care whether Bobby had a bad attitude or not. At first the concept seemed unbelievably mind boggling to Fred, in that in addition to everything else the people of the 25th century could do, traveling through time was within their reach too?

After mulling the idea over in his head while everyone else were going on about *when* they would go to, it made Fred wonder out loud if it were at all possible to go back in time and—save Elisha somehow. But Huey was quick to explain that the laws of physics simply will not allow someone to materialize in the past because just the sudden appearance out of nowhere of some futuristic stranger would be enough to change the course of history and cause a paradox, which in turn could theoretically cause the universe to collapse upon itself. So anyone entering a time portal immediately, automatically, and involuntarily becomes invisible, intangible, and inaudible.

"Like a spirit?" Fred asked as Bobby rolled his eyes unnoticed in the background.

"No," Huey shook his head, "you don't *die*, you enter—*subspace*? And if I remember, subspace acts like a kind of ether that you can push yourself off of so the minute you do go back in time you can literally fly around! Well, *float*, anyway, just like they had Scrooge doing in *A Christmas Carol*. It feels just like swimming in thin air and the whole time cavemen or revolutionaries or famous folks are all passing by—"

"Or passing through you," Marta added.

"Or passing through you," Huey repeated with a nod. "It's better than sex—hey, just kidding, honey! You're going to love it, Fred! Phantom Form Time Travel—like there's any other form of backwards time travel—is the best thing since self-slicing bread. Just kidding, Fred, don't have that yet, just a little future humor there."

* * *

The only point on Saturday the 7th in which the conversation in the Rushes' household did not have something to do with Phantom Form Time Travel was early that morning when a message on the main screen in the living room came over what Huey also termed subspace. According to the type that appeared underneath the image, it was made sometime late Wednesday night, but was delayed because, as Huey illustrated when he instructed the computer to play the message, it was all the way from the planet Bast and his father, John Huggins Rush who had retired there.

"Oh, how I wish I could see this miracle screen to screen right now instead of having to wait for y'all to send a message to me," the image of a Black man in his late 60s, early 70s expressed from behind a desk with a dense tropical jungle behind him. "Even though it was that bastard Batala's doing, I'm sure glad it happened. Fred Rush Senior, my great-times-eight-grandfather, I still can't believe it.

"I'm, of course, Huey's father, John Rush, as I'm sure he's told you about half a dozen times by now and I hope that you're well and you're enjoying everything the 25th century has to offer. After all, your son, my great times seven grandfather, made it all possible, despite all the anarchists' talk of 'the masses being the power behind the throne.' As Captain Kirk once said, 'behind every revolution, there is *one man* with a vision,' and that man was your little Elisha, Fred. I for one want to thank you for giving us him," tears started welling up in John's eyes, "even though I know you never got the chance to see him grow up . . ."

Before Fred knew it, he was rubbing tears out of the pits of his own eyes as Marta stepped up behind him and put her arm around his shoulder. "I'm almost out of time here, we're bouncing this thing off a carrier wave or some such thing," John continued, "I'm about as bad as my son when it comes to explaining tech stuff. I want all y'all to come visit me real soon. Huey, I know you're due some vacation time so you bring my daughter-in-law, my number one grandson, and my ancestor on up here so I can give them a big hug. I love you Fred—"

The screen went blank abruptly and Fred almost sat on a sleeping Mr. Whiskers when he plopped onto the sofa, weary from having cried. "I thought I was going to want to go back and see Elisha but . . . No, I don't want to see him walking around, not being able to see me."

"Then Dealey Plaza it is," Huey enthused, as if oblivious to Fred's mood and state of mind, "c'mon family, let's get in the car. Reservation or no reservation, that line's going to be a 'som-bitch!'"

* * *

Huey took the sky lane above the Kennedy Expressway to get to the Alexandrian Time Travel Consortium, located where Fred remembered the Horizon Stadium being. It took almost a half an hour to find a parking space and the line was just as Huey had described, a "som-bitch." All made up of people with reservations to enter one of the time portals inside, other families, teenagers, and classes on field trips. Then there was the occasional person in the nude either standing in line or wandering about on the grassy grounds, who enjoyed the warmth of the late afternoon for as long as the sun stayed above the horizon and wondered who was the nervous stranger trying to discreetly avert his eyes yet looked anything but casual doing so.

For the next four hours the line gradually edged forward and every once in a while someone would recognize Fred and fall all over him as Bobby's teacher Lori Elizabeth did. They would either ask him to speak publicly or put in an appearance somewhere and each time Fred would either shyly refuse or simply ask if he could get back with them later. One woman wanted Fred's autograph and managed to get it with a bit of persistence while another woman, a scantily dressed White woman, actually proposed to have Fred's baby. Despite Huey's jestful coaxing, Fred refused.

When he wasn't fielding questions about Fred, Huey was giddily describing his past excursions back in time. "Over the years I've seen all my direct male ancestors at one point or another, including you. That's right, you didn't see or hear me, of course, but one time I went back and I was floating right over your head while you were beating the living shit out of this apple tree! God, you should have seen yourself! You sure scared the hell out of this one old woman, dear Lord! What the hell were you doing in her lawn again?"

"It's a long story," Fred mournfully responded.

"Wait—*now* I remember! Junior's first and only spanking! How could I forget *that* story? Jesus! You know, it's a shame no one, me included, ever thought to go back and see exactly what Batala did to you after your trial. Otherwise, we'd have known you were frozen underneath Argonne years ago."

"That's right," Marta agreed apologetically, "everyone just assumed that Batala had killed you in 2030 and I guess no one wanted to know the gruesome details, we're sorry."

"Oh, that's alright," Fred dismissed in a tone no one was sure was genuine or sarcastic, "so I would've only been frozen for 360 or 370 years instead of 380 years, what's the difference?"

"Anyway," Huey steered the conversation back towards his genealogical searches through time, "I've also gone back and seen your father back when he was the Chicago Panthers' minister of defense and caught him right in the middle of a shoot out! Yeah! He got so disorientated he accidentally wandered into a police station! I actually tried yelling, trying to warn him to not go in there, but he couldn't see or touch me, let alone *hear* my ass screaming!

"I also went back and saw that one of our *distant* distant ancestors fought on the side of the Union in the Civil War in one of the all-Black regiments and joined the calvary after the war, a regular buffalo soldier. I've even gone so far back I can tell you, with all honesty, that our clan is one of the few among Black folks that can actually claim that we were descended from a king. Uh huh, it took a while, but thanks to all them trips to the Consortium, I was able to trace our line right down to a guy named Shamba Bolongongo back in *the early sixteen hundreds*!"

"Allah," Fred muttered, sounding very much in awe.

"Shamba was king of the western Congo and was this total pacifist. They called him the King of Peace. They say he came up with a complex and extremely democratic form of government *with checks and balances even* that was divided up into different sectors like the judicial and the administrative—the guy had it going on! And he was your great, great, great, great—"

"Huey," Bobby tapped his father on the shoulder, "you'll be here all night running down the amount of 'greats' on that one."

"Hello, welcome to the Alexandrian Time Travel Consortium," a prim, smartly dressed young girl at the front entrance of the Consortium addressed the Rushes as they finally reached the head of the line.

"I know you must be tired of saying that by now," Huey jibed.

"Actually, my shift just started, but I'm certain I'll be tired of it before I'm through," the girl smiled, "the last name that's on the reservation?"

"Rush."

"Rush . . . Party of four—yes, here you are," the young girl said after checking the readout from a computer panel set on a podium in front of her. "Step right in, pick any one of the free portals, and have a nice trip."

Inside the honeycombed dome that was the Consortium was an enormous circular room with four structures that reminded Fred of the metal detectors that one walked through in 20th century airports only much larger. Two of the four portals were hollow like those detectors of old in the sense that you could walk right through them and all you saw on the other side was the adjacent wall, the other two both had images displayed within the portals' frames. One image showed a being foraging about amidst some foliage who looked as if it were half man and half ape. At first Fred thought this might have been one of the Interstellar Community and then it occurred to him that this had to have been one of mankind's primordial ancestors. So much for Yacub's History, he thought. The other portal displayed bombs bursting in mid air and indicative sound effects could be heard from each of the portals. By each portal sat or stood a team of technicians, all hunched over computer panels connected to the portals either scanning for a particular point in time or maintaining the smooth operation of the apparatus itself.

Bobby immediately took Marta by the hand and led her to one of the portals without an image between its frame while Huey had to lead a nervous Fred to the other. "Now remember what I told you in the car, it's just like swimming, OK? If you start to sink into the ground or something, *don't panic*. Even though we'll be intangible to everyone and everything else, we'll be able to touch ourselves and I'll be able to grab a hold on to you if need be, got it?"

"Got it," Fred meekly said without any inflection in his voice.

"Alright, let's get this party started," Huey turned to one of the technicians, "let me get Dealey Plaza, Dallas, Texas, November 22nd, 1963, 12:27 p.m., and put us right in front of the book depository, ground level."

"A man who knows what he wants," complimented one of the technicians, "here you go . . . Dealey Plaza, one of our most requested hot spots. Knock yourself out, Huey P."

"'Huey P.?' You do come here a lot, don't you?" Fred observed.

"You'll see why in a minute," Huey could barely restrain himself.

Suddenly Fred could no longer see the wall behind the portal. Instead of open space between the portal's frame as before he now saw a crowd of White people, all in very old fashioned clothing, standing in anticipation in front of a very drab looking building. One brunette White man in particular with a dark jacket and light t-shirt looked somewhat familiar to Fred.

"We haven't even stepped in yet and we already have a great shot of none other than Lee Harvey Oswald himself standing right outside the book depo just as the motorcade is about to drive by!" Huey enthusiastically pointed out. "And the FBI had the unmitigated gall to claim that that was some loser named Billy Lovelady standing out there! Ain't *that* a bitch?" Huey looked over at Fred who was taking a couple of steps away from the portal if anything. "You're not scared, are you, old man?"

"No, of course not," he lied.

"Then let's go," Huey reached back and grasped Fred's hand, "we only have 15 minutes with these things." Stepping right up to the mouth of the portal with Fred in tow, Huey bent both knees as if he were about to leap forward and cried, *"vaya con Dios!"*

* * *

"Mr. President, you can't say that Dallas doesn't love you."

"No, you certainly can't," John F. Kennedy answered the rather innocuous statement made by the wife of Texas Governor John Connally from the back seat of his limousine as it, and the motorcade it was a part of, rounded the corner of Main and Houston Streets.

Meanwhile, invisible to all save themselves, Huey and Fred Rush were already levitating above the heads of those on Elm Street waiting for the motorcade to come their way so a view of the President of the United States might be caught. Fred felt like screaming, he was actually floating in mid air! He could still feel Huey's hand hold onto his, just as his descendant said would be the case, but nothing could prepare him for the shock that he felt when the Rushes sank low enough for Fred's foot to accidentally brush by a short, middle aged man holding a super 8 camera and his foot passed right through the camera wielding man's head without fazing the man in the slightest.

Upon seeing this, Fred did scream, and Huey sardonically said after managing to quiet him down, "they can't hear you, Grand X, but you're yelling right in my ear so I can hear you just fine!"

"Sorry," Fred apologized.

"Now come on, we've got the murder of the 20th century to catch!" Huey pointed with his free hand, "you see that fence behind that grassy knoll? That's where we got to be, so let's go!"

When Fred saw Huey kick his legs about like he was a frog underwater to propel himself forward, the 418 year old man emulated. Fred was surprised to see how fast the two of them were moving and wondered how much faster the obviously more experienced Huey would be flying if he didn't have to hold onto his ancestor's hand. Before he knew it, Fred was hovering alongside Huey over the fence in question and hidden behind it were three men. One seemed older than the other two and had on a pork pie hat and a buttoned sweater while the others had on sport jackets. The youngest looking of the trio had on a pair of jeans while the other two wore baggy slacks and they all wore collared shirts. The one thing they did have in common was that they were all armed. The oldest and the second oldest both had long, high powered rifles each with scopes on them to look through while the youngest was armed with only a pistol, spoke quietly into a walkie talkie, and looked as though he were with the other two to stand guard in case anyone tried to walk up behind the trio from the direction of the railroad yard to their rear.

"There, you see?" Huey pointed out the men to Fred. "The two men with the big guns? The one with the hat is E. Howard Hunt, the other one is Frank Sturgis, and 'youngblood' in the back is Dan Carswell, least, that was the name he was going by back then."

"Allah, be merciful," Fred put his free hand over his mouth and gasped, "can't we stop them?"

"How, *Ebenezer*? They can't see, hear us, *or* touch us," Huey reminded. "Besides, even if we *were* somehow able to defy every law of nature and materialize right here and now, you actually think three *White* men from the *CIA* in nineteen *sixty* three are going to listen to a couple of *niggers in spandex*? *Hell*, no! They'd blow our fucking heads off!"

Fred looked behind him to see the motorcade round the corner of Houston and Elm Streets. In the next couple of moments, as the clock within the giant Hertz sign atop one of the buildings on Elm Street read 12:30, Fred was just able to make out which seated figure was President Kennedy. Because as shots could be heard both behind and to the side of the motorcade, Fred could already see Kennedy's head and body jerk to and fro as a man holding a cowboy hat seated in front of him started to bustle about. "Allah! Someone else is already shooting him and these two haven't fired a shot yet!"

"Well it ain't Oswald, that's for cocksure," Huey explained, "those are the other two teams, one in the depository and one in the Dal-Tex Building. But for the final head shot that did him in—" Huey turned Fred's head forward again to see E. Howard Hunt and Frank Sturgis lean their rifles over the edge of the fence, take aim, and simultaneously fire.

Fred screamed again as shots were fired just below his feet, bobbed his intangible body about in fright, and flayed his arms around until he unintentionally let go off Huey's hand and sank into the grassy knoll. The screams became deafening when he found himself still able to breathe and move despite being completely submerged in the ground from not making any effort to levitate himself. The only things Fred could see all around him was dirt, roots, and various stones and pebbles immersed in the Earth.

Then Huey's hand reached into the Earth and pulled his screaming ancestor out of the ground by the shoulder of Fred's bodystocking. "You told me you knew how to swim!" Huey sounded rather irritated. "Do like you would do if you were treading water! Hell, dog paddle even! It ain't that damn hard!"

Fred stopped screaming and starting kicking his legs furiously. Soon, Fred was able to suspend himself in one place in the air alongside of Huey. "What did I tell you, huh?"

After he caught his breath, Fred looked behind the fence and noticed that all three of the men had left the scene of the crime. "They got away!"

"Not quite," Huey corrected, "they just ran and hid in a boxcar on one of the tracks out there and a guy named Lee Bowers thought they were hobos and called the cops on them. The cops came, snatched their asses out of the boxcar, and marched them to the police station. On their way there, a bunch of photos were taken of them which is how we recognize the fuckers as the Plumbers from Watergate."

"So they were arrested," Fred said.

"No, old man!" Huey shook his head. "It was a CIA coup d' etat, remember? They never even *made* it anywhere *near* the police station! Motherfuckers like that are so slick they can walk in the rain without getting wet! Oswald got framed for it, even though he never fired a shot, thanks to the biggest Orwellian snow job since—since Kissinger's eulogy at Nixon's funeral, and it wasn't until we got the National Education Standard in the 21st century 'til they finally got around to making sure it said so in the history books! It *would've* taken until we discovered time travel in the 24th century if it was up to those twin disciples of Josef Goebbels: Gerald Poser and Dan Rather."

"I was fired from my job as a dictator because I told my boss it didn't make any sense that one shooter could have caused all the wounds this Kennedy died from."

"You're boss wasn't named Earl Warren, was he?" Huey saw the confused look on Fred's face and decided to, "forget it. Let's just fly back to the portal, our 15 minutes of fame are probably almost up anyway. Ain't that a bitch? We go back in time and we forget our watches!"

* * *

Huey knew enough to step out of the portal and probably should have told Fred to do the same, for when Fred tried to fly through the portal as he had been flying over the skies of 1963 Dallas, he fell flat on his face upon becoming solid again the instant he came through the portal's frame. The harm was only to Fred's pride as he looked up to find Marta and Bobby standing over him while Huey lent him a hand up to his feet. "So, how did you enjoy your first trip back in time, Fred?" Marta politely asked.

Fred thought back to the shots being fired around him, having sank into the ground, and lied as to not seem ungrateful, "it was very nice. How was your trip? Witnessing the first contact we made with aliens and all?"

"Actually, I wanted to go back to the point when *I* first met an alien, but they won't open a portal to a period of time unless it was over twenty years ago because of the potential temptation of folks going around ethereally spying on people still living being too great. But we didn't go back to see *any* aliens at all," Marta looked down at her son, "because at the last minute Li'l Bobby insisted on going back to see Jesus."

"Really?" Huey spoke up. "Wanted to see how much the old boy looked just like Prince from his second, self-titled album with that long hair riding naked on that Pegasus, huh?" Huey turned to Fred, "he was a Palestinian *Jew*, you know. They were that dark back in the day."

"Not just that," Bobby responded, "I wanted to see how Jesus supposedly healing folks was just a *legend*," Bobby made it a point to accentuate that particular word, "that got started because of him being this Ghandi type and going around defying those anal purity laws."

Fred looked to Huey as if he were the only one to know, "what was a 'purity law?'"

"Let's get out of these people's way first," Huey seemed to be the only one who noticed that the next group of people, a couple of them still naked though it was almost seven o'clock at night, were trying to politely get past the Rushes and to their respective portals. Once the Rush clan followed Huey outside of the Phantom Form Time Travel Consortium, Huey explained, "first century Judaic culture had these hell of strict purity laws that said who you could eat with, talk to, and even who you stand by. Oh, yeah, it was pretty bad. At first they were supposed to be to keep Jews from being assimilated by foreigners, but when all the financial grief from the Romans and the Jewish temple tithes hit, the purity laws got intensified to the 12th power.

"So when it says that 'Jesus touched the sick and they were healed,' it's actually symbolic for him going around pissing people off and going against the system by touching folks like lepers who were branded outcasts. Jesus really stirred up the shit storm in his day, a real rabble rouser. *In fact*, as it turned out, the only thing the Bible did manage to get right about Jesus' life was when it was talking about the time when he went off, took a big stick to that one temple, and started busting up all these religious trinkets they had for sale. About like the way one of my favorite wrestlers, Rowdy Roddy Piper fucked up *The Flower Shop* from the WWF with his crutch back in the fall of 1986 or the way *you* fucked up that apple tree."

At that moment, the expression on Fred's face looked as though he was a child of the 20th century who *had* just been told for the first time that professional wrestling was anything but "real." "So I suppose that—I imagine you're going to tell me that thanks to time traveling it's been discovered that the prophet Muhammad himself was really just an ordinary man and—"

"That's right, Grand X," Bobby cut in.

"Bobby, just a *little* tact, OK?" Marta reprimanded. "Fred, I know I shouldn't be quoting an atheist at this point but right after he become the first man to turn down the Nobel Peace Prize, Jean-Paul Sartre said that Muhammad used other religions that already existed in his time, that all that's basic to the Koran was the work of Jews, and that the Koran was just a transformation of Judaism carried out by some Semitic tribes. I was a philosophy major in college. Anyway, all we're trying to say is—"

"Do you think Islam is evil, *hmm*?" Fred cut Marta off indignantly.

Huey fielded this question, "no, we don't think Islam is evil *per se*, we just don't think it exists." He then turned to his ancestor with a look of curious concern. "Who told you it was *evil*?"

Just then, Bobby glanced at his wrist watch as if to escape having to make eye contact with anyone who might indict him for what he had said to Fred the day before. The watch's animated display read it was exactly 6:59:59 p.m. and the millisecond that changed to seven o'clock, the sound of two notes being played on an old fashioned trumpet could inexplicably be heard blaring clearly from all directions.

Huey, Marta, Bobby, and Fred looked all around them, as did everyone else within sight. For they all heard it, and no one had the slightest idea where the first trumpet blast, or the second, or third, fourth, and fifth was coming from. Something made Bobby think to look at his wrist watch again when the sixth and seventh revelry were sounded and he noticed just as the seventh trumpeting played itself out the display read exactly 7:00:07 p.m. After the seventh, nothing else of the kind was heard, beyond the "echo" of the sound of trumpets playing that a few still had ringing in their heads for some time afterwards. "Man, what the fuck was that?" Bobby exclaimed, not sure at first if anyone would hear him if he spoke any softer.

"I have no idea, son," Huey shook his head, "before we go home, let's head back to the Consortium and see if any of the technicians or anybody in line knew what the hell that was." Huey shooed a couple of persistent and unusually large horseflies away as he led his family away from heading in the direction of the parking lot of the Horizon Stadium and back towards the Phantom Form Time Travel Consortium.

For his part, the sound of the trumpets reminded Fred of the little pair of horns that always used to be illustrated in the top corners of every cover of the one newspaper the NOI would allow in the Lost-Found Nation, *The Final Call*, and wondered . . . No, Fred thought, he'd better not bring up what crossed his mind at that moment, especially not after the discussion he just had with the Rushes concerning the validity of religion. Besides, Fred didn't quite believe the silly little thought he entertained for that instant himself.

CHAPTER EIGHT

"It's *my* house, and if you don't like it..."

Mr. Whiskers, Huey's orange, short haired tabby abruptly leapt onto the Rushes' table either looking for a morsel from its family's Sunday morning breakfast, some attention, or both. Fred was about to shoo the cat away when Huey obliged it with a stroke across its back and broke a bit off of his onion bagel for the feline to eat. Yet another incremental instance in which Fred felt reminded, in at least a minuscule way, that this wasn't his house or his era.

Everyone seemed tired of talking about the sudden, still unexplained blaring of trumpets from the night before, and the clothed-for-Fred's-benefit Rushes had already went on about how novel it was for a Black Muslim to take part in their tradition of having a Jewish brunch every Sunday of bagels, lox, shmear, and fruit-filled knishes, so to take his mind off of how unwelcome he was feeling, Fred decided to bring up some things he had been wondering since he came back from his first trip back in time. "Huey, can one travel into the future?"

"No," Huey shook his head, "at the risk of sounding all philosophical and shit, the future hasn't been made yet, so there's nothing to go to." He then wagged his finger about as if trying to hold Fred's attention so nothing else was said until his mouth ceased to be full and he could speak again, "but besides going into the future the way *you* did, on ice, you can take a ship up into space, fly near a black hole or something without going into subspace or faster-than-light drive, come back, and you will have only aged a few years while centuries have passed down here. That's what this one movie that came out Friday at the Oliver Stone Holoplex is about that I want to take you to tonight called *Beyond the Beyond*. It's a sci fi flick."

"Well, thank you," Fred almost smiled, "I can't remember the last movie I went to, Farrakhan made them nakon so long ago," Fred didn't notice that Bobby had smirked or shook his head at what was just said and continued, "but another thing I was wondering was, well, I take it the Kennedy assassination has been researched and studied in depth ever since time travel was discovered, when did you say? The early 24th century?"

"Yeah," Huey confirmed, "seeing as how we went decades being lied to by the government and CBS news."

"Well, where were all the other 'phantoms' of the different historians and scientists and such who must have went back to that same point in time before we did? We should have seen plenty of other people from this time floating around back then, except it was just you and I out there."

Huey put a hand to his forehead, let it slide down his face, and groaned, "oh, I wish you hadn't asked something so hard to explain,

Jesus! OK, I don't suppose you ever heard of an alternate reality, have you? No? Didn't think so. Alright, back in the 2030s, did Massa Farrakhan ever allow y'all to entertain the 'science fictiony' notion that somewhere just beyond the pale there was a timeline alongside of ours, almost like ours, except in it you could see what the present day would've looked like if Hitler won the war or if the South won the Civil War?"

"Yes, as a matter of fact, we used to wonder all the time how things would've turned out if the Lost-Found Nation was never founded."

"Well, alternate realities *do* exist and there probably *is* a reality out there somewhere in which WAR and the NOI were never funded by corporations. Anyway, there are an infinite amount of alternate realities and 99.9% are not as historically and dramatically severe as 'what if Hitler wasn't so stupid as to think that the A-bomb was Jew science and came up with it first.' In fact, most of them are pretty damn benign. All you need in order to create an alternate reality is to be faced with a split decision, flip a coin, come up to a fork in the road, any instance involving at least 60/40—preferably 50/50 odds. If you flip a coin and it comes up heads, there's an alternate reality out there where it came up tails that diverged from the focal point of you having flipped that coin. Otherwise everything else, historically speaking, in that reality is just like ours. Verbatim, except for the difference of that coin toss, of course. If you roll a die you automatically create five other alternate realities, so you can imagine how many alternate realities get created every day thanks to Las Vegas alone.

"So we went to November 22nd, 1963, right? And they've no doubt already sent somebody back there, right? Well, they can't keep sending folks down the same reality, otherwise you'll have 'phantoms' running into one another able to tell each other what's going in their future, depending on what point in the 24th or 25th century each 'phantom' went back to 1963, and then you'd have a major paradox. To keep this from happening, the technicians you saw with their heads buried in those viewfinders? They scan with these dimensional sensors for a 'virgin' alternate reality," Huey looked to Marta, grinned, and then turned back to Fred, "they find a November 22nd, 1963 that no one has gone to before and *viola*. They'll look back to, say, November twenty *first*, 1963, find some loser playing craps, and say, 'we sent professor so-in-so to a 11/22/63 in which Joe Blow here had rolled a four instead of a five. Now we'll send those Rush boys down a 11/22/63 in which Joe Shmoe rolled a six instead of a five.' The key is to make sure Joe Shmuck or that craps game ain't had nothing directly to do with the Kennedy assassination and it would also help if the nigger didn't live in Dallas either. Which ain't that hard anyway, 'cause like I said, there are infinite alternate realities out there to choose from. Hell, a day in Vegas alone, you know . . ?"

"And the assassination occurs in the *exact same manner* in *each* of these realities?" Fred sounded incredulous.

"Oh, hell yeah!" Huey declared. "Obviously in a reality where Malcolm discovered the Communist Party in jail instead of the NOI the assassination is naturally going to look a *little* different, and in a reality where Hitler won the war the assassination probably never would've happened in the first place, but like I said before, 99.9% of the alternate realties are *not that historically severe*. The assassination in the reality where Joe Whoever rolled a four is going to go down, or *did* go down rather, exactly like the assassination in the reality where the nigger rolled a five. Right down to JFK's head snapping back and to the left," Huey said as he nodded in the affirmative, "back and to the left. And while the non-severe realities are the ones that we study, we ethereally visit the more severe ones that show 'what if the Confederates won,' but usually just for fun."

Marta slowly clapped in a very comedic fashion, "bravo, Huey, bravo. Except that I don't think it's just the Consortium's technicians who keep the realities alternating with every trip you make so the past selves of 'phantom form' travelers don't meet in the past of the same reality and cause a paradox. I think it's *nature itself* that automatically changes realities with each trip. But then, science and physics always were your worst subjects."

"Yeah, well, enough of this treknobabble," Huey stood up from his seat at the table, "Fred, me and the misses haven't been alone—in the *daytime*—for a while now, you know? And we need you to do us a favor: We need you to stay here while we go flying and babysit Li'l Bobby."

Simultaneously, cries went up from both Bobby and Fred, "*what?*"

"Bobby, you're not 16 yet," Huey reminded his son, "so legally you're still a child, and you know *I* of all people know the law."

"I know this," Bobby protested, "that this ain't nothing but another cheap attempt of y'all's to try and leave me alone with—*Grand Wizard X* here so we can, 'get to know each other better.'"

"You can call it whatever you want," Marta remarked, "but if you leave the house while we're gone Fred will tell us, and you *won't* get to go to see *Beyond the Beyond* with us tonight." Marta also instructed Fred as she followed Huey out the front door, "we won't be gone long, Fred, but if you need us, turn to the big screen over here and ask the computer to contact us. We'll pick up the call on our car phone."

"See y'all," Huey called out as the door shut behind him and his wife, leaving Bobby and Fred staring across the table at each other. After an uncomfortable pause that probably wasn't actually as long as they thought, Bobby was the first to speak.

"Look, old man, I—*apologize* for calling your religion evil. Not because my mom said I should last night, but because since there's no God, there's no universal moral measuring standard for what's 'good' and 'evil' anyway, so neither of them really exists as we *traditionally* understand them. How the hell did Hamlet put it?

'There is no good or bad, only what we think is so?' For example, a right-winger says communism's evil, a left-winger says Nazism's evil, the right thought Ralph Nader was a supervillain and Oliver North was a superhero, the left thought Rush Limbaugh was a supervillain and 'The Hunter,' Simon Wiesenthal was a superhero, so in the end, good and evil are only *relative terms* because there's no God to supersede with some measuring standard and say who's wrong and who's 'right.'

"So who's to know for sure the good from the bad? You don't, so each man has to decide for himself is the left 'good' and the right 'bad' or visa versa, which is what they mean when they say that man's predicament is being blessed and cursed with the imagination the animals don't have," Bobby motioned to Mr. Whiskers still lounging on the table, "to assign meaning and purpose to the random chaos that the universe always was. 'Cause the universe doesn't have any meaning except the one our cultures and perceptions impose on it."

Fred's head hadn't spun as fast as it had after listening to Bobby since the last time he heard Baines from the underground rant and rave about politics and the Nation. Even though Bobby's "apology" didn't sound like one so much as it sounded like a platform for his beliefs—or lack of any, Fred was still impressed by the boy's prodigal eloquence. "In all my life, I have never heard of a 15 year old boy using as many big words as you do. Do you have a high IQ?"

"IQ tests were banned ages ago because they were discriminatory," Bobby scoffed, "I'm a philosophy major just like my mom, that's all. Least, I'm going to be next year when I start picking my college prep courses in high school."

For the first time since he laid eyes on the boy, Fred didn't feel as threatened or offended by Bobby as he usually did. Despite the fact that he was clearly what the Muslims used to resentfully call an atheist, a Dahri, this distant scion of his, who looked *so* much like little Elisha, was smart and obviously "going places." Feeling a paternal pride swell within him, Fred tried to lean forward and lay a hand on top of Bobby's from across the table. "I guess we are getting to know each other better."

Recoiling slightly, Bobby stood up from the table with his eyes squinted in suspicion, and looked as though he was going to leave. "You know, all that talk about school just made me remember something I've got to go do—"

"The report that your teacher said was due tomorrow?" Bobby frowned at Fred remembering what he heard Lori Elizabeth remind everyone at the end of her class. "The one on someone Black and famous from the 1920s? Who's it on?"

Bobby sounded as though a secret was being interrogated about him. "Garvey."

"*Marcus* Garvey?" Fred's eyes lit up, the one figure in history the Lost-Found Nation extolled that he had any respect for. A man who came to America from the West Indies with nothing and rose to become the owner of his own fleet of ships. Fred vaguely recalls having done a report on the man back when he was in the Ostrowski Home for Boys and remembered working on the report as being one of the few pleasurable experiences about his stay there. "I'll help you work on it, I used to help Elisha with his homework all the time."

"I don't think so," Bobby stated simply.

"Why not?"

Should he tell Fred the truth, Bobby thought to himself in that instant. That he never had to run anything he did for school by his *parents* let alone some stranger, who was surely looking to be more of an authority over him than his parents ever were? No, Bobby thought, instead he'd give Fred an answer that had a historical basis in fact that the 418 year old man could not possibly dispute. "Don't you think your understanding of Garvey might be just a *bit* skewed after having come up the Lost Nation with all the censorship and book burnings that were going on back then? When we used to live in Detroit and I used to go to Michael Moore Elementary, I was already being tested on things that would've gotten me *killed* if I had said them out loud in your day. Thanks, but I don't think I'll be needing your help, Grand Dragon X."

As Bobby turned to leave for his room, Fred was beginning to feel offended by the boy again but not nearly enough to become indignant. Instead, he merely asked with a semblance of calm and a forced smile, "could I at least *read* what you're doing? Maybe *I* could learn something, seeing as how us Negroes were kept so 'ignant' back in the dark ages."

One of Bobby's eyes squinted while the eyebrow over the other raised as he was deciding internally how to proceed. There was no doubt that Fred was being sardonic, but it *was* a request and not some anal, parental demand, after all. "Fine . . ." Bobby said hesitantly. "Hold on."

Fred suppressed the feeling of authoritative dominance that came over him when the ever-defiant Li'l Bobby went down the hall to his room to retrieve the report for him. The feel couldn't be submerged very well, however, because this was the first time Bobby had shown any amount of respect for him since they met, for when Bobby emerged from the hall with a couple of bound sheets of paper, Fred's arms were folded and his legs were crossed while siting in the same chair that he's been sitting in since brunch. Bobby paused in his walk towards Fred to notice this Henry the Eighth posture that he had subconsciously adapted before finally giving him the report.

"A lot of this is based on the work of Lawrence W. Levine who contributed to a book put out by the University of Illinois Press here in town called *Black Leaders of the 20th Century*," Bobby explained, "I don't suppose you've ever heard of him?"

Fred only looked up to glare at the boy standing over him for a moment and then turned to the report. As Bobby folded his own arms, Fred picked the top of the second page at random to read.

In 1924, Garvey responded to an overture made in good faith by the Worker's Party, a socialist organization, by saying, "we belong to the Negro party, first, last, and all the time." This nearly unwarranted fear of the poor White working class being inherently and helplessly racist, coupled with his affinity for Booker T. Washington's self-help dogma made Garvey's domestic policies extremely right-wing. Garvey was a constant foe of socialism and called anyone who believed in it, "a group of lazy men and women who desire to level all initiative and intelligence and set a premium on stagnation." Garvey claimed socialists and trade unionists were, "more dangerous to the Negro's welfare than any other group at present." Though he didn't come right out and say it, this quote implies that Garvey thought a unionist was more of a danger than the Ku Klux Klan itself, who at the "present" Garvey spoke of were lynching Blacks by at least the dozens. Garvey extolled capitalism as "necessary to the progress of the world" and declared that anyone who went against it were "enemies to human advancement." He also said, "the only convenient friend the Negro worker or laborer has, in America, at the present time, is the White capitalist." Garvey's trickle-down theory was that since the White capitalist's one desire was to increase his profit margin, he would inevitably want the cheapest labor at his disposal—i.e. the Blacks during Garvey's "present time." So Garvey goaded the Black laborer to, "keep his scale of wage a little lower than the White until he is able to become, through proper leadership, his own employer."

"What really makes me sick when it comes to that Napoleon hat wearing, Fat Albert-looking bastard," Bobby expounded, his passion causing him to slip out of his usual intellectual composure and into the same colloquial mode and tone that his father, or Amelia Baines for that matter, would use, "was how niggers in the 20th century went on and on about him like he had something to do with something. He cut deals with the Klan just like the NOI did *and* he was a bootstrap capitalist to boot. *Sickening.*"

"But—you didn't mention his shipline," Fred stammered, sounding very disillusioned, "what about his line of boats . . ?"

"Man, fuck some damn boats!" Bobby exclaimed. "The guy was a fucking fascist! He was going to ship all us niggers off to Africa and make every Klansman's wet dream come true! Thank God they finally busted his fat ass for tax evasion and keeping double books before he could do it, like they would any greedy, hoarding son of a bitch!"

One of Fred's eyebrows raised above the other as he smiled, almost triumphantly. "'Thank *God*, Bobby?'" The catching of what Fred was certain was a major Freudian slip out of the boy was just barely enough to make his Muslim sensibilities forget that a 15 year old child was cursing up a storm with the mouth of a sailor. Especially since everyone seemed to swear in the 25th century.

"Just because someone says 'holy mackerel' doesn't mean they think fish are divine," Bobby rationalized, "it's an expression, a figure of speech, a term of endearment, nothing more. Now if you'll excuse me, Grand Imperial X," Bobby bowed in a mock curtsy, "I've got to go put the final touches on this paper."

* * *

Just as one had bicycle lanes to pull over on the sides of the roads of the 20th century, the sky lanes of the 25th also had sub lanes that one could pull over and park/hover. Huey's red Saturn pulled over to the side of the sky lane directly above Bachelor Grove Woods, a name Huey found so romantically ironic that he decided to make the park in question the spot where he proposed in the spring of 2394 to the woman who now sat beside him in the front passenger seat of his car.

"Computer, play 'After the Love is Gone' by Earth, Wind, and Fire, 'What You Won't do for Love' by George Benson, and 'How Deep is Your Love' by the Bee Gees at about half volume in any order continually." Huey notified his car's on-board stereo system while he gazed into his wife's eyes the entire time. "I call this selection my 'puppy love compilation.'"

Marta grimaced in chagrin slightly while the first notes of "What You Won't do for Love" were being piped in and said to her husband, "if it's not Hanna-Barbera cartoon characters or superhero revival movies like *Popeye* and *Flash Gordon*, it's this—'slow dance on-the-new-kid-in-town's first date' music. You have the biggest late 1970s/early 1980s fetish I've ever seen in my entire life."

"You got a point, make it," Huey grinned slyly.

"For a change, let's pick something a little more . . . I know, computer, play—'Slave to Love' by Brian Ferry."

After the first strands of the song played over the car stereo, Huey pursed his lips and nodded in approval. "I *like* it, very metropolitan," Huey then turned to Marta, "let's get in the back seat and cuddle."

The scarab-like car, suspended in mid air as it was due to its motor being left on, bobbed a bit as the Rushes both crawled into the back of the red Saturn. "Remember when we first met?" Huey asked, knowing full well Marta did.

"We were stuck in a turbo shaft during that blackout with that Jorcon I was giving a tour of the city to," Marta recalled, "one of my first assignments for the Consulate."

"It was raining like a big dog that whole day, that fur of his was soaking wet, and that bad boy stank like a motherfucker!" Huey guffawed.

"He couldn't help it," Marta managed to keep herself from laughing. "All that shaggy fur—"

"Ooooh! Big, ol' polar bear-looking motherfucker sitting there smelling *hell* of funky!"

Marta began to giggle despite herself, "he did smell like a wet dog on a hot day, didn't he?"

"You damn skippy! It was so funny, the two of us being the only other two in the turbo lift, and we're sitting there trying our damnedest not to crack up. The whole time—what was his name? 'Gowl Rahn?' Standing all erect, trying to look all proud like he ain't funky, like he's some proud Jorcon warrior."

"He *was*," Marta reminded, "*and* he had that big blade of his with him. If we had started laughing there's no telling what he would've done."

"Ahh, he wouldn't have done jack shit," Huey waved his free hand dismissingly while the other was holding onto his wife, "I would've whupped that nigger's ass if he tried anything."

"*Anyway*," Marta said, sounding somewhat dismissing herself, "the minute they finally got us out of the turbo shaft we left poor Gowl Rahn in the dust when we both ran out of there like we had to relieve ourselves something fierce and met around the corner to get a breath of fresh air."

"And to laugh our fucking asses off!"

"That's right," Marta agreed, "and then we just stood next to each other, in that doorway, in the rain—"

The repeated sound of something pelting the exterior of the red Saturn interrupted what Marta had to say. Both Rushes looked to see what exactly the barrage was being caused by and found that their car, and the surrounding area, was in the middle of a hailstorm despite the time of year.

"What the hell—" Huey blurted out. "It's March the 8th for God's sake! Weather's not cold enough for this shit!"

"Huey, feel the window! The hail's *hot*, not cold!"

Huey put his hand to the window as his wife had done and suggested, and sure enough, wherever the hail had struck the window that particular spot felt warm to the touch.

"Well if this ain't a mood killer I don't know what is," Huey remarked, sounded very deflated, "let's go back home before this shit fucks up my paint job or one of my sirens. Damn!"

* * *

Fred forgot how long he sat alone in the dining room stroking Mr. Whiskers back, thinking about and trying to bring into focus everything that's happened to him and his life in the past few days. What finally startled him out of his retrospective stupor was the sudden, soft churning of what looked like a sleek cross between a fax machine and a form feeding printer. In back of it was a stack of white paper folded "accordion style" that provided something to be printed on during the seemingly self-activation of the apparatus, which had the brand name "Paper Boy" labeled on it and was sitting next to the front door. Even though the rest of the Rushes didn't think to point the paper boy out to Fred because they took it for granted since it's such a common staple in 25th century households, he was still surprised that he hadn't noticed the paper boy on his own, let alone notice it cut itself on until now.

Fred walked over to see what was being printed and watched until enough of the first sheet made it's way past the printer's tinted visor. He held the sheet along the "teeth" of the visor, tore it off along its perforation and saw that what he had in his hand was the front page of the Sunday edition of *The Chicago Tribune*. The headline was in large, boldfaced lettering and read, "connection between Elijah Muhammad and JFK assassination revealed!"

Fred skimmed through the story underneath that told of how a team of time traveling historians just uncovered how a White Texas businessman named Hunt was a financial contributor to the Nation of Islam who worked through one John Ali of the Nation during the early '60s and that Malcolm X's fabled "chickens coming home to roost" speech on the Kennedy assassination was actually censored by the NOI on orders from Hunt because of the references that made connotative correlations between the assassination and the CIA's removal of third world figures like the Congo's Patrice Lumumba and Iran's Muhammad Mossadegh from power. As strange as the story seemed to him, what Fred found even stranger was how he couldn't bring himself to feel shocked in the least by what he read.

A much smaller headline on the bottom of the front page spoke of the still unexplained seven trumpets that were heard not just over Horizon Stadium but at several other locations all across the city. Before any more could be read, Bobby had pushed his way past Fred towards the paper boy asking, "did the labor section come through yet?"

"*Labor*?" Fred found what Bobby had asked for so curious he forgot that the boy had never said "excuse me." "There's a *business* section, but there's no such thing as a 'labor section' in a newspaper, is there?"

"The labor sections in our papers is bigger than the business sections 'cause there's more to talk about in a labor section than in a business section," Bobby impatiently explained as he stood by the paper boy waiting for the section he wanted to be completely printed. "Nobody wants to hear about folks on Wall Street playing games with other people's money anymore, not that there's even *been* a 'Wall Street' for ages . . ." When the last page of the labor section finally made its way through the printer's toothed visor, Bobby held the pages of the section that were folded like an accordion in one hand and used the other to tear the last of the section off the rest of the *Tribune* which was still being printed.

"Once upon a time—*your* time to be exact, old man, the corporately-owned media used to always center on race whenever it wanted to get people off its back by fooling them into thinking that it tackled all the hard-hitting issues of the time and that they still had a free press after all. This way people either wouldn't even know that the media was corporately-owned or question why it should be if they ever did found out.

"As it turned out, they were concentrating on race, and *never* on *class*, so that minorities would be divided, put too much focus on their racial differences, fight one another, and not address what they all had in common: That their asses were all poor. Which is why they didn't have a labor section in your day, because the corporately-owned media wouldn't have been corporately-owned for long if they didn't continue to distract people and keep them butt stupid by *not* having one. If people back then had a labor section and were all the smarter thanks to it, like they are now, the media back then would've been worker-owned," Bobby ran the labor section past Fred's eyes briefly for his inspection, "like it is in *my* day, Grand Master X."

Fred let the front page fall to the floor as he squinted and glared at the 15 year old who stood before him. It wasn't anything the boy said, *per se*. With the exception of calling Islam evil, something that still seemed only partially apologized for, nothing Li'l Bobby said was ever *technically* insulting in any way. But just the same, it was always the snide tone of voice that Bobby only used when addressing Fred, no matter what the topic at hand happened to be, which couldn't be ignored any longer.

Now Fred finally felt frustrated enough to find out exactly why this distant scion of his had such a problem with him. "What did I ever do to deserve this level of hostility? 'Grand,' 'Imperial,' 'Wizard,' 'X?' I'm not *that* obtuse, I have a good idea of what you've been trying to imply, that I'm just as bad as the Klan somehow. Is that why you have such a bad attitude towards me? Because I used to follow Farrakhan and Farrakhan dealt with the Klan?"

Initially, Bobby was taken aback by Fred's sudden directness. But when he saw that this was *the* opportunity to clear the air once and for all, Bobby sounded off. "Do you really want to know? Alright, I don't want you thinking that you have any say over me. I may be 15, and you may be 418, but that does not mean that you're any kind of a parent or even a relative to me. You're *way* the hell too distant of a relation to exact any kind of parental authority over me. And to be perfectly honest with you? I'm afraid that you're going to start coming up with a bunch of parochial rules for me to follow. Rules I've never had to live by a day in my life and have gone just fine without.

"You already see that we eat naked, 'cuss' at whim, use first names, wear hats indoors, and you can see that we *like* the way we live. You can also tell that we, and the rest of the world's, been living like this ever since—well, ever since we got rid of the last way of living: The way of living *you* were used to, *Fred*! Well, *I'm* telling you right now, what's good for the goose *ain't* going to be good for the gander, so don't try saying what was good in your day is still good today, because obviously it wasn't! Just ask an Australian! The bottom line is I am *not* going to start changing the way I live or the way I speak just to keep you from feeling that 'the youth of today are going downhill' or some such thing!"

"If 'the youth' of the 25th century idolize my son as much as I think they do, then they ought to know that my Elisha was the kindest, sweetest, most polite little boy there ever was!" Fred countered. "And that 'Junior' would never take the tone of voice that you've been taking with me!"

"Oh, nigger, *please!*" Bobby took a step back and paced about as if circling for the kill. "Don't *even* try to turn Junior into some positive male role model for us 'directionless' kids to follow! They tried to turn Malcolm X into some kind of a Mr. T figure just so that lazy parents who didn't want their kids around anyway could use him as a carrot-on-a-string-on-a-stick to keep their kids in rapt attention. Hell, Junior *warned* folks against that very sort of thing!

"And another thing, I don't give a fuck who I look just like, *I'm not your son,* and I will never *be* your son, so get over it! But I'll tell you what *you* are! You are a *guest,* a guest in *my* house, nothing more! So don't start acting like I'm you're son and you're my father, because I already *have* a father! And as you can see, he's bringing me up just fine!"

"What I see is a child without one shred of discipline and without one iota of decency and respect for his elders!" Fred's teeth gritted underneath pursed lips and reddened cheeks as he puffed and panted a bit before speaking again. "At first I thought it was— *arrogant presumption* to think that everyone needed to be guided through life by something bigger than themselves, by a higher power. Well, I see now that *something* ought to be in place to keep at least *the children,* if no one else, from going *completely* berserk!"

"If you're talking about religion you can forget it! Nietzsche said anyone who believes that religion is needed needs to be sincere and say that what they really mean is that they want something that'll *police* people! Well, back when we did let religion police people, people got burnt at the stake!" Bobby then darted to the side of the living room wall, snatched a copy of the King James Bible off of a nearby bookshelf, held up it for Fred to see, and wagged it about. "You see this piece of shit? In *Language and Politics,* Noam Chomsky said this is 'one of the most genocidal texts in our literature.' Is this the sort of thing you want everyone to pattern their lives after?"

"I've never heard of *Language and Politics,* but I *have* read the Bible," Fred put his hands on his hips and scowled. "Have you ever bothered to read it?"

"*Three times,*" Bobby growled, "and it didn't do a damn thing for me! But I can tell you it did plenty for the Amalakites! You remember the Amalakites? The folks God ordered His chosen people to wipe out?" Bobby flung the Bible to the floor before Fred's feet. "Chomsky said, 'people wouldn't be enjoined to do that sort of thing today; they wouldn't want to attribute that to their God today. That's the mark of some sort of moral progress.' Which is exactly why we don't need the Bible *or* the Koran any more! In fact, we've been so morally progressive over the past, oh, *418 years* or so, it's a wonder we ever *did* need them!"

"What's all this damn yelling going on for?"

Fred and Bobby both turned from facing down each other to notice that Huey had returned and was standing in the front doorway with his brow furrowed in an annoyed expression. Marta walked in just as Huey was waiting for an answer to his question and asked a couple of her own, "what's going on? Why is the Bible and the newspaper all over the floor?"

"Your son is the rudest, the most unruly boy I have ever known!"

"I'm not 'unruly,' you just want me to live by *your* rules, that's all!"

"Now just hold on!" Huey held his hands up to silence them both. "I take it you guys have been arguing over religion, right?"

"All I was trying to say was that we're not going to change the way we've always lived around here just so that Grand Poobah X here can feel more at home!" Bobby looked to his parents while pointing in Fred direction.

"I know how much of a Stalinist you can be when it comes to religion, Bobby," Marta chided, "and I can imagine that you've been expressing more than just your fears of Fred overstepping his bounds and ordering you around."

"Well, just tell me once and for all that he's not going to be put in any position of power over me."

"Bobby, you know that Fred is just a guest here, you know that Huey and I will always have the final say in how things are run in this house," Marta assured, "but at the same time you're not supposed to get into shouting matches with our guests either."

"Fine, I won't *shout* at him any more," Bobby looked Fred in the eyes for the first time since his parents returned home, "but that don't mean I have to—*love* him or anything."

Fred's jaw would've dropped to the floor were it not attached from not being able to comprehend what he was hearing all around him. After a pause, Fred's features slowly twisted in disbelief as he said, "I know that this isn't my house, and I know this is supposed to be an AD, anarchist democracy, or whatever, but I cannot understand how you can just let this boy get away with saying any old thing that he feels like. I cannot believe how spoiled and unprincipled you people have let your son become."

Huey was not in the mood for this sort of exchange. The scalding hail that neither Bobby or Fred seemed to notice because of their arguing had stopped, but not before it took the very toll on Huey's car that he had feared. Both of his sirens did in fact get broken and the scars that the hail left on the sides of his red Saturn would take a while to repair—seeing as how Huey would have to pay for the damage out of his own pocket because the Saturn hasn't been official peace officer property since he bought it to own for himself many years ago. All these things, plus having to cut short the quality time he wanted to spend alone with Marta, put the usually happy-go-lucky Huey P. Rush in a rare state. "First of all, *Fred*, my son is *very* principled, which is why he's as passionate about the issues as he is. Second of all, I told you before, if Bobby acts like he's threatened by you, it's because he's been the only child for so long, and . . . Well, you entering the picture is like—"

"When you first bought this holo-thing-a-ma-bob?" Fred pointed to the holographic disk still projecting transparent holograms of golden age superheroes Huey described Bobby being jealous of two days earlier en route to the boy's school.

"And also like him having to deal with a little brother first being brought home from the hospital." Huey finished his thought. "I was the oldest in my family so I know what that's all about."

"Well, I'm not his little brother, I'm a grown man and I deserve some respect!" Fred then pointed angrily at Huey, "in fact, if anybody is acting like they're his little brother it's you! It's no wonder that he acts the way he does, seeing his father go on about— *fictional, fairy tale characters* and *storybooks* as if he were his age!"

"Fred, don't go there," Huey warned, "I'm not in the mood."

"I don't care! It's bad enough that both of you let this boy walk all over you, but when he walks all over me all you do is slap him on the wrist?"

"What would you have us do?" Huey demanded. "Take him out back and rough him up a bit? All he did was talk a little shit and we just told him to take it down a thousand. And that's all we needed to do!"

"'We' nothing! Marta was the one who did all the talking just now while you just stood there and said nothing! And according to Bobby, it was Marta who told him to apologize for calling Islam evil, not you!" Fred took a step closer to Huey. "Then again, that could be because you really *do* think Islam is evil. Friday, Bobby said that you taught him books like the Koran were no more valid than superhero comic books. Is it because you think my religion is evil, Huey?"

Huey filled his chest with air and sighed in frustration, "I'm not going to lie to you, Fred. Next to greed, I think some of the worst crimes in history have been made in the name of God. All religions are guilty of their fair share of atrocities, but it always did seem to me that Islam was the worst of the bunch. In nineteen eighty-eight—not *seventeen* eighty-eight, not *eighteen* eighty-eight, but *nineteen* eighty eight, a woman in Iran was accused of having an abortion when it turned out all she had was a miscarriage and they burnt this woman at the stake, *alive*, in 1988 A.D.

"Yeah, some of our finest works of art and architecture was inspired by religions, but in the 25th century people are taught the good with the bad. And if Li'l Bobby's been centering on only the bad, then that's a one-sidedness on his part and it'll be his loss if he doesn't learn to deal with it someday. But if all he's been doing is pointing out some natural born facts, I am not going to punish my son for telling the truth."

"Then neither one of you are fit to be his parents," Fred seethed, "and you're not man enough to be his father."

There was a hushed stillness in the Rush living room as all the Rushes looked to one another to see who would be the first to break the silence. It turned out to be a very incensed Marta. "I could see if Bobby had physically hurt you in some way, or had stolen or broken something valuable that belonged to you. But we've known about his, how do you say, Huey? 'Mannish' mouth—of his since he came into the world, and I don't care how bad his manners were, you had *no* right to say what you just said."

"I may give my boy a long leash," Huey's voice almost cracked, "but make no mistake about it, he's on a leash. And I know he would never stray so far to the point where he wouldn't hear me if I was trying to say something to him that he needed to know."

"I have consistently had the highest grade point average in every class in every school that I have ever been in and I've won more awards than I can remember," Bobby added, "I have never been in trouble with the law, *ever*, and I can't even recall if I've ever had to be 'grounded' or put on restriction for anything at any time in my life."

"From what I can see, even if you flunked out of school and burnt it down afterwards you still wouldn't be grounded," Fred remarked, "but maybe it's just me, maybe I'm the one that's out of place. This is not my time and I can definitely tell this is not my house. So maybe I ought to just get out of you people's way."

Fred had walked all the way to the front door and opened it before any of the other Rushes either realized what he was about to do or whether he serious about doing it. "Fred, what are you doing?" Marta asked.

"I'm leaving," Fred announced, "I'm a grown man and it's time I made my own way."

"Nigger, come on back in the house," Huey called after his ancestor, "you're talking foolishness, old man. It might start hailing again, and besides, where do you think you're going to go?"

"I've been living in Chicago centuries before you were even born," Fred answered without looking back as he walked across the Rushes' lawn. "It couldn't have changed all that much, I'll manage."

"But you don't even have your things with you," Marta exclaimed.

"I didn't *come* here with anything," Fred called out before crossing the street, "and there isn't anything here I'd want to take with me anyway."

Huey ran onto his lawn and stopped short of clearing it as he watched Fred continue to storm down 79th Street, debating with himself over whether or not he ought to actually drag the 418 year old man back into his house or let him go even while he cried in vain for his ancestor to return. Soon Fred had walked out of his eyeshot and after a long while, Huey finally decided to go back inside. In part because he was just mad enough at what Fred had said about his ability to raise his son to not see much worth in pursuing his great-times-nine-grandfather in his car, but mainly because he held onto the hopeful assumption that Fred would soon come back anyway, certainly before night fell.

But as the sun set that evening, Fred was still on the road, heading for—well, he wasn't sure exactly where he was heading, but it just felt good for him to keep walking. What wouldn't have felt good to Fred at all would have been the knowledge of the purpose of the stranger who was following him from afar just then, and had been spying on the Rush home ever since Fred first arrived there. All the while waiting patiently for an opportunity to catch him alone and outside of Huey's protection.

216

CHAPTER NINE

"The assassination of Islam"
or
"Rush, *die*!"

One thing that helped Fred keep his bearings on his first lone venture into 25th century Chicago is that, as was the case in the Lost-Found Nation, the names of most of the streets and landmarks hadn't changed in over four centuries. In the case of the Nation, the NOI simply hadn't gotten around to changing the names to something more Afro-Asiatic as they'd have liked because the Nation of Islam kept themselves too busy citing and fining couples for holding hands in public view. In the case of the Chicago of 2410 A.D., it seemed that the names were kept the same out of a reverence which no doubt stemmed from this liberal society's obsession with the remembering of history.

The first exception to this Fred cared to take any note of was when he had trekked far enough to the north of 79th Street to reach Marquette Road and found that Jackson Park had been renamed Jesse Jackson Park. But nevertheless, it was still where he remembered it, and as he sat down on a park bench to think his heart stopped beating when he saw something that wasn't human head his way.

Fred was motionless except for the bulging of his eyes as someone who looked like a man that had evolved from a black panther strolled right up to the same bench that Fred was sitting at, sat at the opposite end, and leaned back as if to enjoy the balmy night air. The creature was a Bastian and Fred could tell the Bastian was a "he" because he was naked from head to paw. Somehow Fred didn't feel like trying to run his hands along the Bastian the way he had with the Melkotsurakian in front of peace officer headquarters, but that didn't stop Fred's gaze from running along the cat man instead. The only thing that stopped Fred's eyes from wandering any further was the Bastian making it a point to make eye contact and give Fred a look as if to say, "what are you ogling at?"

The slit green pupils amidst the wide, yellow eyeballs of the cat man staring right at Fred was more than enough to freeze his blood where it flowed. Though the Bastian really wouldn't have cared one way or the other, Fred decided to slowly get up from his seat and relinquish the entire bench to the extraterrestrial. There was no point in staying in the park much longer anyway, Fred rationalized internally, the sun had already sunk below the horizon and he had yet to find a place to stay for the night.

After slowly easing his way out of the park out of fear of the cat man, Fred saw what even his 21st century worldview could discern as a 25th century bus stop and stood by it. Fred remembered Dr. Cohen telling him that public transportation was free, but she said this under the assumption that Fred was to use it to either visit her or return to her care, and the latter is something that he definitely was not prepared to do. The last thing Fred wanted was to go back to being babied or lectured to at the Loyola University Medical Center. And Fred figured if he really wasn't going to ever live with the Rushes again, the hospital, or some sort of museum might be the only kind of home a 418 year old man such as himself would be able to find.

And then something else Dr. Cohen told him came to mind, how housing and food were now considered basic human rights and free. If so, Fred could stay at one of these free houses and have something to eat until he could find a job and pay his own way. Eventually, he would have a place to call his own once again and not have to worry about offending anyone who wasn't as old fashioned as he was or being offended by profane brats.

"If you've been waiting for the taxi bus all this time and you're not just hanging around, you should know you're not going anywhere until you turn on the bus signal first."

Fred jumped from being startled by the sudden voice from behind him. He turned to have his eyes fall on a naked White woman, and not just any naked woman, but the same woman who propositioned Fred and asked if she might have his child while they were waiting in line at the Alexandrian Phantom Form Time Travel Consortium. When Fred recognized her, his embarrassed eyes fell to the ground while a nervous finger scratched behind his ear though there was no itch. When she recognized him, she yelped, "oh my *God*, I don't believe it! It's Fred Rush Senior! Oh my God!"

"Uh," a blushing Fred was trying desperately to think of a way to respond to all this attention from a White woman in the nude. "You were saying about a bus signal?"

"Oh yeah!" The woman reached past Fred, a little too close for his comfort, and touched a touch-a-matic stud on the side of the pole Fred correctly took for a bus stop and on top of the pole was a bulb which glowed a bright red. "Cars fly now, so there's no way they'll be able to detect little bitty us all the way down here unless we send up the bus signal. Now they'll be here in two shakes!"

Fred hoped the bus would arrive sooner than that. He was starting to think his nerves would fare better with the Bastian back at the park than with this woman who was naked, clearly half his age, and "invading" his body space by leaning right next to him.

"I hope I didn't come on too strong back at the Time Travel Consortium. I probably freaked you out. I don't even think I said my name, I'm Scarlett."

Fred trepidatiously shook her extended hand, "how do you do, young lady," he said very authoritatively.

"Oh, I'm no 'young lady,' I just turned 16," Scarlett smiled and batted her eyes. "I'm legal."

Before Fred could finish the doubletake he was in the middle of, something was heard overhead and Fred felt relieved beyond belief as he saw what must have been the taxi bus descend from the starry night sky and land on the opposite side of Stoney Burke Island Avenue.

"Well, that must be for me! I better go!" Fred announced, louder than necessary and then sounded as though he were preparing to hear something disappointing when he asked, "this isn't your bus, is it?"

"No, I was just passing by and wondering why someone was standing next to an unlit bus signal for the longest."

"Thank Allah, I mean, thanks for your help! I have to go! Good bye!" When Fred eased out of Jesse Jackson park in fear of the Bastian, he wasn't so afraid of the cat man to the point where he didn't take his time. When he headed for the taxi bus and away from the 16 year old Scarlett, however, he found himself seated inside the bus before he realized it from having moved so fast.

* * *

The driver of the taxi bus had told Fred that what he was looking for was a "free studio" and a 24 hour a day A.Y.C.E. (an acronym for All You Can Eat) Cafeteria or an ACE for short. The driver also told Fred that her route took her past a free studio complex where the Robert Taylor Homes used to be but if he wanted something to eat first he would have to transfer to another bus that flew towards Daley Center where the nearest ACE was. Already used to being allowed only one meal a day from having lived under Farrakhan's rule for decades, Fred opted to settle in first.

As he leaned back in his seat near the front of the nearly empty taxi bus, Fred thought back to when he would have to subsist on that one meal and realized that now he could go somewhere and eat all he wanted for free should he desire. He recalled all the sacrifices that he and his wife had to make in order to afford the one house they ever owned only to have Nayirah blow it up and now he could stay in a studio apartment at no cost to him whatsoever. Fred even had a White woman who was ready to throw her naked self at him in public. And to top it all off, the sun had long since gone down and Fred had completely forgotten to perform either the Asr or the Maghrib prayers.

On the one hand it was exhilarating to experience things that would've cost Fred his life were he even heard advocating them in 2030. It also made Fred wonder for a moment if this liberal future hadn't made him too decadent and whether he didn't escape the Nation by being frozen in stasis but, since one can only venture etherally and not actually materialize in the past, was permanently exiled as the sentence from his trial dictated after all. Surely that would be how Farrakhan himself would sum up Fred's fate were he alive to see what Fred's life had become. But since Farrakhan wasn't around to judge his life anymore, the only question now was just how many of these new futuristic freedoms, if any at all, was an orthodox Muslim like Fred going to allow himself?

Fred was soon dropped off at a stop walking distance from what was now called the Robert Taylor Free Studios. From what Fred could tell upon first glancing at its entirety, the free studios collectively seemed more like a hotel than an apartment complex. Correctly assuming that it was run very much like one (that was free) as well, Fred searched for someplace that looked like the manager's office, and sure enough, Fred happened upon the 25th century equivalent before too long.

Behind a counter with a desktop computer atop it was a big boned Black man smoking on a cigar. He looked to be at least ten years older than Fred, sported a half shaven beard, and was around Fred's shade, perhaps a little lighter. He was a husky fellow who had a slight paunch but seemed to wear it well underneath his baggy, East Indian ensemble. Fred decided, however, that if this man had a skin-tight bodystocking on beneath the East Indian inspired outfit just as nearly everyone else in 2410 did, he didn't want to see the man in it. One thing that struck Fred more than anything else was that the man had something artificial done to his hair that looked like it could be a jeri curl from the 20th century.

"I know you! I saw you on the TV! You're *Junior's* daddy!" The man reached from behind the counter to pump Fred's hand enthusiastically. "I'm Jake. 'Louisiana' Jake they call me."

"Why?" Fred queried. "Are you from there?"

"No, never been there in my life. My people are though," Jake confessed. "Come from a long line of blues singers but I can't sing a lick. My daddy had a restaurant down there before he died."

"I'm sorry."

"Hell, that's alright," Jake waved a dismissing hand Fred's way, "Ain't no thing but a chicken wing, as he used to say. So what can I do for you?"

"Someone told me that these apartments are actually free—"

"Well, don't say it like you're in line at the supermarket asking the clerk for a price check on some tampons that your wife sent you out to buy! They had supermarkets in the Nation, right? Anyway, *yeah*, all this is free."

Fred turned his head to the side ever so slightly and with half a smile squinted a suspicious look at Jake. "And you don't ever have to pay anyone anything back?"

"No, brother man! We're socialized up in here!" Jake grinned disarmingly. "Boy, they must have put some kind of Horatio Alger/Adam Smith/Napoleon Hill trip on your head back then for you to be worried so about paying something back! Everybody's got a right to have a place to stay, even if it ain't but a no bedroom, no kitchen, mini bathroom having studio. It'd be downright *immoral* to have folks living on the streets in this day and age!"

"How about these naked people on the streets?" Fred nodded towards the door to Jake's office. "You think *they're* immoral?"

"Are you kidding? Some of them women looking *way* fine! Fine as red wine!"

"But what about 'them women?'" Fred sounded as if he were trying to draw something out of Jake. "I mean, what's to stop someone from raping them if they're on the streets butt naked after dark?"

"Didn't they tell you when they woke you up? By the time a young gal is 16 she's required to have at least a first degree black belt in the martial art of her choice otherwise the gal won't graduate from high school. Everybody's all scholarly and in-tel-lec-tu-al now, me included if you can believe it! Folks these days know as much as full fledged professors did in your day, *especially* when it comes to history and politics.

"Why, in Louisiana in 1991, I believe, that Klansman David Duke? He ran for governor and lost, but get this: Around nineteen thousand *Black* folks across the state voted for his ass! *19,000 niggers!* That've been 19,000 ass whuppings if I could *really* go back in time instead of just floating around like some ghost! But can you believe that, though? All 'cause niggers back then didn't know shit from wild honey *nor* did they know their asses from a hole in the ground! Well, all that's changed now-a-days, thanks to that Compulsory Curriculum your boy Junior started up.

"But enough of me preaching like it was Sunday morning," Jake turned to his desktop computer and held his fingers over its terminal in preparation to type. "Let me get down the name people'll be calling you by. There's going to be a computer just like this on the all the desks in all the studios and it'll be what you'll get all your calls and messages from. You can make all the worldwide calls you want, *free*, but you can't call outer space from a free studio."

"Fred Hampton Rush—the First," Fred contemplated asking how would one go about calling the stellar regions except that the only person he knew of that lived on another world was Huey's father, John Huggins Rush. And since his relations with Huey and the rest of the Rushes were currently strained, he didn't any point in pursuing the matter further.

"OK . . ." Jake leaned his head into the computer's screen and squinted at the screen's display. "We got plenty of vacancies so you can have your choice of a room with a view of Lake Michigan, the Loop, or Comiskey Park, which will it be?"

"Are you serious?" Fred's brow furrowed in disbelief. "Shouldn't you be jam packed? These apartments are free!"

"Lord have mercy," Jake shook his head, "Fred—can I call you Fred? Fred, look, when I was a little boy, my momma used to make us the best Rice Krispie Treats you ever did want to taste every Tuesday. Don't ask me why Tuesday, moms was a strange woman. Anyway, me and my brothers used to fight all the time over who had more Rice Krispie Treats than the next. Why? 'Cause they were rare, and if you missed out, you just missed out. Now one day my daddy stepped in and said, 'make some every day, not just on Tuesdays.' Just like that. So moms did like he said and pretty soon, all of us got sick to death of eating them damn Rice Krispie Treats every day!"

"And the moral of this story is?"

"When they first made it official that everybody was going to have a right to a place to stay, a place like this was a damn madhouse, you couldn't get anywhere near here. Finally, after a while, things just naturally died down. And pretty soon, a free studio wasn't so rare anymore. Almost all the businesses were worker-owned by then so jobs weren't being wiped out everytime two companies turned into one or a company took off somewhere because all that kind of corporate stuff was made illegal, and that meant folks had the time to save up enough to buy their own place without worrying about getting laid off before they could do it. That's how come they ain't that many people here, because most folks got their own damn places. Usually, the only kind of people that come by here these days are artists and writers so that they ain't got to work and can do their thing full time, whatever their 'thing' may be.

"And those worker-owned companies didn't duck paying their fair share of taxes like the non-worker-owned ones used to do back in your day so there was always plenty of money to keep these bad boys running, so it wasn't long before things like free studios just became part of the scenery. And speaking of scenery, what you want, boy? The lake, the Loop, or the park?"

"What?" Fred blinked and nodded in surprise, forgetting the choice that had been put to him. "Oh, the lake, I always wanted a view of the water."

"Alright, room 2247. Now, while I'm holding down this 'enter' button on my computer, say, 'computer, this is the only voice pattern you'll recognize as Fred Hampton Rush's,' and kind of loud too, so it'll really take." Noting the look of puzzlement on Fred's face, Jake explained, "it's so that won't nobody but you'll be able to voice activate the lock on your door. Ready?"

"'Computer, this is the only voice pattern you'll recognize as Fred Hampton Rush's . . !' So *that's* how come the computer in my hospital room didn't listen to me when I asked it to increase the lighting. Dr. Cohen must have told the computer before I woke up not to obey any voice but hers."

"Most folks'll just leave it where any old voice can ask their personal computers to place a call, or cut on the TV, or ask what time it is," Jake explained further, "but I figured you want your privacy being famous and all."

"Oh I'm not all that special," Fred grimaced, "but you're right, I'd just as soon have some privacy. Especially from my family."

* * *

The single window in room 2247 filled with gleaming sunlight and the brilliance of Monday morning's dawn kept Fred's eyes from staying closed for too long. He eventually arose from the one bed in the apartment that he had to unfold and elongate from being a couch when he first entered his free studio the previous night, headed for the sink of the studio's cramped bathroom, and began his ablution. True, he had always wanted a view of a great body of water, but what Fred didn't tell "Louisiana" Jake the night before was that if his room faced Lake Michigan, hence the rising sun of the east, then a Muslim such as himself would always know where to face when performing the Fajr or the morning prayer just as he did in his former home during the time of the Lost-Found Nation of Islam, which was situated with its front window facing east along Harlem Avenue.

After the Fajr, Fred wondered if he could keep from having to go out into the world in the same bodystocking that he had been wearing since he left the Rushes without having packed a thing. There was one dresser drawer in the entire studio and Fred opened its top shelf. In it were several bodystockings, but as Fred held them up out of the drawer and into the light for inspection, he couldn't help but feel by looking at the patternless pale gray and white trimmed bodystockings that these were what the people of 2410 A.D. would no doubt consider to be extremely generic.

"Free, but bland," Fred scoffed, until it occurred to him that these people's ethos prescribed that there had to be enough of those unisex, nigh-monotone bodystockings to clothe every human being no matter what world they lived on. He then remembered the schism between rights and privileges being described to him by Dr. Cohen and correctly assumed that while clothing was a basic, human right, style and good taste in fashion was a privilege one still had to strive for.

If he wanted something with more flavor he was going to have to either find some kind of work or go back to the Rushes and ask them for a more colorful wardrobe, and since the latter was out of the question, Fred took to the streets of Chicago on that 9th of March with a fresh resolve: Do as "Louisiana" Jake had said so many others had done in the past, as Fred himself imagined was possible while exiting Jesse Jackson Park; use the free studio as a stepping stone for bigger and better things—

By the end of the day, however, Fred was so drained he wasn't sure if it would be possible for him to pick himself up out of bed again. All he wanted to do was slide off of the taxi bus he had been riding on for seemingly ever, crawl into the free All You Can Eat Cafeteria at Daley Center, and plop down in front of something, anything, that was served warmer than the cold-blooded way the job hunt had treated him.

Though he had been a Chicago resident for literally centuries, Fred had to resign himself to the prospect that he would have to eat alone, at least until he could make some 25th century friends. After he piled his tray full of slices of green melon, two small glasses of apple juice, a grilled cheese sandwich, and a large, piping hot bowl of beef stew, Fred debated internally whether he would even be in the mood for company even if he were to somehow spot someone he knew in the surprisingly spacious and vacant cafeteria to sit with. And then the one bright spot of Fred's entire day since the dawn's early light entered his window occurred when he saw none other than "Louisiana" Jake sitting alone at a round table off in a secluded corner of the ACE.

"Fred! Hey, how you doing boy?" Jake pulled one of the table's extra chairs out for Fred to sit in. "*Man*, you look like somebody done chewed you up and spit you somewhere! What happened?"

Fred slumped into his seat while setting his tray down at the table, took a napkin from a stack in the center of the table, and sighed very deeply. "Before I was—*frozen*, I worked on a newspaper, at a copy shop, and I typed for a living. And at first, I thought the only thing that I'd have to worry about was that the sort of work I used to do was now obsolete. But as I found out *the hard way* today, most of the things I used to do are still done now-a-days in some form or another except that you can't get hired doing *any* of them unless you graduated from one of *their* high schools! *Not* a high school from 400 years ago, and *certainly* not a high school run by the Lost-Found Nation, but one of *their* high schools!"

"Well, hell, nigger, I could've told you that!" Jake's head instinctively jerked back slightly when Fred shot a hard look his way. "Didn't they tell you when they defrosted your ass that you were going to have to go back to school to get your diploma sooner or later?"

Fred felt like strangling both Dr. Cohen and Huey for going on about how key education was to this future society without letting him know that he would eventually have to return to school if he were to truly reenter that society. But then, neither the captain nor the good doctor counted on him leaving either of them as soon as he did. Fred could only guess that they would've gotten around to telling him if he had stayed with one or the other long enough. This wasn't enough to make Fred want to return to the Loyola University Medical Center or the Rush residence, however. "No, no one told me, but it's partly my fault though. I should've been asking more questions about survival and less questions about aliens and time travel."

"I just don't understand it," Jake snorted, "you're the daddy of Fred Rush Junior himself, a 400 year old man! They should've been running around like a chicken with its head cut off trying to hire you! My God, you'd think being famous would get them to let go of them rules of theirs just this once!"

"*Please*, don't talk to me about being famous," Fred held his hand up haltingly, "all I want to do is work a decent job like everybody else, and after they would tell me how I wasn't educated enough to do that, they would *all* say how I should get on a talk show, or go on a lecture circuit, or guest speak. *Allah*, one man even suggested that I *preach*! Well, I don't want to make a spectacle of myself, *or* a specimen." Fred put his head in his hands not to field tears but simply out of exhaustion.

Jake felt along the side of his half-shaven face and stoked his chin thoughtfully. "You know, I imagine you must already feel like the last dodo bird, but if you want to afford something better looking than them freebie, plain Jane, cheap-ass gray longjohns you got on, you're going to have to find *some* kind of way to bring in the ducats."

As Jake spoke, Fred tried to think back to the first time the idea of being in the public eye unnerved him, and all he could come up with was when people would constantly ask about his father, the senator. Was it disturbing because he was tired of hearing about his father or because not enough was heard about him? And if it was the latter, wouldn't being the first 418 year old man in history be the chance to gain some fame of his own? Most would give their soul for the opportunity fate had thrust upon him, so would Fred be—*unappreciative* if he didn't give standing in the public light one last try?

After a deep breath, Fred grudgingly mentioned, "actually, when this man from Chicago State University approached me and I told him like I told everybody else today I was too shy to speak in front of a big crowd, he said that I could just sit there and do nothing but answer questions . . ?" Fred then looked up at Jake from his beef stew. "He said it would be a *Q&A*."

"Well, there you go!" Jake enthused. "I'd get right on that!"

"I think I might," Fred dug into the slit in his spandex bodystocking and produced a slip of paper, "I'll wait till tomorrow to call him. *Professor* Galen's probably gone home for the day since school must be out by now."

"Try him tonight anyway," Jake advised, "he might have a night class if he's teaching at State. And when you get back to your room, cut on the news—"

"Those little desktop computers can pick up TV channels?"

"News and educational channels like CNN, CSPAN, and PBS are the only ones you can get in a free studio. I guess people figure folks'll get *too* comfortable if you could watch all 187 channels for free up in there. But they just had on the news how—did they tell you what an Island City was?"

"Yes," Fred nodded, "they were built because of over-population, right?"

"Yeah, they built one of them things around a dead volcano out in the Pacific and called it Pompeii City. Funny, huh? Except they didn't think so today 'cause the volcano they built the city around just went off!"

"Allah," Fred gasped, "was Pompeii City destroyed? How many people died?"

"They don't know how bad it is yet," Jake related, "and they don't know how many folks are dead either. But here's the thing can't nobody figure out: Every scientist across the country and around the world said that volcano was as limp as a eunuch, they said there's *no way in hell* that bad boy should of *ever* erupted, but it just *did* all of a sudden," Jake shrugged incredulously, "all of them said it was scientifically impossible, like water turning to wine or something."

Fred glanced off into empty space and recalled with a new earnest the silly little thought he entertained after hearing the seven trumpets blaring outside of the Alexandrian Time Travel Consortium. "Yeah, or something," Fred muttered under his breath.

* * *

Fred did get a hold of the bald and diminutive Professor Galen that night just as he was leaving his office for one of his evening classes, which was serendipitous enough. But what Fred really didn't expect was for Galen to have kept his calendar wide open just for Fred's benefit and to ask if the following afternoon during his 21st century history class wasn't too soon. Fred reluctantly agreed, but under two conditions; that his appearance wouldn't be advertised, and that he would be well paid. Professor Galen didn't argue with either request, though he did seem a little surprised at how press shy and avaricious Fred came across to him.

The price of ten thousand ducats (the equivalent of twenty-five thousand American dollars circa 1995 A.D.) was decided upon and approved by the university the next day, which suited Fred just fine. The only thing which worried him was the sensation he couldn't shake that he was being followed on his way to Chicago State. The feeling subsided some when he saw that the route the taxi bus he was taking passed over Huey's neck of the South Side and merely attributed his paranoia to the thought of one of the Rushes having heard about his speaking engagement somehow. Fred wasn't sure if he would be able to go through with the talk knowing that Huey, Marta, or, Allah forbid, Bobby was in the audience.

As it turned out, the only person that Fred recognized in the vast auditorium besides Professor Galen was a certain camera helmet wielding film major he remembered from outside the Loyola University Medical Center, Adam Hecht. Adam waved "hi" to a partially irritated Fred as the goggles that made up the lens of the camera helmet he had on automatically protruded and retracted while adjusting for the lighting in the room. Something made Fred doubt the same Adam Hecht who wanted desperately to make a documentary about him was actually in the 21st century history class, but in the end he decided to pay it no mind.

Fred was told that the auditorium's computer would automatically act as a built-in microphone for anyone standing on the stage and that they could begin the question and answer session at any time since no introduction would be necessary or do justice. The instant Fred seemed to be ready, a sea of arms shot into the air, and after taking a moment to marvel over all the interest these young strangers had in him, he began picking raised hands at random and fielding the students queries. Most of which weren't as personal or intimate as Fred might have feared. The first volley of questions were mainly concerning whether he approved of the LSD system of government of 2410 and was he now a left-winger. One thing Fred did not want to do was preach a sermon, so he briefly and vaguely implied the half-truth that he liked everything about the 25th century well enough. He also said that while he still wasn't sure what exactly it meant to be a leftist, he definitely wasn't a follower of Farrakhan any longer.

It wasn't long, however, before the majority of the questions turned towards asking what "Junior" was like as a youth and soon Fred saw no difference between this audience and those during the turn of the 21st who would always ask about his father, the senator. Fred wasn't telling them what they wanted to hear anyway, because his fond memories of Elisha as a child seemed far too benign to a crowd who wanted to be told stories of Fred Rush Jr. running with the underground alongside the likes of Baines and Eric Blair.

Then the questions began to steer back toward things that centered around him specifically: How Fred found life in general in the former Lost-Found Nation and what it was like to be frozen for 380 years. But before he could answer them all, someone who couldn't be seen clearly for all the people in the auditorium stood by one of the exits and cried before storming outside, "sellout, get the hell out!"

Everyone's attention turned to the slamming door and then back to Fred in anticipation for some kind of a response, who in turn only shook off the startling disturbance without losing too much composure and continued to answer questions until the hour and a half that he was supposed to be there finally ran its course. Afterwards students, Adam Hecht included, rushed the stage and tried to ask him even more, but Professor Galen stepped in to break this up right away, instructing his pupils to give their guest a wide breadth and to leave for the day. The class eventually did so and once Galen had a chance to thank Fred personally (and hand him an envelope with his certified check inside), the two parted ways and Fred left Chicago State for the nearest taxi bus stop with the feeling that he could do this sort of thing again if he had to, even if Fred wasn't sure how soon he'd feel up to it.

He had gotten as far as 95th Street when that feeling of apprehension came over him again despite not having seen any of the Rushes. Was the voice that cried out in the auditorium James Finley, the 25th century Klansman? Didn't that old Nazi realize Fred was never all that loyal to Farrakhan even when he did live in the Lost-Found Nation? Could it be that Fred sounded too far to the left during the Q&A for Finley's tastes and the "sellout" outburst was made when the ex-lawyer simply couldn't hear any more?

Someone brushing against him from behind disturbed Fred's train of thought, but before Fred could say "excuse me," that someone spoke first, "As-Salaam-Alaikum, my brother."

Fred whirled around to face who said that all-too familiar phrase and saw a middle aged Black man not in a skin-tight bodystocking or in a baggy East Indian Kurta-Pyjama but in a 20th century three piece suit—and bowtie. Fred looked down and almost gasped when he saw the man held something poised at Fred's abdomen that looked as much like a "laser gun" as anything ever did.

Fred couldn't believe that the first thought which came to his mind at a moment like this was, "how could this man think of killing me in broad daylight," with it being barely four in the afternoon. Especially since he knew full well from Baines that Malcolm X was killed earlier in the day than 4 p.m. and in front of an audience no less.

In the next split instant, the second thing that occurred to Fred was how he should have expected this. Dr. Cohen said that the Nation of Islam still existed in the 25th century and James Finley was living proof that people could still believe in what Farrakhan did all those centuries ago. The only question left was how much of a chance did Fred have of escaping this fate? Though he wasn't what he would consider to be a hero, he had faced pain and death before, so if he was about to die anyway, what would it matter if he—

"What the—" The Black Muslim suddenly went from feeling no sensation save his index finger slowly squeezing on the trigger of his gun to having to marshal all his energy towards wresting his armed hand free from Fred's grasp. Thanks to a last minute surge of desperation, Fred was barely managing to forcibly redirect the gun and the hand which held it away from him and towards the pavement. The two stood in the middle of 95th Street with the few bystanders that were around stopping to look from afar to try and discern what two Black men were struggling so intently over. The two looked equally matched at first, however the Muslim, having mentally prepared for this moment a lot longer than Fred had, was better able to get the best of the situation. With a final burst of strength, the Black Muslim threw Fred off of him and onto the sidewalk while reaiming his weapon at his downed victim.

Fred looked up, certain that this Muslim standing over him pointing a gun at his torso, and a couple of shocked passersby, would be the last sights that he would ever see. But then from the periphery of his vision, Fred saw a foot shoot out from the left of the Black Muslim and knock the laser gun to the ground.

The Muslim made the mistake of turning to see who would dare interfere in his business before retrieving his gun and only saw the fist of Captain Huey P. Rush fly out of nowhere and crash land in the middle of the Black Muslim's face, knocking him even farther away from his laser gun. When the Muslim saw that his new opponent wore the skin-tight uniform of a peace officer, the battle took on a whole new light; it would be his personal honor versus the power of the state. Rather than make another attempt for his gun still lying on the sidewalk, the Black Muslim stood and fought, which was his second mistake.

Huey blocked every one of the Muslim's punches and kicks before returning in kind with some blows of his own. Within the span of a couple of seconds, Huey had let loose with a volley of left hooks and right crosses that were almost too fast for the eye to follow which left the Black Muslim barely able to stand on his own two feet.

Fred meanwhile had gotten back up and grabbed the laser gun when he spied Adam Hecht not too far in the distance from the scene with his camera helmet on no doubt capturing the fight on film that seemed one-sided in Huey's favor from the onset and ended with one last kick to the Muslim's midsection that sent the would-be assassin to the ground unconscious.

Huey was standing over the fallen Black Muslim and cracking his knuckles when he noticed for the first time that Adam had been filming him for the first time. "Goddamn it, boy! Get the hell out of here! I told you before we don't want to do no damn documentary right now!" Huey stood and glared menacingly in Adam Hecht's direction until he saw that the young man had finally scurried off back in the direction of Chicago State University. Huey then walked over to Fred and took possession of the Muslim's gun. "Are you alright?"

Fred didn't know what to say at first, he wasn't sure if he should still be angry with Huey and ignore him but then Fred figured he shouldn't be too terse with someone who had just saved his life. "I'm fine."

"You don't know this asshole, do you?" Huey pointed at the Black Muslim sprawled on the pavement.

"No," Fred felt at the back of his neck and then looked at his direct male descendant suspiciously, "how did you even know to be here? Did you find out about me speaking at Chicago State? Have you been following me since Sunday?"

"Well, not since *Sunday*," Huey's eyes fell to the ground in chagrin.

"I don't believe this . . ." Fred became incensed. "So I'm not free to go about my business without the peace officers following me around everywhere I go?"

"It ain't about the POs, it's about *me*, I was worried about you, alright?" Huey glared at his ancestor. "Jesus H. Christ, you'd think that you'd be thanking me for, oh, *I* don't know, keeping this nigger from blowing your fucking head off!"

Fred couldn't look Huey in the eye from feeling petty when he muttered, "you're right, I'm sorry, I apologize," Fred then met Huey's stare, "thank you for—saving my life."

"If you really want to thank me come back home with me."

"What?" Fred couldn't believe how opportunistic Huey just sounded. "No, I'm not going back with you, I've got my own place now!"

"A free studio?" Huey ignored the dirty look on Fred's face for knowing where he was staying from following him. "I thought you Muslims hated living off the state?"

"I never said I hated it," Fred corrected, "and besides, what's the difference between living off the state and living off your fam—*relatives*?"

"The difference is . . . Look, both of us are obviously still pissed at each other for what happened this weekend, emotions are obviously running pretty high right now thanks to this guy lying here, so let's just—calm down."

"Actually, captain, officer, sir? Unless I need to file a report at peace officer headquarters or some such thing, I'll be on my way."

"Damn it, old man, don't be such a *snit*!" Huey looked past Fred and Fred followed his gaze to what resembled a 20th century public pay phone in its structure except there was a TV screen where the phone would be and no place to insert a coin. Huey then darted back to the still unconscious Black Muslim, grabbed him by the back of his collar like a sack of potatoes, and drug him over to Fred.

"My guess is this motherfucker was probably following the both of us ever since word got out that you got defrosted, just waiting for a chance to catch you far enough away from me, 'cause he knew I'd whup his ass. And if that's the case, the minute the folks who sent him, and we all know who they are, think that I'm out of sight, they're going to try again. So if you're going to 'live on your own' with your bad self, then they're going to have to think that you're as much a bad ass as I am if they're going to leave you alone while you're 'living on your own.'" Huey then drug the Muslim past Fred and over to the public "phone" while beckoning Fred to follow and ordering the phone, "computer, get me the Chicago Temple of the Nation of Islam."

* * *

"If you take the word, 'democracy,' and break it down into its basic roots," the old Black man in a suit, bow tie, and African pillbox hat said before his audience of half a dozen as his knarled, wrinkled hands scrawled with a pen upon the huge board behind him, "what you have is two words, 'demo' and 'cracy.' Now, the word 'cracy' is Greek for 'a form or type of government.' But 'demo?' Look at it now, 'demo' is only missing one, tiny, little letter to spell—you guessed it, *demon*, from the Latin, *demos*. A letter that was purposely taken out by that White devil slavemaster way back yonder in slavery times to hide the *fact* that the word 'democracy' really means 'a form of government for demons' or 'demon government!' And what is a demon but another word for devil, *a blue eyed, White devil*. So the next time you hear them go on about a libertarian socialist democracy, remember what those liberals really mean to say; libertarian socialist demonic government! And that's what you're living in, Black man, a government run by the devil himself!"

"Minister Christopher," an unassuming young Black girl in an all white chador meekly interrupted when she quietly eased to the minister's side at the head of the class he was teaching. "There's a call for you from a peace officer named Captain Huey P. Rush. He says it's urgent."

Minister Christopher frowned and sighed, "I'll take it in my office, Ieisha," before leaving his congregation of six for a doorway off to the side of the room draped by a red curtain. The old minister parted the curtain, sat behind a desk in the tiny enclave, and saw Huey with Fred Rush Senior, alive, standing behind the captain on the screen of his desktop computer.

"This belong to you?" Huey held up the barely conscious body of the Black Muslim he had soundly defeated for the minister's inspection once he saw the old man's face come into view on the screen of the public phone on 95th Street. "Don't try to deny it either, don't nobody but you temple niggers still wear suits and bow ties these days."

"I won't try to deny it as you say, Captain Rush," Minister Christopher responded, "I recognize that man as Brother Johnson."

"Well now that you're in a rare mood to tell the truth," Huey scoffed, "why don't you tell us how you ordered Brother Johnson here to kill my great-times-nine-grandfather?"

"I shall do no such thing," Christopher declared, "because if Brother Johnson did in fact try to assault your ancestor, it was on his own compulsion. He didn't receive any orders of the kind from the Detroit temple or myself."

"Yeah? Well, that *Mission Impossible*, 'we will deny all knowledge of your expendable existence,' crap may have worked 400 years ago back when everybody was afraid of your Mafia acting ass, but it won't work now." Huey then held the groggy Brother Johnson even closer to the screen at his end. "You may think as fucked up as this nigger is that *I* was the one who tore his ass up, but believe or not, it wasn't me for once.

"Oh sure, I was trailing my boy here, but before I could even show up on the scene, Fred Hampton Rush aka Elijah Isiah, the baddest motherfucker in the 21st century had *already* beat me to it, and as you can see, this nigger's natural ass has been whupped like a narc at a biker rally!" If Huey wasn't blocking Minister Christopher's view of Fred with Brother Johnson's crumpled form, the expression on Fred's face of surprise might have exposed Huey's overt lie. So Huey quickly shot Fred a look as if to say, "let me do the talking and go along with what I'm saying."

"Really," Christopher raised one of his eyebrows over the other, "I never knew that Fred Rush was so formidable."

"How the hell do you think Fred Rush *Junior* learned how to fight and grow up to be the super Black revolutionary he turned out to be?" Huey let Brother Johnson fall to the ground. "Shit . . . Didn't I have to pull your ass off this nigger, Fred? Wasn't I screaming in your ear, 'let the law handle it, Fred, *let the law handle it*!' "

Seeing that this was his cue to take part in this facade, Fred answered in a gruff tone that didn't quite suit him, "yeah . . . Yeah, that's right. Sure you right."

"I see," Minister Christopher mused, "you know, all this posturing on both of your parts is completely unnecessary, captain. For you see, though we would just as soon see Fred Rush be punished for being a race traitor, you won't have to worry about the punishment coming from us. Allah will take care of Fred Rush and all who opposed His will, the liberals, the communists, the anarchists, the *gay*, the White devils, the Jewry, and even the mixed-up, half breed mongrels such as yourself, *captain*, will all be swept away in one fell swoop! The signs are all around us, all you have to do is look and see the writing on the wall . . !"

"Uh . . . *Yeah*," Huey rolled his eyes, "well the *street* signs ought to tell your monkey ass how to get to PO headquarters to come see your boy Johnson 'cause his ass is going to jail. Computer end transmission." When the screen on the public phone went blank, Huey requested another call, "computer get me the desk of Cheshta Castelblanch at peace officer headquarters."

In an instant, the tawny, buxom woman Fred remembered from his one trip to Huey's place of work appeared on the screen. "Lieutenant, I have an attempted murder near the corner of 95th Street and the Dan Ryan Expressway near Chicago State. I'm on foot so I'm going to need a lift to HQ."

"You got it, captain," the lieutenant assured, "Castelblanch out."

Huey looked down at Brother Johnson still lying at his feet. "Damn, *you* must have hit this nigger harder than *you* thought, Fred! *You* must not know *your* own strength!"

Fred ignored Huey's joke and inquired, "the minister called you a half breed, do you know each other? And what are you mixed with?"

Huey turned Brother Johnson over and tied the assailant's wrists with something—"futuristic" he had pulled from his pocket that Fred didn't recognize and sighed. "Well, with all of us Rushes having been named after Black Panthers for the past 400 years or so, you figure that in that time somebody *long* before me would've been named after Huey P. Newton, the biggest, baddest Panther of them all. But it just happened that none of the past Rushes were, until my dad, who was a taxi bus driver, before he retired on the planet Bast, met Jennifer, my mom on his Detroit-to-New Jersey route. She was Jewish," Huey stopped to note how stunned Fred looked upon hearing this, "and only after they had me did it occur to them to name me Huey because Huey Newton himself was part Jewish.

"The only reason why that scum-sucking bastard Christopher knows any of this is because when I was 21, my little 18 year old sister, Elaine Brown Rush, actually wanted, for some *unearthly* reason, to join the NOI and *marry* one of them temple niggers. None of us could figure it out for the life of us why, no, *how* the hell she could be so masochistic. Especially with our family history and all, seeing as how the Rushes and the NOI were like the McFlys and the Tannens from *Back to the Future*, but she wouldn't listen.

"My folks didn't try as hard as I did to talk her out of it because they were about as 'star crossed' as they came. When Farrakhan and Metzger first came to power, thousands of Jews who tried to get out of Aryan Amerikkka would literally come up missing, and in the end it wasn't nothing but pure spite that kept WAR and the NOI from just letting them leave the country alive. Most of the Jews in the world became isolationists after that. Even to this day, a lot of them don't appreciate folks intermarrying with them. Not because they're racist mind you, but because they're afraid that by the 26th century there won't be any Jews left. So you can imagine what they must have thought when this Black taxi bus driver shows up at this Kibbutz in Jersey and wanted to marry one of their women.

"Because of all the flack that my folks got about getting married, they practically stood by and watched *Brother Jerome*, this damn temple nigger, marry into the Rushes. And the first stone cold, stomp down fist fight that I, Captain Huey P. Rush, ever got into was when Elaine came home crying one night about how *Brother Jerome* found out that she was half Jewish, and how *Brother Jerome* acted like he had the superhuman ability to beat one's DNA out of them!"

"Dear Allah," Fred shuddered, realizing just what Huey had meant by that comment.

"I went over to that nigger's house and by the time I got done beating the living shit out of him for hitting *my* little sister they had to call the peace officers on *me*! *Minister Christopher* tried to have me locked up or, at the very least, kicked out of Chicago State. But I beat that rap, just like I beat the shit out of that no good brother-in-law of mine."

"That sounds like when I took that bamboo stick to Sister Sweanea's apple tree," Fred almost cracked a smile, "I guess there's no accounting for what one will do if someone hurts a member of your family."

"Really?" Huey tilted his head to one side coyly, "I didn't knock you around when you hurt me and my wife by calling us bad parents."

Fred knew this was coming, but was too ashamed to bring the subject up himself. "Huey, I am so sorry. I should never have said what I did and I didn't even mean it at the time either. It's just—that son of yours attitude about Islam is what got me so upset, that's all."

"Marta and I understand, Fred, and we had a long talk with Bobby after you took off. I don't know if it did any good, *but . . .*" Huey shrugged and bore a sheepish grin. "But the thing you have to understand is that most of the people in the 25th century are either agnostics or outright atheists, and while it would be Stalinisticly hypocritical for any of us leftists to fuck with you about your beliefs, you're going to have to also remember that it's hard for people to take what you believe in too seriously, what with Phantom Form Time

Travel and all. Malcolm X once said in a speech how we need to keep our religions at home, keep our religions in the closet, and keep our religions between ourselves and our God in order to keep from getting into arguments that'll keep folks from coming together, and for once the old boy was right and not just right-wing."

"Well maybe that's been the people of the 25th century's problem," Fred put to Huey, "I hate to bring this up because I can imagine how much this is going to make me sound like Minister Christopher, but I know what he meant when he was talking about 'the signs are all around us.' Think about it; the trumpet sounds we heard at the Horizon Stadium Saturday night, the hail you mentioned Sunday, and yesterday the volcano the Island City was built around that scientists swore could never possibly erupt—*erupted*. None of these things have been explained, but the hearing of *seven* trumpets, a hailstorm, and 'a burning mountain in the sea' have all been described in the Bible as the first of the seven signs of the apocalypse."

Huey simply looked at his ancestor, and after a long pause, he finally said, "you've been smoking the *kind* bud behind old uncle Huey's back, haven't you, old man?"

"I'm serious! Maybe, just maybe, Allah doesn't appreciate how 25th century society has 'kept religion in the closet.' Maybe He figures 16 years old is too young to be to be able to sleep with someone, especially someone older. Maybe He doesn't approve of public nudity, or drugs, or everyone knowing *just* how the world was created thanks to time travel. You say that everybody's an intellectual in 2410, well maybe you know too much. Maybe you've gone so far to the left to the point of being like—Sodom and Gomorra . . ."

Huey's sudden bellowing laughter both interrupted and infuriated Fred. "They said the same thing about 'Sin Francisco!' Look, Fred, I'm sorry, but you're *way* the fuck off base here! I know about the volcano at Pompeii City yesterday, and I know all too well about that damn hail, which is why we're waiting for Lieutenant Castelblanch 'cause my fucking car's in the shop because of it. But I'm telling you, those seven 'trumpets,' or whatever the hell they were, were not announcing the end of the world!

"If you ask me, all this is is that old Rush insatiableness. That's right, your pop, Bobby Rush was a moderate when he was in the House and became an even bigger one in the Senate. This other Illinois Panther, Bob Brown used to call him, 'consistently inconsistent.' And my guess is that it's because your granddaddy Jimmy was an ex-con and a Black Muslim that they eventually had to put in the nut house and your grandmomma Cora was a Sunday school teacher who used to sell corn bread and fish sandwiches on the corner."

"My father used to walk barefoot and pick cotton for spare change when he was a boy in Georgia," Fred fumed, "if you have a point, make it."

"Because he came up in that kind of a James Carville/Mary Matalin mix, your father wound up with the split sensibilities he had till the day he died, *and you're the same way.* You obviously weren't happy in the Lost-Found Nation—hell, who *would* be—because it was so far to the right, and now you're seeing omens everywhere because you're anxious about the present 'cause we're so far to the left. You're easily spooked by extremes just like your daddy was, Fred. But I'm telling you, there's no need to be."

"You can rationalize it all you want," Fred shook his head, "but the bottom line is both you *and* I both better hope that I'm wrong about the signs."

"You?" Huey seemed surprised. "As diligent a Muslim as *you* are?"

"You heard Minister Christopher, I'm a race traitor, a sellout. If Allah is on Farrakhan's side and not on Malcolm's, and I'm right about these—*occurrences* being the seven signs, then I'll be just as damned when the end comes as, well, I'm sorry to say, *you'll* be."

Huey peered up at the sky and recognized Lieutenant Castelblanch's peace officer vehicle veering off of the skylane that was directly above 95th Street in order to descend near his position. He then looked back at his distraught ancestor and sighed. "Fred, you're not a traitor, OK? Clarence Thomas, he was a traitor, David Horowitz, he was a traitor, but not you. I've been called a traitor of one kind or another all my life. They said I betrayed my people by marrying Marta because she ain't Black, they say I betrayed my people by not becoming a practicing Jew, they even say I betrayed my people by deciding to be a peace officer. Well, I'll let you in on a little something I found out a long time ago: Black folks aren't my people, Jewish folks aren't my people, hell, the Rushes, my own family aren't my people. You heard me! My sister Elaine? She may have divorced Brother Jerome, but she's still a member of the NOI to this day, and you know they cocksure ain't my people!"

"So who are your people?" Fred inquired. "Those on the left?"

"Close," Huey lifted Brother Johnson onto barely conscious feet as the peace officer vehicle Lieutenant Castelblanch was finally landing across the street from the Rushes and their would be assassin. "My *friends* are 'my people,' and—I consider you my friend, Fred. Which is why I wish you'd come back and stay with us. Marta still wants to take you to her work and we still haven't seen Beyond the Beyond because we wanted to see it *with you* since it'd be your first holographic movie ever."

Fred smiled, and even blushed, but he knew he couldn't deal with what his descendant was proposing. "Huey, I—appreciate that, and I *would* like to go places and do things with you, and Marta, but Bobby—I'm sorry, I can't move back in with you. Despite what Bobby may think, I don't want to change him—*much*, but at the same time, especially with these signs coming true, I don't want him changing me either. If something *is* happening, my faith might be the only thing that'll shield me from what's to come, and I don't want that blasphemous boy of yours weakening that shield."

"Oh, for—oh, for *goodness* sakes!" Huey proceeded to sling Brother Johnson over his shoulder in much the same manner as he did hostage-taker David Kornblatt nearly a week before as he saw Lieutenant Castelblanch jog around her vehicle and head his way. "'The signs,' 'the signs,' there ain't no damn signs, Fred! They're coincidences, and I'm certain there's *a logical explanation* behind each and every last one of them!"

"Captain, I just got a call from Major Byrne while I was on my way here," Castelblanch ran up to her superior officer sounding out of breath, "as soon as we drop this guy off at PO HQ we have to fly out to the Chicago River. There's *blood* in it, they don't know how much, but they say it's a lot! Maybe *tons*!"

Fred narrowed his eyes and slowly turned to his direct male descendant, but before Fred could make any snide remarks, Huey first said to him without quite looking in his direction, "to quote Charles Napier from *The Blues Brothers*, 'don't you say a *fucking* word.'"

CHAPTER TEN

After Fred was dropped off with Brother Johnson at peace officer headquarters to file a report, he went back to his free studio and called the Rushes' residence with the desktop computer in his room. Luckily for Fred, Marta answered instead of Bobby and when Fred apologized to her about Sunday she waved the matter off with a dismissing gesture while inviting him to have lunch that Friday with her and one of her friends from the Interstellar Community Consulate; a Melkotsurakian.

Fred accepted her invitation and asked if Huey had come home yet. He had, and when Huey stepped into view of Fred's small computer screen he related that it was in fact real human blood, type O and disease free, which was suddenly and inexplicably polluting the Chicago River almost to the point of discoloration, from Lake Michigan to as far inland as New Chinatown (since the river gained its fame by being the only one to ever flow backwards as it has ever since it was jury-rigged to do so in 1900). According to Huey, the cleanup was already underway and proceeding smoothly but no one had any idea how the blood got there in the first place.

Fred no longer felt in the mood to harp on something on the order of "I told you so." Rather, he felt a chill run through him and though Huey wanted to talk more, mainly about how there was nothing to worry about, Fred abruptly cut the conversation short. Though he still had another hour until it was time for the 8 p.m. Maghrib prayer, Fred dropped to his knees before his eastward view of Lake Michigan and began to pray anyway.

Fred had been skipping prayers since he had awakened from his 380 year hiatus. Several times he had gotten up in the middle of the night to urinate and didn't bother to perform the Isha prayer but that had changed after he heard from Huey. On Wednesday the 11th at precisely noon, after having searched in vain for even a menial job (figuring "idle hands are the devil's handiwork," Fred tried to go on with his life as if the end time might not come) that wouldn't require him to have a 25th century high school diploma, Fred picked a spot on a sidewalk, in public, smack in the middle of the Loop in downtown Chicago to kneel to the east and pray. His fear of what the primarily liberal residents of 2410 A.D. would think of him was balanced, if not surpassed, by the fear of what might happen to him if he didn't perform the Zuhr prayer at precisely noon. But what Fred didn't realize was how he wasn't the only one who was as concerned, or at the very least, as affected.

Most, like Huey, had more on their minds and in fact had already written off the unexplainable events as fluke occurrences. But the significance of the exact order in which the events had occurred and the religious ramifications of the events themselves weren't lost on everyone. Though the media of the 25th century had long since been broken from perpetuating or concentrating too much on stories that were tabloid or trivial in nature, the fact that the trumpets, the hail, the eruption of the volcano on the Island City, and a bloodied river had all been described in the Bible as signals that the end of the world was near were reported nonetheless. So far, most of the strange events have been localized only to Cook County, but when the news of the Chicago river broke, people, however few in number, from across the country and around the world were all talking about, if nothing else, how quaintly *Biblical* it all seemed. Copies of the King James Bible that had been sitting on the shelves of many a personal library for ages were being dusted off and cracked open. But while people were turning straight to the Book of Revelations by St. John the Divine in anticipation, said anticipation hardly ever rose above the level displayed when one opened a sports program to see who was to compete against who next.

The events did generate more than a mere passing interest in some, however. The further to the right on the horizontal political spectrum one dared venture, the more you found those who took what was going on in the Chicago area very seriously. The few right-wingers left in the World Government of 2410 called that "a state of spiritual emergency" be declared. Those that weren't subjected to immediate recall by their constituents for suggesting such a ludicrous thing continued in vain to enact something similar yet diluted. Commentators of all ideologies mulled over the issue on telecasts and in their individual columns with the leftists predictably dismissing the strange events as freak coincidences, the far right swearing they're much more, and the moderates not having any more of an opinion on the matter than they ever had on any issue in history.

Protests with varying degrees of nonviolence and civil disturbance against the Compulsory Curriculum were being held outside of schools and colleges under the pretense that God was upset over the "godless" and "liberally biased" education their children were forced to receive. While in the darker corners of 25th century society, book burnings were held by the likes of the Ku Klux Klan and the Nation of Islam far from the roving eye of the peace officers where works such as *1984* and *Fahrenheit 451* secretly went up in flames for encouraging the anti-authoritarianism that they felt surely led to the libertarian socialist democracy's disregard of the authority of God.

Membership in churches and temples grew slightly (though Fred never so much as entered one for fear of running into a member of the Nation of Islam), sales of religious novels went up a bit, and all eyes were on Friday the 13th, not only for the date's long renowned reputation in the annals of superstitious lore, but mainly because of something that everyone who had an almanac for the past year had known already: A full solar eclipse was due on that day and according to the Bible the next of the seven signs was to be "a blocking of the sun and the moon."

Fred heard about this on the morning of the Thursday before the 13th and cared just enough about what would be thought of him by the Rushes to not cancel his luncheon date with Marta and the Melkotsurakian because it fell on the day in question. Frightened as a small part of him was, he was bound and determined not to give the sacrilegious "Li'l Bobby" the satisfaction of thinking that Fred was afraid to go out because of what would surely be considered nothing more than "barbaric superstition."

But Fred needed something to take his mind off of both the signs and his failure to find a job short of the public appearances he was (in light of the assassination attempt) still reluctant to subject himself to, so he called Huey Thursday afternoon and asked if the Rushes still hadn't seen this new holographic movie, *Beyond the Beyond*. As it turned out, Huey and Marta hadn't but Bobby had already went to see it with some friends of his earlier in the week and didn't like it enough to see it twice. Fred asked if Huey and Marta wanted to see *Beyond the Beyond* that night and they both said yes, all the while concealing his delight over the prospect of Bobby not accompanying them. Fred then asked for directions to the theater where it was playing so that he could meet them there since he felt that if the Rushes saw how cramped of a place the free studio he lived in was they might try and convince him to come back to their house. Huey told Fred the Oliver Stone Holoplex was off of Halsted Street near Brighton Park where the International Amphitheater used to be and Fred understood where his descendant was talking about.

Fred was late in his catching of a taxi bus to the Holoplex because of his performance of the Maghrib but luckily Huey and Marta were already there holding a place for him in line. Once inside and seated Fred tried to think back to whether movie theaters had stages and not screens. When he asked Marta about the lack of a curtained silver screen she informed him that the stage he saw in the front of the theater was where the holographic show was to be projected. Fred took her word for it and wasn't exactly sure what she meant until the lights dimmed and the show actually started. What looked like actual three-dimensional figures and objects in full living color suddenly appeared on the stage as though they were live actors and props about to perform a play of old. This initially startled Fred a great deal and prompted him to visibly shudder, which in turn reminded Huey of the days when motion pictures were first shown and the unsophisticated actually screamed when they saw a train or a horse approaching on screen. After the previews for coming attractions were finished displaying themselves, Marta noted Fred's discomfort and leaned over to whisper in his ear assuredly how the holograms on stage were just as intangible as the projections of superheroes and pro-wrestlers that Huey's disk emitted in their living room.

No sooner than Marta explained this, the panicked cry of "fire" went up from at least two thirds of the movie goers, Huey included. And no sooner did Fred leap out of his seat did everyone in the theater burst into laughter. At first Fred fumed, angrily thinking he had been recognized because of his celebrity status and that everyone had decided to pull a prank on him but then Marta calmed him down and whispered how one of the most commonly used arguments for censorship in the 20th century was how if free speech was unlimited, as it was in 2410 A.D., then one could yell fire in a crowded theater and anarchy would ensue. So sometime around the 23rd century a tradition began out of spite of that argument where people would yell "fire" during movies at whim. Fred felt too sullen and deflated to ask what one would do if there really had been a fire in the Oliver Stone Holoplex. Instead he just sank back deeper into his chair and tried desperately to escape and immerse himself in the story being shown.

But even that was to be denied Fred. He bristled at one of the first scenes in the movie which showed the protagonist, a gay space explorer, kissing his lover goodbye before entering a one man starship on a mission from which he would never be seen by anyone he knew ever again. What the explorer volunteered for was to fly his ship as close to a black hole as safely possible, where only a matter of weeks would pass for him, and then return to Earth, where many centuries will have passed because of the laws of relativity.

"Just like Fred Rush!" Someone young in the front row cried out, and when Huey chuckled along with everyone else in the theater at the blurted out comment it only added to Fred's embarrassment.

Once the explorer returned to Earth after having only aged a month within his small starship while orbiting the black hole, it was the year 3007 A.D. and the 31st century. 95% of the human race had long since left the planet to colonize greener pastures since a second ice age had forced the world's few humans to move to countries along the equator. Flying his ship towards the West Indies, he first found those who had many similar journeys there and were in effect stranded since there still wasn't a way to tangibly travel backwards in time. The explorer's predecessors introduced him to the humans of 31st century Earth and explained that centuries of intermarriage had made the last humans on Earth a homogeneous (and all nude) race of tan skinned, flat featured, dark eyed, curly haired brunettes who had eliminated ducats altogether and lived on tribal collectives all along the Caribbean.

Did everything these people do have to try and slap Farrakhan across the cheek at every turn, Fred thought as he was watching this, how many more ways can these people derive pleasure from rubbing their freedoms in a dead man's face?

The movie concluded with a depiction of the sun finally dying out in 3010 A.D., marking the end of life on Earth. Fred found himself hoping that the end of the movie wasn't prophetic in any way as he left the theater with the Rushes but parted ways with them as a taxi bus was seen descending from the sky across the street from the Oliver Stone Holoplex. Though Huey and Marta talked only about how Fred was to meet her and the Melkotsurakian for lunch the next day, both their facial expressions surely spoke of how they wished Fred would come home with them instead of going back to his studio.

* * *

Fred was pensive the entire morning of Friday the 13th, 2410. He decided against looking for a job that day, opted to stay in his free studio apartment all morning, and intently watched his desktop computer screen for those few news channels that were covering the full solar eclipse due at approximately 1 p.m. central time and commentating on its religious significance. With every comment describing how the eclipse must surely be the fifth sign, Fred's stomach grumbled and became slightly acidic from nervous stress. He had followed what coverage there was on each channel he could before the subject would invariably change to more pertinent topics such as how unions were continuing to trepidatiously oversee the introduction of robotic labor or the making of current cloning ethics even more restrictive.

"Damn it, I'm new to this century and even *I* already know it's illegal to clone people," Fred yelled at his small computer while slapping the side of it, "so, by Allah, I want to hear more about the eclipse! The eclipse!"

After his noon prayer, Fred finally left his apartment for his date with Marta and the Melkotsurak, as they're sometimes called for short. He was to meet them at an outdoor seafood cafe on Lake Shore Drive near Grand Avenue that was specially equipped to serve Melkotsurakians, but before he left Fred stopped by the front desk of the Robert Taylor Free Studios complex to chat a bit with "Louisiana" Jake.

"Jake, do you mind if I asked you what faith you follow?"

Jake stroked his half-shaven chin thoughtfully for a moment before replying, "I guess you could say I'm a non-church going, non-born again Baptized Christian with a touch of 'nostic, Fred."

Fred leaned against the edge of the counter Jake was sitting behind. "You don't seem too worried that all seven signs of the revelations are coming true."

"They ain't *all* come true *yet*," Jake reminded, "besides, colored folks done already been through something similar to this anyway. Back in Louisiana."

"*In Louisiana*?" Fred almost sneered from disbelief.

"Hell, yeah! I never will forget my great granddaddy telling me the story of how it up and decided to snow, yes, *snow* in Twisted Cross, Louisiana on Saturday, July 27th, nineteen forty *nine*! That's right, it was snowing like it was Christmas in Connecticut smack dab in the middle of the summertime—in Lou-is-i-*ana*! Shit . . . Come Sunday morning, every old Negro preacher in the South was talking about how the world was coming to an end! The preachers in Twisted

Cross had more money put in their collection plate that week than they ever did see in their entire *lives*, but," Jake shrugged slightly, "aside from a couple of lynchings, nothing apocalyptic happened. So after a while everybody went on about their business and watched the last of the snow melt."

"You're going to tell me you think every-last-one of these signs is just a—" Fred searched for the right phrase, "*freak of nature,* just like whatever happened in 'Twisted Cross?'"

"Or it could've been that God just wanted to let folks know He's still out there, that's all," Jake grimaced, "it don't necessarily have to mean it's the end of the world. If it did, world would've ended back in 1949, but Black folks survived Twisted Cross, Louisiana, we'll survive this right here too."

"I wish I could be as easygoing as you are," Fred nodded as he headed for the door, "you're wise beyond your years, Jake."

* * *

Huey wondered for a moment as he stood by his lieutenants and corporals just behind the force field fence the peace officers erected around the Alexandrian Phantom Form Time Travel Consortium if his guarding of the Consortium from the two thousand or so anxious protesters would be looked down upon by his revolutionary ancestors. He contemplated this for only a moment, because it was hard to feel as though he had sold out somehow when the protesters he was protecting the Time Travel Consortium from all consisted of Nazis, Klansmen, Black Muslims from the Nation of Islam and other members of the Religious Right from all over the midwest. Each and every one of them, including two Huey recognized as James Finley and Minister Christopher, seething with the intent of tearing the Consortium apart with their bare hands if given the least little opportunity.

"All this goes to show you can legislate that folks learn some knowledge but you can never account for some folks' lack of morality," Huey said loudly so that Lieutenant Castelblanch could hear him over the angry crowd's yelling even though she stood at her post right beside him.

"*You're* the one who's lacking in morality!" Cried one of the Nazis who was standing on the other side of the force field from Huey and managed by chance to overhear what he had just said.

"*As I was saying,*" Huey glared at the Nazi and then turned back to Castelblanch, "all we can do is teach folks all sides of an issue and hope their inherent morality kicks in and pick the right side instead of the right-wing side. Obviously, the system works, 'cause if it didn't then these assholes would be in charge again. Instead, there's only a few of them left in the world and they're all right here today; getting on my damn nerves."

"Maybe you shouldn't antagonize them, sir," Lieutenant Castelblanch murmured, "this force field isn't sound proof." She then looked to the black and gray poles that were dug into the ground around the Horizon Stadium which kept the thin fields of transparent static discharge between the poles energized. "It's not even over seven feet high."

"I'm not talking to them, I'm talking to you, Cheshta," Huey assured, "I mean, you can require the truth be taught about the Kennedy assassination, but they'll always be someone who'll think JFK *deserved* to be shot by the CIA, and I guess you just can't change the fucked up way some folks think about things. You've never heard of anyone ever trying to change the way folks *think* about history, have you lieutenant?"

"No, sir."

"*No . . !*" Huey narrowed his eyes at the mob on the other side of the force field from him. "We've just tried to *teach* history, that's all!"

"You've tried to force it down our throats!" James Finley shouted after having made his way to the front of the crowd with a boy in his mid teens by his side.

"Finley, that better not be your son Daniel out here on the middle of a school day!" Huey bellowed.

"You see?" Finley whirled around, flaying his arms about dramatically to the protesters behind him. "All they can think about is throwing my poor son right back into that den of iniquity they call a *school* so he can be peer pressured into turning his back on God! Now His wrath has been brought down on all of us, thanks to their *teaching of history*!" Finley hissed.

"You're just pissed because we've had 400 years of everybody being exposed to every-single-solitary-viewpoint there *ever* was and in those 400 years there hasn't been one—*not one* generation who's wanted to go over to your side!" Castelblanch cried out, sounding very flustered.

"My *Lord*, lieutenant!" Huey smiled as he laid a hand on his broad chest in a mock effort to appear faint. "'Least we not antagonize the natives, shall we?'"

"You have some gall talking about the Lord, captain!" Minister Christopher called out as he wormed his way through the crowd to Finley's side.

"Nigger, you ought not be saying jack shit 'cause it took us 400 years to clean up the mess you and your proud, Aryan brothers out here done made! 400 years—four *hundred* years . . !" Huey purposely left his voice trail off in order to better satirize the afrocentricly theologian oratory the minister and his ilk were known for.

Several feet away, standing at their posts on the peace officer's side of the force field, Lieutenant Harlan Kendle turned to Corporal Tercel Jackson and asked, "has everyone been evacuated from the Consortium?"

"Yes, sir."

"Good," Lieutenant Kendle sighed before thinking out loud, "'cause it's going to be a long day . . ."

Fred knew there were certain forms of seafood his Black Muslim code forbade him to eat, and he had intended to make sure he didn't order anything which would've violated that code. Except that he was so entranced by the Melkotsurakian who sat across from him and Marta that he wound up ordering and eating catfish without realizing it until lunch was over. Fred only hoped the Melkotsurakian, a young one named Nim, didn't mind how he stared at it as it ate by sticking its head in a large tank Marta explained was filled with microorganisms that the waiter had brought to their table.

Marta had given Fred her spare universal translator headset to wear when he first sat down, but beyond introducing himself Fred wasn't sure of what else to say to Nim. Fred certainly didn't want to bring up how he had ran his hands all along one of its compatriots outside of peace officer headquarters and he was likewise glad that Marta hadn't brought it up either. But after lunch, when Marta decided to go for a walk from the cafe in the southwards direction of the still somewhat bloodied Chicago River, it prompted Fred to think to ask Nim something he had always wondered was true and something he was sure only an extraterrestrial would know for sure.

Fred nervously felt at the tiny microphoned bulb at the end of the thin, black wire that came around his head and was part of the headset before speaking into it. "Uh, *Nim*?"

Fred saw the half man, half dolphin creature turn its head his way, and as Nim moved its "lips" to speak into its own headset, Fred heard through the headset's one, small headphone covering his right ear, "yes—Fred—Hampton—Rush?"

"Ahem," Fred cleared his throat and looked back at Marta for a second before addressing Nim again, "Nim? In my time? 400 years ago, our leader Farrakhan?" Nim nodded to assure it knew what Fred was referring to. "Farrakhan said that in the fall of 1985 he had a vision, like Ezekiel's vision of a 'great wheel in the sky' in the Bible. Farrakhan said he was carried to a mountain top in Tepotzlan, Mexico when a *wheel-shaped plane* came down and used a *beam of light* to bring him on board."

Fred looked around for any of the disparaging kinds of looks he has come to expect from the likes of Li'l Bobby and when he found none continued. "Well, *he* said that a pilot escorted him to a room with a speaker at the center of the ceiling. And the voice he said he heard come out of that speaker was the voice of none other than the Honorable Elijah Muhammad himself. Now according to Farrakhan, Elijah Muhammad told him that the President of the United States met with his generals to plan a war, with the country of Libya I think, and ordered him to hold a press conference to tell the world how he got this information from this *wheel in the sky*.

"I guess what I'm asking, Nim is . . . Was Farrakhan right? I mean, was he really beamed up by one of the Interstellar Community?

They told me you—*people* were secretly monitoring us back then, so could it have actually happened . . ?"

At first, Nim stopped in its tracks. It took a moment for it to fully register what exactly was being asked and another moment to decide if Fred was in fact serious. Once Nim saw it had heard everything Fred had to say, it laughed long and it laughed hard. Not a human laugh, but one only a Melkotsurakian could utter; a sound consisting of dolphin-esque shrieks and screeches that caused Marta to spring to Nim's side to see if it was in pain. Nim waved her off and bore what could only be taken as a smile.

"I—am—alright—" Nim assured. "That—has—got—to—be—the—funniest—thing—I—have—ever—heard!" Nim "laughed" some more before saying, "I—thought—the—stories—of—the—Interstellar—Community—supposedly—arranging—the—rocks—at—Stonehenge—or—mutilating—cattle—or—abducting—humans—and—probing—them—were—funny—but—*this* . . . Has—got—to—be—the—most—*ludicrous*—thing—I—have—ever—heard—in—my—entire—life! We—hid—from—your—radars—and—your—sensors—for—as—long—as—we—did—because—of—your—barbarous—inclinations. Why—would—we—possibly—want—to—let . . . No—*invite*—barbarians—onto—our—ships?"

Fred felt as if he had been talking to Li'l Bobby after all and wondered if a simple "no" couldn't have sufficed. Fred wasn't sure why he was internalizing Nim's laughter so, he didn't believe the tale of Farrakhan's vision when he was being tested on it in school any more than this alien did. Perhaps his heightened sensitivity was due to the three of them drawing ever closer to the once bloody river. Because when Fred saw as they passed Lake Point Tower the last remnants of what must have been the clean up efforts Huey spoke of, it reminded him of the signs that were still to come and the costs that might incur from scoffing at them. Fred then stopped walking and looked up at the sky.

It was one o'clock, and he could tell without looking at a watch or asking a room's computer because he could see, as Nim and Marta had once they looked up to see what Fred was looking at, that the sun was slowly but surely being blotted out by the moon just as the almanacs and the calendars and the weathermen had predicted and anticipated. As the sky dimmed and finally darkened as if it were much later in the day, Fred had to fight the instinct to drop to his knees and beg forgiveness for—well, he wasn't exactly sure what for. All he knew was what he felt, which was a wave of apprehension that eclipsed his logic as the moon had the sun.

Under the cover of the sudden midday darkness, four burly, White male youths lurked in a nearby alleyway and glared at Nim the Melkotsurakian with a contempt brought even further to the forefront of their consciousness by all the alcohol they helped themselves to earlier. All of them had come from a survivalist enclave outside of Peoria to the big city for the day. Chock full of the ideas their parents could get away with filling their heads with thanks to their enclave being hidden far away from the irreverence of the Compulsory Curriculum. Ideas about how times were better when man thought the Earth was the center of the universe and how the existence of aliens ended those days of man's supremacy over his own world. In fact, the aliens' presence posed a mortal threat to the survival of the human race. Sure the Interstellar Community claimed to be only interested in peaceful coexistence, but with all the advanced technology they had at their disposal, *and their refusal to share with the more "barbarous" members of the human race*, the Interstellar Community could enslave the planet overnight if they wanted to.

The four young survivalists, like their parents, spent their lives making sure they were always prepared to fend off an alien invasion should it ever reach Peoria. Raised to believe in God and the Book of Revelations, the youths had come to the city for one last day of drinking and carousing before the end (and the invasion) came. And while taking out the one alien the four unarmed youths could find on the streets that day wouldn't make that much of a dent in any armada they were surely planning, at least there would be one less dolphin man the world would have to worry about.

Nim was still doubled over with laughter when the four burly young men lunged out of the eclipse induced darkness and pounced towards it. When Marta tried to intervene she was immediately slapped down to the ground and once there, two of the boys proceeded to stomp at her sides while the other two were beating at the force field that Nim had cast barely an instant before they could actually lay their hands on it. Which left an initially stunned and then enraged Fred, who leapt to Marta's defense assuming that Nim was safe for the moment only to be felled with a single yet very well placed right cross from one of the boys across his jaw. The blow sent the back of Fred's head crashing onto the pavement behind him and kept Fred unconscious for the duration of the onslaught. In which time, Marta had sustained nearly a dozen kicks to her ribs, hips, breasts, and head for having worn a bodystocking the boys recognized as the typical dress of an Interstellar Consulate employee while Nim fared much worse. The few witnesses in the vicinity called the peace officers on the nearest public phones but by the time they had arrived it was too late.

It seemed that in order for a Melkotsurakian to levitate itself within one of their force field bubbles, let alone maintain a force field bubble under duress, a certain level of maturity and experience must be attained first, and the young (teenage by human standards) Nim was unfortunately lacking in both. Soon its force field collapsed, and once it did, the two boys who had been pummeling Marta for being deemed a traitor to the planet Earth turned their attentions to Nim, making it four against one. The skin of a Melkotsurakian is just as tender as that of a dolphin and after the severe beating Nim had inflicted on it, it was all Marta could do to keep from crying as she could tell, even in her semi-conscious state, that the young Melkotsurakian who was lying stiff and still beside her had been killed by the four youths who were all chased down by the peace officers when they arrived on the scene.

* * *

The moon blocked the sunlight of the sky over the Alexandrian Phantom Form Time Travel Consortium bit by bit until finally everything looked as though a dim cloak had been draped over the world. For a moment, both the peace officers on their side of the force field fence and the fascist protesters on the other side of said fence ended the dirty stares or the periodic bouts of caustic rhetoric they had been exchanging across the force field and looked up at what was happening to the midday sky.

Tensions had been running very high ever since the protesters first showed at the Horizon Stadium earlier in the day only to find that the attention surrounding their protest of the Time Travel Consortium's debunking of past religious icons had given the peace officers enough notice to install a force field. Being who and what they were ideologically, they didn't make too many bones about their main goal being the total destruction of the Consortium. The fascists didn't exactly advertise this bit of knowledge, but a simple search through the crowd would've revealed that they also didn't take great pains in concealing the homemade and illegal explosives that some had brought with them should the opportunity ever arise.

All the protesters, even the social darwinistic Nazis, followed the word of God to at least some degree. Meaning that the occurrence of the eclipse (within the context of the past week's revelations) gave them just the excuse they needed to try something defiant and insane. In their frame of mind, it was just the sign from above they were waiting for.

"*Let's rush the force field!*" James Finley declared, raising his walking cane to the darkened sky as a calvaryman of old would lift his saber before a charge. "*They can't stop us all!*"

Finley's ulterior motivated logic had some basis in fact. The peace officers' field was only seven feet high, and though the discharge from the static energy generated by it could surely repel a few dozen people trying to ram past it, the force field was never designed to withstand the better part of two thousand bodies all shoving against it at once. The first wave of protesters, including the lame James Finley, the elderly Minister Christopher, and little Daniel Finley had to feel the bonecrushing brunt of being pushed by those behind them into the seemingly electrified sheet of transparent energy. The laws of physics dictated that they be bounced back immediately, but the laws of God (as they perceived them to be) would see the protesters all rot in hell should they cease and desist. To the astonished eyes of the peace officers on the other side, the energized fence actually began to buckle in, as far as they knew, a scientifically unprecedented way. Until finally—

"What the fuck—" Huey and his junior officers all instinctively jumped back as an immense deluge of the protesters writing in pain spilled through the portion of the force field fence which had been pressured by the sheer weight of hundreds, if not thousands, into collapsing. The black and gray poles that kept it operating were unearthed from where they were dug in and toppled over as the protesters behind the first wave trampled over those they had to thank for breaching the field and stormed past the peace officers. That is, the majority of the protesters stormed past anyway, the ones with explosives hidden on their person most definitely. But a good number of them decided to stay and fight with the peace officers, not necessarily to keep them occupied while the explosives were being set, but just because.

For himself, Huey managed to hold at bay five to seven of the Nazis, Black Muslims, or Klansmen at a given moment amidst the swirling chaos. However the less formidable lieutenants and corporals barely held their own and it took all of their individual fighting prowesses to keep from being completely bowled over. But the battle royal at the Horizon Stadium was soon to be over, for just as enough of the Muslims had managed to trip Huey up from behind and wrestle him onto the ground, the Alexandrian Phantom Form Time Travel Consortium was heard from behind the peace officers position going up in flames in a series of thunderous blasts. Small explosions were heard detonating from all sides of the honeycombed dome that was the Time Travel Consortium and pillars of fire amongst huge plumes of jet black smoke were seen rising high above the dome shaped building which was now riddled with gaping, crater-like holes.

White hot fury shot through Huey's body and the surge of anger and adrenaline gave him just enough strength to throw the six Black Muslims that were piling onto and pummeling him off of him. Seeing that the Consortium was now in smoldering ruins, the Muslims, along with all the other protesters, collectively felt what they wanted was accomplished and that it was time the protesters all scattered to avoid capture. The sun had also begun to slowly emerge from its eclipse, which only further killed the mood the fascists were in and had used to excuse their actions. The battle weary peace officers weren't in a condition to restrain any more than a few of the fascists and most of the ones they did manage to capture were the more elder members of the siege, namely those who were in too much pain from being pressed up against the force field fence such as James Finley and Minister Christopher.

Battered and bruised, Huey angrily limped over to where Finley and Christopher both laid semi-conscious and quivering in agony from their close encounters with the force field's static discharge next to an unconscious Daniel Finley and several other protesters, all of whom were in similar critical conditions. "Serves you right, you old bastards," Huey spat. "What the fuck did you think you were doing? You sons of *bitches*! Look at what y'all done *done*!"

"Frankly, captain," Christopher weakly and barely audibly groaned, "we don't feel like hearing one of your 'sermons on the mount' right now."

"Look into my *eyes*, Chrissy!" Huey took his right index finger and peeled down on his bottom eyelid for a moment for effect. "Does it look like I give a *fuck*? You claim to know so much about Mother Africa, about Egypt? Do you know what this Consortium was named after? *Alexandrian*, as in the library of Alexandria? The biggest baddest library there was back then *and they burnt it down!*" Huey's fists were shaking from anger over being too injured to chase any of the thousands of protesters down, anger over the destruction of one of his favorite places ever, and from anger over this self-professed expert on history that lay before him either not seeing, or worse, not caring about the significance of the Time Travel Consortium's namesake. "They burnt it *the fuck down!* And now your dumb-ass done repeated history, just like you did in 2006! Boy, you are *so* lucky this wasn't the only consortium in the midwest, 'cause if it was, *I'd take y'all off the planet!*"

"Captain," Lieutenant Castelblanch said mournfully as she staggered wincing from her injuries towards her superior officer, "you have to get to the hospital right away."

"Don't worry, Cheshta, I'm not *quite* as bad as I look," Huey sounded deceptively calm after having cussed out Minister Christopher, "but I suppose all these losers lying here have some major internal bleeding going on and they're going to need—"

"I'm not talking about that, sir," Huey saw something was wrong and leaned towards her to pay closer attention, "I just got a call from Loyola Medical Center when I was putting these Nazis in one of the PO cars; your wife and your ancestor were jumped by—"

That was all Huey needed to hear before defying the aches and pains that cascaded across his form as he dashed for where his red Saturn was parked.

* * *

For a very brief and fleeting moment, Fred thought all of the things that had happened in the past nine days; Huey coming to fly him away, time travel, Li'l Bobby's blasphemy, the seven signs of the Biblical revelations, the attempt on his life, had all been part of an elaborate dream since he found himself awaking in the very same bed suspended by anti-gravity in the very same hospital room that he had awakened in a week and a half ago with Dr. Joanna Cohen once again dotingly standing over him. Then Fred felt a sharp pain on the back of his head which reminded him that the aforementioned events were real and they in fact explained why he would be right back in the hospital.

"Where's Marta? Is she alright? And Nim—"

"Take it easy, Fred," Dr. Cohen soothed, "Marta's down the hall resting. She was beaten pretty bad, but she'll be fine. The Melkotsurakian however," Dr. Cohen's eyes fell to the floor, "didn't make it."

"Allah be merciful," Fred muttered. As he sat himself up, Dr. Cohen laid a hand on his shoulder. Sensing she was about to tell him to lay back down, Fred stated, "I want to see her."

"You have a concussion and I want you to stay here overnight for observation," Dr. Cohen sternly ordered, "which means *no* gallivanting off with Huey after he's finished seeing Marta."

"Fine, come show me which room they're in," Fred grunted.

Dr. Cohen led Fred down and across the hall she spoke of to a room where another doctor, a young Black male, stood off to the side as Huey was standing over Marta holding her hand. Fred noted that the hospital must have already healed her wounds on a cosmetic level, as they did him, but from the look on her face there was clearly more internal healing that had to be done.

"Hey, Grand X! I was going to see you next, they were just about to put Marta to sleep," Huey turned to his wife who grimaced at the remark, "just kidding, actually they were just about to give her something so she can rest for the rest of the day. Which is why I didn't get Bobby out of school 'cause she'd be asleep anyway, as I'm sure you're glad to hear."

Fred saw that Huey feeling at his side and favoring one leg, "are *you* alright?"

"They just got done patching me back up, I'll be back up to snuff in a couple of days. There was a riot at the Time Travel Consortium and it got—well, I don't want to talk about it."

Fred came around to the other side of Marta's floating bed, took the hand Huey wasn't holding, and noticed the tremor in his voice as he spoke. "Marta, I am so sorry I couldn't fight those bastards off. I'm so ashamed of myself, I got knocked out before I could even get one hit in while you—"

"Fred it's not your fault, it's mine," Marta squeezed Fred's hand assuredly and smiled, "I was just telling Huey how when I was growing up in India I used to fake doctors' excuses to keep from having to learn martial arts in school. I don't know if anyone told you yet, but part of the Compulsory Curriculum requires that all girls have the equivalent of a first degree black belt by the time they're sixteen, and—I always thought being taught martial arts would make me feel like a victim somehow. But I see now I was coy for thinking I was so clever because I kept anyone from finding out how I had gone without ever learning it. I just hate I had to find out how wrong I was the hard way, and at the expense of you and—*Nim . . .*"

Fred's next question was in fact going to be had Marta found out about Nim but the tears welling up in her eyes was more than answer enough. "I think we better leave Mrs. Rush alone so Dr. M'Benga here can administer the sedative," Dr. Cohen said while motioning to the young Black doctor who had been quietly standing off to the side.

Huey and Fred left without saying a word and stood out in the hall until Dr. Cohen and Dr. M'Benga exited Marta's room. M'Benga headed for the end of the hall and rounded the corner.

Before Cohen followed the young doctor, she glared back at Fred and wagged her index finger at him as a warning. "Remember, you're to stay here o-ver-night."

After she had walked out of sight or earshot, Huey smiled and quipped, "so what y'all going to be doing *overnight*?"

"Huey, do you know anything about the four boys who beat us up?" Fred asked, ignoring his descendant's lewd comment. "Were they skinheads or something?"

"There hasn't been a 'skinhead' in 300 years," Huey pointed out, "but don't worry, the POs did manage to catch them. And from what I heard on the way over here, they were from some survivalist camp."

"Survivalist?"

"They think the Interstellar Community are cannibals from outer space," Huey grinned somewhat, "and they're all holed up in these little camps getting ready to go to war against the IC in case of an invasion or something."

"Well that's ridiculous," Fred exclaimed, "poor Nim was peaceful and gentle and—*Allah*, people like that ought to be rounded up and had something done with them!"

Huey's brow furrowed from being puzzled over Fred's vehemence. "I just told you we caught all of them, old man."

"No, I mean the *rest* of them, holed up as you say in these camps! Maybe the Melkotsurakians can fly down and wipe the whole lot of them out!"

"First of all, the Melkotsurakians would never take revenge on the survivalists only to make every paranoid preconceived notion these insignificant assholes have ever had about the IC come true," Huey sighed in frustration as if Fred should've somehow already reached this conclusion, "second of all, you can't just bust a whole bunch of folks just because a couple of them fucked up."

"How can you say that?" Fred sounded both incredulous and incensed. "They killed Nim! And they beat your own wife!"

"The POs said that the four of them were all piss-ass drunk too. So are you going to illegalize alcohol? Because a case can be made that they wouldn't have done what they did if they weren't drinking. And if you do that, then we'll have to illegalize everything else that might prompt folks to fight, from watching violent TV to wearing gang colors. Until we look up and find ourselves right back in the Lost-Found Nation of Islam in North America."

"That's not fair," Fred frowned, "I wasn't talking about going that far into the extreme."

"Isn't it?" Huey shot back. "Boy, you *are* a moderate just like your dear old dad if you think just a little good old fascist—sorry, *fashioned* law and order'll go a long way. Well let me tell you something; 'just a little' law and order can turn into too damn much before you know it."

Huey felt at his temple for a moment before speaking again. "Look, anytime you illegalize something, you have to make sure no one has it, does it, or even *flaunts* whatever it is, no matter what the cost. Otherwise there's no point in having made 'it' illegal, is there? The problem is, if you're seen running around like a chicken with its head cut off trying to enforce a billion and one different laws, and ordinances, and edicts, and so forth, then the people, especially young people, will have all the less respect for law and order. In other words, you only police just what you know you *can* police and police *well*. Otherwise you wind up burning yourself out trying to police every-little-thing.

"This is why we have as many freedoms as we do now-a-days, because we realized a long time ago that freedom—is a lot like *alcohol*. Most folks can get plastered and not need another drink for the rest of their life, and then there are a few folks who—well, a few folks who are natural born alcoholics and fuck shit up. Now, is it *fair*, as you say, to take alcohol away from everybody else and waste ducats making sure no one ever has it just 'cause *a few* folks can't handle their shit? No, of course not. Is it *fair* to illegalize public stripping and waste ducats making sure no one ever does it just 'cause *a few* folks can't take no from a woman for an answer and can't keep their dick in their pants? No, of course not."

"But—but we're not talking about drinking or naked folks," Fred shook his head and fanned his hands as if Huey had missed the point he was trying to make, "we're talking about a murder! And an *assault* . . ?"

"*Look*, I have enough respect for my feelings not to let them get all riled up by something as emotionally charged as this. White folks in the 20th century used to be goaded into falling for this kind of shit all the time. In fact, that's actually what my favorite holographic movie of all time is about; *Three Strikes and You're Dead*! It came out a couple of years ago and it's about this guy who's daughter was killed by some big time crook and he whipped folks up into this big frenzy to pass this skull-fuck stupid law where if you were caught after doing any three crimes; big crimes, little crimes, medium crimes, didn't matter, you went to jail for-*ever*. So the folks like the dead daughter's father built this big space station, like the Death Star from *Star Wars*? Except that it was a penal colony, and pretty soon it got so full of small time crooks who were in there for minutiae that there wasn't any room left for the very kind of big time crooks who killed dude's daughter in the first damn place!

"But you couldn't tell folks shit, 'cause if anybody tried and let anyone who was jam packed in the penal colony for minutiae go, they got branded 'soft on crime' by folks like the daughter's father, and in the movie being branded was like the kiss of death. If anybody with the least bit of sense tried to say how stupid the whole situation was, they were made to look all cruel and shit 'cause folks like the father would come up and say something emotionally charged like, 'if it had been *your* daughter, you would do anything for law and order . . .' Well, this went on and on until eventually the penal colony got so damn crowded folks finally started killing off the prisoners one by one to make more space, hence the title of the movie, and made the killings look like accidents or racial prison fights. And if anybody told the truth about it, they were called a conspiracy nut or—"

"Alright, alright, already, I get your point," Fred rubbed his temples as if the act in of itself was a sign of surrender. "I've been beaten in yet another debate, satisfied?"

"Fred, it's not about beating you, it's about teaching you," Huey took a calming breath and managed a half-hearted smile before continuing. "There's nothing wrong with getting a little hot under the collar like you just did. Hell, today at the riot, I said some things to a certain minister I probably shouldn't have. But the key to it all is to remember everything I just told you the next time you feel like coming down hard on somebody. Now I've got to go home and see about Li'l Bobby and you better hop back into bed so you won't keep Dr. Cohen waiting. Wink, wink, nudge, nudge."

CHAPTER ELEVEN

"R u s h   t o   j u d g m e n t"

Fred never knew if Dr. Cohen had ever checked in on him to see whether he had gallivanted off with Huey or not. Because after his descendant had left, Fred felt so weary from everything that had happened on Friday the 13th that he decided to sleep for the rest of the day and the night.

It wasn't until Fred awoke the next morning that he realized his room, the very hospital room he had awakened to the 25th century for the first time in, was just as utterly sparse as he remembered. Fred then asked the room's computer for the time of day and received no audible response. Surely Dr. Cohen didn't think she still had to keep him in the same bare and viewless room (devoid of any technology save the reclining anti-gravity bed) where he first came to after 380 years in order to prevent any futuristic stimuli such as verbal access to the room's computer (which Fred correctly assumed that she must have initially "locked out") or a telephone/television screen from inducing culture shock? She simply must not have gotten around to sprucing the place up any in the time Fred had been gone, or perhaps putting him in his old room was all her idea of a joke. Either way, Fred wanted access to a computer screen or some other means by which the news of the day could be related to him. He remembered from the Bible that the next of the seven signs of the revelations were to be a deluge of locusts and wanted to see if any such plague had been mentioned on the news.

Fred recalled noticing a fairly wide screen on the wall of Marta's room and proceeded to walk down the hall in hopes that she was both awake herself and in the mood to watch the news as well. He found however that while she was up, she wasn't exactly alone. In addition to Dr. M'Benga, four Melkotsurakians were standing over Marta's bed and all turned to face Fred as he stood in her doorway before speaking through their universal translator headsets again. It seemed that whatever conversation they were all having was wrapping itself up despite Fred's intrusion, for Marta had bid the Melkotsurakians farewell before slipping her translator off and Dr. M'Benga began to politely usher the aliens out of her room. Marta assured Fred that the members of the Interstellar Community Consulate who had just left were running late anyway and had only stopped by to say how they didn't blame either Marta or Fred for what happened to Nim.

Fred sensed there was something Marta was omitting and upon further pressing she finally admitted that in the 60 odd years that the IC had kept in contact and lived with the human race, no human had ever murdered an alien for any reason. And though Nim was the only extraterrestrial casualty from the previous day's violence, there was already serious talk of the Melkotsurak breaking off contact with Earth altogether. Marta also told Fred that while they were talking she tried to explain how the timing of the eclipse unfortunately coincided with the Biblical context of the other "revelationary" events of the past week and contributed to the drunken mood Nim's killers were in. Marta hoped that the Melkotsurakians would see how such a rare set of circumstances were far from the norm on Earth and would surely never happen again or result in another alien death.

Rather she saw that her argument had only added to theirs when they told her how inexcusable it was for anyone to allow themselves to be so "emotionally charged" by some unexplained phenomena and that being so "excitable" only went to show that man hadn't changed since the days he claimed a White man with a long beard was responsible for throwing the lightning bolts which were seen across the night sky over a millennium ago.

At this point, Fred felt ashamed of the original reason why he came to Marta's room in the first place, which was to see if any other of the seven signs had occurred. But before he could leave without letting Marta in on the intent of his visit or his shame over it, Marta invited him to stay and watch the news with her, allowing Fred to save face in a sense. He was surprised by her charitable gesture, but not nearly as surprised as when he found out after eventually finding a news or educational channel that bothered to cover something other than labor news or broadcast something other than a history lesson (the channel selection in 25th century hospitals was just as limited as that of the free studios) that instead of the sixth of the seven signs—a swarm of locusts—the seventh sign, what the Bible predicted to be "a falling star," was about to take place instead.

Fred silently wondered why God had all the other signs occur in order besides this one while a pair of anchorwomen reported how at two a.m. that morning astronomers discovered that a meteor the size of a football field had suddenly and inexplicably veered off its natural, scheduled course towards Venus and was now headed straight for the eastern coastal tip of the state of Florida. Given the meteor's rate of acceleration, experts predicted that it would land at approximately noon the next day, Sunday the 15th. Every square mile between Miami to Key Largo was being evacuated for they anticipated that the impact might be comparable to that of one of the first atomic bombs ever made.

When Fred incredulously asked how could coverage of this magnitude be so hard to find, Marta shrugged and simply responded by describing how while in the 20th century something on order of a ship sinking, a plane crashing, or a meteor landing would monopolize every airwave and distract the public from more important issues, in the 25th century media priorities had changed, and such an event was only considered "local news" since it wasn't happening in the Midwest. Since evacuation procedures in 2410 were so impeccably streamlined that any loss of life the meteor might cause was certain to be absolutely minuscule, and since society in general was no longer materialistic enough to harbor too much anxiety over the costs of property damage, Marta pointed out that the Chicago press probably wouldn't have reported the Florida disaster at all were it not for all the other, primarily local religiously significant disasters as of late.

After spending all morning and most of the afternoon in Marta's room searching the channels for testimonies from scientists about the meteor or commentaries about its significance, Dr. Cohen finally checked in on Fred during a late lunch and reluctantly prognosed that he was medically free to leave. When she tried to inquire as to what Fred had thought of 25th century life so far, he anxiously sidestepped conversing with Dr. Cohen altogether, thanked Marta for having him in her room so long and said his good byes to them both. Fred then caught the first taxi bus heading for the Robert Taylor Free Studios, went straight to his studio, cut on his desktop computer, and resumed searching for any channel with any other information about the meteor. Just as Fred had found a segment of a newscast with a fascistic commentator he immediately found very obnoxious who swore that God had sent down "the Rock of Ages" to punish the Jews and that the lack of "solemn and reverent" coverage of the seven signs was tantamount to censorship, the computer's feminine voice spoke over the commentator's voice and informed Fred that he had a call coming in from Huey Rush.

Fred anxiously bit his lip as he tried to catch as much of the fascist commentary as he could despite how abrasive the commentator came across to him before finally telling the desktop computer to put Huey's call through. Huey made a joke Fred didn't understand about how he was sorry if he had interrupted Fred's following of something called "the OJ trial coverage" before stating how he and Li'l Bobby must have just missed Fred at the hospital when they both came to visit Marta. Fred asked why didn't they come by the hospital sooner and Huey explained how he spent the morning at a gym working out some frustrations despite how tender he still felt from the few, insignificant injuries he sustained at the riot outside the Time Travel Consortium.

Huey went on to say how he wanted Fred to come have the Rushes' traditional Sunday Jewish brunch with the family in Marta's hospital room since she would be bedridden for another couple days still. He then said how while Marta approved of the idea, Bobby explained how he didn't want the Jewish brunch in a hospital since part of the tradition was that the brunch has always been held at home. Huey saw this was just an excuse once it was suggested that they had the brunch at home after all and *still* invite Fred over. At which point Bobby then snapped his fingers and claimed he just remembered how he had other plans for Sunday morning anyway but refused to say what they were.

Fred really didn't mind that Li'l Bobby wasn't looking forward to seeing him again because the feeling was mutual and told Huey that if Bobby "had other plans" not to keep the boy from them on his account. Fred also said that he also didn't feel like going back to the hospital anyway because of Dr. Cohen's "mothering" bedside manner despite the fact that he's no longer a patient of hers. Huey grinned wide and almost knowingly at this before finally telling Fred to come on by the Rush house first thing in the morning, stating that if the Sunday Jewish brunch wound up only consisting of the two of them then that's how it would be.

* * *

"You know, if you were going to eat brunch with me here in the hospital after all, then Huey and Fred might as well have come along too."

Marta dabbed the corners of her mouth with a napkin after only barely touching one of the warm blueberry knishes that her son Bobby had brought from home in a satchel along with several other Hasidic delicacies for the both of them to eat. "Yeah, it's a shame Huey can't be here, isn't it?" Bobby lamented.

"You know what I mean, Bobby," Marta narrowed her eyes at her son and sighed.

"Marta," Bobby threw up his hands almost in exhaustion, "you said he sat up in here with you and watched coverage of the meteor coming down all day yesterday like he was some poor White trash housewife from the 20th century worrying about Tonya Harding's guilt. If he was in here right now, I'd have to keep myself from talking shit about how much he was getting worked up over some damn rock falling from the sky a la Chicken Little. I wouldn't even be able to digest my food properly if I had to listen to him constantly hooping and hollering, '*Lawd* have mercy' the whole time like it's the end of the world or something."

"Life hasn't been very fair to Fred, Bobby," Marta offered, "before he was your age he was accidentally left in the Lost-Found Nation where he was eventually arrested, beaten, separated from his only son, frozen alive, and now he has to adjust to life 400 years from the only time he's ever known. Considering everything that he's been through, plus the fact that Farrakhanism was all that he's ever been exposed to in his adult life, I think Fred's coping with the unfair hand life's dealt him and all these—*revelations* the best way he can. Which is why you ought to give him the benefit of the doubt."

"There's nothing 'unfair' about what happened to him at all," Bobby amended, "because since there's no God, life is fair."

"*This* is a new one," Marta sat up with peeked interest in her levitating hospital bed floating three feet off the floor via anti-gravity, "is this principle the subject of another prize-winning paper of yours?"

Bobby ignored his mother's comment and began to explain what he had meant. "Since nature is indifferent and existence is chaos, then any events, or series of events—*whatever the hell they happen to remind people of,* only occur completely at random. So what could be more fair than that? If a baby comes in the world deformed at random 'cause of bad DNA, then so it goes, but if it turns out it was 'Allah's will' or some such thing that decided it'd come out deformed, then *that's* unfair. There's-no-*way* I'd let a decision that's going to affect a baby's whole life rest in the hands of someone who thinks like a human (and some say looks like one too) with that much power! No way in hell!

"To this day, you're still not allowed to pick the sex of your babies or abort them if you find out the fetus'll be homosexual, so why the hell would we trust that kind of power to somebody we've never met, let alone can't even see? If power corrupts and absolute power corrupts absolutely then God must be infinitely corrupt because he has infinite power—"

"Spoken like a true anarchist," Marta grinned.

"Anyway, it's not fair to have some—*guy* running around with that much power deciding our fate, it would be much more fair if everything in life all happened at random. Sure, that means there won't be a God to help you out of a jam, but on the other hand it means there won't be a God to *hurt* you either.

"Besides, what's fair about spending *all eternity* in Hell for committing a sin that took 30 seconds to do? Even the judges from that movie *Three Strikes and You're Dead*! weren't that anal! The only way the afterlife would be fair is if it didn't exist at all, and have everybody; 'good' or 'evil'—just black out forever. Like you told me death was like when I was little—*permanent unconsciousness*; with no awareness or sensation of the passage of time."

"Sounds like to me you just *hope* there's not a God," Marta teased, "'it would be much more fair if *this*,' 'it won't be much more fair than *that*,' it doesn't sound like you sound too sure He doesn't exist."

"Sure I'm sure!" Bobby fumed, sounding as though a nerve of his had been struck.

"Are you really?" Marta wagged her finger at her son. "Because it sounds like to me you weren't just worried about Fred telling you what to do, Fred's also reminding you of all those nightmares you used to have about dying and going to Hell."

"I don't think so, Marta," Bobby fanned his hands dismissingly. "I think you're reaching."

"Am I? When you were little, vampires and werewolves never fazed you, and you even used to say how the Mummy wasn't scary because he moved so slow, you remember that? Huh?"

"Yeah," Bobby shrugged admittingly.

"The only shows that did scare you were *Heaven Can Wait*, *Here Comes Mr. Jordan*, *Highway to Heaven*, and any *Twilight Zone* episode with an angel or someone selling their soul to the devil. Even *The Kid With the Broken Halo* kept you up for a whole week. Which is why Huey sat down with you with those comic books one night and showed you, in his own indelible fashion, how if you could go back and somehow convey to the ancient Vikings that *The Mighty Thor* would be nothing more than a title from Marvel Comics in their future they'd never believe you."

"And then Huey showed me the latest issue of *The New Adventures of Jesus* and said how no one in the 20th century would believe that Jesus would be just a comic book hundreds of years in their future any more than the Vikings would believe Thor would. I remember, I remember."

"That's right. He explained that given enough time, people can overcome their fears, and I think that it's only fair if you give Fred some time to overcome his."

"Nice of you to worm that in," Bobby said with a slight snarl. "Trying to get me and him to . . . Wait, you're not going soft on me now, are you? All these so-called signs aren't making you doubt your atheism, are they Marta? You didn't have one of those out-of-body-experiences when you were hurt Friday, did you?"

"*No*, you know those silly things were debunked 200 years ago," Marta waved her hand at Bobby for him to perish the thought, "but Fred, and a whole lot of other people out there, are just as afraid as you once were." Marta paused a moment before saying, "*I'm* even a little scared, not because I think God's 'coming to get me' but simply because I don't know why all these things are happening any more than you or anyone else does. And it's perfectly natural to fear the unknown."

"Now wait-a-minute," Bobby held up his hands, "I know exactly what's going on: A bunch of scientific flukes, one after another—"

"No, Bobby, you don't know that for sure. You have no proof, no one does. There's no way to tell one way or the other, which is the one thing both you and Fred have in common: Neither one of you knows what's going on and both of you, whether *you* want to admit that *you* are or not, are scared half to death. This is what I meant by giving Fred the benefit of the doubt."

"But there's no way it could be what he thinks it is!" Bobby exclaimed. "It's not scientifically possible!"

"Correction; you *hope* it's not scientifically possible," Marta added. "But that's OK, I'm hoping it's not scientifically possible too. We all are, and I'm pretty sure you're the one who's right about—" Marta looked about her wildly, "*all this*, but you're not helping your case any by feeding into the stereotype Fred's been taught most his life by the Lost-Found Nation of the Stalinist *Dahri* who burns down temples because he's afraid of something. And if you're *not* afraid of anything then don't act like it by shouting down someone like Fred who clearly isn't as intel—well, let's just say as *well-read* as you are. You only make yourself look like a bully that way. Just think about that the next time—alright, *if* you ever see Fred again." Marta laid a hand on Bobby's shoulder and squeezed. "Now, I want you to take all this brunch stuff and *go straight home*, alright? Not everyone in the world knows how to handle their fear as well as some and for the first time in decades the streets of Chicago aren't safe anymore."

* * *

"You know, so much has been going on I forgot to ask you something I've been meaning to bring up since we saw *Beyond the Beyond*," Huey spread some peppered lox on the onion center of a bialy he had heated while conversing with Fred across his dining table. "I noticed you—I don't know, *shuddered* when the hero kissed his boyfriend goodbye at the beginning of the movie. I mean, I know you came up in the Nation and all and there's no reason why you shouldn't still be at least a little homophobic but—I'm just curious; *are* you?"

Fred looked as though he were looking inside himself for an answer and said, "I remember that's all they talked about back at the Ostrowski Home for Boys; who's a fag, who might be, who's turning into one. I remember after a while I got tired of hearing about it, but I never . . ." Fred shook his head slightly and shoulders in mild disgust. "I don't know, I've just never seen two men kissing before."

"Well, get over it," Huey warned with a smile, "'cause believe it or not, it was proved ages ago that homosexuality always was genetic and not some kind of perverse sin. They also say it's nature's way of keeping the population down since people don't have strict, involuntary mating cycles like animals do."

Fred stroked his chin thoughtfully for a moment. "I wonder what Khallid Muhammad would say if someone told him that fags were part of the natural order?"

"I'm telling you all this because I don't want you embarrassing yourself the next time you see two dudes kissing in public. And even though there's no PC police running around correcting folks' grammar or anything, unless you want one of those 'fags' to whup your ass, you better call them 'gays' instead."

"Khallid used to tell us they were too feminine to fight." Fred wondered even as he was saying these words whether Huey would mistake what he had said for bravado.

"One of my lieutenants, Harlan Kendle is gay," Huey pointed out, "and you should have seen him beat the living shit out of these Nazis who were all around him after they broke through the force field at the Time Travel Consortium riot—" Huey then paused and sank his head in his hands in angst. "*Man*, I can't believe those—i-*di*-ots, burning down the Consortium like that! Goddamn it! One of my favorite places . . ."

"Well, while we're on the subject of reactions to the signs," Fred opportunistically said, taking a hint from Huey's own obliviousness to other people's bad moods, "can we turn on your screen and watch the news?"

"And here I thought you came to see *me*," Huey said sarcastically before looking up at his wide screen in the den across from them both, "computer, cut it on—hell, I don't know, any damn channel covering that comet shit."

Fred shot Huey a look of disdain for not taking the meteor landing (or Fred's interest in it) seriously before turning to the screen to watch the meteor, which the media took to calling the Rock of Ages, begin to enter Earth's atmosphere from the point of view of the camera helmet of a rocket jockey flying as close to it as safely possible. The commentary from the newscasters sounded rather dry and merely reiterated what they were being told by the scientific community and experts on the subject. Huey rested his head on the palm of one hand and leaned into it, causing his elbow to slowly slide down his table under his weight a little. The frown on his face indicated his boredom and maybe even some hidden frustration over the fact that none of his fellow peace officers, locally or abroad, had any explanation behind these Biblical phenomena besides the obvious religious one.

Even though the Rock of Ages was said to be traveling at hundreds of miles an hour, on screen it looked as though it was moving at a snail's pace. So eventually, Fred himself became bored with just watching the underbelly of the Rock of Ages become red with heat from its entry into Florida airspace and verbally commanded the screen to search the many channels within its range of reception for any additional coverage of the revelations. The newscasts Fred watched varied between stories of a despondent few who committed ritual suicides in despair that the world was coming to an end to images of mass prayers held in the middle of street traffic. A couple of the stories however took an even more sordid turn. In Tulsa, Oklahoma, a newborn baby boy was killed by his parents who thought he was the Anti-Christ because of an odd shaped birthmark on his head and in Turlock, California a family of four who wanted to escape God's wrath purposely burned themselves to death because they believed that they had to pass through a fiery death in order to be reborn on an unheard of planet known as Sirius. To wit, Fred thought to himself, were they *serious*?

"Man, I'm sick of this," Huey's voice startled Fred out of the entranced stupor he was in from watching the screen without any conversation between them for several minutes. "Change it."

"I can't believe you or anyone else in this time," Fred huffed as he turned from the screen to face Huey, "anytime anybody has something to say about a union, or a co-op, *or* a collective, or how bad the Nation used to be, folks around here are all ears. Historical documentaries on *this* channel, political debates on *that* channel, but this," Fred pointed at the screen and sounded shaken, "this could mean the end of the world! It could mean that we're all going straight to Hell! And it doesn't seem to faze any one of you people in the least!"

"Well, not *me*, anyway," Huey snorted with a slight grin, "look, I'll put it like Martin Luther King did, *a preacher* no less. He said, 'I'm much more concerned with this life than the life after. I'm not concerned with the temperature of Hell or the furnishings of Heaven, but with the things men do here on Earth.'"

"So the intrepid *Captain Rush* is not the least bit frightened," Fred folded his arms, "not in the slightest?"

"Martin Luther King *also* said, 'no man is free if he fears death,' and that he'd, 'rather be dead than afraid.' For someone Black folks always wrote off as some kind of wimp, he was one bad motherfucker. But the thing is, even if I thought there was a heaven I wouldn't want to spend eternity with a big an asshole as God! Look at His track record! The guy tells Abraham to take his only son to the mountain top and 'kak' his ass. So Abraham goes up there, the whole time he's crying like a big dog wishing he didn't have to do it, and just as he's about to plunge the knife, God shows up at the last minute and says, *psyche*! You didn't have to do it, Abe! I was just testing your faith, that's all!'" Huey paused and purposely gasped for effect. "'Testing my faith' *my ass*! There's no way in *hell* I'd even *think* of sacrificing my only son over some shit like that . . ! It's worse than *Sophie's Choice*!"

Fred didn't say anything of Huey's blasphemous tone but instead sighed and thought out loud, "I had to sacrifice my only son."

"Yeah, I guess you did," Huey was silent for a long moment before asking Fred, "I bet you've been so busy watching for 'the signs' that you haven't even seen one of the movies made about Junior, have you?"

"Actually, except for when we flew past that mural of him when you took me hom—*here* from the hospital, I haven't seen any footage of him."

"*What*?" Huey sounded as incredulous as he ever had in his life, "why the hell not? That's your boy! He's a legend! He molded our whole damn society with his bare hands!" Huey illustrated briefly with sculpting hand movements. "He was 'pimp' as fuck! And you haven't seen *any* footage of him in action, any at all?"

Fred merely shook his head, "I guess I just want to remember my little Elisha as—as *my little Elisha*, that's all."

"Well Li'l Elisha done grown up, son," Huey turned from Fred to his screen, "computer, cut this Sunday morning Rapture testimony off and play me a little something from *Tales of the Reconstruction*; the documentary that came out right after Fred Rush Jr. died. Any scene with Junior styling and profiling in it."

It took a moment for the computer to discern what exactly its master had requested but an image soon replaced the coverage of the meteor's descent with a Black man in his mid 20's with a goatee who was wearing a blue and black Asiatic, possibly Chinese robe and had his dreadlocks bound behind him in a ponytail. Fred's jaw gaped open in shock when he saw the figure move on screen and speak with just enough of the same intonation he remembered his son having so long ago for the man's voice to sound painfully yet amiably familiar.

"Junior" had his arms folded as he sat in a director's folding chair across from a balding and disheveled White man with horn rimmed glasses. Before them both was an audience of around a hundred and they were all on their feet with their hands eagerly raised. "Yeah, you in the back," Junior stately addressed.

"Yeah, *Junior*, since it hasn't been proven once and for all that the CIA killed JFK, shouldn't you say that it's only your opinion that they did it before you go around calling for an end to all military intelligence?"

Junior furrowed his brow before raising one eyebrow above the other in frustrated angst over the extremely snide inquiry. "It sounds like to me that you don't know enough about poli sci to tell the difference between a fact and an opinion, so let me give you a little civics lesson: There are facts and then there are opinions *based* on said facts. For instance, it's a fact the Holocaust happened and there are opinions based on that. The left-wing's opinion is that the Holocaust should never happen again whereas the unpopular opinion of the far right is that the Jews supposedly got just what they deserved. But you can't say it's your *opinion* that the Holocaust never happened at all because that would be a flat out lie.

"The same thing with JFK. It *is* a proven fact that a coup d' etat went down on November 22nd and the left's opinion is that the CIA should be strung up for their part in it. While the opinion of the right is that E. Howard Hunt and Frank Sturgis ought to be given medals. So don't tell me I need to go around with some kind of damn disclaimer hanging around my neck because I'm supposedly so biased, huh, pal? Because when I say the CIA killed JFK, it ain't nothing but truth. And if the truth so happens to turn people away from the right and towards the left because their inherent morality finds something reprehensible about 'military intelligence' then so it goes. Next question, *please*."

"Junior, the World Socialist Party has said that if they were powerful enough to be in a position to require an equal time rule to begin with, then they wouldn't bother with such a little thing but they'd go after bigger and better things like ending capitalism itself. What's your response to that?"

Junior scowled, not at the young man who asked the question, but at the very thought of those he knew all too well who the man was referring to. "The problem with them niggers is they still don't know something even a Muslim deal-cutting moron like George Lincoln Rockwell knew, who said, 'the first phase is to reach the masses; you can do nothing until you've reached the masses.' I'm sorry, y'all, but we couldn't have a socialist revolution today even if we wanted to. Now for the first time in a long while the left has the firepower to *attain* it (which is exactly why the boys in the WSP vanguard are all power drunk), but none of y'all are educated or intellectual enough to *maintain* and *sustain* it, not yet anyway.

"Which is why we need an equal time rule, so y'all can get exposed to enough and be well-rounded enough to know how to put mechanisms into place that'll continually sustain the gains of a revolution generation after generation. And if you ever doubt an equal time rule should be our first priority, just think back to what the powers that be used to tell us back in the 20th: That if people really wanted to find out about Noam Chomsky or the Peace and Freedom

Party, they would take advantage of the so-called free press, go out of their way to those 'conspiratorial' underground bookstores everyone used to malign or marginalize, and find out about the far left for themselves. 'We have a free marketplace of ideas,' they used to say, 'if people wanted to hear Chomsky as much as they hear Rush Limbaugh, then the market would've demanded it.' Well as I just got done saying at Berkeley, *you can't choose what you don't know exists!* *All* a man's choices must be *clearly* laid out before him if the choice itself is going to mean anything. If I set a glass of water and a glass of weak lemonade on a table and I'm hiding a beer behind my back—unless your ass has x-ray vision, you are *not* going to get that beer!" Laughing rolled throughout Junior's audience. "The right knew this, even if the WSP still doesn't, which is exactly why Reagan struck down the Fairness Doctrine in 1987. Because, unlike the WSP, I bet Reagan read his Shakespeare before his memory finally gave out." This line garnered some laughs from those who were old enough to remember the inference Junior had made.

"He must have recalled that scene in *Julius Caesar* where Cassius is telling Brutus' dumb-ass, 'don't let Marc Anthony speak after you! He'll sway the people!' But Brutus didn't listen, and after Brutus got the crowd all whipped up into a frenzy thinking Caesar *deserved* to get killed . . . See? Even *Brutus* didn't try to lie and claim some lone defector did it!" More laughter came from the audience. "Anyway, after Brutus had the crowd convinced the assassination was a good thing, my boy Marc Anthony took the mike, appealed to that *inherent morality* y'all always hear me talk about, turned that crowd around 180 degrees, and had *all* them Roman motherfuckers running Brutus and Cassius out of town on a rail!

"The whole time they were running? I bet Cassius was saying, 'if we ever get out of this, I'm going to join the GOP so I can strike down the Fairness Doctrine someday!'" Junior waited until the laughing from his joke died down before continuing. "And I know Brutus must have said, 'yeah, and in the future, I'm going to go join the WSP, so I can go on about how meaningless an equal time rule is in case anybody tries to bring it back!'" At this point, Junior's audience was clapping and cheering as well as in hysterics while some were on their feet and crying, "Ju-*nior*! Ju-*nior*! Ju-*nior*!"

Fred on the other hand was saddened by what he had just seen and Huey order the screen to shut itself off when this was noticed. "He was a great man, Fred, you got a lot to be proud of. He was the best." Huey looked to see that Fred wasn't crying so much as he was merely somber and saw this as an opportunity to say some more about Junior. "Here's a little known fact; the motto that Junior lived by, 'with great power comes great responsibility' actually came from a line in the first comic book Spiderman ever appeared in. Junior used it to teach that if the corporate elite in y'all's day had 10 times the power that elected officials had (since they paid for those leaders' campaigns) then the elite ought to have 10 times the responsibility too. And the use of that power/responsibility quote always did go over real well, but for the longest no one knew it was ol' Spidey who had coined the phrase."

"I remember Spiderman!" Fred looked over to Huey's holographic disk still projecting holograms of various heroic figures from pop culture. "I remember in the underground, Baines had Elisha watching 'Spidey' on a program called *The Electric Company* she had on 'video tape' while I was talking to her! But—Allah, that was the last day I ever saw Elisha—"

Huey scratched the back of his head while he thought for a moment and then proposed, "you know—you need to take your mind off of this seven signs shit, and frankly, I'm getting sick of hearing about it. So let's take a trip down memory lane! Let's see if we can find where your old house used to be before Nasrin . . ?"

"Nayirah," Fred said flatly.

"Yeah, before she blew it up! What was your old address again?"

"Actually, Huey, I don't know if I feel like seeing my old house again. And besides, there wouldn't be anything left to see of it anyway."

"We can see what's been built over it, and then we can see if we can try and find where the apple tree house was!" Huey enthused. "You know, the one where you went off on that old woman when she hit Junior!"

"Why don't we try to find the underground's secret tunnels while we're at it?" Fred snorted.

"What? Do you remember where they are?" Huey implored until he saw that Fred was just being sarcastic and then he sighed, "aw, hell—I just can't believe I never got around to time traveling Phantom Form to see a young Junior being schooled by the underground. But then, I have been just about everywhere and every *when* else. Boy, I hope they get the Consortium rebuilt soon, I don't want to have to go all the way out to Michigan . . ."

"Huey, if you don't want to watch any more about the signs, I can go back to my apartment and—"

"No, nigger! Where's you sense of adventure? You need to get out of the house, not be all cooped up watching *more* coverage, quivering in fear over whether or not Gag and Maggot are 'gonna getcha.' C'mon, man, let's just hang out, you know?"

"That's Gog and Magog," Fred corrected as he stood up out of his seat, stretched a bit, and grunted, "and they're . . . Oh, alright, I guess we can fly around a little before you drop me off."

"*Cool*," Huey leapt up from his chair at the dining table, "I needed to get out of the house anyway. It's so lonely in here without Marta and—"

Bobby stopped in his tracks when he saw Fred as he interrupted what his father's was saying when he came through the front door. Fred looked at Bobby once, let his eyes fall to the floor, and then turned to Huey as if to avoid having to look at the boy. "Y'all going somewhere?" Bobby asked.

"We're about to head out," Huey answered, "we're going to go see Fred's old stomping grounds. Want to come?"

Bobby glanced at Fred before responding, "no, that's alright, I'm going to stay in and study."

Huey sighed when he looked at both his son and his ancestor and shrugged, "OK, it's your loss. Don't forget to change Mr. Whiskers' litter box."

As Fred followed Huey towards the front door, Bobby stood stock still for a moment with his back to the senior Rushes, and then startled the both of them when he called out, "Fred . . !" Huey and Fred whirled around to see what the boy wanted and after Bobby huffed a breath and bit the inside of his mouth he said, "there was this hell of obscure Black radical writer back during the Kemp Years, I can't remember his name for the life of me, but he managed to break into the talk show circuit and used to talk about how if the media is the fourth branch of government then it ought to have checks and balances too—or words to that effect.

"Anyway, what this guy was saying was dead on and way ahead of his time, but he had this *really* bad attitude and would always have to be 'bleeped' on any show he was on because he'd cuss a lot. Eventually it got to the point where people used his bad attitude as a cheap-ass excuse not to listen to him, even though everything he had to say was coming true. It was a classic case of folks losing out on an important message because they were alienated by the messenger. I guess what I'm trying to say is don't make that same mistake niggers in the 20th century did; disregarding the message because of the messenger." Before anything else could be said by anyone present, Bobby left a stunned Fred and Huey in the front doorway and walked down the hall to his room.

No words were spoken between Huey and Fred until they had both gotten in Huey's red Saturn and began to lift off. "Well, ain't *that* a bitch!" Huey exclaimed. "I do believe that hard-headed boy of mine was trying to kiss and make up with you, Grand X!"

"I've heard one of his 'apologies' before," Fred scoffed while surpressing a grin, "and this sounds like yet another one of his philosophical run arounds."

"Those *are* how his apologies sound!" Huey explained. "And I declare, that boy surprises me more and more every day!"

"He . . ." Fred searched for the right words even as Huey leaned over and stared wide-eyed at him with a smile. "He's—an *alright* boy, it's just a crying shame he—I don't know. When I was a boy, I had a—sense of wonder about the world. The universe still held some mystery for me, but it seems like to me the boy thinks he knows everything, and—well, I just can't imagine growing up without believing that miracles couldn't ever happen and that life was just some cosmic accident. It all seems so cold and sterile somehow."

"Let me tell you something, ancestor-of-mine," Huey said with his tongue in his cheek, "every time we fuck we create a miracle. When Bobby was born, Dr. Osterman used to tell me and Marta that with every ejaculation, a thousand million sperm are sent after just one egg. And each and every one of those sperm is at least a little different than the next even though they're all coming from the same guy, but only one can penetrate that egg. That means the odds of *you* and *only* you being born were a thousand million to one. Now you figure if that went on every time your descendants/my ancestors got to fucking, then you have to keep multiplying those same odds over and over and over again, couples having *this* precise son, *that* precise daughter . . .

"Until you finally came up with me and *I* come up with Bobby. Which may not seem like much, until you figure what you're talking about here is the distilling of a form as specific as an individual human being from all the mass chaos going on whenever those thousand million little buggers get to swimming after that one egg. It's just as improbable a miracle as air turning to gold or water turning to wine, but it goes on every time folks fuck."

"But . . . That could be said about everybody in the whole world," Fred stammered, "who ever lived."

"Oh, yeah. But the world's so crowded with folks that, I don't know, the value of the miracle goes down like supply and demand or something. So sometimes you just have to take a step back and look at the world from another angle, from afar, like this," Huey then motioned for Fred to look out of his window and see Chicago's teeming masses sprawled on the streets below, "just to remind yourself that even though the human race may be a scientific miracle, it's still every bit as—*miraculous* as some old fashioned, stereotypical miracle."

* * *

As centuries of fate would have it, 2247 Harlem Avenue, the location of Fred's old residence had become the address of Andrew Bub's Buds and Shrooms. When the "coffee shop" came into full view of Fred from his seat in Huey's red Saturn which was descending to park, Fred was almost too mortified to speak. Huey on the other hand seemed pleasantly surprised, got out of the car to take a closer look, and eventually strolled inside the establishment much to Fred's silent dismay.

Fred decided to stay in the car until Huey emerged several minutes later with a small shopping bag puzzled that Fred hadn't taken the opportunity to roam about the area that was once his neighborhood. A stoic Fred folded his arms and offered no explanation as to why he remained seated as Huey sat back behind the driver's seat and began to search for the house that formerly belonged to "Sister" Sweanea where the course of Black history was changed forever when Fred attacked her apple tree.

After going by Fred's vague and reluctant recollections of his one visit to Ishmael's house and the subsequent frantic search for a lost Elisha, Huey finally managed long after the sun had gone down to find the exact location where Fred's outburst on an old woman's front lawn 380 years ago garnered the attention of the underground and set in motion a series of events that gave a revolution its leader. There was no longer a home where Sister Sweanea's house once was, but an empty lot undergoing construction. A nearby hologram read that an antique store called Blast From the Past would soon be opening on that spot. However there was a tall tree, albeit gnarled from age and without a single fruit or leaf for that matter, which had to be the fabled apple tree Fred took a bamboo stick too.

"I imagine with all the carnage from the counter revolution of 2045 that was going on, they missed out on the chance to memorialize this place," Huey lamented. "It's a shame how fucked up the tree is, now it looks like one of the tree monsters from *The Wizard of Oz*."

"What do you expect after 400 years?" Fred put to Huey. "Come on, let's go back to the car."

A distinct rumbling was heard and then felt underneath the Rushes' feet. Huey and Fred looked to one another, as if either had an explanation for why the ground under them was trembling. But as much as their bodies were being shaken up, the old decrepit tree was shaking even more, until both the Rushes were knocked off their feet by the sheer force of a hoard of locusts suddenly erupting from the top of the tree. The swarm flooded the sky over Fred and Huey's heads for almost a whole minute before finally flying off to the north and northwest.

When the last of the locusts had flown out of sight, Huey sat up from having been bowled over and slapped his left fist on his right hand's palm as if something had just occurred to him. "Ah *ha*! I knew it had to be something like this!" Huey turned to a still dazed and confused Fred. "Don't you see? Locusts don't live in trees! I don't know how, but all those signs have been faked!"

Huey sprang to his feet, leapt onto the side of the tree, and climbed it until he could peer past the branches and into the middle of its trunk. "Ah *fucking* ha! It's hollow! There's a tunnel under here!" Huey looked back at Fred who was still on the ground. "And here I thought God lived in the sky and *the devil* lived underground!"

"You can't be serious!" Fred cautiously stepped toward the tree, literally staggered by the concept that the judgment day he was sure was en route might now be averted if not eliminated as a possibility altogether.

"You damn skippy I am! And if some asshole has been causing all this shit to happen somehow, there's going to be hell to pay!" Huey then spat down the hollow middle of the tree, listening for the wad of spit to make impact, which he heard within a couple of seconds. "Good, it's shallow. Stay here, call the POs, and tell them to meet me out here. I'm going in!" Without another word, Huey climbed over the edge of the branches and disappeared into the center of the tree itself.

Fred was about to follow Huey's instructions and then he thought back to how helpless he felt after he found out the survivalists had knocked him unconscious with a single punch while Marta was being beaten and Nim was being murdered. She was now in the hospital and—*it* became the first alien to ever die on Terran soil because he couldn't lend a hand. Maybe he wouldn't have been able to make a difference even if he was conscious, but that would always be something Fred would never know for sure.

Fred also thought of all the advancements that he'd been exposed to thus far in the 25th century and wondered, could it be technologically possible that someone had been playing God this entire time? And if so, why would someone do something so blasphemous? After having followed what coverage there was of the seven signs, Fred was far too curious to simply stay put as Huey instructed. Surely as long as he stood by his descendant as he did in the home of James Finley nothing would happen to him, so Fred turned to the nearest and seemingly unresponsive bystanders at the scene, called out for them to call the POs, climbed up the aged apple tree, and descended into it.

* * *

Whoever had hollowed the inside of the apple tree didn't line its interior with anything such as metal or concrete, so the well, as it were, was lined initially with the inner wood of the tree itself and then dirt. The dirt surrounding the artificial well (almost four feet in diameter) below the actual length of the tree had various roots and twigs protruding out of it that Huey and then Fred were able to hold onto. Which in turn had slowed each of the Rushes' descent and halved the distance of what would have otherwise been a 30 foot fall into a hole in the ceiling of what looked like an old, abandoned subway tunnel.

Though his ankles in particular regretted the drop, Fred tried his best to ignore the pain that shot through his legs upon landing on his feet, and attempted to discern which of the two directions the tunnel stretched in Huey had traveled down. In the short time Fred took to decide whether he would join his descendant, Huey had only traversed a few dozen meters, and Fred could tell that the peace officer had taken the path ahead of him because he could barely see in the distance the light illuminating from a new cigarette lighter that Huey must have just bought from Andrew Bub's.

Fred cried out for Huey to wait for him to catch up and once he had, Huey turned to his ancestor and smiled, "believe it or not, I'm actually glad you came down here. You know what this means, don't you? This means you're my sidekick now, *Kemosabe.*"

Fred rolled his eyes but before he could say anything of Huey's ill-timed frivolity, two unusually large horseflies appeared from no where and flew in wide figure eight patterns around the Rushes. "Those goddamn—" Huey stepped ahead of Fred and towards the flies. "Remind me of the same motherfuckers from outside the Consort—"

Huey felt the ground give from under him at that moment and saw only darkness all around him because he dropped his cigarette lighter from being caught off guard when he suddenly found himself sliding down a slick, pitch-black chute. He fell through a hole in the roof of a dim, blood stained cell of a room with semi-skinned bones of livestock and poultry littered about. The dank stench was enough for Huey to contend with, but when he looked over at what was lumbering toward him out of the shadows of the corner of the room, Huey realized that the scent and the decor would be the least of his problems.

The trap door on the tunnel's floor had sealed itself shut once Huey had fell through it and Fred's instinctive stomping on it didn't help matters any. After screaming pleas for his descendant to answer, Fred felt the now familiar sensation of a gun's nozzle being pointed against his back. He slowly turned around, hoping it was one of the peace officers but instead it was a Black man in an African dashiki. An all too recognizable man who now looked to be some twenty years older than Fred remembered him to be.

"Batala," Fred gasped.

CHAPTER TWELVE

"Climbing Yacub's ladder"

"As-Salaam-Alaikum, Mr. Isiah."

Fred couldn't believe that the man he had turned around to face who was holding him at gun point, and had just said "peace be unto you" in Arabic was none other than Dr. Batala himself. Fred shook his head a brief second out of stunned amazement and tried to speak, however the shock he was experiencing caused Fred to be short of breath which initially kept any words from forming. Once this was overcome a moment later, Fred stammered, "you can't possibly be Batala, you're dead! You've been dead for 400 years!"

A huge, proud smile seeped across the doctor's face, "I'm so glad you recognized me. I, of course, remember the only man on this miserably decadent planet who could call himself a contemporary of mine. Elijah Isiah, the man whose frozen carcass helped make it possible for me to become practically immortal."

Fred scowled at being called by his "slave name" and immediately corrected Batala, "that's Fred Hampton Rush, and speaking of us Rushes, what did you do to Huey?"

"The peace officer? Oh, he's just fine, he's in a cell of mine right now."

Fred took both a breath he hoped would be emboldening and a rather brave step towards Batala, despite the fact that the doctor still had a gun trained on him. "Well, get him out of there!"

"I'm afraid not. You see, while an old man such as myself should be able to keep you at bay with *this*," Batala motioned to his gun, "I doubt I could keep both you *and* a 'PO' in check. And I couldn't very well have him use his 'martial artistry' to knock my gun from my hand so he could escape and return from the surface with reinforcements to apprehend me."

"How do you know the POs aren't *already* on their way?" Fred tried to counter.

From a pocket in his dashiki, Batala produced a black box with an antenna, a miniature TV screen, and several touch-a-matic buttons. Upon pressing a couple of those buttons, the two "horse flies" that buzzed about Huey before the subway floor opened under him flew in front of Batala before becoming stationary in mid air. "Because all you did before you so foolheartedly leapt down my secret passage after your friend 'Huey' was yell for a couple of oblivious passersby to call the peace officers without explaining why. Thanks to my Spy Flies, I was able to see that the people you blurted out to simply walked off, no doubt thinking you were a tad off."

"'Spy Flies?'"

"*These*," Batala beamed, "little *miraculous* devices of mine act as my eyes to the outside world. And while I haven't been able to program the Spy Flies to pick up sound yet, I have been successful in enabling them to broadcast it. I know this will sound familiar." With a flick of a switch on Batala's remote control, the sound of a single trumpet blast blared throughout the subway tunnel. Unprepared as he was for the sudden burst of volume, Fred's hands immediately shot straight for his ears.

"For the most part, however, they're my scouts, and I had one that neither you or Huey noticed while you were outside, which leads me to ask: Why in Allah's name were you and your companion gawking at the tree for so long? I needed to release the locusts under the cover of darkness and I couldn't keep them pent up for too much longer. Yet you two were the only people who were looking in this direction let alone paying any real attention to the area; why?"

Fred wasn't about to relate something as personal as his involvement with the tree's historical significance to the likes of Dr. Batala, so the only explanation he offered the doctor was, "it's a long story."

"Well, I have a rather long story to tell as well." Batala kept his sights and his gun aimed at Fred while he rested his palm against the side of the subway tunnel's wall. A moment later, a section of that same wall parted in two, as a double doorway would, and revealed a stairwell the wall hid that wound downward. "If you would just walk this way—"

* * *

Huey's mother Jennifer used to tell him the old Jewish fable of the Golem, a man made essentially from pieces of either clay or solid rock. What Huey saw before him in the dismal, fluorescently lit metal tank of a cell where he had landed looked as if it could be a Golem made from patches and chunks of human flesh, even though what trudged Huey's way hardly seemed human at all. It—the Golem, was naked and had several stitched scars and long, pulsing varicose veins lining various portions of its body. The off-white skin of the Golem looked as if it would be clammy to the touch and had very little body hair to speak of. Like a pear, the Golem's head almost came to a point and had a couple of strands of blond hair stemming from the base of the skull. Underneath a rather thick and perpetually furrowed brow were two feral eyes with pin drop pupils that gleamed blood red as though whatever else the Golem was, it might also be part animal. When the Golem gaped open its maw to hiss at Huey, the peace officer realized that the skeletal remnants of both beast and foul that littered the dim cell had to have been gnawed into their current state by the fangs that the Golem bore.

"Holy shit!" Huey said out of reflex. "What the fuck kind of freak are you?" But the peace officer had already decided in the back of his mind that the Golem could only be the product of illegal eugenic tinkering and whoever had created this mistake must surely be the same individual who has been artificially engineering the Biblical revelations as of late. Huey fully intended on bringing that individual to justice except that their creation was blocking his way to the only visible door in the room, which looked to him like the entrance to a bank vault. The hole in the ceiling that Huey had fallen out of was far too high for him to try and leap for, which meant he would have to duck around the Golem to reach the one door in the cell.

Huey used the instant he had before the Golem's inevitable lunge for him well. The Golem wasn't as slow as he assumed it would be, but Huey still managed to slip past the creature and scramble for the door's lever. Once Huey grasped the lever, however, he quickly found it would only give so far before becoming immobile.

"Locked!" Huey cried out, and with the Golem already spinning on its bare, callused heel to face him again, the peace officer realized no further attempts at an escape were going to be possible until the threat of his new cell mate's advances could be neutralized. Huey quickly mentally sized up his opponent, and while trying to recall if he had ever taken on someone or something as big as the approximately seven foot, 500 pound Golem, Huey only found himself drawing a blank.

* * *

"Since you are already privy to the knowledge that only a genius of my high caliber could have possibly been behind the orchestration of the so-called signs, you might as well now know how I managed to fool the entire world if not this corner of the galaxy. As you've just heard, the 'trumpets' you, that peace officer's family, and everyone else I saw through my Spy Flies outside that horrid Consortium heard last Saturday night, came from the combined speakers of my Spy Flies working in, dare I say, *concert*?" Batala chortled at his own little joke as Fred walked just ahead of him down the winding stairwell. "How very droll of me. Anyhow, the hail that rained the very next day was made possible by firing a rocket of my own design into the clouds that exploded and released my own special brand of dry ice. I fired a similar exploding missile into the volcano of Pompeii City and I launched yet another projectile to explode along the side of what has now been euphemistically dubbed the Rock of Ages, which I sent it hurtling down from the heavens off course and onto terra firma. I didn't mean for it to even land in this hemisphere, and if I didn't have to operate in secret with such jury-rigged, contraband equipment, I would have been able to better determine an exact target. But at least it didn't land in Chicago, eh, Elijah?"

A stunned Fred stopped walking down the stairs of the secret passage for a moment to turn to face Batala and stammered, "you couldn't have possibly been firing missiles at whim at all those things! They would have spotted them a mile away and traced them right back to you!"

Batala waved his gun a bit as if to tell Fred to keep moving. "You're still thinking like a 21st century man, which is good in many respects given how depraved this society is. You're assuming that the people of this frivolous era still give a damn about the integrity of airspace as we naturally did in our time, but they don't. At first, I was certain I would've had to find a way to cloak my rockets somehow, but then I found out how little respect these people had for their own borders. They don't have any radar stations, any spy satellites, in fact, they don't have anything beyond simple air traffic control to keep their precious flying cars from bumping into one another. Well, here we are."

An open entrance almost like the mouth of a cave lay before them and once Fred walked ahead of Batala through it, he saw what reminded him of one of the subway stops the underground operated from so many centuries ago. There were rusted railways but no abandoned streetcars. Instead, Fred saw an immensely wide variety of lab equipment and scientific apparatus he couldn't begin to cognize or fathom the purposes of, where the underground would have had their many boxes of books, compact discs, and video tapes if were they using this subway depot. Among the tanks of water, the enormous vat of red solution placed against a wall, the tables covered with test tube racks or desktop computers, and the half-finished armatures and exo-skeletons, the only things that seemed the least bit familiar to Fred were the truck parked next to the vat of solution and the huge deep freezer with shelves containing test tubes that protruded out from the freezer's doors which were left open.

Batala prompted Fred with a wave of his gun to walk further into the stopgap laboratory and said, "I fired those missiles from a secluded patch of land just outside of Joliet, but this," an added touch of pride slipped into his tone of voice, "is where I created life itself, time and time again."

Fred slowly looked behind him to accusingly ask the doctor, "those weren't *real* locusts, were they? You . . . *Cloned* them, didn't you?"

"Very good, Elijah!" Batala patronizingly sounded as though he was teaching a class and Fred had given the right answer to a question. "I *did* create the locusts—among *other* things . . ."

* * *

As Huey sparred with the Golem around its cell, he had to fight back the cocky notion that facing the creature would be some glorious challenge to stand toe to toe with. He had no idea how powerful this abomination truly was so Huey decided his best strategy was to "stick and move." Which in essence meant striking as a mongoose would; hitting hard and particularly fast any perceived weak spots while staying out of the opposition's reach.

Huey proceeded with his strategy under the assumption that the Golem's anatomy would be as vulnerable in all the same, familiar places as a human's, and for the most part he was right. The blindingly quick karate chop Huey sent to the creature's Adam's apple garnered a painful grimace on its face, the swift kick he then aimed at the Golem's solar plexus did make it gasp, and a second rapid fire kick to the creature's nether regions actually produced from it an audible groan. But Huey soon realized that though the three blows would have had far more of an effect on a normal human being, the creature's leathery epidermis was obviously twice as thick as that of any ordinary man, and as a result, the Golem didn't slow down nearly as much as Huey felt it should have.

Huey's blows did manage to infuriate the Golem, however, but the nimble peace officer was also able to keep safely out of the creature's grasp. Yet every time the Golem tried and failed to grab a hold of Huey, it would become more and more agitated. To the Golem's feeble mind, this red, white, blue, and tan skinned stranger had fallen down the hole where its food usually fell *and had struck it first.* The Golem didn't have the faculties to acknowledge that it would have surely torn the stranger apart whether he had been completely immobile or not, all it knew was that it had yet to respond to the stranger's stinging in kind and that made it blush a sickly pink hue with rage.

The Golem's arms had been trying in vain to grab at Huey long enough for what could almost be called a rhythm to develop; a rhythm of the creature's arms constantly ensnaring inward. But because of its increased frustration, there came a brief point when the rhythm became erratically disrupted and reversed; when the Golem's arms had mistakenly flown outward instead of in, one arm flung back in the form of a slap. Which was unusual, since beyond either instinctively choking or bear hugging, it never needed to know any other technique of subduing any of the prey that fell down its hole. But the Golem's meager intellect decided it would have to remember to fling its arms back sharply more often, for that move of all moves finally made contact with the stranger and knocked him flat against the wall.

Huey felt his jaw smart when the creature accidentally back handed him, but what really hurt was when the force from said back hand sent his shoulder blades flying into the side of the cell's metal wall. As though the creature wanted to practice a new trick, it stepped up to Huey just as he had regained his footing and caught the side of his face with another slap, knocking the peace officer into the cell wall once again. The Golem would've attempted yet another slap except it was far too impatient to see if it could squeeze the life out of the stranger just as it had everything else it'd ever known to fall down the hole, so the creature dove for the peace officer's throat and began to choke him.

But Huey saw this coming and after some straining he was able to break the choke. He then took advantage of being so close to the Golem's face and poked both of its eyes with his fingers. A deafening howl went up and reverberated throughout the metal cell, but instead of blinding the creature the maneuver only reddened its already blazing eyes while causing them to tear up. The pain heightened its fury and also put an added adrenaline surge of speed in its movements. This quickening allowed the Golem to clasp onto both Huey's shoulders before he could slip away despite its somewhat blurred vision, and much to Huey's fright, the creature abruptly drew him to its chest and began to squeeze—hard.

Huey's jaw clenched and his teeth gritted from feeling as though he were within the grips of an iron vice that was slowly being tightened. Huey hadn't completely healed from having to fight his way through the riot at the Time Travel Consortium and here he was being subjected to a level of excruciating pain he never knew possible. But then the pain started to give way to a numbness that Huey had had some experience with in his many battles which he recognized right away as the insensate beginnings of unconsciousness.

* * *

"You seem surprised, Elijah, if not—repulsed by the idea of me taking advantage of the eugenic technology those liberal milquetoasts on the surface were too cowardly to explore." Batala gazed up for a moment at the ceiling of the subway depot he had converted into a laboratory as if he could see those on the surface he spoke of so disparagingly walking above him. "They have the power to create a veritable Black superman, or recreate the Original Men of the tribe of Shabazz, something that would have done Minister Farrakhan *proud*, and what do they do? Duplicate seeds for plants and grow new gall bladders in petri dishes!" Batala then motioned for Fred to follow him. "Come here, look at what can be done when someone with a vision takes the helm!"

Batala wagged his gun hand about and steered his captive audience of one toward the enormous vat of red solution against the wall of the underground depot and the truck that was parked next to it. The truck also faced an empty tunnel which was too long and dark to see where it led. On the floor in between the vat and the truck was something Fred didn't notice before, a dark red sphere with a runny, pulp-like surface, the size of a gymnasium's medicine ball, with a viscous pool of red liquid under it. As it turned out, this was exactly what Batala wanted to call Fred's attention to. "Taste this," Batala slyly grinned.

Fred was about to protest, and was also contemplating trying to wrest the gun from Batala's hands at this point, since for all he knew the ball of red pulp could be poison. But Fred remembered how unsuccessful he proved at taking Brother Johnson's firearm away after his speaking engagement and figured if Batala wanted him dead the doctor would've shot him already. So Fred did as he was told and found the red ball to be very bitter—and sickeningly familiar. "What in *Allah*—what *is* this?"

"It's blood!" Batala announced as Fred spit onto the ground no less than six different times. "Disease free, type O blood cloned many times over! In this vat, I congeal the blood until it becomes almost gelatinous. Do you remember the frozen orange juice concentrate of our day? Well this is made from the same principle! Ingenious, isn't it?"

"And this is how you made the Chicago River look as though there was blood in it?" Fred still looked disgusted from his tasting of the ball of concentrated blood.

"There *was* blood in it! I loaded a dozen 'balls' just like this one onto the truck and drove them to the surface down the tunnel. The balls simply dissolve when immersed in water and viola! 'And lo, as it was written, the rivers shall flow with blood!' I did it all, Elijah! All except the eclipse on Friday the 13th of all days, of course. That was Allah's small contribution to my grand design, something I picked up on in the almanacs from the very beginning and found simply too opportune and too novel of a natural occurrence not to arrange the rest of the signs around."

Fred couldn't quite believe what Batala was confessing so calmly to, and sounding both incredulous and incensed, he fumed, "'Allah's small—' Do you hear yourself? You've been playing God! Even worse, you've been—been genetically engineering things! Which makes you just as bad as Yacub himself! If you were ever really a Muslim, you'd see just how blasphemous all of this is! If you really did set off that volcano and make that meteor crash into Florida somehow, then that makes you a mass murderer, you madman!"

Batala shook his head, narrowed his eyes at Fred, and scowled, "you naive, little man . . . You don't honestly think that blood wouldn't have been spilled at all if Allah Himself were actually behind these revelations, do you?"

"Then *why*, why would you do—all of this, *any* of this in the first place? Huh?" Fred was so distraught over the ramifications of what was being described to him it was an effort to find just the right words, let alone articulate them well because of the lump in his throat that came from being "choked up." "What could possibly be worth all the deaths that are on your head and the blood that's on your hands, *doctor*?"

Batala paused for a long, silent moment before using the nozzle of his gun as an indicator of sorts to point out a nearby chair for Fred to sit in. Once a sorrowful Fred wearily sat down, Batala leaned against the edge of a long table that was in front of the chair as if he wanted to relax but still be standing over Fred at least somewhat to remind his captive of who had the upper hand between them. "To answer that, I'll have to go back to the beginning. Which in this case, would mean some 380 years ago, right after I put you in a state of suspended animation. The CC 100, the name of the cryogenic unit I placed you in, was only the prototype. And because even my supra-genius was bound by the constraints of 21st century technology, it would take me another 15 years before I could construct the CC 101; a chamber suitable to place the Honorable Khallid Muhammad himself into. I must say in retrospect, Elijah, that the information your—*volunteerism* provided proved to be most invaluable."

Fred bristled in his chair at the doctor's flagrant and repeated disrespect for his name and blurted out, "for the last time, the name is—"

"Fred Hamilton Rush, or something. Yes, yes, I know. Anyway, the year was 2045, and the rebellion your son led had descended upon Chicago. Bombs were bursting everywhere and the Honorable Khallid Muhammad chose to invoke the better part of valor and take his leave of the wilderness of North America for Libya with the other ministers instead of placing himself in suspended animation as a means of surviving his enemies—which meant I was free to use the CC 101 myself. At which point, I should confess— *Frederick*, I was about to take an axe to the glass of your chamber just before I entered mine."

Fred folded his arms and quipped, "I can imagine."

"Except that luckily for you, one of the bombs landed near enough Argonne to cause a cave in at that exact moment, separating me from your chamber. And up until I heard otherwise on the news two weeks ago when they accidentally found you underneath Argonne, I thought the cave in had crushed you to death for sure."

"But when I woke up they told me they found you dead."

"Ah, *that*," Batala smirked. "Well, I imagine they also told you many a discrediting thing about me, my experiments, and sullied my reputation even further upon your revival. The project that your son's *White* friend, Eric Blair was involved with? I'm certain they claimed that I tortured him or some such thing. The truth is, like you, Mr. Blair and the others provided me with a great deal of valuable information. Not insofar as recreating Yacub's race splicing experiment, as I'm sure you've been misinformed, but as far as providing important material on eugenics."

It didn't take but a moment for Fred to take what the doctor had said and correctly place it within the context of everything that had been shown and described to him so far. "You cloned your own body—just like you cloned those locusts, didn't you?"

Batala nodded and sighed, "once again, 21st century technology proved to be an impediment to my creativity. The best I could come up with was a dead clone of my body, and sadly, the only use I managed to derive from it was in the faking of my own death so no one would think to pursue me. I then prepared the CC 101 and set the timer to automatically revive me in exactly 360 years. I figured since Allah had 360 degrees of knowledge, in 360 years the social climate on the tumultuous surface of 2045 A.D.—a hundred and eighty degrees from the way life *should* be—would have turned around another 180 degrees by 2405 A.D., when I calculated life should have once again returned to the way it was back in our day. It wasn't a very scientific calculation, I grant you, but determining future sociological climates is at best a frivolous 'science' to begin with, so . . .

"After the CC 101 defrosted itself five years ago underneath Argonne I sneaked above ground and found that I had awakened to the same nightmare I'm sure you must have when you were brought out of stasis: Wanton, unveiled women! Public nudity, urination, and excretion! Children using foul language and committing blasphemy at whim! Open drug use! Legal homosexuality! *Interracial marriages*! A society of no morals, no family values, *no religion*, and no drive or initiative! They have free housing and free dining but no free enterprise! I know! Try as I might, I couldn't find anyone who was both traditionally minded *and* wealthy enough to covertly subsidize my work for the life of me, which left me with no recourse but to resort to stealing or counterfeiting ducats to fund myself! *It's all so tediously insane*! The marketplace today is so weighed down with rules and regulations that it can't expand in the slightest while the few big businesses that are left in the world are controlled by the minions and not the masters? *Let's just put the monkeys in charge of the zoo, why don't we*?

"But the worst was their time traveling! Actually allowing people to go back in time and invisibly spy on the Prophet himself, letting them come away with the erroneous impression that he was just an—*ordinary man*?"

For a couple of moments, Batala seemed lost in thought grumbling incomprehensibly while clenching his free hand into a fist and banging it onto the table he was still leaning against. In that time, Fred had concluded that all the things about the 25th century's libertarian socialist democracy which had either annoyed or alienated him had pushed Batala over the edge of insanity that the doctor evidently must have been teetering on as far back as the 21st century.

"If only the laws of physics were different in our dimension," Batala muttered and lamented, "if only I could *physically* go back in time—*materialize* in the past. I could warn Minister Farrakhan and the Honorable Khallid Muhammad that the future we fought so hard for became a—a cesspool for Sodomites! I even looked into the possibility of whether or not there was an alternate reality just beyond the pale in which the Black Republic was still in existence in some parallel 25th century, dimensionally adjacent to ours. But according to those *precocious technicians*," Batala hissed the last two words with a caustic sarcasm, "there would have had to have been at least a 40 percent chance of the Lost-Found Nation surviving your son's onslaught for such an alternate reality to exist. And apparently, in every possible alternate past time line in the space-time continuum, the Nation—*falls* by the end of the 21st century for one damn reason or another." Batala then lowered his head as if in mourning but still kept an eye and his gun leveled on Fred.

"So that's what this is all about? Space and time themselves have told you that 'the Black Republic' can't possibly remain intact for long, and yet all *this*," Fred waved his hands about him as he snidely crossed his legs in the chair he was sitting in, "all the pain, suffering, and *death* that you've caused was just to con people into wanting to go back to living like they did 400 years ago anyway? In another Lost-Found Nation? Who would be in charge of it, *you*?"

"It's bigger than the Nation of Islam, you fool! It's about morality itself! Do I have to spell it out to you? *It was all to put the fear of God back into the populace!*" Batala waited until he calmed himself down before he spoke again. "If you were a minister, such as I was, you were privy to certain—materials. Nakon to everyone else but permissible to us ministers so long as we kept whatever it was we had to ourselves. What can I say? Membership has its privileges. The nakon material would usually be music of some kind, occasionally a video tape or two, but sometimes it would be works of literature which didn't get disposed of. I received as a gift when I was first made the minister of science and technology a novel entitled *The Brothers Karamazov* by Fyodor Dostoevsky. In it, one of the brothers, an unbelieving *Dahri* named Ivan, told his father's servant that there supposedly wasn't a God, and since there wasn't, there wouldn't ever be any spiritual consequences to face for one's actions either. Well, I hate to spoil the end of the story for you, but I'm afraid I'm going to have to to make my point: Ivan's father's servant takes Ivan's blasphemy to heart and kills the father. And why not? If there's no Allah, then obviously there won't be any price to pay for committing a sin, and if there's not even the *hint* of a threat of some form of divine retribution, then what's to keep mankind from slipping into total *anarchy*?"

Fred let the rhetorical question hang in the air unanswered while he contemplated what must have been the moral of the story Batala was trying to leave him with: That whether or not there was ever any truth to all the religions of the world, religion itself needed to still be in place within a given society in order to keep its people in line. Fred thought how that directly conflicted with what Li'l Bobby had told him last Sunday about how the cry for there to be a religion was in fact a call for a kind of moral policing agent. Then Fred remembered what Dr. Cohen said of his son's philosophy: That man's *inherent* morality would kick into gear when given choices as to how to live and that a knowledge of history would help the choices to be seen clearly or would keep mankind from making any of the bad choices all over again. It was at this point when Fred saw what must have happened.

"You're plan hasn't work, *has* it?" Fred abruptly shot up out of his chair but had to remind himself to be very wary since he was still being held at gunpoint. "You expected every last one of these people to be so scared the world was coming to an end that they'd be stampeding like a herd to their nearest churches and temples in hoards by now. To repeal every last one of their radical laws and put some old fashioned ones in their place. Instead, you only managed to put fear into a select few with all your—*special effects* and even fewer have actually acted on that fear. Even though they may not know for sure if the signs have been faked or if *you* were the one behind of all this, most of these people simply don't give a damn! They think it's—distracting trivia, that's not worth giving too much media coverage to. And at least one man I know in particular has even gone so far as to say they wouldn't want to spend all eternity with any God that would be willing to send them to Hell anyway.

"It makes so much sense now. Baines was right, the Nation did try to limit people's choices and you're the proof! You *had* to have been one of those scientists they approached back in the 20th century. Maybe you were even some student somewhere listening to Farrakhan speak about how Black folks didn't need to learn about history or politics because those were Jewish specialties, but only had to know about math so they could make money for an all-Black nation, or know about engineering so they could build things for an all-Black nation. And they found you, a prodigy to be sure, but with little if any knowledge of basic civics! Like any scientist, you're naturally going to think things like social studies aren't scientific, but being a scientist for the Nation of Islam only made that bad attitude worse.

"Don't you get it? You said yourself it wasn't scientific to think that things would be back to the way they were in our day after 360 years just because 360 degrees happens to make a circle, so obviously political change isn't cyclical. If you had spent as much time learning about ethics as you did learning about cloning, it wouldn't surprise you that these people haven't made Black super Original Men yet. If you knew as much about their trusting, peaceful nature as you do about rockets, you would have had some clue as to why these people didn't have the means to detect those missiles you fired anymore. And if you had studied the history of those who have used the Bible or the Koran as an excuse to hurt people as much as you studied what was *in* those books, you would've known that you shouldn't have been playing God in the first place!" Fred took a breath and felt pleased if not a little shocked with himself over the outpouring that had just flowed from him which he had attributed to 25th century life finally rubbing off on him. Now, Fred thought, all that was needed was a coy, parting line: "The bottom line, doctor, is that these Dahri have outsmarted you and they don't even know you're alive." There, Fred mused to himself, that'll do.

Batala paused, and sat on the edge of the table he had been leaning against, very surprised at (if not the tiniest bit suspicious of) Fred's confidence and grasp of the subject at hand. When the doctor broke his stunned silence, he sounded more as though he was talking to himself than to Fred. "I still can't believe I spent five years of my life—the planning, the exhausting workload—I was 50 when you met me in 2030 but I was 65 when I froze myself in 2045 *and*, of course, when I awoke five years ago, which makes me—too damn old to have made the amount of the sacrifices that I have in vain! The only break I seemed to have received from Allah after I revived was stumbling upon this subterranean network not too far from the cave I had dug underneath Argonne, which I imagined was once the—'hideout' of your seditious, subversive friends that had gotten you in so much trouble way back when. Deliciously ironic, isn't it? Had I only known at the time . . ."

"If the underground knew what you've been doing here, they'd all roll over in their graves." Fred smugly quipped, still riding high off of the rush from his soliloquy.

Batala paused again, this time very suspicious of Fred's tone. "I know you're still a practicing Muslim, I heard so on the news, so why are you sounding so much like these people? I mean, I hope that they haven't actually swayed you in any way. It would be a shame if the one contemporary from my time were to cross over into the darkside."

"Why do you ask?" Fred cautiously queried, sensing a deadly earnestness in the doctor's voice.

"Fred," Batala noted the raised eyebrow and the distrustful look given him at his first sincere usage of Fred's name but proceeded with the proposal he was about to make anyway, "I want to know once and for all where your loyalties lie. You see, I prepared for the eventuality of the seven signs not being enough to scare some values into this debauched populace. The signs were only supposed to be warnings after all, and what good is a threat if it turns out to be empty? So since I couldn't very well have the Prince of Peace Himself put in an appearance after the seventh sign, I applied my supra-genius in eugenics and bionics toward the creation of the Four Horsemen themselves."

"The Four Horsemen of the Apocalypse?" Fred thought back to what he was taught about those legendary emissaries of doom in the Ostrowski School for Boys and shuddered at the notion of them actually being brought to "life" by the likes of Dr. Batala of all people.

"Actually, *three*," Batala shrugged with the first sign of modesty Fred has ever known the doctor to display, "I didn't have the means to finish the fourth one on time. But yes, if I can't put the fear of God into these heathens then by Allah I can definitely visit the wrath of God upon them! And since the Second Coming is about to come, I need to know now I can trust you. Do I have to kill you now to keep you from telling the world what you've learned here, or will you join me, and watch as this demilitarized Gomorra tries to contend with a wave of destruction its been warned of but has scoffed at for centuries? Tell me now, *Fred*."

"Now?" Fred found himself wanting to stall for time though he wasn't sure what good it would do. "As in right this second? I mean, you haven't even sent out the Horsemen yet or anything, and you don't have to either. You can still change your mind."

"Fred, you wound me," Batala dramatically laid his free hand flat on his chest, "I'm not some fictional villain who explains his masterstroke in every detail so the *hero*," Batala looked Fred up and down while smacking his lips dismissingly, "will know exactly how to stop it. The Horsemen were programmed to take to the air fifteen minutes ago. The end is nigh, Fred Hamill Rush. The only question is, do you want to live to see it?"

* * *

The Golem's bear hug was incrementally sapping the consciousness out of Huey, and since letting his mind go as limp as his pain racked body would surely mean blacking out entirely, Huey made doubly sure to keep his head filled with thoughts. A negative thought might have sped up his slip into unconsciousness, so Huey refused to even consider there was a possibility that he could lose to the Golem. Instead, Huey lied to himself by thinking about how much stronger than the creature he was. He imagined how within his chest beat the heart of a lion, how within his chest literally beat the heartbeat of America. How he was Captain Huey P. Rush, direct descendant of a Black Panther, a buffalo soldier, and an African king, the latest in, and the top of a long line of revolutionary warriors. Which meant that he himself was a warrior, and if that was the case, there was no way in hell he could ever allow himself to be beaten in any way by the likes of the Golem.

It all seemed so clear, so utterly obvious to Huey that the creature's arms should simply fly off of his torso with the merest shrug. But strain as he might, Huey still couldn't call upon the strength necessary to break free of the Golem's grip. All he had managed to do was build up his ego, which made Huey realize what he needed to do to tap into his inner reserves was to make himself very, *very* angry.

So Huey risked taking a precious moment to imagine a future in which he died broken in this creature's arms. He pictured Fred eventually falling into the clutches of whoever was behind this scheme to recreate the Bible's descriptions of the Rapture, a scheme Huey took a stab and assumed was designed to scare the world into reverting to fundamentalism. He thought of his wife lying helpless in a hospital bed as Dr. Cohen stood over her dressed in a white chador about to administer leeches instead of the usual 25th century medical fare. Huey envisioned Phantom Form Time Travel Consortiums all around the world simultaneously going up in plumes of hell fire while books by the volumes were being thrown into the flames by crowds of fascists surrounding each engulfed Consortium.

And then an image came to mind of Li'l Bobby in an overcrowded, underfunded classroom, wearing every part of a parochial school uniform of old except for the traditionally dark colored shorts which were pulled down around his ankles in order to expose his bare ass to the swats of a wooden ruler being wielded by a decrepitly old nun. As Bobby (who had never experienced any form of corporal punishment in his life) was being beaten by the nun, he was repeatedly asked by her in Huey's brief and horrid vision to confess that a God existed. An orphaned Bobby's only response were the pleading cries, "Huey!" "Huey, where were you?"

"*No!*" New life flooded from the core of Huey's being to the ends of every extremity. Goose pimples from Huey's moral certainty and his renewed sense of purpose sprang forth and peppered the back of his neck letting him know just how inspired he was. And a divine wrath took hold of his very soul as opened his enraged eyes wide and glared right into those of the monstrosity who was trying to squeeze the life out of him.

Huey felt as though he were a man of steel powered by lightning that flowed through his veins. Huey's arms, once pinned to his sides by the Golem's hold, began to slowly but surely pry open the vice-like grip of the creature, who's usually twisted facial expression actually registered a look of genuine shock at this sudden turn of events. Its food had never tried to resist to such a degree before, and the Golem's lack of experience with a being so willing to fight back left the creature unprepared for the ravenous onslaught that a dangerously furious Huey had unleashed upon it once he was free of that bear hug.

Huey showed none of his usual practiced fighting form when he used his right fist as a sledgehammer to unrelentingly pound into the eugenic mistake, like it was so much meat, and eventually drive the creature first to its knees and then to the cell's metal floor as if it were a railroad spike. The peace officer had maddened himself to the point of being a man possessed with a berserker fury that hadn't been rivaled since the days when the Teutonic Vikings would allow themselves to become caught up in the heat of battle. Huey's blows soon broke the Golem's thick skin, and as it bled the creature began to wail in a manner that even the least canny could tell was for mercy. It was never taught to form the words, so after almost five minutes of solid abuse, the Golem finally cried for Huey to stop the only way the creature knew how; by yelping as though it were an injured dog.

But Huey had psyched himself up too high and too well, and the peace officer literally couldn't stop until he could tell he had finally pummeled the creature into the very unconsciousness it had tried to permanently dispatch him to. As the Golem's body laid in a heap, already beginning to visibly bruise in several places, Huey leaned back against one of the cell's wall and trembled as if he were shaking loose any residual Herculean energy left in him. After some very deep breaths of the metal cell's stale, stench-ridden air, Huey staggered over to the door and gave its lever another try. Still locked, he thought, and then it occurred to Huey that with all the noise he and his cell mate had been making, it wouldn't be long before *someone* from outside would check in on them. Huey would simply have to find the strength to prepare for what might happen afterwards and hope that his opponent didn't come to before that point. For as drained as he was feeling, Huey wasn't sure if he would be able to conjure up enough energy for a second round.

* * *

Fred wasn't sure what exactly Batala meant by "joining," because he knew he definitely wasn't mechanically inclined enough to help out in a scientific capacity. Simply staying with the doctor in the underground laboratory for the rest of his life was certainly not desirable, and Allah only knew what machinations Batala would employ to guarantee Fred's silence were he ever allowed to return to the surface.

Which left Fred with only one option that felt right to him: Defiance, because he wouldn't have wanted to be a party to Batala's wave of destruction or blasphemy should the real Allah decide to appear some (judgment) day anyway. And since he opted to be defiant, Fred figured that he might as well make a demand as well. After all, Fred thought, if you're going to be a bear, be a grizzly.

"I want you to free Huey from your cell, Batala, or whatever you said he was in, and for the both of us to be let go right now. It may be too late to stop your Horsemen, but at least we can warn people about them and have you arrested."

"And you called *me* mad?" Batala asked incredulously. "Didn't you hear what I said? My Horsemen are going to try their damnedest not to leave anything left alive up there! And besides, even if by some remote chance those milquetoasts up there have enough teeth to actually do some damage to any one of them, do you honestly believe those liberal social deviants of yours truly give a damn about you?"

"Oh yeah, as if *you* ever did," Fred spat, "unless you've already forgotten that the only reason why I'm alive today is because I was your *guinea pig*?"

"And you should be *grateful*! How many men get to live to be over 400 years old? I just wish neither one of us had to awake to this futuristic Sodom and Gomorra; where you're persecuted if you're a Black Muslim and happen to demonstrate the least amount of respect for Minister Farrakhan!"

"That's not true, these people give everyone the freedom to believe whatever we want," Fred's thoughts then turned to Li'l Bobby and his temporarily sour facial expression reflected this, "granted, there are some who attack religion—but I have the freedom not to stick around and listen to those types of folks, who are a lot fewer in number than you're trying to imply! Just like I have the freedom to not join the likes of you, now let's go free Huey!"

"I hate to break this to you, *Fred*," Batala motioned with the hand which had Fred at gunpoint to walk ahead of him, "but 'Huey' is so much ground round by now, thanks to Yacubstein."

"What—what are you saying?" Fred began to choke up at the prospect that something might have happened to his descendant.

"Oh didn't I tell you about Yacubstein? He—or should I say it, is kept in the same cell your friend dropped into when he fell through that 'trap door' which is actually where I drop *its* food." Batala steered a somewhat despondent Fred toward the farthest end of the laboratory. "And since you've expressed a—*certain interest*, I think it's time you visited Yacubstein yourself. It should be finished with the peace officer by now and it might want a traitor for desert."

The two walked in silence until they reached a metal door embedded in the side of a subway wall that reminded Fred of an entrance of a bank vault. "It can only be opened from the outside," Batala mentioned as he motioned for Fred to stand beside the door as he went to pull on the its lever, "so don't bother trying the lever on the inside once you're in there."

The fear induced lump in his throat made it difficult to ask the question, but Fred still queried, "what exactly is a 'Yacubstein?'"

Batala grinned, leaned forward slightly, held the gun closer to Fred as he stopped working the lever for a moment to answer. "Well, let's just say if it wasn't so savage and misshapen, it might have been the fourth Horseman."

Fred's heart sank as Batala slowly drew the metal door toward him with one hand and waved his gun for Fred to enter the cell with the other. But before Fred could take a single step inside, the door abruptly swung outward, hitting Batala in the face. A dazed Batala readied his gun, thinking his creature had forgotten both its place and how painful a laser was at close range. Yet the doctor was shocked to find that the door suddenly swinging open wasn't due to Yacubstein trying to wander out of its cell but because Captain Huey P. Rush was taking advantage of an instant-long opportunity to escape. Huey snatched the gun from Batala's hand, and in the same motion, yanked the doctor by the arm, thereby flinging him into the cell. Batala stumbled backwards uncontrollably from being flung until he tripped and fell over Yacubstein's crumpled yet stirring form. The last thing the Rushes managed to visibly catch right before Huey slammed the door shut was the creature regaining consciousness because of the doctor falling over it.

As Batala's cries for help and Yacubstein's growls could barely be heard from outside the door, Huey quickly darted his head all around him out of reflex, pointing the doctor's gun first to his side and then behind him to see if there was anyone else he needed to contend with. For his part, Fred couldn't restrain himself until Huey could see if all was clear and threw his arms around his descendant, hugging the peace officer for dear life.

"Huey! Thank Allah!" Fred almost sobbed. "Thank Allah you're alive!"

Huey reluctantly returned his ancestor's embrace and waited a moment before gingerly pulling Fred off of him. He still looked nervously about him and demanded in a serious tone, "anybody else around here?"

"No," Fred explained assuredly, "it was just Batala. *Doctor* Batala, from the 21st century!"

"What? You mean that old bastard I just threw in there was *the* Batala?"

"He froze himself just like he froze me," Fred apprehensively looked at the cell door and listened to Batala's screams barely audible through the metal door, "is that thing in there going to kill him?"

"Maybe. But I fucked it up pretty bad, so as long as he keeps moving, it'll probably only rough him up a bit," Huey commented, sounding very unconcerned. "*Batala* was the one who faked all those revelations?"

Fred's eyes widened with fear when he remembered, "*the Horsemen*! Huey, Batala created these monsters and they're supposed to be like the Four Horsemen from the Bible! He already sent them out to kill everybody! We've got to do something!"

"Then what are we standing around here for? Let's get the hell out of here!"

Fred grabbed Huey's shoulder before the peace officer could move and asked, "what about Batala?"

"Do you want to stop the Horsemen or do you want me to waste time seeing if I can get that thing off of Batala?" When Fred failed to answer Huey right away, Huey said before jogging off, "I didn't think so."

290

CHAPTER THIRTEEN

"The final call"

"Did you see which way did they go?"

"No," Fred answered as he jogged alongside of Huey towards the core of Batala's laboratory, "but he said they'll 'take to the air' so I guess he's found out a way to make them fly just like the Bible said they would."

"Great," Huey smacked his lips in chagrin and then stopped in his tracks once he reached a long table covered with various test tube racks, desktop computers, armatures, and blueprints. "Now, what's the quickest way out of here?"

Fred pointed at Batala's truck and called attention to the subway tunnel it faced. "Batala said he drove these blood balls to the surface down that tunnel."

"'Blood balls?'" Huey gave Fred a peculiar look as he and Fred sprinted for the truck's cab. "Actually, don't get into all that, what I really need is some idea as to where those Horsemen'll be."

"I don't know for sure," Fred apologetically called out to Huey as he ran around one side of the cab to get into its passenger side while Huey was heading for the driver's seat. When they were both seated, Huey busied himself with the "hot wiring" of the truck while Fred stared thoughtfully into space until he recalled something from his youth. "Wait—I remember at the orphanage I was in, the ministers told us that the Four Horsemen would come from all directions; the north, south, east, and west. Of course, their interpretation of the Bible—"

"Or the Koran for that matter left a lot to be desired, yeah I know," Huey interrupted as he managed to get the truck started, "but at least that's a start. If Batala sat through the same bullshit sessions that you did, then maybe he sent these bad boys north, south, east, and west from *this* location."

"Actually they would only be flying in three of those directions," Fred amended, "Batala said he 'didn't have the means' to finish the fourth Horseman."

"Good," Huey lamented as he floored the pedal of the truck and raced it down the tunnel, "one down, three to go."

* * *

Huey eventually reached the end of the long tunnel and drove through one of Batala's secret passages; a subway entrance with a closed down construction site built all around it to act as a camouflage. In the distance, the Rushes could barely see where Argonne National Laboratory was being cleared away and converted into a park. Despite it being closed, Huey noted that the construction site announced the coming of an antique store called Blast From the Past—just as the construction site near the infamous apple tree had.

"You see this shit?" Huey pointed all about him. "'Blast From the Past' my ass! The fucker must have thought he was being cute! He must have found some kind of way to make an old fashioned 'dummy corporation' without getting busted, sneaky son of a bitch!"

Instead of engaging the truck's flight mechanisms, Huey found an exit onto La Grange Road, stayed on it, and drove due north until the surrounding area began to look familiar to Fred. "This is Ishmael's old neighborhood," Fred noted, "why are we—"

"Hold on," Huey held a free hand up to silence Fred for a moment, "computer get me peace officer headquarters at Hilliard Center."

The small computer screen just above the truck's stereo blinked on a second later and displayed none other than Lieutenant Cheshta Castelblanch.

"Cheshta, I want every PO and their momma up out of bed two seconds ago, we've got something major going down! Listen very carefully: There are three, count them, *three* eugenically engineered supermonsters made to look like the Four Horsemen from the Bible, I imagine they're probably armed to the teeth and bionicly enhanced to boot, so consider them *extremely* dangerous. They can fly, and they may have been airborne for as long as a half an hour, we're not sure. Each of them are heading either north, south, east, or west from their point of origin, which was somewhere between where the new Argonne National Park the Agrarian Party called for is going to be and La Grange Road and 55th Street or so.

"Near La Grange and 55th you'll find a construction site for an antique store called Blast From the Past but it's an old style *dummy corporation*. There's a big old tree with no leaves that's hollow in the middle and leads directly underneath the site to a bunch of old, abandoned subway tunnels. In one of those subways you'll find the lab of the asshole who's been *artificially* creating all these 'signs from above' lately. There's also a metallic cell down there with one of the asshole's eugenic nightmares inside, so approach with extreme caution. You got all that?"

"Yes sir," Lieutenant Castelblanch dutifully said, "and if may say so, it'll be nice to have to wake Major Byrne up at four in the morning with a story like this. It's the least I can do to repay him for giving me the nightshift the one weekend my boyfriend is up from San Salvador."

"You may say so at that," Huey repressed a grin, "Rush out."

Huey stopped the truck in the middle of La Grange Road when he reached the curb where he had left his red Saturn parked. Fred looked at his descendant with incredulous eyes for making such a move. "You came all the way back here for your car?"

"First of all, it wasn't all *that* far," Huey corrected as he leapt from the truck's cab and headed for the back of his Saturn, "and second, if these motherfuckers are as bad as I think they are, I'm going to need a little extra something. You know what I'm saying?"

Fred ran to catch up with Huey who had opened the trunk in the rear of his scarab-looking car to reveal an array of armament the likes of which Fred had never seen outside of a work of science fiction.

"And in case you're wondering—no, none of this stuff is standard peace officer issue." Huey fished around for a weapon he thought would be appropriate. "In fact, I know a lot of this shit is probably illegal, but I forget which ones are and which ones aren't." Huey finally decided on a couple of weapons from the wide variety he had to choose from in his trunk and held each of them up to the full moon's light for inspection: A long nozzled gun with a targeting laser and a launcher of some kind with a very large muzzle. "Now let's go make glue out of them Horsemen, and since a Muslim got us into this mess, we'll try the *east* first to see if any of them things are heading downtown."

* * *

"Louisiana" Jake didn't mind working the front desk at the Robert Taylor Free Studios during the nightshift. The slow foot traffic after dark gave him a chance to stand outside of his office and gaze at a starry sky he knew from his history wasn't always clean enough to see the stars come out. He looked with a sense of pride at the structure he managed then slowly looked up to let his roaming eye run the full length of the studio apartment building. Once his eyes reached the building's crest, however, he saw something he couldn't believe was real not just flying but galloping overhead.

As far as Jake could tell, it was a man on horseback who was somehow flying at a level as high up as the top of the apartment building. And though the figure wasn't trying to land on the roof, the man seemed to notice Jake standing outside, and dipped out of its flight path slightly. Because of his naturally hospitable personality, a part of Jake actually wondered whether the man had come to see him in particular, which made what was to happen to him all the more sad. The man on horseback was trying to visit upon Louisiana Jake, but the Horseman wasn't about to impart good tidings.

He—or as Jake thought once a better look could be glimpsed of—it, since *it* didn't look much like a man at all with its gleaming feral red eyes, produced what looked like the nozzle of an old fashioned fire extinguisher, and sprayed the area in front of the Robert Taylor Free Studio's front entrance with a yellow gas. Garbed as it was with headgear and a sickly green light body armor chain mailed to an exo-skeleton, the Horseman arched his robotic steed back onto its original (and programmed) eastward flight path. The Horseman then bore fangs in a lipless smile, satisfied that the human it had just doused and left coughing on his knees back on the ground would be suffering from its non-lethal-but-very-painful recipe of fever, lesions, and lethargy soon enough.

"Bogie at twelve o' clock!" Huey rolled down the driver's side window of his red Saturn as he flew within visual distance of the

Horseman. "About time we found it! That motherfucker's dead ahead and just got done spraying something," Huey then turned to Fred sitting pensively in the passenger seat, "you're the Muslim, what do you suppose that yellow shit was?"

"I don't know," Fred looked irritatingly at Huey, "maybe that's supposed to be the Horseman who brings disease to mankind."

"*Biological warfare*," Huey shook his head angrily, "that fucker Batala really *is* a Blast From the Past, ain't he? Son of a bitch, if that thing reaches Lake Michigan—" Huey pulled from the floor of his car the laser gun with the long nozzle and held it up to examine it. "Well, we're going to have to head it off at the pass. Fred, it's going to be your job to hold the steering wheel straight anytime I'm shooting."

"What?" Fred sounded more scared than he had ever known himself to sound before. "Doesn't this thing have an auto pilot?"

"No," Huey answered, "don't worry, Kemosabe." Huey then flew his Saturn under the buoy-lit sky lanes of traffic and proceeded to intercept the Horseman's course. "Alright, this is it. Computer, play Wagner's *Ride of the Valkyries* and put it on continuous loop." Huey spied the expression of shock and disdain on Fred's face, anticipated his response, and quickly added, "computer, until further notice you will respond to *no* other voice other than that of *Huey P. Rush*."

"Understood," the computer's feminine voice coolly articulated.

Fred sat silently for a long moment as he tried in vain to comprehend the thinking of the man who sat to his left before saying, "I cannot *believe* you came from any loins of *mine*. How can you *possibly* think of playing music at a time like this?"

"*Listen* to the music," Huey implored, "this isn't just any song! It's the *perfect* song for an aerial dogfight! Just as that kid from that Louis Gossett Junior movie, *Iron Eagle*, needed to hear Queen whenever he flew into battle, I-need-motivation!"

"What you need is *help*," Fred snorted, "you need *so* much help. I cannot believe that you're—what's the word? *Indicative* of 25th century life!"

"Get ready to hold the wheel!" Huey looked out his driver's side window and saw that he was beginning to match the Horseman. When the Horseman looked to its right to see the first person to ever try and fly alongside of it, the creature aimed its gas dispensing nozzle at the red Saturn.

"On second thought, *give me the wheel*!" Huey grasped the steering wheel and made a sudden, hard right. Causing Fred to scream because the car was suddenly tilting on his side, which made him feel as if he might fall out of the Saturn even though his seat belt was on and the car door was locked.

The yellow gas the Horseman spewed missed the car completely and that incensed it since the creature had yet to miss a target in its brief tenure of consciousness. When it saw the strange, scarab-looking vehicle come about, the Horseman realized it had a challenge worth relishing on its hands.

"I'm going to keep making passes from afar till I cut this fucker down," Huey informed Fred. "Luckily, that gas doesn't have the spray reach that this bad boy has," Huey patted his gun, "otherwise we'd be suffering from Batalaitis by now. Get ready!"

As he announced, Huey steered his Saturn to swing around toward the Horseman's left side even as it was re-aiming its muzzle. Huey stayed true to his plan and didn't fly nearly as close to the Horseman as he had initially. The Horseman sprayed and almost seemed surprised when the gas didn't reach the approaching car. Huey pointed his gun's long nozzle out of his window and fired. The first shot missed but the second sliced by the Horseman's shoulder blades and the last shot hit its robotic steed in the buttocks. The horse buckled a bit but it didn't lose its control of anti-gravity.

Huey made another pass from behind, this time he saw that trying to include Fred in the process of fighting the Horseman was becoming too distracting, since Fred's hold on the steering wheel proved to be very fleeting and trepidatious. So instead of asking if Fred would participate again, Huey held onto the wheel himself and re-aimed his gun with his left arm which he hung out of his open window, despite the fact that a gun of that particular model fired best with two hands wielding it.

The Horseman was in the process of turning its artificial mount around to face the red Saturn coming up fast behind it when Huey fired again. Huey gripped his gun tight and braced his one arm to either absorb or ignore the gun's slight "kick" as his right hand steered his car. Only two of the five shots he managed to get off before flying past the Horseman actually struck the creature, but the damage the shots caused it were fairly severe. One shot struck the Horseman in the shoulder, leaving a smoldering laser wound, while the other knocked the muzzle and the small canister it was connected to out of its hands.

The Horseman made its first verbally audible sound ever when it shrieked as its one weapon fell to the ground below and shattered to pieces, even the horse seemed distraught from the loss. What little of an emotional program Batala bothered to install within the Horseman produced a feeling of utter disdain for its opponent in the flying red scarab which was so powerful the creature no longer cared if it carried out its programming. Since the Horseman could no longer spread its precious virus, the creature saw no point in—continuing, and decided to ram straight into the infernal scarab upon its next, inevitable pass in hopes of mutual destruction.

"What the hell does that thing think its doing?" Huey thought out loud as he swung his Saturn around for another pass. "Damn thing looks like its trying to charge us!"

"You didn't think it was going to keep floating around in one spot so you could keep hitting it and not fight back, did you?" Fred asked in a very frantic, panicky way.

"Well, kind of," Huey shrugged sheepishly before boasting, "it don't matter, though. If that motherfucker wants to joust, we'll joust his fucking ass!"

It wasn't until Huey had increased his speed while driving straight for and not around the Horseman as he had before when it had occurred to Fred what his descendant had meant. Tales of knights and chivalry were nakon in the Lost-Found Nation, so it took a moment for Fred to realize in horror what the word "joust" meant. "Are you *crazy*? *Pass*! Pass like you've *been* doing! *Don't crash into it*!"

"*Trust me*," Huey hissed in frustration over Fred's lack of faith in him, "and hold the wheel this time! I'm going to need both hands to get this just right!"

For once, Fred held the wheel steady as Huey leaned both his arms and his head out of the driver's side window to better aim his gun. Not only were the Rushes heading straight for the charging Horseman, but it was Fred's job to keep the car from steering off of the dangerous flight path they were on, and a very frightened Fred didn't appreciate the irony one bit.

"When I start firing, *veer right*! *Got it*?" Huey called out over the sound of the wind resistance surrounding his car since his head was still poked outside his window.

Fred was able to hear him, however, and cried, "got it," but only out of a sense of duty and not as a sign of approval.

A second later, Huey was squeezing off a volley of laser blasts at the Horseman's upper body, and without any real means of retaliation, the creature took the scathing shots that didn't miss it all along its body armored torso. But as the Horseman's laser riddled form drew dangerously near, Huey wondered why the car wasn't moving away. As it turned out, Fred had become so entranced with the sight of the Horseman's mid-section flaring up from laser fire he forgot his station. At the last possible moment, Huey managed to snake his right arm back inside the driver's side window to steer the car away from the Horseman, who for its part had kept charging more out of reflex and inertia than anything else down the flight path the red Saturn had been scarcely an instant ago. The Horseman galloped another few dozen meters across the sky before finally sliding off of its saddle and falling onto the pavement of Michigan Avenue below. When this happened the horse slowed somewhat, but never actually stopped, and continued its flight towards the east unable to decide upon any other course of action.

"Man, *why didn't you veer right*?" Huey howled once he pulled his head back inside the car. "I thought you were the one who *didn't* want to crash into it?"

"Can you just drop me off, please?" Fred pleaded. "I'm not a peace officer, I'm not cut out for this sort of thing."

"Can't," Huey stated tersely, "no time. We've got two more to go, you're just going to have to remember to hold onto the wheel, I may need my launcher and I know that's going to require both of my hands. Now . . . If there *is* one heading west, we can't go after it 'cause that'll mean flying the distance between here and its starting point at Batala's *and* whatever distance 'the Wicked Horseman of the West' has covered between the time it first took off and now—or whenever we managed to catch up with it, rather. So that's out." Huey turned to a very shaken and uncomfortable Fred, "which way do we go, old man? North or south?"

"*Home!*" Fred scowled with contempt.

"Alright, south it is," Huey then brought the car about, cut on its sirens, and illegally flew underneath the grids of floating buoy-lit sky lanes to better reach the South Side of Chicago in a short amount of time.

* * *

As much as it would like to think, the crimson body armored Horseman did not have an inexhaustible reserve of napalm, which meant its targets were going to have to be discriminatingly chosen. In the short time since the Horseman first felt the programming to take to the southern skies and wreak havoc come on line in its head, the creature had flown on its bionic horse over many a place of residence or business, but the Horseman realized its glorious mission would be all too brief if it had tried to burn down every house and building in its path. So in the interest of being selective, the limited independent artificial intelligence of the Horseman had decided to only set aflame any of the parks it came across that these humans seemed to hold so dear, and the first garden spot the creature happen to come to was—

"*Bachelor Grove Woods!*" Anger welled up from within Huey and his heart felt as though a fist was closing around it when he first spied the back of the Horseman from afar trickling a discharge of napalm over a small section of woodlands setting it ablaze from its floating robotic mount. "This is where I proposed to Marta! That motherfucker . . !" Huey then slowed his red Saturn's descent from the northeast to a mid air stop which he calculated would be within firing range of the creature and grabbed his launcher from the back seat of the car.

"I ain't got but two shots with this bad boy," Huey explained to a fuming, nervous, and silent Fred, "but since its back is to us, maybe one shot is all I need." Huey rolled down his window and prepared to aim the launcher. "Alright, you asshole," Huey muttered to himself under his breath as though he knew if the Horseman would hear an utterance made any louder, "don't-turn-around . . ."

What the Horseman did managed to hear was the sound Huey's launcher made when he fired, and the brief time the laser torpedo needed to spend covering the distance between its point of origin and its target provided the creature with just enough of an opportunity to barely duck out of its way. The Horseman then brought itself about and aimed its napalm emitting muzzle at the red scarab that had fired upon it.

This Horseman's muzzle reminded Huey of the previous Horseman's means of spraying its toxin and that caused him to make a very grave assumption. "Don't worry," Huey remarked to Fred once he saw the red armored Horseman aim its weapon at him, "this one may not even have as much reach as the last one. Boy, these things are stupid."

FLOURRISHHH!!

Both Rushes screamed as a pillar of flame cleared the distance between the Horseman and Huey's Saturn, and like the creature, Huey scarcely had enough time to get out of harm's way without becoming any more than singed. After making a hard left and dipping his car out of the line of fire, Huey quickly found himself fighting an unanticipated defensive battle. The Horseman decided to stop setting Bachelor Grove Woods afire for a moment and concentrated on incinerating the red scarab that had fired upon it. And to avoid being engulfed by the confined streams of flames being spewed at him, Huey darted about in the air and flew his Saturn in "figure eight" patterns very much like the insect the car's design reminded the creature of.

"I need to get my other shot in before we crash!" Huey cried out while trying to gain altitude without being torched by the Horseman, who was descending upon the car and seemed to be trying to force it to fly lower and lower toward the part of the woodlands that was flame engulfed by cutting off any of Huey's attempts to ascend.

"We need to get the hell out of here!" Fred countered as he clutched alternately at either his seat or his seat belt in terror.

Each time the Horseman would fire a bolt of flaming napalm, Huey and Fred could either see the stroke or even feel it stream across a side of the car. But as Huey tried to keep the Saturn from flying too close to the partially smoldering park, both Rushes looked at one another when they noticed that a couple of moments, a few seconds, and then at least a dozen seconds had gone by without seeing, feeling, or even hearing any bolts of flame sear from above them.

Huey leveled off his car and dared to take the time to peer his head through the window to see five rocket jockeys encircling the Horseman as angry insects would, peppering the creature and its steed from a safe distance with a barrage of lasers. Except Huey could tell the Jockeys weren't just some gang of teens or a bunch of rank and file civilians, but that all five of the rocket backpack propelled saviors were—

"*The peace officers*! Fuck yeah!" Huey cheered. "Here comes the calvary!"

"Thank Allah," Fred felt at his heaving chest and almost shed tears of joy.

Their revelry was to be short lived, however. For the Horsemen knew full well that enough laser fire would soon burn through its body armor, so it pulled on the reins of its bionic mount, arched straight up, and headed for higher ground—which in this case meant the clouds far above the Chicago pre-dawn sky. Before long, the

Horseman's silhouette crossed the still visible full moon and disappeared into the cloudy heights, outflying the peace officers who had been hovering about it and still fired their rifles in the direction it ascended to.

"What's wrong with them?" Fred demanded. "Why won't they fly after him?"

"How fast and high do you think them rocket packs are supposed to carry a human being?" Huey snorted as he reared the Saturn up toward the same cloud cover he saw the Horseman fly into. "That not-quite-Human Torch might be able to go wherever the fuck it wants, but there are limits as to where you can fly with just a pack without getting yourself killed, you know. No—the POs loosened the jar lid, now it's time for *us* to screw it off!"

Something within the Horseman didn't like the idea of having to hide above the clouds, but it knew that logically the move was strictly a tactical retreat, and not an admission of defeat. At any rate, the creature could still finish burning down the woodlands below even from its current height. And even though the clouds obscured its view, which would mean other things (or beings) beside the park might catch on fire, the Horseman probably wouldn't have cared even if it had the capability to do so within its programming.

The Horseman galloped across the floor of the clouds for a couple of strides while looking itself over and didn't find any of the damage it had just sustained to be too extensive. The Horseman then pointed its muzzle at the clouds under the robotic steed's hooves and was about to open fire when the creature noticed in the corner of its eye that familiar red scarab rise from the floor of the clouds.

The driver's side window was rolled down on his red Saturn and Huey's head, arms, and launcher were leaning outside of it as Fred held the steering wheel in place. A millisecond before he pulled the trigger, Huey muttered sternly, *"peek-a-boo . . !"*

The laser torpedo rang out and shot forth straight and true. It found its target and utterly obliterated both the bionicly constructed horse and the eugenically engineered rider in one fell swoop. The pieces of both cascaded and sprinkled all over the partially burning Bachelor Grove Woods in the form of smoldering debris.

And Huey couldn't help but to feel really good about himself. Reading Captain Marvel as a child after school, winning the first fist fight he was ever in, kissing Marta for the first time, and watching Li'l Bobby emerge from her womb were all good feelings Huey was certain would never know their rival until that moment. The thrill of victory from watching the Horseman explode coupled with the overwhelming sense of closure about the entire affair he felt was nothing less than wrapping oneself in pure joy for Huey. Which was why Fred had to tug at his shoulder especially hard to get his attention. "Huey—*Huey*! I think there's smoke coming from the trunk!"

"What the—" Huey looked behind him to see the tiniest wisp of smoke emanating from the crack of his car's trunk, and then the peace officer thought of his secret cache of banned weaponry. "Oh, *shit*! My stash! Fucking firefight! We got to land this thing!"

A sudden burst was heard stemming from the rear of the Saturn that sounded like a car backfiring, then wicks of flame could be seen fingering their way out from the inside of the trunk. Huey divebombed the Saturn through the cloud cover with the smoke from his trunk temporarily fusing with the clouds themselves to make a fiery trail stream behind the car for a few moments which gave the vehicle the look of a comet.

The peace officers were first shocked and then frustrated that there wasn't anything they could do to stop or at least slow down their fellow officer's fall from the heavens. Huey tried to steer the Saturn past the parts of the park still in flames and aimed his car for a particularly muddy pond next to a tall hill he remembered chasing Marta around and eventually wrestling with her in once. For his part, Fred was too petrified to even characteristically pray, and as the edge of the pond came closer and closer into view, he cried out despite himself, "oh—*shit*!"

* * *

When Fred came to, he was nearly covered in mud and being carried across a staggering Huey's shoulder up a grassy hill. His head was facing Huey's back and when Fred looked up he could see behind his descendant the red Saturn sinking in flames into a muddy bog. Once the Rushes had reached the summit of the hill, Huey had gently laid Fred on the ground beside him and knelt by his ancestor's side. Fred sat up, shook his head, and noticed for the first time both the touch of blood on his temple and the splitting headache which throbbed from the interior his skull. A couple of the peace officers who had been flying with rocket packs and had engaged the Horseman came to a landing on the slope of the hill, both of which Fred could recognize as Lieutenant Cheshta Castelblanch and Lieutenant Harlan Kendle.

"Sir, are you alright?" Lieutenant Castelblanch asked as she ran to the hilltop to the Rushes' side.

"You better call a doctor—" Huey tried moving his arm in a circle, and when he could manage half of one without wincing, he added, "for the *both* of us. We still have to get that last Horseman, though—"

"No need, captain," Castelblanch nodded in the negative, even as Fred was about to moan over the prospect of being dragged into yet another aerial battle, "we took out the last one before we got here. Some farmer out in Hinsdale reported a guy on a flying horse dusting his crops with something that made them *rot*, but like I said, we got it but *good*, sir."

"*Famine*," Fred muttered as he sat sprawled on the ground.

"They also found that lab, sir," Lieutenant Castelblanch continued, "you didn't tell me the 'asshole' in question was none other than the Black Mengele himself, Dr. Batala! The POs on the scene reported how they managed to pull him out of that—thing's cell just in time. He's scarred up pretty bad, and they say he might not walk again, but he'll live. Speaking of, we better get you two to a hospital."

"Better have something to say to them first, 'cause they're not going to let you leave without a quote," Lieutenant Kendle motioned behind him to an armada of camera helmet wearing members of the media descending upon the hill either on foot or landing from the sky onto the hill as a rocket jockey would. "Unless, of course, you want one of us to field their questions, sir?"

"Kendle, you're forgetting who you're talking to," Huey beamed, knowing full well this would be his moment to shine. "You know this is what I live for. Besides, I won't be but a minute."

In a matter of moments, the two Lieutenants, Fred, and Huey were surrounded by dozens of reporters and journalists all speaking at once. It was almost too much for Fred to take after everything that had happened, but Huey looked as though he were swimming deep in his natural element. Unbelievably, when the expression on his face indicated in the slightest that Huey was about to speak, a sudden hush fell over the hill. As the morning sun of Monday the 16th slowly began to rise behind him, Huey gazed into the crowd he was about to address and thought of how Batala might have easily won if these people—and their fears had *let* the doctor win. And if they *had* all given in to fear, there wouldn't have been a blessed thing one lone, albeit stalwart, peace officer could have done about it. It was this *almost* humbling thought which coursed through Huey's mind when he offered these words as his official statement to the press:

"Once upon a time, the extent of the general population's knowledge of—*anything*, was limited to the trials and so-called tribulations of a bunch of rich jocks gone schiz. Just as the Roman Empire kept its people distracted with bread and circuses, the general populace was made addicted to tabloid fluff by America's corporate empire so they wouldn't notice that fiscal nightmares like NAFTA and GATT were being passed right under their noses. Hell, most folks didn't even know what the damn acronyms stood for, but I bet you the fuck they knew every intimate detail of the personal lives of any celebrity involved in a scandal! All the while giving up way too much power to a select few who happen to be more 'into' politics than they were, which as y'all know is dangerous—even if that few are on *your* side. And once upon a time Dr. Batala's evil scheme to frighten civilization back into the dark ages would've worked like a charm. Yet it didn't, not just because I managed to save humanity once again—"

Huey knew from the groans he could hear throughout the crowd that he would soon lose his audience if he didn't get to how he really felt and fast, "—but because *we* saved humanity! That's right, we *all* did! We saved it by making sure that every-single-last-one of us was smart, and smart-alecky enough, to see right through what was going on, and not panic or not tear each other apart. Our logic, our intelligentsia, our very imagination was what saved the world.

"So instead of worrying about whether or not somebody's getting power hungry because they consider themselves a hero, just remember that so long as each of us continues to expand our minds, broaden our horizons, and learn all that is learnable, we'll *all* be heroes. Each and every last one of us: The history teacher at the local junior college, the recycler who separates our garbage for us, the cynical, fatalist anarchist living on some remote collective keeping the naive of the world in check, even the new kid in town just trying to find his niche," Huey caught a quick glimpse of Fred, who in turn looked as though he could tell who "the new kid" was supposed to be. "We're all superheroes in our own little way!

"Once upon a time, you had only a couple of rams off in left field shepherding a big herd of sheep in the middle of the road and it was the rams' job to defend those ignorant sheep from the few bulls you had that were coming from the right. Nowadays, our societal demographic is made up of almost *all* rams, which is why the bullheaded like Batala will *never* beat us, *because we as a people simply won't take none of that old fashioned bullshit any more*! We-the-*people*: It's a *group* 'thang,' and like the old song goes, *it's got a funky 'swang!*' "

Huey's last words had their desired effect, in that they roused the crowd of usually objective journalists to the point of laughter and then cheering, as if the peace officer were instead a stand up comedian or a Black preacher of old. After the cheers had died down, compliments began to circulate among those gathered on the mount about how much Huey's words invoked memories of old Fred Rush Junior speeches. Huey was about to be helped by his lieutenants through the crowd to a peace officer vehicle which had pulled up at the bottom of the hill to be driven to a hospital just as Fred was waving away any efforts to help him to his feet. Instead, Fred Hampton Rush Senior remained on his weary knees, turned to face the sun rising in the east, held out the palms of his hands as if catching rain, bowed his still somewhat bloodied head, and prayed to Allah as he never prayed before. As if no one else was around.

Huey planted his feet and stopped his junior officers from ushering him any further down the hill while he looked back for a moment to see both this and a group of reporters capturing the spectacle on film. Huey then cleared his throat so that the same group would turn around and pay him heed. Once this happened, Huey took the opportunity to say, "Look, I'm going to tell y'all what I told my son the night I first brought Fred home—'let's leave him alone.' "

EPILOGUE

"What a rush!"

"So you see—wait, what was your name again? This 'stoner memory' of mine . . ."

"Adrienne."

"So, *Adrienne*, the population of any given country is always at least half female, and since women have been 'dissed' so throughout the eons, if they all had become feminists back in the 20th, or even before then, there might have been some 'sho nuff' changes going on which would've made the men in charge feel like wardens locked in their own prisons overnight. 'Cause believe or not, not all women back then were feminists. In fact, some of them were down right masochistic, which is hard to believe in this day and age."

"Mm *hmm*," Adrienne answered.

"There were two ways of keeping women in control back then: With an iron hand like in 20th century Saudi Arabia or in the Lost-Found Nation—"

At this point Fred turned around in his seat slightly on board a Kiwi Starlines shuttle about to launch from the Earth to overhear what the young man sitting behind him had to say about his former temporal residence.

"—or control could've been maintained with a *slow* hand, like it was in the *old* America, where you had women kept brainwashed like in *A Clockwork Orange*. Except instead of keeping folks all doped up, you kept them on a diet of crap the then corporately-owned media had on the TV from dawn to dusk for women who stayed home to watch: Morning 'news' magazine shows, trashy talk shows, home improvement shows, game shows, *court* shows, soap box operas, *more* talk shows, and tabloid news shows to top the day off. None of which said a damn thing about the world around them that they really needed to know, and kept women butt stupid 'till the 21st century or so. It's just like Chomsky used to say, 'propaganda is to a democracy what brute force is to a dictatorship.' And in women's case, it was *fluff*, at least, that's what my master's thesis at Chicago State was on. Where do *you* go to school?"

Huey returned from the bathroom to his seat next to Fred's, noticed a peculiar look on his ancestor's face, and asked consolingly, "*still* nervous about flying to Bast? Should we call up my pops and say we can't make it? Should I just go home or back to work and give up my vacation time?"

"As if you *would*," Fred snorted in jest, "but this time, it's not me being afraid of going into outer space, it's—" Fred looked around him, leaned over to Huey's ear, and whispered, "I accidentally eavesdropped on this young man back here coming on to this girl and, I don't know. Call me old fashioned, but I just don't think it feels right to have politics—what's the word? *Permeate*, every pore of a society to the point where even the fine art of propositioning a lady has to be political."

"*Everything* is political in some way *anyway*, old man," Huey explained. "Look, you've already lived in an era when everyone was apathetic and no one gave a damn about anything, and I'd think that you'd be grateful you were frozen—*not* grateful for everything you had to go through in order to *get* frozen, obviously, but that you're able to see within your lifetime the rewards for all the sacrifices that've been made over the years."

"What do you mean?" Fred knew when he asked the question that the answer would be in the form of a typical, 25th century soliloquy, but was too curious to let the subject just drop.

"Well, I imagine the underground railroad must have wondered all those times they were hiding from the slavemaster's dogs if things would ever get any better for Black folks. I imagine the Partisans of Vilna must have asked *them*selves back when they were hiding in the forests and blowing up Nazi railroad tracks if it was worth all they were going through. Hell, I *know* folks must have thought the end was near during the Reagan Years! Constantly having to worry about whether that senile fuck was going to nuke them all to Kingdom Come! But enough folks took to the streets, the Berlin wall fell, and eventually all them damn missiles got taken apart.

"And now *we* ain't got to worry about any of that shit any more because of the sacrifices that *they* made. Our colleges are free because too many students in your time had to drop out because it was too expensive and work in slophouses just to survive. We *fly* in our cars because in your day enough homeless families had to *sleep* in theirs. Everything that we enjoy today is built on the foundations of all the sacrifices that the folks who came before us made.

"But—even though most of them didn't mind doing what they did, sometimes I feel a little guilty, you know? Sometimes I wish I could *materialize* back in time and just—*let them know*. Go to them, in their darkest hour, and say, 'it's not going to be for nothing, come 2410 A.D., everything's 'gonna' *be* alright!' That's what *I* wish! Like I said, I figure most of them would've made the sacrifices *anyway*, but *still*, I wish I could be of some comfort to them just the same. Not to mention act as a warning to those who either wasn't doing jack shit back in the day, or worse yet, was causing the shit to happen in the first damn place."

"So in other words, if a girl has to listen to a guy ramble on about politics—" Fred turned to see if the couple behind him were listening and saw that they were too into each other to pay anyone else any mind. "She should just deal with it."

"She should *participate* in it, like Marta—" Huey laid a hand on Fred's shoulder and sighed,"*damn*, it's a shame she has to work and Bobby has to go to school. It's been a week since Batala's trial and it's been *two* weeks since '*the Rapture*,' but they could still use a break, and pops would've liked to see them too."

"Yes," Fred nodded, "I'm glad *Marta's* made a full recovery too."

Huey shook his head, frowned, and took his hand off Fred's shoulder. "You can't possibly still be mad at Li'l Bobby?"

"I came by to visit one day while you weren't home and that boy of yours was watching some perverse 23rd or 24th century computer animated cartoon called *Psycho Cinema Starring the Maniac Psycho*. A cartoon character that's a serial killer! A crazy man! The episode he was watching actually showed this—*Maniac Psycho* going around killing all the beneficiaries, the lawyer, and the executor of his grandfather's will who had kept him from his inheritance! I never thought a *cartoon* could be so—*gory!*"

"I remember that episode from when I was a little kid," Huey reminisced, "that shit was *funny . . .*"

"You should have seen the look he gave me when I just *suggested* that he turn it on something else—"

"Well, you're coming to his 16th birthday party April 9th, whether you like it or not." Huey declared.

"So long as I don't have to buy him a gift."

"You can afford one with all that money you're making from guest speaking. Speaking of, when are you moving out of that free studio? You ought to be able to buy a house by now."

"As soon as Dr. Cohen says 'Louisiana' Jake is well enough from that disease the Horseman gave him to be up and about—oh, didn't I tell you? I've been helping him manage the building while he's been sick." Fred glowed with a sense of accomplishment.

"Good," Huey patted Fred's shoulder, "glad to hear it. You're finally starting to feel like you're at home in 2410, huh?"

"Well, I didn't say all *that*," Fred shrugged.

"Good afternoon passengers, welcome to Kiwi Starlines, still worker-owned since our start in 20th century New Jersey." A steward stepped forward from a hatch at the head of the shuttle and announced. "We will be taking off momentarily for Space Station Roddenberry where you'll connect with your flights to Bast, the Melkotsurakian homeworld, or Space Station Bradbury, so if you'll please fasten your seat belts we'll be on our way." The steward then made direct eye contact with the Rushes. "Captain Rush, we would be honored if either you or Fred Rush Senior would make the first song request to be played on the onboard stereo for our journey."

The individual quiet conversations that had been heard throughout the shuttle suddenly ceased as all eyes fell on the peace officer and the 418 year old man sitting together. Fred blushed from the attention, but before he could say anything, Huey said without a pause, "'Ooh Child' by the Five Stairsteps." Fred glared at his descendant for a moment, but then thought, he's just being Huey, and in the end, we must all do the things that makes us who we are.

The stewardess then looked upward and spoke into thin air, "computer—play 'Ooh Child' by the Five Stairsteps."

As the computer piped the first strands of the song through the shuttle's speakers, Fred tried to settle back in his seat amidst the trembling of the shuttle itself that only he seemed to find unsettling. Once Fred could sense that they were airborne, he quickly turned to Huey who only smiled calmly back at him. When Huey had lain his head back and closed his eyes, Fred tried to do the same.

Fred then thought about what Huey had said to him about feeling at home and wondered had he ever felt at home at any stage of his life. Did he feel at home in the South Side of Chicago of the 20th century? Clearly, Fred didn't feel at home during the 21st, but what *about* the 25th? The laws of physics dictated that he couldn't physically go back to any *past* home of his, and Fred couldn't go into the future unless he flew near a black hole as the gay space hero had in the movie he saw, *Beyond the Beyond*, because the future hasn't been written yet. So in a sense, nature itself had determined that Fred Hampton Rush Senior was to spend the rest of his life in the 25th century, and thanks to the sacrifices made by the likes of the son he left behind and all those who came before (and after) him, that wouldn't be such a bad deal for Fred after all.

No sensible decision can be made any longer without taking into account not only the world as it is, but the world as it will be—and naturally this means that there must be an accurate perception of the world as it will be. This, in turn, means that our statesmen, our businessmen, our everyman must take on a science fictional way of thinking, whether he likes it or not, or even whether he knows it or not. Only so can the deadly problems of today be solved.

Issac Asimov, who has been quoted as saying that *Star Trek* was the only television program he ever watched.

At this stage of history, either one of two things is possible. Either the general population will take control of its own destiny and will concern itself with community interests, guided by values of solidarity, sympathy, and concern for others, or, alternatively, there will be no destiny for anyone to control.

Noam Chomsky

THE PRICE OF LIBERTY IS *ETERNAL* VIGILANCE

THE END

ACKNOWLEDGMENTS

First and foremost, I'd like to thank Anne Bevilacqua for teaching me that political/social science is just as "hard" a science as physics or chemistry. Mad Max from Berserkly (he knows who he is, there can be only one) for the off-hand comment he made while working on his car about a 21st century America regulated to third world status while still having the world's biggest nuclear arsenal, thanks. A shout should go out to my proofreaders—the *A.D.* Team: Erika Dyquisto, Jesse Falk, and Sandra Square, thanks y'all.

Razor Ramon, El, and Carlos the *Sixth*, is it? Thanks for letting me into your home. The Berger family, thanks for not stopping your number one son from helping me survive "the Year of Hell." Maile, Big Mac, and Alex G. back at room 121 at Solano, thanks for the memories. Mr. Segal, thank you for being a far better teacher than that big, black cauldron of disinformation, Thurston. Martin Mini, for being quite simply the greatest community college counselor of all time. Tim Blaskovich, for being the greatest film teacher of them all. Thanks should also go to my mother, JFK investigator extraordinare Paul Kangas, "Mr. Modest" Mike Cariglio, Professor Goldner, Rob the Slob, Davids Mitchell, Hoffman, and Weitz, Art Evans, Bill Meyers, Kevin McCarthy, and Rachel Goldstein for being there. Jack and Roz Kirby, Sebastian says hi.

I imagine in the years to come there will be those who'll say that I concentrated on the Nation of Islam too much and not enough on the corporate elite who truly run this country (into the ground). The Black Muslims are just pawns near the bottom of the political totem pole as it were and I'm being petty for singling them out while not focusing on the obscenely rich, people'll claim.

First of all, all one has to do is read this book to tell I am *no* fan of bootstrap capitalism. Second of all, if I *do* hit the talk show circuit, we'll see if the hosts, those purveyors of tabloid fluff, will let me talk about capital flight, regressive taxation, mergermania, and so forth. Because rest assured, I will try to bring those things up. I owe that much to all of the Black Panthers. Those long gone, those still around—and those yet to come . . .

310

311

313

Anarchist Fiction From
III Publishing

The Last Days of Christ the Vampire by J.G. Eccarius
ISBN 0-9622937-0-9   192 pages, 4.25 x 7"
$7.00
The book that broke the silence about the vampiric nature of Jesus Christ
and his fundamentalist zombies. Jesus has set his sights on converting some
teenagers in Providence, Rhode Island, but instead they resist and set out to
hunt him down before he can release his Apocalypse upon the world.
Arguably the best religious satire of the 20th century. Jesus Lives; vampires
never die.

Virgintooth by Mark Ivanhoe
ISBN: 0-9622937-3-3   192 pages, 4.25 x 7"
$7.00
There is no escape: at death every soul is swallowed up into the abysmal
hunger of the feral vampires. Elizabeth, however, has not exactly died: she
has been made into a vampire. Now she has not only the problems she had
when alive, and of avoiding the feral vampires, but she must also get along
with the other human vampires. At times terrifying, at times hysterically
funny, Virgintooth will horrify and delight you.

Geminga, Sword of the Shining Path by Melvin Litton
ISBN 0-9622937-4-1   5.5 x 8.5", 256 pages
$9.95
In a world poised between a superstitious past and a surreal future of
bioengineering, virtual reality and artificial consciousness, Geminga surfs on
the winds of the present. A product of genetic engineering, this bird has
been trained since infancy to assassinate the enemies of Peru's Sendero
Luminoso. Now she's come with her best friend, Jimmy the Snake, to
California Norte.

This'll Kill Ya by Harry Willson
ISBN 0-9622937-2-5   192 pages 4.25 x 7"
$6.00
The anti-censorship thriller that will have you laughing out loud and
examining your own reactions to materials that surely should be censored.
Caution: If you believe that words can be used as weapons to harm people,
reading these pages may be hazardous to your health. Willson has a
devilishly delightful sense of humor that should place him in everyone's
library.

(Continued next page)

We Should Have Killed the King by J.G. Eccarius
ISBN 0-9622937-1-7   192 pages 4¼ x 7"
$5.00
Jack Straw and hundreds of thousands of other English peasants rebelled
against their overlords in 1381, killing nobles, lawyers and tax collectors.
Ultimately they were crushed, but the spirit of rebellion was reborn in
America in the punk/anarchist movement during the 1980's and Jack Straw
was there. A stunning look at the underground in the USA.

My Journey With Aristotle to the Anarchist Utopia
by Graham Purshase
ISBN 0-9622937-6-8   128 pages 4¼ x 7"
$7.00
No government? No taxes? No police? Wouldn't that be anarchy? In
Australia in the near future coal miners meet in a town to determine how
to deal with economic collapse. They are attacked by police who attempt to
force them to work the mine. One worker, Tom, is bashed by the police
until they leave him for dead. Recovering, when Tom emerges from the mine
he finds himself a thousand years in the future. The mine is abandoned but
he encounters Aristotle, who leads him down to Bear City. There he sees
how human life can be organized without government or bosses of any kind.
The inhabitants of Bear City live in harmony with nature and one another,
yet have a highly developed civilization.

Non-fiction:

Vampires or Gods by William Meyers
ISBN 0-9622937-5-X   192 pages, 8.5 x 11"
$15.00
Vampires living thousands of years, commanding legions of human wor-
shippers. The stuff of horror novels? No these vampires are right out of
ancient history books. Every major ancient civilization was associated with
an immortal claiming to be a god. Egypt had Osiris, who rose from the dead
after his body was hacked to pieces. He reigned for 3000 years. Asia Minor
had Cybele, whose followers fed her their blood. She was thousands of years
old when she saved Rome from Hannibal's army in 204 B.C. Greece had
Dionysus and Hercules, Rome had Quirinus, and the list goes on. Altogether
the most powerful conspiracy in the history of the world. With illustrations
and extensive quotations from the ancient historians.

Available at bookstores not run by zombies.

To order direct from III Publishing send cash, or check or money order for
the listed price (postage & handling is free for orders of $7.00 or more in
the US; otherwise add $2) made out to III Publishing, P.O. Box 1581
Gualala, CA 95445. Or send $1.00 for an up-to-date catalog.